Awakening Curry Buckle

Michael Donnelly

Blue Works
Port Orchard ◊ Seattle ◊ Tahuya

Awakening Curry Buckle
copyright 2005 by Michael Donnelly
published by Blue Works

ISBN 1-59092-226-3

9 8 7 6 5 4 3 2
First edition October 2005

Cover art by Mark Adams, in collaboration with the author.
Map by Charlie Wise.
Interior design by Blue Artisans Design.
Blue Card™ concept by Grace M. Garcia.
Ratings Block™ concept by Grace M. Garcia.

For information about film, reprint or other subsidiary rights, please contact Mari Garcia at mgarcia@windstormcreative.com.

Blue Works is an imprint of Windstorm Creative, a multi-division, international organization involved in publishing books in all genres, including electronic publications; producing games, toys, videos and audio cassettes as well as producing theatre, film and visual arts events. The wind with the gear center was designed by Buster Blue or Blue Artisans Design and is a trademark of Blue Works.

Blue Works
c/o Windstorm Creative
Post Office Box 28
Port Orchard, WA 98366
curry@windstormcreative.com
www.windstormcreative.com
360-769-7174 ph.fx

Blue Works is a member of the Orchard Creative Group, Ltd.

Library of Congress Cataloging in Publication Data available.

to Cori

Acknowledgments

Special thanks to Poulsbohemians
Alice, Celia, Cheryl, Dee, Marylyn, and Sue,
to Ellen (E.T.), my first and most generous ally,
to Dr. Don, a.k.a. "The Nub" for myriad acts of kindness,
to Tamara for her sage advice,
to the sleep-deprived staff at Windstorm Creative
for their dedication and commitment,
and to my wife, Cori, who understands
a novelist must always live in (at least) two worlds.

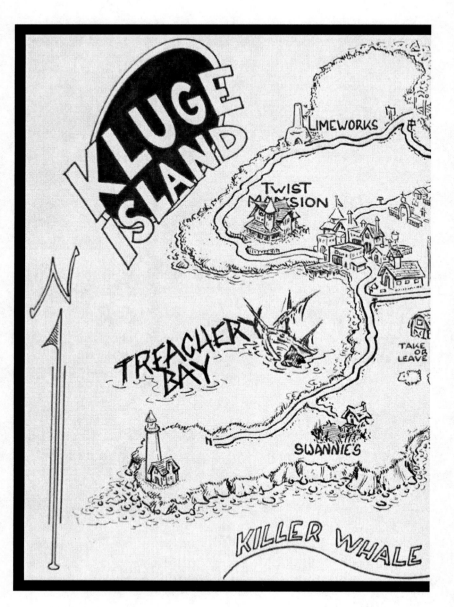

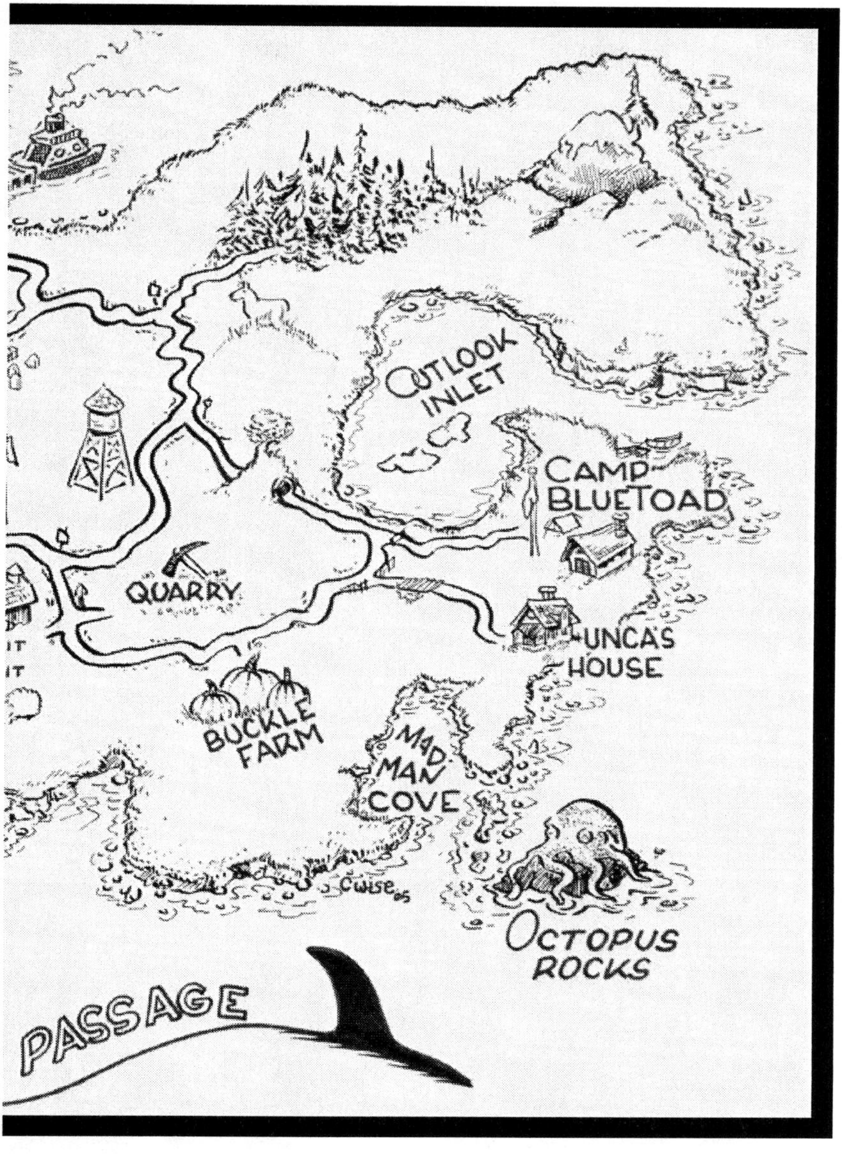
OUTLOOK INLET
CAMP BLUETOAD
QUARRY
UNCA'S HOUSE
BUCKLE FARM
MAD MAN COVE
Cwise 05
OCTOPUS ROCKS
PASSAGE

Awakening Curry Buckle

Michael Donnelly

Whence come the wondrous and secret things I reveal to you? Things past and likely to be? In the bosom of ongoing creation is the Hall of Akashic Records, the vibratory chronicles of every act by every being in the universe. Every thought leaves its vibration. Every emotion, taste, smell, sound, touch. Every nuance of a being's existence is written in light; nothing forgotten or expunged. Every possible variation of the future may be glimpsed by whomever finds the way to Akasha.

—Swami Curryban Bucklananda

Chapter 1
Curry Lands on His Feet

My first glimpse of Curry Buckle's astonishing powers came the day we dumped him from his chair in sophomore biology class. Like most teachers at Kluge Island High, Mr. Flatski taught two subjects. Science courses all day—becoming snarlier with each passing hour— then he coached football. We called him Old Flattop because of his haircut: upright bristles thick as a doormat. I say *we*, but I'd arrived that summer from off-island and hadn't blended in. I carried a notebook with *Darwin Bownes* written in block letters so people would learn my name, but I think they already knew because of my dad taking over the newspaper, which got everyone stirred up. Anyway, the class avoided provoking Mr. Flatski because he could go off like a gaffed halibut.

On this particular September afternoon, he had his back turned, drawing the double helix of a DNA strand on the board. The classroom looked like a theater, with desks on four curved terraces facing a long counter fitted with sinks and gas burners. I always sat in back, on the top riser where, through the rear windows, I could see the wing with the girl's shower room. The frosted shower room glass had a corner missing from one pane and I always hoped to see something interesting but never did. As Mr. Flatski drew rungs in the double helix with different colored markers, I noticed Curry Buckle had fallen asleep at his desk using his book as a pillow. Curry was short, stocky, with no neck to speak of. Quiet guy, but good-natured, often wearing a doofus expression of amusement as if absorbed in some private joke. I think my real reason for sitting in the back is that I felt safe sitting next to Curry. Safe that he never sneered at me or pretended I didn't exist or made snide comments. He had this aura of dorky weirdness about him that made others leave him alone.

But not that day.

Choker Durant sat immediately in front of me, one riser lower. Biology didn't interest Choker. Not the kind you learned from a book. He was the alpha male in the patch of hallway by the Coke machine where the sophomores hung out, his tight polo shirt revealing a self-inflicted skull tattoo on a thick biceps; his loose 'board-baggies revealing an inch of butt cleavage. Curry Buckle didn't belong to Choker's crowd. In fact, he probably ranked *numero uno* on Choker's loser list.

I must have been on a different kind of list. Three weeks into the term, classmates should have loosened up toward me. But no. Our family moved here from the mainland that summer when dad bought the weekly newspaper: the *Kluge Island Whalebone*. People acted like dad had ripped out the island's beating heart for breakfast. It didn't help that the prior editor, who at age eighty-two had slumped dead over his last editorial, had been a character in the local islands for decades. The grudge carried over to me. No one wanted me at their lunch table, so I brought sandwiches from home and ate outside on the bleachers. Even among a sophomore class small enough to fit in one room, I felt invisible. So when Choker turned to me, his thick-featured face parted with a canine grin, and recruited me to humiliate a fellow classmate, well... it's not that I wanted to be Choker's friend, but if I could just show everyone I was up for a little fun... Curry Buckle seemed a small sacrifice.

Choker pointed to the right rear leg of Curry's desk. I hesitated, hearing the squeak of Mr. Flatski's marking pen over Curry's light snoring. But Choker egged me on with a gesture and I caved and hunched over to grab a rear desk leg. Choker took the front leg. At his nod we both lifted.

Had Curry not been leaning toward the open side of his desk, he might simply have plopped to the floor like a bag of dog food. But he *was* leaning, and Choker gave Curry an extra shove, causing him to pitch forward and tumble down to the next terrace, and his momentum carried him all the way to the ground level, where he did a face plant before the studly alter to science, behind which stood Old Flattop, hands on hips, face hot enough to fry an egg.

"Buckle?" Flatski said between clenched teeth. He never called anyone by their first name.

Curry looked up, groggy. "Yessir? Um, sorry sir."

"Do I not talk loud enough for you, Buckle? Do you need to sit closer?"

Flatski wasn't exactly yelling, but it looked like every cell in his body wanted to.

"Yessir. Nosir."

Then Flatski looked in my direction. "You two—Bownes is it? —and Durant."

My blood heated like soup.

"Bring that desk down front so Buckle can hear better."

We did.

"That's right, make yourself comfortable. Now in all the commotion, I've forgotten where we were. Buckle, remind me."

Curry looked up and swallowed. My chest tightened and I wished I could have taken back what I'd done.

"Sir," I said, rising from my seat.

"Bownes?"

"I, uh... that is, we..."

Then Choker Durant turned and gave me a fierce scowl that promised if I said one more word, he'd wait for me after school, as long as it took, and would pound me beyond recognition of my own mother.

"What is it Bownes?"

"Er..." I gulped. "His book. He's dropped his book."

I picked it up and stepped down the risers to hand it to Curry. I avoided his eyes at first, but my guilt forced me to give him a brief look of apology. He blinked hard as I held the book out. Then, with a nod of thanks, he accepted it.

"Well, Buckle? Where were we?" Flatski said.

"Ummmm." Curry looked at the whiteboard, looked down at his

book, then looked back at the board, and blinked hard. "Well, I guess that would be your basic DNA strand. Dee-oxy... um... deoxy... ribonucleic acid?"

Curry had never impressed me with a special grasp of biology, or any other subject. In this case, Mr. Flatski had yet to tell us exactly what he was diagramming. But from the bulging look on Flatski's face, Curry must have guessed right. The bulging look also told me Curry would have done himself a favor if he'd guessed wrong.

"So, Buckle, you know so much about it, you can clown around during the lesson. Maybe your classmates aren't as smart as you. Why don't you step up here and finish the lesson for them?" Mr. Flatski held a marker over the lab table, cords of muscle lacing his hairy arm.

"That's all right," Curry said, leaning back from the marker.

"No, it's not all right. Get up here. *Capiche?*"

Curry *capiched.* We all did, I suspect. We *capiched* that anyone who upstaged Old Flattop must be trashed before the show could go on. Curry stood, took the marker, looked at the unfinished diagram on the board, then did an open-mouthed head-tilt of pure astonishment. He stood flat-footed for the longest time, frozen in position as if sculpted from Spam. Blocky head, bad haircut, and wire glasses bent and re-bent. Then, never taking his eyes from the board, he shuffled past the lab table, and began labeling parts of the double helix.

"The sides of the ladder are made of sugar and phosphate molecules," he said. "They alternate. The rungs make a code for genetic information, and there are four different chemicals. The red is cytosine." He wrote *cytosine* on the board. "Green is guanine. You see, the cytosine will bond only with the guanine, and not with the thymine or adenine."

Mr. Flatski's jaw sagged.

Curry stepped back from the drawing and frowned at it. "Actually, this shows the helix twisting to the left, but it always twists to the right. This is true for all organisms, but we don't know why."

Curry turned to see if he should continue, but Mr. Flatski's mouth seemed stuck in the open position.

Then the class brainiac, Keeley Uncas, waved her thin arm. I'd heard somebody say she'd been homeschooled the last couple years by her father, a doctor, and she knew her stuff. At least her father used to be a doctor—supposedly he'd been de-stethoscoped for being a quack. Somebody important had died. Keeley always seemed to be waving her chicken-bone arm, especially if someone else answered correctly, then she'd add her two cents.

"Curry," she said in an uppity tone, "did you know if you straightened out the DNA strands from one cell, expanded them to the thickness of spaghetti, and laid them end to end, they'd reach to the moon and back six times?"

Curry again blinked hard. "Well, yes, it does say that in a footnote at the bottom of page forty-nine. Just one time, actually."

"Hey Keeley, your noodle is overcooked," someone said.

The class giggled.

Keeley's fine black eyebrows bunched up over her piercing dark eyes and her mouth turned down.

Old Flattop just glared like a man unsure whether he's been set up. He waved Curry back to his seat, gave us an extra-long assignment, then the bell rang. We didn't stampede out as usual; everyone paused to look at Curry as they filed past, as if he was a traffic wreck.

I slipped out hurriedly and went to my locker just to have something to do. Just down the hall by the soda machine five or six guys gathered around Choker Durant, listening to his inhaled bray of a laugh.

"Did you see me roll that smeg down those steps? Heenk heenk! He's my new roll model. Heenk!"

I headed over, thinking I'd earned the right to join in. I hesitated outside their circle, but decided to keep going.

"Hey, smeggo!"

I turned, saw Choker and his trolls looking at me. He had a broad face and a smirking smile that could, in an instant, turn fierce.

"Wudden't you say Curried Butthead makes a good roll model?"

I shrugged. "All we got out of it is double homework."

"Homework? Do I look worried?" He folded his thick arms over his polo shirt and slumped his weight to one leg. "Maybe you wanna help with my double homework, huh?"

"I don't know." It dawned on me that dumping Curry Buckle had been only a down payment on membership in Choker's club.

As lockers clanked and slammed around us, Choker scratched his head as if remembering something. "You weren't about to squeal on the Choker in there, eh smeggo?"

"The name is Darwin." I turned before Choker could answer. Nagged by my conscience, I headed back to the science lab.

Keeley Uncas had her back to me, blocking the doorway with elbows spread, thumbs hooked under her belt. Her black hair in a boyish cut came to a point at the back of her neck. She stood almost as tall as me, looking willowy in her India-cloth blouse and flares. Old Flattop had gone, but Curry remained, trapped by Keeley who looked down a couple of inches at him. "Don't give me that sardine slop, Curry Buckle. I've known you too long, and you're not stupid, but you don't apply yourself, either." She jabbed a finger in his face. "So how did you know that DNA stuff?"

Curry opened his toothy mouth, shrugged, and yanked his ear. He could probably hear worms crawl with it already, and it would only get bigger if he kept at it. Keeley shifted to see who'd come up behind her, gave me a suspicious look, and stood where she could keep an eye on both Curry and me.

"I can't explain," Curry said. "I went to sleep on the book, and then I could see the pages in my mind."

"Bullgoobers!" Keeley jutted her finely shaped chin. Her flower-petal complexion didn't need the corpse-colored gook that most girls experimented with.

"Really. Test me if you like."

The tip of Keeley's tongue poked between her lips like the neck of a clam. She opened Curry's textbook to the middle. "Okay, on page one-thirty-three it talks about the Law of Superposition. What is it?"

Curry pressed his eyes shut. "The lowest layers of rock were deposited first." Curry opened his eyes and smiled brightly. "Therefore, scientists can date fossils by—"

Keeley slammed the book shut. "Whatever you did, it's cheating. If you keep doing it, don't think I won't report you."

Keeley brushed past me in exasperation. As she blended into the hallway bustle, I exchanged impressed looks with Curry. "She's bent on being class valedictorian," he said. "Already working on her speech." He started to shuffle off.

I caught him. "Do you have a class?"

"A free period. I usually go down to the stream. I have permission because of a science project."

"I've got study hall. I'll cut it."

Curry stared somewhere far away. "I guess I've been expecting this."

The stream gurgled through an alder and maple thicket. Devil's club arched over the path, spiky leaves backlit by late September sun.

"Why is Keeley so bent on being first in the class?" I asked.

Curry shuffled through fallen leaves. "Something to prove maybe."

"Like what?"

"Oh, like restoring the family name I suppose. Her dad, you see, is Doc Uncas."

"What about Doc Uncas?"

"My aunts say he lost his medical license. Before Doc and Keeley came here, he treated a girl with a concoction used by an Amazon tribe... and she died. The dead girl's father went on to become governor."

"Big shot with a grudge."

"Yup."

"So Keeley's from off-island too," I said. Maybe she could be an ally, as we had something in common.

Curry faced me as he held a springy branch out of the path. "It hasn't been easy for her." It sounded like he understood what it felt like.

"Is it true," I said, "what you told Keeley about sleeping on your book?"

Curry nudged a toad with his sneaker. It sprang into the bracken. "It's happened a couple of times, like nodding off reading a magazine or a book, then when I continue reading it later, it's like... like I've already read it."

We walked on, leaves crunching underfoot like huge cornflakes. A gust brought more of them down, rocking, spinning, each with its own special motion. I caught one in mid-flight, broader than my hand.

"You realize of course why you fell out of your chair?"

Curry cocked his head as if I'd asked a trick question. "Well... I fell asleep."

My throat felt made of concrete as I forced the confession out. "That's not all of it."

When Curry stopped and looked up at the autumn canopy, I did too. My stomach fluttered like the leaves. "You mean Choker did it?"

"Yeah."

"I thought I fell out on my own."

"No." I took a few breaths but there didn't seem to be much oxygen in them. "And the thing is, well, I helped him."

When I worked up the nerve to look at Curry, he was still arching his stumpy neck to stare into the moss-hung maple.

He pointed up. "You know, Darwin, there's a screech owl that lives up there. I took a picture of him once with my telephoto lens. Want to see it?"

"Did you hear me? I'm sorry."

"I know. I'm trying to figure it out."

"Just a little joke. It was stupid."

Curry looked up at me, with something like puzzlement in his eyes. "No, forget it. It's just... just that... well, before you came to Kluge Island, I had a dream... with you in it. Several dreams actually."

I took a step back and felt a shiver—almost a convulsion—go through me. Part of me wanted to make some excuse to slam out of there, but the rest of me wanted to know more. "When I asked if we could talk, you said you expected it. Did you mean...?"

"In the dreams," Curry said, "it seemed we knew each other, a long time ago. And then, this summer... never mind."

The rattle of dried leaves in the breeze had a clarity that set off my nerve endings. I checked my watch. "Five minutes until next class. I'd better go."

"Darwin..."

He waited until I stopped and looked back at him.

"Why don't you come to dinner? Mom always roasts a lamb on Friday night."

If there'd been a single note of pleading in his invitation, or any weirdness, I would have refused. But he looked certain of my answer, as if it would fulfill a *déjà vu,* and I said the words that formed in my mind.

"Some days it doesn't pay to be a lamb."

Chapter 2
A Fly in the Nostril

*A*fter school we stopped by the newspaper office so I could tell mom I'd be going to Curry's for the evening. In the pressroom, we watched Dad tinker with the drying unit of the old Miehle. When ready for testing, he hit the start button and the monstrous press powered up to its operating rhythm. I powered up too. The thing had a deep groove that set my hips pumping and my chin bobbing. A bass question and treble answer. I added some elbows and knees to encourage Curry to get into it, but he didn't so much as tap a toe. Yet, he seemed transfixed by the printing press, the drum flying around, all the moving parts dancing in complex rhythm, and he stared unblinkingly.

Dad seemed satisfied with the press and hit the kill button. As the machine wound down, so did I.

"Funky, huh?"

Curry nodded. "Hypnotic." He blinked a few times as if trying to clear his focus. "We probably ought to get going."

I followed Curry on my bike, working my 36 gears hard on the rolling hills, keeping up with his sputtering motor scooter. He lived out past the water tower, the abandoned lime quarry, the sheep meadow. I knew the territory. My parents had worried I'd get bored on Kluge Island. The town was so small it didn't even have a name, just *the village*. No mall. No cable TV (and we couldn't afford satellite). No daily newspaper. Not even a movie theater. The gas station closed at five, and didn't open on Sundays or holidays. A lot of my old friends couldn't have hacked it. One of the trade-offs was you could thumb a ride anywhere. Even little kids hitched. And nobody locked anything. We didn't get a set of keys when we bought our house; the sellers couldn't remember ever having any. For bike riding, the empty roads, gentle hills, and jagged coastline suited me fine. Legs pumping, I hunched over the bars and squinted into the wind, feeling like a hawk gliding over the hayfields.

We made another stop before reaching Curry's place. He turned at a hand-lettered sign that said *Take It Or Leave It*. At the end of a short road stood a dilapidated barn with its doors flung open and stuff literally spilling out. It looked like the mother of all garage sales. A van had backed up to the barn and two guys were unloading it. One of them had white dreadlocks past his shoulders. He looked albino.

"That's Leon," Curry said. "Ever been to the Take It Or Leave It?"

"No. What is it?"

"On islands, you want to recycle as much stuff as you can. So people leave things here and take other things home."

"Free?"

"Yup. Never know what's going to show up. It's where I got my telephoto lens. My shoes too."

I peeked at the clothes and tools and furniture and books and toys and dishes. An urn of hot-spiced cider couldn't mask the smell of fermented body odor in the old clothes. There might have been a trace of pot smoke in the air too. A small sign said *Let go your possessions; take back your soul.* I noticed the van driver handing a drum to Leon.

Leon chuckled. "You didn't keep it very long."

"I decided someone else could get more use out of it."

"You're the third person who's decided that," Leon said, nodding. He set the drum on a table.

"Yeah?"

"Sarah? She took it home for a week and said the crazy drum would start vibrating on its own."

The driver massaged one hand with the other and seemed unsettled. "I'm not saying I heard anything, you know. It just made me... uncomfortable. It's weird but I can't keep a steady beat going—it's like it wants me to play something else."

"I'll take it!"

The words were out of my mouth before I'd even thought about it.

The two men looked at me. I squirmed under their stares, then went to examine the drum made of hammered metal, the size of a large kitchen kettle, and etched with spiky symbols joined in a horizontal line, like writing in a strange language. The drum head looked intact, though darkened by use, and tough sinews around the perimeter kept the skin taut. I gave it a couple of slaps and got a rich, resonant sound. "I'm a drummer," I said.

The two men looked at each other and shrugged.

"What do you think, Curry?" I asked.

He smiled. "That's how stuff gets—"

He stopped abruptly and turned the drum to inspect the etching. He looked up. "Where'd this drum come from, Leon?"

"Troutigan. He brought it back from the Kumba Mela in India."

Curry nodded. "Yes, Darwin. I think you should keep it."

We rode on another two miles with the drum strapped behind Curry on the motorbike, and turned down a gravel drive, through acres of ripening pumpkins to a rather shabby farmhouse. The Buick in front looked ready to join the row of junkers in the side yard. A scrum of dogs emerged from under a Studebaker, jostling for a share of a gnawed Frisbee.

With the drum under my arm, Curry and I climbed the porch stairs. There, three old women in rockers sipped an oily-looking fluid from small, stemmed glasses and disagreed about going to someone's funeral. The smell of roasting meat and onions wafted from the house. Curry waited for a break in the argument to introduce me to his mom and his two aunts. Aunt Iris—tall, lanky, hair like spider webs collected on a dust mop. And Aunt Pansy—a squat toad of a woman, eyes full of mischief. I'd seen them before: they ran the antique shop in town. The Twist Sisters Junque and Vintage Girdle Emporium. Though I figured Curry's mom to be the youngest, she looked like a vitamin deficiency case, head bound in a scarf, skin slack, eyes that had seen as much of the world as they cared to. Crowd noise and the excited voice of a ringside boxing announcer filtered through the screen door.

The three sisters looked me over. Pansy said, "You're a healthy looking boy—maybe a bit knobby, wouldn't you say, Iris? Kind of like you? Knobby?"

"Worse things than being knobby." Iris seemed intent on acting dignified despite Pansy, and despite whatever it was they were drinking.

Pansy asked me, "A little splash of amontillado? You look almost old enough."

"No thank you," I said, clueless about amontillado. "I just look sorta old for my age."

"So do we," Pansy said, laughing. "Iris is seventy-three, but she doesn't look a day over eighty-two, does she?"

I just smiled.

"Well, if I was sixty years younger," Iris said to me, "I'd chase you around that pumpkin patch, I would."

Pansy snorted, "Iris hasn't caught anything but a cold in sixty years."

"That's rich coming from an old turnip like you."

"Chaste makes waste," Curry's mom said and they all laughed. The amontillado had them lit up.

"Anyway," Iris said, "getting back to the point of disagreement, I'm going to Bumpy's funeral tomorrow, with or without the both of you."

Pansy looked even more toadish when she puffed up. "But we never go to funerals unless there's an estate sale afterwards. With Bumpy's wife still living, what's the point? And that new undertaker makes my flesh creep. The expressions he puts on those faces, my lord! Don't you dare let him near me when I'm gone, Iris Twist. I will not go to my grave looking constipated."

"Well, there's always the taxidermist," Iris said. "And you've already got the one glass eye, so we'd only have to get one more."

As Pansy swiveled her right eye, her left remained staring straight ahead. "Anyway, I don't know why you'd go to Bumpy's funeral. You've hated him the last forty years."

Iris paused. "I'm going, and that's that."

Curry's mom chimed in, "Let her go, Pansy. She was sweet on

Bumpy once, if you recollect."

"How could I forget all that moping and carrying on."

Curry sidetracked things long enough to ask, "How's Drano doing, mom?"

"You'd better go check on him."

"Be right back," Curry said to me, so I waited on the porch, though I would rather have gone with him to the barn.

"That Curry sure does love his animals," Iris said.

His mom drawled, "Yeah, he stayed up all night with Drano, pulling porcupine quills out of her mouth."

"Drano is a dog?" I asked.

"Yep."

"No shortage of dogs around this place," I said.

Curry's mom looked over the fields with dull eyes. "Since we cleared this land, we've raised a lot of punkins and a lot of kids and a lot of hounds. Not much to show for it."

"Eleven of 'em," Pansy said. "And not one with the sense to pour pee out of a boot—with directions on the heels."

"Dogs?" I asked.

"Nooo, kids."

"Each one of 'em named for something out of the spice rack," Iris said, a note of disapproval in her voice. "Ginger and Dill and Basil and Rosemary, et cetera."

"Good names," I said, to be agreeable.

"Except for that poor runt, Dry Mustard," Pansy said. "No wonder he turned out simple. He'll always be a minimum-wage boy."

"Not likely to get elected president with a name like that," Iris said.

Curry's mom shrugged. "Should have named them after fancy cars, I suppose. Like Lincoln." The three sisters giggled.

"At least you didn't call them what's under the sink," Pansy said.

Iris explained to me, "Those are the names the poor dogs got."

"Anyway, not a dab of enterprise in the lot of 'em," Pansy said. "The kids nor the dogs."

"Except Paprika," Iris said, finger in the air.

Pansy nodded. "What enterprise there is in the family, Paprika's got it."

"Speaking of which... " Curry's mom said.

A speeding pickup raised a plume of dust off the driveway and skidded to a halt next to the Buick. A curly-blonde guy got out, his football jersey cut to show his abs. He walked slowly, arms angled outward. He'd just come from practice, no doubt, and his shoulders were too broad and muscles too pumped for his arms to hang naturally. His tongue lolled as if there were too much of it to fit in his mouth. Curry's sister, Paprika, who'd followed the ape-man out the driver's side, led him up the stairs as if she'd found him in the wild and tamed him.

Dan Klatt. A senior. He took up a lot of space at school.

"Enterprise," Iris whispered to me. "A born schemer."

Paprika was a hard girl not to notice. Two grades ahead of Curry and me, a cheerleader with a flounce of reddish hair, she carried herself with jaunty confidence and knew how to pose her bust to great advantage. I'm sure she'd put in plenty of mirror time getting it right. Her mom's tired eyes brightened in a way they hadn't for Curry, and Mr. Buckle came out to greet her and Dan Klatt. He'd been in the living room watching a fight from his recliner. He didn't notice me. Neither did Paprika. Klatt did. He gave me a gloating look that said *I know you'd like to be me, but that's your tough luck.*

Mr. Buckle embraced Paprika, then shook ape-man's hand. "You taking good care of my pride and joy?"

"Yessir."

"That's the right answer. Come in and watch the fight. I'll get you a cold one."

"I'm in training."

"Good man. How 'bout a root beer then?"

Klatt inspected me again briefly, then went in, apparently satisfied that I posed no threat to the women.

Curry returned from the barn. "I think Drano's going to be fine." C'mon Darwin, I'll show you my room. And bring that drum, will you?"

Curry's second floor bedroom had an old-book smell to it. The wallpaper had blistered, and water stains bled around the light fixture. His mattress sagged and wires held his wooden chair together. A threadbare Persian rug covered some of the painted slat floor. He kept the place neat, but nothing looked new. The eleventh kid living in a world of hand-me-downs.

Something made the room feel too empty. Maybe the lack of the usual stuff: music posters, stolen road signs, dirty clothes, sports gear, model trains. No clues about hobbies except some old cameras and a few black-and-white pictures of malformed pumpkins. A stone elephant in lotus posture anchored the corner of his writing desk. And—probably the weirdest thing—an ironing board. His shirts may not have been new, but they didn't have wrinkles.

"Do you mind looking at something for me?" He pulled a curious brass-colored birdlike creature from under his shirt. I'd seen the thing around his neck in the shower room at gym class. The weird bird had colored stones in its crown, but before I could get a good look, he turned it over.

"See the writing on the back?" The tightly knotted thong was too short for Curry to look at the medallion directly.

There were some faint markings. I moved my head to get a better angle to the light. "Yeah. In fact, it looks like the decorations on my drum."

Curry nodded excitedly. "Look at them side by side."

He squatted next to the desk while I compared the two inscriptions. "Pretty much the same thing," I said. "Heck of a coincidence, I'd say."

I could tell from the hollow look on Curry's face that he was trying to make something more of it.

"What is that fungdingus around your neck anyway?"

"An amulet. It was a gift."

"What does the writing mean?"

Curry continued staring at the spiky script on the drum. "Don't know. But it's about time I found out." He rubbed his thumb over his medallion and asked, "Can you play that thing?"

"What?" I said. "I got my first drum kit at age four because I was beating the crap out of the furniture."

"I heard you got permission to play electric guitar in the school band."

"Hey, if it makes noise, let me at it. I'm your man. And they already had too many drummers." I settled cross-legged on the rug and began experimenting with the drum to see what kinds of sounds I could get out of it, striking the head in different places, with slaps and finger taps, bumping with the heel of my hand, rim shots, whacking the metal sides.

Just then Paprika flung the door open, rushed to Curry who'd stacked his pillows against the headboard and settled in. She flopped her hand in his face. "Look! Dan gave it to me. A Mexican fire opal."

I began playing softly; the framework of a rhythm emerged and while my hands refined the groove, I began to think of ways to fill it in, hoping Paprika would appreciate my prowess. As Curry examined the ring, Paprika killed time by looking me over. Her eyes were radiant green, like cross-sections of kiwi held to the sun. They seemed tender enough when she looked at her brother, but when they scanned me, I felt microwaved.

"Is it true Curry fell asleep in class?" she asked.

Absorbed in the opal, Curry appeared not to hear the question. I hesitated at embarrassing him, but got my first taste of Paprika's power to get what she wanted. I nodded yes.

"Poor thing."

Curry continued his hold on Paprika's hand, shifting the ring against the light. I played on, teasing the elusive, exotic beat from my subconscious, no longer trying to impress anyone. Suddenly I realized where the riff had come from. The Miehle press at the newspaper. Pleased, I explored the question-and-answer rhythm on the drum. I looked at Curry to see if he recognized it, but his eyes looked half shut. Zoned out. Then his hand slipped away from Paprika's, and his head tilted back against the headboard, eyes closed.

Paprika said, "That's what you get, nursing that wingnut dog all night." Then she looked at me with a chirping laugh. "He loves to stare at sparklies."

My hands settled into the drumming without me paying them conscious attention.

"Anyway, I heard he scuttled Old Flattop. Were you there?"

"Yeah."

Paprika sat on the end of the bed and leaned near enough for me to see little bumps under her makeup. She smelled like Juicy Fruit.

"Tell me."

Curry looked sound asleep. I stopped drumming. "Well, he dozed off on his book, and when he woke up he knew everything in it. Stuff we haven't covered yet."

"Hm." She nodded as if this somehow made sense, and her tongue crept along her lip like a snail. "That gives me an idea." She rummaged through her purse, and showed me a glossy entry form for a contest sponsored by Blubbergum. Everyone was chewing the dang stuff recently. It gave off carbon dioxide and blew its own bubbles. You could glomb it to the corner of your desk and it would inflate to the size of a cantaloupe by the end of class. People would draw faces on the bubble and watch them become grotesque as the gum swelled unevenly.

"Guess the number of Blubbergum balls in the Blubbermobile," I read aloud. The picture showed a red convertible filled with colorful gumballs. The winner got the car.

"I'd give anything!" Paprika said, taking the form back. "Do you suppose, if he can sleep on his biology book... ?"

Carefully she tucked the form between Curry's skull and the headboard. "Now Curry," she said softly, "I want you to sleep on that picture so you can tell me how many gumballs are in that car."

Then, just as I'd rolled my eyes, wondering what kind of fruitcake factory I'd stumbled into, Curry, his eyes still closed, spoke.

I say he spoke, but his voice sounded distant, thickened with age. It sent through me the same kind of shudder I'd felt in the woods that afternoon when he'd mentioned his dreams.

"*Yes, the automobile is before me.*"

Just for a second, Paprika's eyes grew round. Then she quickly narrowed them. "Very funny Curry. Okay, smart aleck, how many gumballs?"

Curry lay still for a moment, looking more like a wax figure than a live person. His mouth barely moved when he answered. *"Not as many as it may seem, as the other prizes lie hidden under the gum."*

"You mean all the Blubbie Dolls? They wouldn't do that. That's cheating."

"Things are often not as they seem in this world."

Paprika wrinkled her face at Curry. "Well, mister know-it-all, give me a number."

"Twenty-one thousand, two-hundred and twenty-one—but the winning answer will be one less because a gumball is wedged in the driver's air vent and likely won't be counted."

Paprika screwed her mouth up in thought, then retrieved the entry form and wrote the number down. "I suppose it's as good a guess as any. Now stop your clowning around."

"Beware the cost of desire."

She slapped her brother on the leg. "Beware your smart-mouth comments."

He didn't stir.

"Curry!" This time Paprika pinched his arm. He still didn't move. "Sleep your whole life away. I'm going to get Aunt Iris's opinion." She scooted out the door and bounded down the stairs.

Curry lay still. A fly landed on his cheek. "I think you had her going," I said. The fly walked over to his lip, then explored a nostril. My own nose tickled just watching, but Curry didn't so much as twitch.

Chapter 3
I Make an Enemy

*T*he call to dinner didn't wake Curry either, and I shook him without result. I told Curry's mom, who didn't seem concerned. "There is no Godly limit on how much a teenager can eat, sleep, or pile up the laundry."

I eyed the roast lamb coming from the oven, and said, "I suppose I'd better be off."

"You're welcome to stay, but suit yourself."

"Of course you'll stay," Aunt Pansy said, steering me to a chair. "Can't let an eligible gentleman escape."

I scooted my chair to the table, feeling odd sitting next to Curry's empty plate. After the blessing, Pansy leaned her amphibious face toward me and said, "If three little moles crawled into three little holes, what's the last thing you'd see?"

"I don't know."

"Mol-asses!"

Pansy's taller sister, Aunt Iris, rolled her eyes. "That one's old as your toes and twice as corny." I smiled and Iris winked. The others took little notice of me—Mr. and Mrs. Buckle, Paprika, Dan Klatt, and Curry's older brother, Basil—but the Twist Sisters seemed pleased to have a fresh audience for their moldy jokes.

"Speaking of holes," Pansy said, "someone's been sneaking around at night, digging on our property. Well, I've got news for them: I got Uncle Cyrus's gun out, and I'll make a few holes of my own if I catch 'em."

Dan Klatt, Paprika's buffed-out boyfriend, stopped chewing. "You wouldn't shoot someone just for digging holes, would you?" His words garbled through the wad of meat in his mouth.

Pansy puckered her wrinkles. "You just watch me. Besides,

someone was prowling inside the house. One day we came home and it smelt like a man in there. We haven't had a man in that house for a long time, and I have a highly developed sense of smell. Then I found the toilet seat up—that clinched it."

The subject switched to Mr. Buckle's giant pumpkin, The Big McGillicuddy. "I think she's going to top nine-hundred pound," he said. Everyone agreed that would be a county record. For the rest of the meal, Paprika and Dan mostly held the spotlight. Dan carried the football for the Kluge Island Gooeyducks. Their helmets pictured a mighty gooeyduck clam bulging from its pathetic shell. As I reached for seconds, Dan told about the secret reverse they were going to run against the Hoag Island Hooligans.

After dinner, I found Curry still napping against the headboard. I pulled him out flat by the heels so he wouldn't get a whang in his neck. His shallow breathing didn't so much as change cadence. I thought about waking him, but decided against it, and went downstairs to help clean up. I washed dishes as Mrs. Buckle scraped dinner scraps into the dog pail. I asked, "Has Curry ever said anything about knowing what's in books without reading them?"

She stopped in mid-scrape. "You mean ESP?"

"Yeah, I guess so."

"No... " She frowned. "Just a creepy feeling sometimes. Like he's in another world, know what I mean? I think that foreigner put a spell on him."

"What foreigner?"

"The one on the ferry when Curry was just out of diapers. He had a turban on—the foreigner, that is. I don't want to think about it—it gives me goose flesh."

The next day, Saturday, mom urged me to go to the Gooeyduck/ Hooligan game that evening. I didn't want to go alone, but mom said, "How are you ever going to meet people if you don't mix?" I wanted to say *if everyone on the island didn't hate my parents for taking over their newspaper...* but I didn't. Wasn't their fault. I considered phoning

Curry but wasn't sure about chumming with a dorkfish in public. I'd be admitting social defeat. Besides, I'd probably run into him there and could at least say hi. Paprika would be there, bouncing around with her pompoms, kicking up the pleats of her skirt.

Dan Klatt swept fifty yards around end the first time he touched the ball. Everyone except me stood and cheered insanely, but I didn't feel any school spirit. I didn't see Curry so I meandered down to where the six lusty cheerleaders were hopping like fleas on a skillet, chanting *Dan, Dan, he's our man, if he can't do it, no one can.* Gag me with a gym sock. In ten years, Dan Klatt might be castrating farm animals for a living, and I might be discovering a new subatomic particle, or laying down stinging leads on my Fender Stratocaster in domed stadiums. I'd never have a bevy of cheerleaders worshiping me, but so what. Maybe if Dan could see beyond the floodlit gridiron, he'd gladly swap his fortunes for mine.

When the nubile sisterhood finished flapping about Dan, I got Paprika's attention. Her cheeks glowed in the chill evening and her uniform filled as she panted for breath.

"Is Curry here?"

"My brother?"

Like, how many Currys were there? I nodded.

"The little gomer is still asleep. Can you believe it?"

"You mean he never woke up? Since before dinner yesterday?"

Paprika nodded, pursing her lips petulantly as if Curry had slept twenty-four continuous hours for the sole purpose of annoying her. "Mom even jabbed him with a knitting needle. He has chores, you know."

"Maybe some tsetse flies snuck in on a shipment of giraffes."

"Huh?"

"Never mind. I just hope he's okay."

Paprika turned to watch the next play and I evaporated from her life. I milled behind the bleachers, feeling conspicuously alone, got in line at the snack bar, not because I wanted anything, but it gave me a few minutes break from wandering aimlessly. Then, with blue sno-cone in hand, I set out to walk around the field.

Just past the bathrooms, something sailed through the air: a paper cup, crimped at the top, trailing a stream of dust. Some kid imitated the sound of a plane going down. The cup landed at my feet. A familiar voice called out, raising a prickle of apprehension at the back of my neck.

"Hey smeg-head. Darwin Boner."

Out of the shadows of the lavatory came four toughs in denim jackets, trying too hard to make their cigarettes look casual. Choker Durant blocked my path.

"I wasn't finished with you yesterday."

I figured nothing I could say would make a difference.

"Let's see, we were talking about homework." He crossed his arms. "Just trying to be friendly to the newbie. But you know what? I got plenty of friends already. I don't need any more friends. What do you say to that?"

I checked my peripheral vision hoping to see other people approaching. But it sounded like the Gooeyducks were about to score and everyone had flocked to watch. My stomach felt sour. "I'm glad somebody likes you," I said.

"Whoooa!" one of Choker's pals said. "You gonna let that slide?"

Choker took a drag on his cigarette. "Whatcha got there, a sno-cone?" He tapped ashes on it.

"No, it's penguin poop."

Choker flicked away his cigarette though it was only half smoked, probably because it seemed the tough thing to do. "You know, you're not so smart after all. Lucky for me you're not doing my homework. But I do have a lesson for you, smegoroid. We want you to appreciate our island, don't we boys."

The boys agreed I should learn to appreciate the island.

Choker picked up the cup that had landed at my feet, uncrimped the top and poured fine dust over my sno-cone.

I gritted my teeth. A greenish light lit the washroom area, casting stark shadows. Two girls behind the concession counter waited on a small kid. Hoots of encouragement rose in a crescendo from the bleachers. Why didn't Dan Klatt score and get it over with so people would come to relieve themselves and buy popcorn and I could melt into the crowd?

"Let's see if you can develop a *taste* for our island. Eat up."

I heard a roar and horns honking from where cars could park on the opposite side of the field. We'd scored, but too late. Choker's thugs were circling me, pushing me into the shadows. I decided to take my best shot, though Choker alone had me by twenty-five pounds of brawn. I tossed the sno-cone straight up and when Choker's eyes followed it, I shot my fist into his gut. I tried to run, but someone stuck out a leg and tripped me. By the time I scrambled to my feet, they had me by the arms. Choker measured me for the first punch and swung for my face. I couldn't duck fast enough to avoid a stinging blow to the ear. Then punches started raining in from all sides and I tried covering up and twisting away but they kept finding unguarded places. Choker landed a payback shot to my midsection that buckled my knees, but I fought against going down because I knew I'd get kicked. As his next fist came out of the dark, I could see the glint of a massive ring on it, and tried dodging but someone shoved me into the punch which landed high, above my eye, metal on bone. I dropped to a knee while a flock of crows tried to find their way out of my skull. The punches seemed to have stopped, but time had slowed and other fists were probably on their way. Then my vision cleared and I saw the thugs slinking into the shadows.

Other people milled nearby without seeing me crouched in the shadows. Somewhere a toilet flushed. Blood ran into my eye, and I blinked and groped for a hanky. Some old guy shouted to a friend, "Say, how 'bout that Klatt kid. A real thumper ain't he." If only Klatt had thumped in for a score three minutes earlier, maybe I wouldn't be bleeding all over my new jacket and my face wouldn't be swelling up like a wad of Blubbergum.

When the flushing stopped, and people went back to the game, I got up, aching everywhere from the kidneys up, and went into the washroom. I bathed the cut over my eye and examined it in the scratched metal mirror. The cold water slowed the bleeding, but my eye was swelling shut. I ground my teeth in anger and thought how this mess of a face would make mom sorry she forced me to go to the game. Maybe dad would pause five minutes from his work to see the results of moving me away from my friends to an island full of knuckle-draggers. I threw my hanky away and pressed a damp paper towel over the cut. I took a deep breath. The anger passed, and I felt shaky and small. My parents hadn't beat me up, and I didn't have the right to tell them where to live. I'd made friends before and I'd make them again, but I wouldn't forget Choker Durant, and his time would come. That was a promise.

After the pep talk, I wanted only to get home without being seen or questioned, so I stayed in the shadows. My tongue probed a loose tooth and I spat some foamy blood among the garbage under the bleachers.

"Darwin? Is that you?"

I knew her voice, but couldn't put a face to it. It jolted me to be called by name. Peering over the top row of bleachers at me, I recognized the pointy jaw and wide-set eyes of Keeley Uncas.

"Oh gosh!" She looped her leg over the backrest, found a foothold, and climbed down. "Great bullwankers, what happened to you?"

"Visit from the welcome wagon."

Keeley pulled the compress away from my forehead and grimaced. "This needs stitches." She pursed her lips in thought. "You'd better come with me."

She took my arm, led me to the parking lot, opened the door of an old-style Volkswagen Bug and told me to get in.

"Where're we going?" I asked as she fired up the engine. "You're not old enough to drive, are you?"

Keeley just smiled and dropped the stick into reverse, backed up, got us out on the road, jamming gears like a pro.

"You've done this before," I said, fumbling for the seat belt.

"Father hates to go out, so I do the errands. I've been driving since age eleven. He helps Missus... " Keeley paused. "Let's just say Sheriff Biggs owes dad a favor, so as long as I don't massacre someone's cow, the license thing isn't a problem. My dad can stitch up a face like nobody's business."

As Keeley downshifted into a curve, I groped for the armrest.

"I'm not bleeding to death," I shouted over the clatter of the engine.

"I know just how fast to take every curve on the island."

God help us.

"Hold on!" Keeley cranked the wheel, swerving onto a graveled road in a four-wheel slide. I braced against the dash, and found the blood had become sticky enough to hold the paper towel against my eye. With rear tires spraying gravel, she accelerated, fishtailing shoulder to shoulder. I began to relax—she really did know how to drive that thing. Ahead, reflector posts marked a small bridge crossing an irrigation canal. The whole thing ramped several feet higher than grade because of the dikes. When Keeley floored it, I knew she was trying for air. We hit the approach at about sixty, and for a quiet, endless second we were free of gravity. Then each of the punches I'd absorbed cried out as we bottomed the suspension on the other side.

"EE-HAW!" I managed to say.

Keeley backed off on the gas and looked over at me with obvious pleasure. And maybe a little surprise, too, that I wasn't curled in the fetal position, sucking a thumb. She turned up a long driveway, slowing to normal speed, probably not wanting her father to know he'd raised a stunt driver.

Doc Uncas let us in the door of their modest house, an intent man with a brush of chin whiskers, who would have been tall if not hunched. Eyes dark like animal caves. He said nothing, but arched a questioning eyebrow at Keeley.

"A pack of bullies beat him up. His name is Darwin. Darwin Bownes. He's new here."

Doc Uncas replied in slow, hoarse syllables. "Of course. The newspaper." He pulled me under the light and eased the compress from my wound. "This could stand a bit of knitting. You should see a doctor."

Logs crackled in the fireplace and the room smelled of alder smoke and pipe tobacco. A fat book lay open on the chair by the fire.

"I think we can trust him, dad," Keeley said, almost in a whisper.

The Doc looked at me and shrugged. "I don't have a piece of paper on my wall saying I'm a doctor."

"Keeley says you're the best."

He seemed to function at about a quarter the speed of his daughter. I counted four breaths before he reached for the phone and handed it to me. "I need to hear it from your parents. I can't have the newspaper saying that Doc Uncas is performing surgery without a license."

I made the call.

Mom didn't get overly hysterical when I told her I'd fallen out of the bleachers. I'd put her through a lot over the years.

"So you split your skull open?"

"Not that bad."

"How many fingers am I holding up?"

I grinned. "Three."

Pause. "How did you know that?"

"You always hold up three fingers."

"I do? Well, how much blood did you lose?"

"Less than a gallon."

"Any brain damage?"

"No, I landed on my head."

"Okay, put the doctor on."

"That's kind of the point, mom. He's not currently a doctor—but he *is* a doctor."

I handed the phone to Doc Uncas.

"Ma'am... What? You always use GooeyGlue... Right, I know, stickier than barnacles... No, this cut's too deep for that. Good old needle and horsehair."

Keeley hid a smile behind her hand. Her dark eyes sparkled.

"Mm, no, sorry Mrs. Bownes, there's really nothing I can do about the nose. It's out of my line."

He said goodbye and hung up, and took me into his den which smelled of rubbing alcohol. He disinfected the wound and sprayed something to ice it, but I still felt the prick of the needle and the tug of thread being pulled through my brow. Mostly to divert my mind from it, I said, "I heard something about Governor Bigelow's daughter dying."

Keeley scowled at me, but her father didn't seem to mind the question. "Uh huh. Of course, he wasn't governor then. Just attorney general. I got convicted of criminal malpractice." Doc clipped the thread. "A girl died and somebody had to pay. I'm lucky he didn't railroad me into prison." He shook his head. "Lucky—not exactly the right word for it."

"Had you done anything wrong?" I asked.

"No he did not!" Keeley said.

"I tried an experimental treatment. Something I'd learned from an old shaman in the Amazon. Her condition was desperate."

"Dad was an outstanding doctor. All the hopeless cases came to him—the cases nobody else could cure. And they still—" Keeley stopped herself.

Doc cleared his throat. "Even now, Governor Bigelow would like to check me into the iron bar hotel. If I get reported for practicing without a license, well... I hope we can rely on your discretion."

Chapter 4
Raising the Dead

J woke the next morning with too many aches to count. I dressed, pulled my cap visor down to cover my bandage, and went for a bike ride. Started slowly, out of town past the pond, outlines of ducks in the fog, rushes hung with dewy spider webs. Crows acting in charge of the world. They made me think of Choker and his goons. When my bruised muscles loosened up, I pushed it up to workout speed headed up Boneyard Road, waving when a car went by, a family dressed for church. Drivers on Kluge Island waved at everyone—even Conrad Bownes' son. Six or seven miles mostly east, I took a swing through Camp Bluetoad to look at the lodge and the rustic cabins by Outlook Inlet. Every student with a 'B' average or better got to spend the last week of school at camp. Sounded like a hoot.

I rode wobble-slow past a row of overturned canoes and imagined Choker dumping one at sea and begging me to save his worthless life. *What? Big bad Choker can't swim? You sure can whimper though. Louder, so everyone can hear, then I'll knock you with my paddle to calm you down and save your candy butt.*

I had to shake out of it before grinding my teeth to nubs. If you wanted something bad enough, did it have a way of happening? Heading home on my big loop, I passed Curry Buckle's mailbox, and, on a whim, carved a turn and went back. He might like some help with his chores, and I thought I'd show him the stitches over my eye.

Curry's mom opened the door two inches and peered through the gap. I wasn't looking my best, but she recoiled as if whatever happened to my face was contagious.

"Is Curry home?"

"Did you give him any drugs?" she demanded.

"What?" My mouth dropped open. "Of course not. Why?"

"He still hasn't woken up. We think he might have got drugged."

"You mean he's been sleeping since Friday night?"

"Lying still as those punkins in the field."

I frowned with concern.

"Who is it mum?" came a boy's deep voice. The door opened further and a freckled, gap-toothed face appeared. Curry's older brother, Basil.

"Just Curry's friend," she said, as if he had only one.

"Darwin," I reminded them.

"Might as well come in," Basil said. "I'm just about to wake him up."

By that time, Curry's dad had moseyed over. "No more firecrackers Basil, you hear?"

"Sure dad."

Mr. Buckle chortled. "Basil's got a scientific mind. He once resuscitated a dead chicken using the electric fence."

When Basil and I got upstairs to Curry's room, I found he had something similar in mind for his brother. With the smell of gunpowder hanging in the air, Curry lay on his back, a peaceful look on his face, bare feet protruding from his blanket. Basil had wrapped a stripped wire around one big toe. The wire ran to a black box with a dial on it. Basil set to work attaching a second wire to the box.

"It's a modified train transformer," he said. "We can crank the juice until he wakes up, like jump-starting a jalopy."

I shuddered. "Oh?"

Basil held up the remaining end. "Where should we attach this other lead? We could shave a patch on his scalp—the current should arc through the brain, don't you suppose?"

"Um, seems kind of drastic. Does your mom know...?"

He whispered, "I'd rather surprise her."

Oh cripes. "What else have you tried so far?"

Basil cracked a diabolical smile; I'd never seen so much space between a person's teeth. "I'll show you." He picked up a feather. "Curry's ticklish just about everywhere, especially on the bottom of his feet. He's never slept through this before." Basil demonstrated. Curry didn't move. "Now check this out." He gripped a large sewing needle with pliers, and picked up Curry's hand.

I felt paralyzed with disbelief. "No," I said. "Please don't."

"You have to see this. I pushed it halfway through a few minutes ago. He didn't even flinch."

My stomach knotted. "You don't need to show me. I'll take your word for it."

"It's like a miracle in our own house. Hey, I know! Darwin, you open his mouth and hold this wire to one of his fillings. I'll dial up some juice."

"Ah, maybe we should call a doctor. He might be really sick. Give me five minutes, okay?"

He shrugged and I rushed downstairs.

"I'm worried about him," I said to Curry's parents, interrupting the big-haired evangelist on TV. "Have you thought about calling a doctor?"

Mr. Buckle, from his recliner, hit the mute button, then hooked a thumb behind a suspender. A bit of shirttail poked through his fly. "You learn after raising eleven kids there's no point getting panicked—most of the time. Am I right?" He looked to Mrs. Buckle.

"Of course, Neil, but I am getting worried. We should call the clinic."

"Clinic's closed. Nurse Williard's out of town."

"Well, there's Doctor Slather."

Mr. Buckle shook his head. "No insurance." He pronounced it *in*surance.

I didn't know how long Basil could restrain himself. I asked with some urgency, "Can I make a phone call?" I dialed the only Uncas in the thin phone book and got Keeley.

"How's your head, Darwin?"

"My head? It feels like it's on spin cycle with a dead cat inside."

"Normal, considering."

"That's a relief. Can you get your dad?" I explained the problem. "Basil's ready to light Curry up with a train transformer." I watched for Mrs. Buckle's reaction and saw her eyebrows go up.

"Bullpucky!" Keeley said.

"I'm serious!"

"Hold on." I heard Keeley passing on the facts to her dad. He took the phone.

"What do you think, Doc?"

"He's been sleeping for what, about forty hours?"

"Yeah, about."

"Same age as Keeley?"

"Right."

"Has he missed any sleep recently?"

"Well, he stayed up with a sick dog Thursday night."

"There you have it."

"But they've been sticking him with pins and blowing off firecrackers."

"What! Hmmm. He just went to sleep normally on Friday evening?"

"Well, sort of. His sister was showing him a ring and he kinda sorta spaced out."

"Showed him a ring?"

"An opal. Before that, he almost went to sleep on his feet at the newspaper shop, watching the printing press. Then I played the same rhythm on a drum I got at the Take It Or Leave It, and... " I stopped, realizing it must sound like nonsense.

"Opal ring? Drum? Hm... I once saw a shaman in Peru follow flute music out of his body, and hours later his assistant piped him back in."

I held the receiver away from my ear for a moment, then said to Doc Uncas, "I've got an idea. I'll let you know if it turns out." I hung up and took the stairs two at a time. But when I got to Curry's room, Basil had the transformer dial halfway up and Curry's eyebrows were quivering like electric toothbrushes.

"Stop!" I said, and pulled the plug. The wrinkles went out of Curry's face. "There's something else we should try."

"But he was just about woke up," Basil said.

"He was just about medium rare. Now, where's Paprika?"

"Rika?" Basil looked at his watch. "If it's before noon, you'd be finding her in the bathroom."

It wasn't even ten-thirty. By noon Curry could be a science project gone tragically wrong. "It can't wait." I passed Mr. and Mrs. Buckle as they came into the room, hustled down the stairs and knocked on the bathroom door. "Paprika, it's Darwin."

"Who?"

"Darwin Bownes."

"Go outside and use a tree."

"Curry needs you right now."

"Get real."

"I am. Only you can help him."

"I'll strangle him, and you too, if you don't leave me alone."

"Please, it's important."

"Does the term 'get lost' have any meaning to you?"

Suddenly mad, I grabbed the doorknob, thinking only of rattling it. But the door swung open and there stood Paprika, hair in pins, face spotted with zit ointment, eyes made up in two different color schemes, her mouth gaping in outrage. The sight of her could have scared the shell off a turtle.

"You... YOU... LITTLE RETARD!"

"C'mon," I said, grabbing her arm. Once I had her beyond sight of the mirror, its spell seemed broken and she stopped resisting.

"What? He's dying?" Paprika demanded.

I didn't answer and she hurried up the stairs. In Curry's room, Basil got one look at his younger sister in her unprocessed state and his face stretched in mock horror.

Paprika pointed to the door and stomped. "Out, you spasticated idiot!"

"I'm going," Basil whimpered. "Anyone who hasn't had rabies shots, stay at your own risk."

Basil slipped nimbly by Paprika before she could scratch out his eyes, and lurked safely out of reach.

Paprika looked Curry over anxiously, then scowled at me. "He looks the same."

"What did Doc Uncas say?" Mrs. Buckle asked.

"He gave me an idea. Maybe he needs to hear the drum again to find his body, but also, Paprika, do you remember how you told him to sleep his life away? Maybe if you tell him to wake up... "

Paprika rolled her eyes.

Basil said, "If Curry wakes up and sees her, he'll go back into a coma for a week."

Paprika threw the first thing she could lay her hands on—the train transformer—and it might have hit Basil but for the wire wrapped around Curry's toe.

As I unwired the unfortunate toe, Mrs. Buckle shooed Basil away and closed the door, then collapsed in the chair beside the bed. She took Curry's hand and patted it.

Then I focused on the tarnished medallion at his throat. I took a closer look at the strange bird wearing a crown with three colored stones in it. From the wear on the raised areas, and the dark grunge on the rest, it appeared to be very, very old. I'd never seen anything like it, and couldn't help handling it. It felt heavy and warm.

"That's Curry's omelet," his mom said.

"Amulet," Paprika corrected. "I looked it up. It's a magic charm."

"That's what I said. Omelet. At least that's what the foreigner on the ferry called it."

"The one with the turban?" I asked, remembering her comment after dinner Friday. "You thought he might have put a spell on Curry."

Mrs. Buckle nodded. "A stranger character I've never beheld, wouldn't you say, Neil?"

"Oh my Lord," Mr. Buckle said. "Strange ain't a proper enough word for it."

"He had this wide nose and orange robe. We was riding back from Anacortes when he came right up and asked to sit down. There were scads of empty seats. But he seemed polite. Curry had just turned two and the stranger took a real shine to him. Then he said, 'Madame, you have been blessed with a special son. I have something for him, if you will permit.'"

"What happened?" I asked.

"He took out a leather bag with a bunch of these doodads in it, and spread them on the table. Little Curry stood up on the seat and made a grab for this one here. I tried to make him turn loose of it, but the foreigner just laughed and said it was rightfully Curry's."

"Something about protecting him from evil," Mr. Buckle added.

"Wow," I said.

"Yep. We thought he'd get tired of it like the rest of his toys, but, like you see, he always keeps it close."

"Mmm." I looked at Curry, deep in slumber, and wondered if the amulet was giving him sweet dreams. Then I said to Paprika, "I'm going to play the drum and you just speak softly in his ear. Tell him to return to his body now and to wake up."

She'd been spitting on a tissue and wiping off the zit cream. "Really, I don't see how..."

"It sounds crazy, but what can it hurt?"

I sat on the edge of the bed, wedged the drum between my legs, listened in my head for the question-and-answer beat of the printing press, letting it come out through my hands.

Paprika shook her head, but leaned over her sleeping brother. "Curry, do you hear me? It's Rika. I want you to come back to your body now. Please come back."

I played the phrase over and over, the groove getting deeper with each repetition.

"Curry, you goofball, are you here?" Then Paprika tensed. "His lips moved, I saw them."

I stopped drumming and pressed near the bed, and sure enough, saw his dry lips part, and heard the words come out in that distant voice. "*I am here.*"

"Well thank goodness," Paprika said. "I thought I'd hypnotized you into a vegetable."

"*This is not hypnosis. It would be wrong, and possibly dangerous, to turn one's mind over to another.*"

"Stop talking so weird. If you weren't in your body, where the heck were you?"

"*Wandering the halls of Akasha, where all things are written in light.*"

All this became too much for Mrs. Buckle, and she wagged a finger over Curry. "Stop clowning around and get your butt out of bed."

"*You may always awaken me by chanting OM in my right ear.*"

As I was on his right, I did as he instructed. Mrs. Buckle also leaned forward, and Mr. Buckle craned over the top of her. And when Curry's eyes flickered and snapped open, everyone, including me, drew back as if alarmed by the magic of it.

Curry sat up and looked around. "Why's everyone here? Jeez, Darwin, what's been gnawing on your face? Is dinner ready? I'm starving."

Chapter 5
Choker's Wild

I caught up with Keeley in the hallway at school Monday—I had to run because her legs were as long as mine, and she walked like she drove. I couldn't wait to tell her about Curry's recovery. "It's like your dad thought. He was in some kind of trance."

"Well, he must have an awfully weak mind. It runs in the family, as far as I can tell. They probably snack on paint chips off the house. Anyway, how's the cut?" She leaned close and ran a finger over my swollen brow. I'd taken the geeky-looking bandage off. Her short black hair had a spicy smell to it. "No signs of infection."

"I owe your dad one... and you too."

Her gaze shifted past me and she stiffened. I looked around to see the goon squad coming, Choker in his purple sneaks doing his dipping, bent-knee walk that his ankle-biter friends copied. I hoped they'd pass on by.

They didn't.

"Check this out," Choker said, looking at the stitches above my eye. He nodded, apparently satisfied with his work. "Looks like you got a zipper installed, Bownes. What, you had a little accident? You should be more careful."

"And you should be ashamed of yourself," Keeley said.

"What's this?" Choker said to his smirking friends. "Birdlegs, sticking up for the zipperhead."

"Yes, and I'm going to report you to Principal Krogstrand for beating people up and cheating on your homework."

For a moment Choker lost his cool and glared at Keeley with clenched fists. "You want trouble? Maybe your pretty little orange Volkswagen gets busted. Or maybe Frankenstein here gets a matching zipper."

"Bullfeathers!"
The five-minute bell rang. "C'mon, Keeley," I said.
"This isn't over, zippy," Choker said.
No it isn't, I vowed silently.

In biology class, I tried ignoring Choker but he didn't like being ignored, so he called me names and gave me the evil eye. Curry slunk in right at the tardy bell—the first time I'd seen him that day. I guessed he wasn't eager to face Old Flattop, but coming in last just made it worse. Mr. Flatski, hairy arms folded across his white shirt, watched Curry all the way to his desk. The Gooeyducks had lost Saturday night and I'd heard whispers that Flatski would be growly, being the coach. Everyone seemed to be watching for something to happen.

It didn't take long.

"Put your books away and take out a sheet of paper," he said.

Everyone groaned.

"Let's see how many of you bothered to read your assignment this weekend." He turned and rolled up the anatomy chart he'd used to cover the pop quiz question on the board: *Explain the basic elements of Charles Darwin's theory of natural selection. Give examples.*

"You have exactly," he waited for the second hand to reach the twelve, "twenty minutes. Go."

He reached for his smokes as he headed to the door, taking a last glance to note who was writing and who was lolling their head as if recovering from a lobotomy. Choker Durant played it cool until the door closed, then looked about frantically.

That told me something important about Choker. It had never occurred to me that he actually cared about passing his courses. But he did. He cared a lot. Maybe his parents had thumbscrews and knew how to use them. In that instant I made a rash decision.

When Choker turned in my direction, I nodded, pointed to my paper with a scribbling motion, then pointed to him. He smiled and seemed relieved. After all, I was named after Charles Darwin—I should know the answer, right? Choker spent the next ten minutes twiddling his pencil while I scribbled furiously with mine. When done, I let the page fall off my desk. It landed near Choker and he snatched it up. I glanced over at Keeley, hoping to find her absorbed in her writing, but she was looking squarely at me, looking disappointed. Knowing how she felt about cheaters, I cringed. With time running short, I dropped my pencil out the rear window and switched to pen for my own quiz, changing also from a crabbed cursive script to the brisk printing I usually use. I glanced up to see Choker signing his name to my work and hoped I hadn't made a terrible mistake. I'd almost finished when Flatski returned.

He collected the papers starting at the far end of the room, taking a quick glance at each. You could basically tell who screwed up just by the length of their answer. Keeley had written four pages, single-spaced, while some had barely covered a half-page with headline-sized writing. My nerves glowed like wires in a toaster as Flatski glanced over Choker's paper. He froze, eyes squinted for a closer look, the little muscles around his mouth tightening, the veins in his temple swelling.

He handed the paper back to Choker. "A most original piece of work, Durant. Perhaps you'd like to read it out loud."

Choker glanced around helplessly, probably wondering if this was a good or bad development. But he went ahead. You didn't cross Coach Flatski.

"How natural selection works. For example, it is natural for the toughest guys to get all the best women."

There were a few snorts of laughter.

"It's always been that way, because in the old days, the tough guys killed the most dinosaur meat and could feed more women. There weren't many scrawny guys then because they got eaten in battle."

I had to bite my lip to keep a straight face. Choker pressed on cheerfully, probably thinking the chuckles were for his witty writing style.

"Nowadays, there's more scrawny people because the tougher guys killed all the dinosaurs, so then the wimps lived and started making baby wimps."

"Silence," Mr. Flatski barked to quiet the laughter in the classroom. "Continue, Durant."

"And the longer that went on, the uglier the wimps got, because they could only get the ugliest women. This means evolution is going in reverse. The proof that humans are turning back into apes is there are more hairy people..."

I think Choker knew, then, he'd been had, because he looked up at Mr. Flatski, who stood before him like a monument to testosterone, drumming his fingertips against his biceps. Even the backs of his fingers were hairy. Choker turned to me briefly with a puzzled look. Flatski noticed, and looked me in the eye. I looked away.

This time the class's laughter quickly dried up.

"Very amusing, Durant." Mr. Flatski ran a hand over his bristle-cut then jerked his attention back to me. "Bownes, did you write this?"

If he'd drilled me with a football just above my gut, it would have felt pretty much the same. I took a breath, then leaned forward for a look. "Looks like it's written in pencil," I said lamely, and handed him my quiz. "I only have a pen."

Flatski scanned my paper then looked back at me, eyes burning with suspicion. I probably wouldn't get an 'A', but my payoff came when Old Flattop slid a red pencil from above his ear and scrawled a fat 'D-minus' on Choker's paper. "The only reason you're not getting an 'F', Durant, is because you showed an instinct for survival. And why not? Everyone in this room runs on high-octane genes tested mercilessly for a half-billion years. Each of you is a finely honed survival machine, hair or no hair, and don't you forget it."

He took Curry's paper next, snatching it in a manner that suggested he hadn't forgiven Curry for upstaging him Friday. Mr. Flatski scanned it, then pushed out his lower lip and read more carefully. Curry still seemed a little dazed, probably from his long sleep, and I noticed he hadn't been laughing along with everyone else. Soon Flatski's mouth pursed into a grim smile.

"Did I say this was an open-book quiz, Buckle?"

"No sir."

"In fact, didn't I specifically say to put your books away?"

"Yessir."

Mr. Flatski's neck reddened like a steamed crab, and he jabbed Curry's page with a stiff finger. "You copied this answer straight from the book. No doubt about *this* being cheating. You know what happens to cheaters, Buckle?"

Curry's Adam's apple bobbed. "But I've never even read... I mean, I didn't..." Curry raised a finger and tapped his melon. "It's all in here."

Like a trout hitting bait, Mr. Flatski had Curry by the ear. "You know what I hate worse than cheaters? Liars. Let's find out what Principal Krogstrand thinks of liars and cheaters in his school."

When Curry's ear got dragged out the door, the rest of him wasn't far behind.

Chapter 6
Curse of the Mummy

Curry Buckle a cheater? I had no way of knowing for sure, yet somehow I did know for sure: he wasn't. I hustled to the door in time to see Curry dragged up the stairs that led to Mr. Krogstrand's office. Just the thought of our principal made me shudder. He looked like an unwrapped mummy in a three-piece suit, his shrunken skin pulling his mouth into a painful smile. Just enough leather on his triangular face to upholster a bicycle seat. And he had a nervous habit of jerking his head around as if trying to catch someone in the act. He rarely came down the narrow staircase from the old bell tower he'd converted to his office.

A few others joined me at the door.

"Curried Butthead really smegged up this time," Choker said, drawing a finger across his throat.

"You should be the one getting your ear stretched," Keeley Uncas said. She stood tall enough to look Choker in the eye, but his wide shoulders made her look like a beanpole.

Her comment reminded Choker of the joke I'd played on him and he bared his teeth at me. A strand of drool made the snarl convincing. Then his little buddy, Jimmy Colvin, the ankle-biter who'd help bash me at the game, said, "That was a real harfer you came up with, Choker. Ultimate, man, a real harfer."

Choker saw other kids agreeing that his quiz had been the ultimate harfer, so he said, "Yeah, Old Flattop didn't know whether to fart or go blind." But when he turned back to me, his mood darkened. He crumpled up his quiz, said, "Keep your D-minus," and crammed it in my shirt pocket. I heard something rip, but didn't look. I was looking at a set of knuckles with a sharp-edged ring displayed in my face. "You better pray to whatever god you believe in, Bownes, 'cause you're going to get oblubberrated."

"You know, Choker," I said, my heart thudding, "I think two syllables is your upper limit." I looked at Keeley to see if she approved of my wit in the face of danger.

"More like guttural grunts," Keeley said, taking my arm. "C'mon," she whispered, "before he realizes how big of an ass you made of him."

"Let's go see how Curry's doing."

"Huh? Upstairs?" Her eyes got big. "Bullslobber! There's nothing we can do." She tensed her chin, raising a dimple. "You go." She made it sound like a dare.

"Well, all right then." I shouldn't have talked so big, but couldn't wimp out. I walked boldly to the stairs then paused. The school building was a long wooden two-story with a bell tower in the middle. Mr. Krogstrand had modified the bell tower into his office. The narrow stairs went up a half-flight then doubled back; the dark paneling smelled of polish.

Each stair made a faint creak, no matter how carefully I stepped. At the upper landing, I paused outside a frosted glass wall. Just reading the fancy gold letters—*E. Krogstrand, Principal and Superintendent*—raised a clammy sweat that made my shirt stick to my back. I peered through the open door into a small, windowless room, and saw the principal's secretary, Mrs. Muldoon, cupping her ear toward a circular staircase, which, no doubt, led up to Mr. Krogstrand's private office. She had a notepad and pencil in hand, which she concealed when I entered.

"Curry... he didn't cheat," I said.

She held a finger to her lips.

I heard Mr. Flatski's deep voice, something about an honor code and copying answers from the book. Then came Mr. Krogstrand's staccato response. "What are you shaking your head for, Buckle? Calling Professor Flatski a liar?"

"Sir," Curry said, his thin voice wavering. "It just came to me. The answers."

"Just came to you. Word for word, full born in all its glory and splendor, just like in the book."

"Yes sir."

"Space aliens whispering in your ear."

"I—I don't think so."

Mr. Krogstrand raised the pitch of his voice. "Buckle, do I look like an idiot?"

"No sir."

"Then spare me the lame excuses!"

The cutting remark affected me like a gulp of sour milk.

"No place in this school for cheaters and liars. Know what happens to cheaters and liars here?"

The contempt in his voice when he said 'cheaters and liars' set my teeth on edge. When he said it the second time, I became furious. Not mad—instantly furious.

Curry didn't get a chance to answer the question. I barged past Mrs. Muldoon, up the spiral stairs, the cast iron treads ringing like dull gongs. They twisted me in a 360 and I emerged, slightly disoriented, in a different world. My feet sunk in thick burgundy carpet. Windows ringing the circular office allowed Krogstrand to spy in any direction. Rich sofa, model ships, huge walnut desk. Before me, at parade rest, stood Mr. Flatski. As he recognized me, his scalp reddened through the bristles.

Curry rubbed his stretched ear. "Darwin!" Then his joy at seeing me crumpled into concern. I followed his gaze across the bunker-like desk to Mr. Krogstrand.

Still juiced by my fit of anger, I said, "Mr. Krogstrand, Curry's telling the truth. He didn't cheat. I would have seen it."

"And you are...?" Krogstrand glared with such force I couldn't even draw breath. His eyes never blinked.

My mouth went dry.

"He's Darwin Bownes," Mr. Flatski answered for me.

The principal's head twitched, and he scanned me with a sideways look. "Newspaperman's boy."

"That's the one," Flatski said, stroking his chin. The grating of his stubble unnerved me and the shakes began replacing my anger.

"Sticking up for your friend, are you? How noble." Krogstrand held up Curry's paper. "Explain, if you can, how he wrote the answer word-for-word without looking at the book."

"Um, well, actually, the truth is... Curry *is* psychic."

His face pointed at Curry, but his eyes strained sideways at me. If he kept that up, both eyes would migrate to one side of his face like a halibut. "Did... you... say... *psychic?*"

I nodded. "You can test him for yourself—ask him anything from the book."

"You think my time is something to be squandered?"

"But it's to find out the truth."

Never blinking, he said, "I have all the truth I need."

There is something unnatural about eyes that never blink.

Then Mr. Flatski made things worse. "Since it's truth we're after, I think Bownes here had something to do with writing another boy's quiz."

A sparkle of glee lit Krogstrand's eyes. I felt numb, as if outside my body; in that moment, I understood the game. Flatski twisted the joke I'd played on Choker into something uglier. The set-up. Now the knockdown.

"Well, Bownes?" Krogstrand asked.

It would do no good to explain. I knew that if Krogstrand were in my shoes, he'd lie. But he figured I probably wouldn't. That was the game. *Come to the dark side, Luke.* Either way, Krogstrand won, so why not be honest about it. "I wrote Choker's answer."

Krogstrand shook his head slowly. "It's a black day for Kluge High, Mr. Flatski. Punishment?"

I hoped Old Flattop would slip into his football coach mode and assign us to run laps.

"Ahem! I'll leave that to you, sir."

Krogstrand spoke through his teeth, "These boys have earned failing scores today. Can't imagine this wouldn't impact their biology grades for the term—by at least one full grade."

"Undoubtedly."

"In our day, Mr. Flatski, that would have been getting off easy. Next offense, expulsion. Understood?"

Both Curry and Mr. Flatski nodded their heads. I gritted my teeth for a moment, then turned to leave.

"Bownes!"

I gulped in a breath and held it.

"Do I recall approving a request for you to play electric guitar in concert band?"

My breath still hadn't come unstuck, so I didn't answer.

The corner of his mouth curled in a false smile. "Been giving it more thought. Guitar isn't a proper band instrument. Now clarinets... every band needs clarinets. You can't ever have too many clarinets."

Chapter 7
Camp Bluetoad

We only had a few minutes before the end of biology period, so we got some fresh air instead of returning to class. "Dang," Curry said as we shambled out toward the bleachers. "I should have just put down the wrong answer and saved us both a lot of trouble."

I picked up a rock, threw it at a power pole. Missed. "If it's inside your own head, don't you have a right to use it? Some people have better brains; nobody gets worked up about it. Or photographic memories. Nobody says that's cheating. So you're psychic. What's the big deal?"

That got a glimmer of smile out of Curry. "You'd make a good lawyer, but I don't know, somehow it does seem like cheating. Anyway, sorry about your grade and about band."

Of all my classes, I looked forward most to band. I threw another rock, harder, and this time plugged the pole. "Clarinet! I'd rather toot a dead rat's ass." I followed that up with the foulest word in my vocabulary.

Curry cringed and looked away. "Could you use some other term in the future?"

It never occurred to me another guy might get offended. But Curry was a shy owl. "Like what?"

"How about *drat!*"

"*Drat?* Get real. Sorry, but *drat!* doesn't cut it."

"Well," he folded his arms, "there's always *double-drat!*"

After that, I didn't feel like cussing any more anyway. "Yeah, that's much better. Kinda has that dead-rat thing going for it."

"Anyway, I'm really sorry. You might have given Keeley a run for head of the class. She's worried, you know." He gave me a knowing glance, as if he thought I cared what Keeley thought.

Then we heard an announcement over the crackling PA system—

Mrs. Muldoon's nasal voice: *All students and faculty will meet in the auditorium at one o'clock for a brief assembly.* She repeated it, but didn't say why. For a second, I wondered if it had something to do with making a public example of Curry and me, liars and cheaters that we were. Clamp us in stocks and have everyone spit on us as they filed by.

"Want to go see Troutigan with me at lunch?" Curry asked.

"What for?"

"Maybe he can tell us something about the markings on your drum. Remember, at the Take It Or Leave It, Leon said Troutigan brought it back from India?"

"You want to find out what that amulet of yours is all about."

Curry nodded, a worried sag to his eyes. "Lately, I feel caught in some kind of rip-current, and I don't know where it's sweeping me."

I'd been meaning to ask him something. "Hey, when you were asleep for almost two days, did you like... go somewhere? Do you remember anything? Dreams?"

Curry twitched, almost a shiver.

"A dream. I'd forgotten about that weird dream. And you were in it."

"Yeah? Tell me."

"We'd been swallowed by something huge, a whale or something, and I thought we were goners but you weren't worried. You took out a knife and carved a big chunk out of the whale and ate it, and kept at it until I could see light from the hole you made, and I flew through it and escaped. I just flew and flew, everywhere...   That's all I can remember."

Old hippie Troutigan ran a lunch stand at the waterfront. He wore his gray-streaked hair in a ponytail, and his bushy moustache covered most of his mouth. For a cook, he was suspiciously skinny.

"Interest you in a couple of gooeyburgers?" he asked.

Curry held up his sack lunch and gave an apologetic smile.

"It's cool, dude," Troutigan said.

"Darwin here picked up a drum at Leon's, and he said it originally belonged to you."

Troutigan looked me over carefully, but didn't comment.

"We've got some questions about it," Curry said.

"Me too, believe me."

"You got it in India?"

"There's this Buddhist monastery out by the Ajanta caves. Bunch of monks who fled Tibet when the Commies invaded. I traded my blues harp for that drum, and went through all kinds of hassle getting it home."

"Then why'd you give it away?" I asked.

He shrugged and began shaping some clam patties. "My cat didn't like it." He seemed almost embarrassed to admit it.

"What do you mean?"

"Well, it's tuned just right that it picks up vibrations from other things and starts droning on its own."

"Like what other things?"

"I don't know, the refrigerator, or a boat motor, or even the wind. It scared Cleopatra, so I had to get rid of it."

"What about the weird marks on the side?" Curry said.

"Yeah, that's what intrigued me. It's Tibetan writing. Some kind of mantra I suppose. I've seen that kind of thing carved on prayer stones."

"Mantra?" Curry said. "What exactly is that?"

"Something you chant over and over until it purifies your consciousness and gets you high."

Curry seemed deep in thought over it. I checked my watch. "C'mon, we've got eight minutes to get back for the assembly."

For a small school, we had a decent auditorium. They must have gotten a deal on the seats when some other place upgraded. The floor and ceiling slanted toward a stage that was almost as large as the audience area, if you included all the space behind the wine-colored curtains. The acoustics were good and everyone kept shouting louder to be heard. Then Principal Krogstrand walked onto the stage and flicked his fingernail against the microphone, sending sonic booms through the hall until we all shut up.

"Students of Kluge High. I have unfortunate news." His gaze swept back and forth like a lawn sprinkler. "This school has a long tradition of excusing all 'B' students and above to attend Camp Bluetoad at the end of the school year. However," he twitched his neck, "the Camp Bluetoad property is to be sold."

A collective gasp rose from the students. I'd heard that all but the dullest of them scratched out a three-point average, not wanting to miss camp.

"Expenses have increased, and the camp no longer meets safety codes. Regrettably, the school can't afford the upgrades. We have a generous offer for the property—an offer that will allow us to construct a new gymnasium. Not to worry, we'll continue to reward good scholarship. Perhaps a bonfire on the baseball diamond or—"

Groans drowned out whatever Mr. Krogstrand had in mind.

"Going to have to live with it," he said. "Now back to class."

As he stepped away from the microphone, one of my teachers, Ms. Dozier, rushed up the stage stairs. She taught English comp, a blocky woman known behind her back as Bull Dozier. She had an oddball spirit I liked, though it came out in questionable ways. For instance, she wore the same dress every day: a loose Hawaiian muumuu.

"A moment, sir?" she said into the microphone. Krogstrand turned. "There must be something we can do? As you said, this is an honored tradition here, and we can't let it die. What if we somehow raise the money to fix whatever needs fixed? Couldn't we keep the camp?"

She took the microphone off its stand and held it at arm's length toward the principal. For a moment he resisted, but Bull Dozier had put him on the spot.

He tried to make light of it. "By all means, Ms. Dozier. Pass the hat. When your nickels and dimes add up to twenty-five thousand dollars, then come see me."

Ms. Dozier's seemed stunned by the amount. "How much time do we have? Six months?"

Krogstrand shrugged. "Six weeks."

Ms. Dozier swallowed, her formidable bosom heaved within her muumuu. She raised the microphone to her lips and faced us. "Well, we're not going to cry 'uncle' are we? No way. We can do it if we all pitch together. Are you with me?"

I felt a fighting spirit burn in my chest and I added my voice to the booming "Yes!" that stopped Krogstrand cold on his way off the stage. He jerked his head around as if we'd done something wrong.

After school that day, Curry and I cornered Keeley Uncas at her locker.

"We want to find out what the writing on Curry's amulet says," I explained. "We think it's a Tibetan mantra. Any ideas?"

Curry showed her the reverse side of his amulet.

"Have you tried the county library?" We must have had blank looks on our faces because she added, "Need directions?"

"You think they might have a book on Tibetan mantras?" Curry asked.

"If not, they have high-speed internet access. Oh, meet me there in ten minutes. I'll get you started."

I searched the library catalog for anything having to do with Tibet or mantras while Keeley worked the web. Curry thumbed through the books I pulled. We finally got traction when Keeley searched on *amulet + Tibetan + mantra* and found a site with photos of dozens of ancient amulets, none exactly like Curry's though. A number of the artifacts were labeled as from the Arkenstone Collection, so I took a shot at searching the catalog for Arkenstone and got a hit.

The oversized book was checked in and proved to be mostly pictures of an extensive collection of Asian art, including amulets. Some amulets had inscriptions, similar, but not the same. But Curry continued leafing through the book.

"Here's something about mantras in general," Keeley said, and read from the screen:

> "Mantras use the powerful vehicle of sound to transport consciousness, using sacred syllables from

the ancient Sanskrit language of India. The Indian
Rishis believe that Sanskrit was given by God during
a higher age, and that the words have a vibratory
power which connect the speaker with powerful
astral forces."

Keeley clicked on several more links, but it felt like we were losing
momentum. Curry looked exasperated, too, and finally he slammed
the book shut. He slumped back in his chair with a sigh, blinked
twice...

Then his eyes widened. They were looking at the back cover photo
on the Arkenstone book.

"There it is!"

Everyone in the library looked our way to see what the fuss was
about.

Curry jabbed his finger excitedly at the photo of a carved cylinder
mounted on a handle. Keeley took the book from him and opened to
the inside flap.

"Says it's a Buddhist prayer wheel. The rest is covered up with this
library sticker."

My pocket knife made short work of the plastic book cover, and
Keeley continued reading the fine print on the flap. "The powerful
mantra inscribed on the wheel is *Tat Savitur Varenyam Om*. It invokes
the divine and nearly incomprehensible Light of enlightened
awareness shining forth from every mote of Creation."

Two days later, I left my sandwich in my locker and went through
the serving line in the cafeteria. Today was pig-in-a-blanket. Mom calls
it mystery meat in a coffin, but I like it. And I like the way the hallway
outside the cafeteria always smells like pig-in-a-blanket whether
they're serving it or not. I found Curry sitting alone and joined him. I
said something disgusting about the creamed corn and he couldn't
help but smile.

Then the room got quieter and I saw Ms. Dozier's familiar muumuu,
printed with bird-of-paradise and other jungle flowers, stationed before

the serving line, her hand waggling for attention.

"Okay, here it is. Some of us teachers, and the student council, have come up with a plan to save Camp Bluetoad." We all hooted and whistled, and she raised her arms for quiet, flab swinging under them like socks full of marbles. "But it won't be easy. Everyone has to pitch in. We're going to set up a bazaar on the school grounds every Friday afternoon until we raise the twenty-five thousand dollars. We'll have booths, and make things to sell, and we'll get people to donate things to sell—second hand furniture and clothes. We'll sell garden produce. A dunk tank. A raffle. Some of us teachers will be auctioned into slavery for a day," she made a wide-eyed look of apprehension, "including me."

"I bid a nickel," someone shouted.

Ms. Dozier gave him a crusty look. "Now, what other kinds of booths can you think of to raise money?"

Someone offered to sell homemade ice cream.

"That's the spirit." Ms. Dozier shook a fist.

"I can dye people's hair—whatever color they want," a girl called out. Three other girls who were always experimenting with trashed-out clothes offered to hack blue jeans, or whatever else the customer might be wearing. The football jocks said they'd do a car wash. A guy with a long neck would give unicycle lessons. Then Choker flagged his hand. "Ms. Dozier, Ms. Dozier, I'm going to run a freak show!"

She looked over her half-glasses with suspicion.

"Where you going to get a freak on short notice?" someone said.

Choker stood, looked around as if expecting to find one lurking about, then pointed to Curry Buckle. "Him!"

Too many people laughed, and my ears got hot.

Curry tried to smile, but it looked feeble.

Just then Mrs. Muldoon's voice came over the PA. "Paprika Buckle to the office please. Urgent phone call. Paprika Buckle to the office."

Red hair bouncing like springs, Paprika made for the door. Curry got up to follow his sister, but Choker blocked his way. "Not you, freak."

"It's probably no big deal," I whispered to Curry. Reluctantly he sat, but fidgeted while Bull Dozier lectured Choker about no put downs, then went on with her spiel. Finally, Curry cocked a droopy ear toward the hallway, and I too heard the clop of shoes running on hardwood. Sure enough, Paprika burst into the cafeteria and interrupted things with a shout.

"I won! I won the car! I won the Blubbermobile!"

Unable to contain her joy, she broke into a cheerleader routine by the serving line, shaking handfuls of napkins like pompoms—"Shish boom bar, I won the car! Rah rah ree, send me the key!"—until her friends surrounded her in a power hug. "I guessed how many balls of Blubbergum were in the car!" Paprika took the picture of the little red convertible from her purse and waved it over her head. "They said I got the exact number of gumballs: twenty-one thousand, two-hundred and twenty! They asked me how I came up with that number, and I said we figured they'd hidden the other prizes under the gum, and took that into account, and they said that was smart because that's exactly what they did, and..." her face went blank, "just like my brother Curry said when I... omagod!" Her eyes bulged. "He really is..."

The room buzzed like a hive. Curry and I made our way to Paprika.

"Rika," Curry said in a low voice. "I have an idea. Since we need to raise money, you could donate the car for a raffle, and we might make enough just on that to save Camp Bluetoad."

Paprika pushed Curry away. "Huh? Did your brains just turn to creamed corn, or what? I won it fair and square and I'm keeping it. In fact, you darling little twit," she whispered, eyes glinting slyly, "we're going to enter every contest on the face of this planet. I'm going to have a whole fleet of cars. One for every shade of nail polish."

Curry looked away. His jaw slack, his eyes pinched shut.

Chapter 8
Fate Takes a Twist

*W*e talked that afternoon in study hall, and Curry asked—practically begged—me to come to his house after school. I wasn't much in the mood. I'd just come from band, where I learned that Mr. Krogstrand made good on his threat. Mr. Apostle, the teacher, pulled the plug on my guitar and handed me a battered clarinet case. He looked shaky and sad-eyed. I liked him a lot because he'd given me a chance to audition on my guitar, then got me an exception to play it in the band.

"I'm a drummer too. Can't I play drums?"

He shook his head. His sad eyes apologized to me. His shakiness looked like held-in rage.

I pushed the clarinet away, grabbed my decal-covered Stratocaster case, and headed for the door. Biting my lip to keep my eyes dry, I turned to Mr. Apostle.

"I'm dropping out."

I didn't really want to see Curry, but didn't want to go home either, and ended up pedaling my bike out by his place. I slowed to look at The Big McGillicuddy. Though it was near the house, sheltered under a plastic tent, growing in chemically balanced soil, with its own drip watering system, I could easily see the monstrosity from the road. Something told me I should at least pop in for five minutes, so I did. After tapping on the door and poking my head in, I immediately found out why he needed me. Paprika's boyfriend, Dan Klatt, had Curry pinned back in Mr. Buckle's recliner. Curry's parents crowded in, and some half-dozen dogs circled around them on the frayed rug as Paprika held her opal ring two inches from Curry's nose. "Hello!" I said, and let myself in. If anyone noticed me, they didn't show it.

Curry's eyes were crossed and he struggled to break free.

"Look deeply," Paprika intoned.

Curry tried to look away but Klatt, tongue lolling like one of the dogs, held Curry's head in a vise-like grip.

"Relax, I told you."

"I don't want to."

Paprika appealed to her parents. "Make him relax."

"Now Curry," Mr. Buckle said. "If you win us some contests, mother and I maybe could retire. And this Hawaii contest would be a good start. So what do you say?"

Curry twisted away from Klatt and saw me for the first time. "Dar!" He aired his spade-like teeth in a smile and said to me, "I've been trying to explain that I don't want to cheat on contests. It wouldn't be fair to everyone else."

"How can you say it's cheating?" Mrs. Buckle said, ignoring me.

"It just feels like it."

"Young man," she said, fists on hips, "your dad and I have raised you good and you've never gone hungry."

In the short time I'd known Curry, it seemed he'd received less attention than the pack of mutts that had the run of the place. Certainly less than The Big McGillicuddy. Of course, they'd raised ten other kids before him, so we're probably talking burnout.

"I know mom, but..."

"Seems like you'd want to pay us back, if you could."

"Well, yes, but..."

"But what?"

Curry blinked several times, but couldn't answer.

"Son," Mr. Buckle said. "You want to make your old dad proud, don't you?"

Curry nodded, but looked suspicious.

"Then you need to show the world what you can do. Am I right?"

Curry made five different expressions in five seconds. "Maybe, but if I really do have a special talent, I want to help people with it."

"Well, help us then," Paprika said, arms flung wide.

"I don't mean contests."

"Yo? We're listening."

Curry turned to me for help. I didn't really see the harm in winning contests. What riled me was his parents forcing Curry to do something *he* believed was wrong. I cleared my throat and did my best for him.

"Um, yeah. You remember the story of the golden flounder, how the fisherman released him and the flounder granted a wish?"

Blank looks all around, except Paprika, who said, "So?"

"Then the fisherman's wife asked for too many things until the flounder got torked off and took everything back."

I got some puzzled looks, including one from Curry, but Mr. Buckle seemed to get the picture. He nodded thoughtfully. "So we should be asking for one big thing," he said. "Instead of dozens of little things."

Curry rolled his eyes at me as if I'd made things worse.

Just then we heard tires crunching gravel.

Klatt's eyes widened as he glanced out the window.

"It's Sheriff Biggs!"

He stepped back from Curry and thrust his hands in his pockets as if they'd done something felonious. Curry couldn't get out of the recliner fast enough.

Paprika folded her arms defiantly. "We didn't break the law. I won that car fair and square and I'm not giving it back. I'll sue."

The dogs squeezed out the door to bark at the two officers, who both took their hats off as they climbed the porch steps. I knew by the slow way the hats came off that it couldn't be good news.

"You should have a seat, Mrs. Buckle," said Sheriff Biggs—the older one—after being invited into the living room. He had so much gear hanging off his belt he had to hike his pants every few steps. "I'm afraid it's your sister. Pansy Twist."

"Oh," Mrs. Buckle sat and clasped a veined hand to her heart. "She's fallen through that rotten porch. How bad is she hurt?"

"She didn't fall, Mrs. Buckle. She, um... she was shot."

"Shot? With a gun?" Mrs. Buckle's mouth sagged in horror.

"Yes ma'am. Murdered."

*   *   *

Pansy. The squat aunt, face creased around the eyes and mouth from laughing at her own puns. The one who'd been so kind to me when I'd come for dinner. She'd scratched her glass eye with a fork just for a laugh. The Sheriff's words echoed in a hollow place within me and I wanted to believe I'd heard it wrong, or that it was a bad joke, but Mrs. Buckle's reaction left no doubt. She clutched at her flannel shirt, then her eyes rolled up and she slumped to the floor. Mr. Buckle and Dan dragged her by the armpits to the recliner where Mr. Buckle fanned her with a magazine, and when that failed to bring her around, he punched the vibrator button, and seemed pleased with himself when, within seconds, she came to.

Curry meanwhile had gone white and wobbly on his feet.

With Sheriff Biggs and his deputy perched on the edge of the sofa, and the dogs looking suitably glum, we learned the details.

"We think it was a robbery," the sheriff said. "Miss Twist—Pansy—left the junk store—excuse me, antique shop—early this afternoon—according to Miss Iris—saying she wasn't feeling well. When Miss Iris came home at five-thirty, she found Miss Pansy on the living room floor, dead. Shot through the heart."

Mrs. Buckle's eyelids fluttered and I thought we might lose her again. Paprika patted the back of her hand while Mr. Buckle stood ready at the vibrator controls. Curry swayed, and I put an arm around his beefy shoulders to steady him. I could feel the cold sweat through his shirt.

"Miss Iris phoned the station. Later she discovered her sister's purse had been rifled. She thought there might have been thirty or forty dollars in it."

"Oh God," I uttered past the lump in my throat. A murder on this sleepy island? And for a measly forty bucks? I'd lived in the 'burbs near Seattle most of my life and never got close to this kind of news.

"But who could have done it?" Paprika asked.

"One of those migrant field hands," Dan Klatt said, clenching his fist as if wishing he had the scoundrel's neck in it.

"We're checking all possibilities," the younger officer said. " Miss Iris has offered a ten-thousand dollar reward, so I imagine we'll solve this one soon enough."

"Oh, poor Iris," Mrs. Buckle wailed. "Whatever is she going to do? Those two were a matched set."

The deputy inched his fingers around the brim of his Smoky-the-Bear hat. "I'm afraid she's quite distraught, ma'am. She's down at the station right now, and the doctor is there just in case, but she'll need a family member to stay with her awhile."

"Of course," Mrs. Buckle said. "Rika, pack my overnight bag—I don't have the strength. And Pa, there's enough goulash in the freezer to keep the rest of you alive for a couple days. Alive! Oh, poor poor Iris. What are we going to do?"

Chapter 9
Warts and All

*M*y dad gave it the boldest headline since the cannery fire of '87. He had to search the morgue—past editions of the *Whalebone*—twenty-eight years back just to find the last killing on the island. A duel fought over a riding lawnmower, whose engine conked the first day after a guy traded his hunting dog for it. Sheriff Biggs' staff screened everyone leaving the island by ferry, and got a zillion tips because of the ten-thousand dollar reward, but, after a week, he still hadn't locked anyone up. He said the murder weapon was a medium-caliber handgun, fired from close range, but it hadn't been found.

The following Saturday, Curry stopped by my place and said he needed to deliver some pickled beets to his Aunt Iris. Would I like to come along?

"Truthfully?" Truthfully, I'd rather suck snot out of an aardvark's nose than spend all morning trying to cheer up Curry's aunt—at the scene of the murder.

"We won't stay long, and there's lots of cool stuff to look at," Curry said. "My great-uncle Cyrus Twist built these amazing machines. But if you don't want to..."

I shrugged. The old Twist House at the edge of town did look intriguing from the outside. "Let's just make it quick, okay? Drop off the beets, say 'have a nice day', and zip out of there."

Autumn had arrived and the morning had a snap to it. The Victorian-style Twist House had an oversized turret which resembled a lighthouse. It had been a classy address once, but, as we drew near, its shabbiness made me feel creepy. Moss pushed the shingles up, and the siding had weathered to bare wood. A patch of flowers looked scrawny and neglected.

We knocked, let ourselves in, and found Aunt Iris in her rocker, afghan over her lap, listening to old records stacked on a spindle. The place smelled like dry rot and mothballs. I couldn't help visualizing Pansy in a pool of her own blood before the fireplace. The soapy harmonies on the record must have been cheery once, but all the scratches made it seem spoiled, like everything else.

Iris barely seemed to notice us. She was the taller of Curry's old-maid aunts, more refined than Pansy--the dumpy one with the dorky jokes--had been. Curry turned the music down so they could talk while I wandered through the clutter of antique furniture and knickknacks. Rectangles of clean wallpaper marked where pictures had recently hung. I noticed there were no photos of Pansy in the room. Iris probably couldn't stand being reminded.

Good to his word, Curry made it short. But before we left, he showed me a contraption his great-uncle Cyrus had made: a mechanical solar system with belts and gears that moved the planets. The brass base had a loopy 'T' engraved on it for 'Twist'. "Old Cyrus loved gadgets and puzzles," Curry explained. "There's still talk about gold he might have hid somewhere."

The musty smells and the creak of Aunt Iris's rocker were working on my nerves. "Let's beat feet," I whispered.

Walking in the sunshine cleansed me of the gloom, but Curry remained in a funk. We stopped at a bench overlooking the marina. Gulls squawked and halyards clapped against aluminum masts. I figured Curry was bummed about his Aunt Pansy, so I kept quiet. But after a while, he said, "I want you to try something."

"Yeah? What?"

"I want you to try putting me in a trance."

"Are you sure? I thought..."

"I just didn't want my sister doing it. I don't trust her."

People often seem to trust me for no good reason, but something about Curry's trust made me feel good about myself.

He pulled a knee up and rested his chin on it. "I need to find out more about... you know."

"Your ESP?"

He nodded. "If that's what it is. I hope that's what it is."

"What do you mean?"

"My great uncle Cyrus..."

"Yeah?"

"He died in an insane asylum."

"Tough break. So?"

"Maybe it started out like this for him."

"Curry, whackos don't know what's in books without reading them. They just think they know. But you proved it, right?"

"But that doesn't mean it's a good thing. And when I'm under... I don't even remember telling Paprika the answer for that Blubbergum contest."

"Hey," I said, "if it works, we can find out who killed your aunt."

"No!" Curry said.

"Why not? We can split the reward money."

From the somber look in Curry's eyes, I knew it had been the wrong thing to say.

"No."

Sounded totally non-negotiable.

"What if I got it wrong? I wouldn't want to make trouble for an innocent person."

"Sure," I said, unconvinced. Did Curry have some other reason for refusing? "Well, let's give this trance thing a try. But how?"

"Remember Paprika's opal ring? All those colorful flecks sort of became a door that I could step through. Maybe we can find something like that. And I want you to write down the answers."

We went to my house, and in the privacy of my room, Curry took off his shoes and glasses, and got comfortable on a big stuffed chair. I tried several things from around the house: cut crystal, a sapphire ring of my mom's, crumpled foil. Curry tried, but finally sat up and shook his head. "It's not working."

"Maybe if we play some spacey music," I said. "Mom has some new age CDs."

An idea came to me as I took a disk from its case. I had Curry lay back, and held the disk before him, the side with the prismatic colors, and tried to think of what a hypnotist might say. "You're becoming deeply relaxed. You have no body, just an infinite mind. There are no boundaries to what you can see, no boundaries to what you can know."

I sounded like something from a comic book, and was about to laugh it off as a failure when Curry's eyes turned up, and his lids quivered.

It spooked me. "Curry? Can you hear me?"

Then he jerked violently, his face contorted, and his tongue shot out.

I jumped back, every muscle tensed. "Curry!"

Then he opened his eyes, saw me standing in stark terror, and started laughing.

"You butthead!"

"Sorry. Couldn't help it. You sounded like you were trying to hypnotize me."

"Well, isn't that what we're doing?"

"I don't think so." He shook his head earnestly. "I think I'm trying to escape from the belly of a whale."

He waited for me to get it, but I didn't get it. Not then.

"I need you to open up a hole. For just a second I saw a shimmering light, but I couldn't concentrate on it. I think maybe if you play your drum again. Do you remember that same rhythm?"

"Trapped in your own mind, huh? I hate it when that happens. Well, let's open that baby up." I got the drum and noodled around until I found the beat. Curry got comfortable again. Then I remembered the markings on the drum. "What about saying the mantra? If you remember it."

Curry stared at me, his mouth round and surprised. "Of course! Have I been a bonehead or what?"

I concentrated on the beat, getting the inflections just right. As I did,

Curry chanted, *"Tat Savitur Varenyam Om... Tat Savitur Varenyam Om... Tat Savitur Varenyam Om..."*

And it fit the beat like a key in a lock.

After a minute, Curry's chanting became softer and softer, until I could hear the mantra only in my head. And it began having its effect on me. I got so deeply into the groove that my body felt like a perfectly-adjusted printing press with its hundreds of moving parts, and I seemed to be watching it function from a distance. I could have played on and on—but remembered Curry and thought I should check in on him.

He appeared to be sound asleep, except he wasn't snoring. In fact, I couldn't detect any breath at all, and I felt a jolt of terror.

"Curry? Can you hear me?"

A voice answered, but it was not Curry's. It sounded older, craggier, and lacked the halting cadence of Curry's speech.

"I am with you."

I stood and backed away. If his head started doing 360's, I'd be streaking for the door. But he remained peacefully asleep. "Do you know who I am?"

"Better than you know yourself, Darwin Bownes."

I felt dizzy, as if the world had cracked open below my feet and I might topple in.

"But... who are you?" I said.

"I am that which Curry Buckle will become."

I remembered Curry wanted me to take notes so I jotted it down. "You don't sound like Curry. Where is he?"

"The ego will do anything to keep the soul captive in the body. It is distracted for the present."

"So you're the real Curry and the one I was talking to five minutes ago is a fake?"

"The ego cannot comprehend the soul."

"You got that right," I said. "Anyway, may I ask you some questions?"

"If you can live with the answers."

My neck hair bristled. Hello, was that a warning? Now I just wanted this over with. Curry had suggested that I test him first, so I asked, "I have something wrong with my body that hurts. Can you tell me what it is?"

"Shall we begin with the pimple on your forehead?"

"No," I said, touching the recent eruption. "You can skip the zits."

"A condition known as a plantar wart on the sole of your left foot is causing some distress."

My mouth gaped open. Only my mom knew about this, and it had been getting worse lately. The goo from the drug store hadn't helped. "Yes, that's right." I decided to really put Curry, or whoever was doing the talking, to the test. "What's causing the wart and how do I make it go away?"

The voice did not hesitate. *"The condition is a manifestation of an endocrine imbalance, caused by drinking too much milk. The milk is produced by dairies who feed estrogen and other hormones to the animals to stimulate milk production. The body is irritated by the foreign chemicals and is expressing its irritation through this growth."*

I gave my head a scratch. "But my mom looked it up. A plantar wart is caused by a virus."

"The body tolerates the virus as an agent of expression."

This didn't sound like anything Curry could have made up. "Should I keep using the salve to cure the wart?"

"Have you been listening? Even if the salve reduces the lesion, the body will find another way to express its irritation. Chemical and hormone infused milk must be avoided. Also, the condition has become lodged in your subconscious mind. You must dislodge it by visualizing the lesion subsiding. Do this for seven days. Understood?"

It sounded like a command.

"Yes."

Time to move on to Curry's question.

"Curry wants to know if he's going insane."

The slow laugh sounded like a boulder rolling down a mountain. *"To the contrary, the entity known in this incarnation as Curry is about to embark on a journey to sanity."*

I remembered my notepad and scribbled it down. "But what does it mean to become sane?"

"You are not only more than you imagine, but are more than you can imagine."

"Okay, but is this dangerous for Curry?"

"Has not a token of divine protection been bestowed?"

I puzzled over the answer for a few seconds. Then it hit me. "The amulet." Curry's mom had described a 'foreigner' who'd claimed it would protect Curry from evil. I eased closer and pulled it from under his shirt. "Who was the man in the robe who gave Curry this when he was a baby?"

"He who will straighten the road."

"Who is he? Where does he live?

"He dwells in this world, but not of it."

The voice had a quality that made me both trust it and cower before it. I trusted he had good reason for giving a slippery answer. Perhaps we couldn't have understood. I should have asked more questions, but could hardly wait to tell Curry about the amulet connection. And I remembered how he'd slept through an entire weekend, and worried about not being able to bring him back.

"How do I wake Curry out of his trance?"

"This has been given before. Chant AAAUUUUMMM in his right ear."

I leaned over. "AAAUUUUMMM... AAAUUUUMMM... AAAUUUUMMM."

Curry took a sharp breath and his body moved, then he yawned, opened his eyes, and rose to his elbows, blinking.

"Did I say anything? What time is it anyway? I feel wasted, like I just loaded a truckload of punkins. And, man, could I go for a serious gutbomb!"

Chapter 10
The Blubbermobile

*N*o leftovers in the fridge so we headed to Troutigan's. Despite the season, he wore a tie-die muscle shirt; it hung loose over his scrawny chest. Curry was broke so I sprung for two gooeyburgers.

"Check this out," Troutigan said while he fried the clam patties, "I'm thinking of renaming these things *murderburgers*—to cash in on this unsolved case. You know, Pansy Twist getting greased? Might spark some business, right?"

Curry looked stunned.

"Oh, she's your aunt, right?"

"*Was*," he said.

"Right. Well, I'll make this big sign," he spread his arms. "Murderburgers! Keep pressure on the fuzz to crack the case."

We took the burgers to our bench. I let Curry finish eating then told him what the *voice* had said.

The news vacuumed the air and color right out of him. He groped for the amulet and clutched it tightly. "I knew it! I knew this had a meaning. You're sure about this?"

"It's here in my notes." I gave him the pad.

He studied the notes. "And what about this plantar wart?"

I cranked off my shoe to display the lima bean-sized wart.

He shook his head. "How can this be? Maybe I subconsciously noticed a slight limp. But I don't even know what a plantar wart is, and I certainly don't know what they're caused by, or how to cure them."

"Do you know anything about what they feed dairy cows?"

"Cows? They've been known to eat grass."

"I'm talking chemicals, drugs."

"Not a clue." Curry gave crumbs to a waiting gull. "I just don't know whether to believe... it's all too fantastic. You know what would be really scary?"

"What?"

"If you stop drinking milk and that blasted wart goes away."

A week later I toweled off from my shower after gym class, and realized something. "Curry, come here!"

Curry, always fussy about hygiene, seemed unwilling to break off his routine. He probably went through a can of talcum powder a month, and had barely begun dusting himself.

"It's important."

"All right!"

Just then Choker strode by, naked as a buzzard neck, and snapped his towel at Curry, landing a shot to his back. "Hey!" Curry cried. He put up a forearm to defend against the next shot. It hit the can of talc, sending a cloud of powder into his face. "Dang you, Choker!" Curry said, coughing.

"What, freakshow?" Choker didn't work out, but had plenty of natural muscle. He sighted another victim and moved on.

Curry came over taking his pressed undershirt from a hanger—he actually gave that ironing board in his room a workout. I held up my foot. "It's almost gone."

"What's almost gone?" Curry rubbed at his back. Wearing just a towel (and the strange old amulet around his stubby neck) he didn't look as soft as you'd suppose seeing him fully clothed. His broad chest, thick arms, and stocky legs may not have been sculpted, but he looked like he could carry a load.

"My wart. Look. There's barely a callous where it used to be."

His attention sharpened, and he felt the spot for himself.

"I've been laying off the moo juice. Visualizing, too."

"Maybe it was the salve."

"I stopped using it."

Curry checked the soles of both my feet. "Holy pig-snouts, are you telling me...?"

"Curry," I said. "We've got to do some serious talking."

*   *   *

We skipped geometry class and walked up the lane toward the cemetery. Curry had never cut class in his life, so I figured it would do him good. Two or three more misses for me and I'd get scrubbed out of the course. I'd have to think of something else—earphones maybe. Our geometry teacher, Schwartzie, was a nearsighted certifiable moron with a German accent, who'd forgotten that sophomores already knew how to divide and multiply. I had no problem keeping up, and Curry could always sleep on his book.

We took turns kicking a pebble up the crumbling pavement.

"There's no doubt any more," I said. "You've got the goods."

He caught up to the pebble and kicked.

"It's just a matter of what you're going to do with the goods."

"I'm not sure I want to do anything."

I stopped in the road. "Why not? That would be like Batman saying, 'Yo, Robin, let's take the bus.'"

Curry looked down. "You heard Choker. He keeps trying to recruit me for his freak show. I don't want to be a freak."

"What, you're going to let that mental midget rule your life? He's a speed bump. He's a wart on a speed bump's butt."

A hawk on a fence post watched for rabbits, and he didn't fly off when we passed.

"If I use my talent—my gift, whatever you call it—it should be used for good causes."

"Right," I said. "Like helping to cure my plantar wart, but not helping Paprika win more prizes."

"Exactly."

"Does that mean you don't want to be stinking rich?"

"Rich? What do you mean?"

"C'mon, Curry, don't be such a mullet-head. You could pick stocks, or horses." As I said it, my lungs inflated with excitement. If Curry and I hit a zillion dollar jackpot, we could buy a Hummer with a killer sound system, and when school's out, hire a chauffeur and buy every CD ever made and head to the Grand Canyon, or wherever, because we'd be disgustingly rich.

"No," he said.

"No to being rich?"

We lost our pebble so he kicked a dried horse turd and sent it rolling. Road apples, they called them here. "I have a strange feeling about it, like you don't get something for nothing. Know what I mean? Like the story of the golden flounder you came up with."

"Maybe more like the monkey's paw," I said. "Remember? The guy makes a wish on the monkey's paw for money, then his uncle gets chopped up in a machine and the guy inherits the precise amount."

"Yeah, exactly. There's always a price to pay. I had this terrible feeling when we heard about Aunt Pansy. It came right after Paprika won the car."

"Now *that's* horse pucky. There's no connection."

My turn to kick the road apple. So, no zillions. The new Marshal amp would have to wait. But Choker's idea about a freak show gave me an idea. "Do you think saving Camp Bluetoad is a worthy cause?"

"Sure," he said without hesitation.

"So if you were to use your goods to raise money for the camp, you'd be okay with that?"

He kicked the apple too hard and it broke into pieces. "Well..."

"Okay, I've got just the thing!" But before I could explain my brilliant idea, the vroom of an accelerating car approached and we angled toward the shoulder. The car screeched to a stop even with us. Behind the wheel of the tiny red convertible sat Paprika, coppery hair tied with a black ribbon.

"I just got it!" She displayed every one of her perfect teeth. "Hop in."

We didn't bother with the door—just climbed over. I took the back seat. Paprika punched it before we could buckle in, and we flew past the bone yard, out toward the park.

"Isn't it outrageous?" Paprika shouted above the wind. "I just love it to pieces, don't you?"

I would have loved it more if she'd slowed down and didn't turn to look at us every time she had something to say, which was almost constantly. I felt way more comfortable riding with Keeley Uncas, and discretely tightened the seat belt.

By the time she parked back at school, we'd spooked a couple of horse riders and hit a bird. When Rika got out, I leaned over the driver's seat and probed the air vent with a finger. Sure enough, I found it. A single blue gumball. "Look!" I called, holding it up, but Curry had just teased the body of a finch from the grill. He cupped it in his hands, and, downcast, looked at his sister.

"It should have known better than to fly in front of me," she said.

Then I saw Curry's face change. He continued looking at Paprika, but his eyes squinted and his head tilted as if struggling to understand.

"Rika," he said.

But students on lunch break gathered around the car and touched it and pleaded for rides.

Curry and I ceased to exist in Paprika's life.

Chapter 11
A Swami is Born

"Hold still," I said during my fourth try at winding a turban on Curry's head.

He frowned at himself in the mirror. "Jeez, it looks like a brain diaper."

"Looks fine."

He flapped his arms under the orange robe. "Can't I do it without the circus get-up?"

"People want their full five bucks worth. It's to save Camp Bluetoad, remember."

"But you're not wearing a costume—except that dumb skullcap."

"Hey, I'm just your humble helper. You the man. Now, let's dangle that amulet over your robe." As I pulled it out by its thong, Curry reached protectively for it. Something in his gesture warned me to back off. I asked, "The foreigner in a robe who gave it to you, do you remember him?"

He nodded. "It's my first memory. He had a wispy beard and deep eyes and a pouch of wonderful things, but this particular amulet, I knew, belonged to me." He laughed, "I used to bite my brothers and sisters when they tried to touch it."

"But who the heck is he?" I imitated the *voice*: "*He dwells in this world but is not of it.* What kind of double-talk is that?"

He rubbed the weird bird symbol with his thumb. It looked worn, as if others had rubbed it too, over many centuries.

I looked more closely—without touching. The unearthly pot-bellied, bow-legged, winged creature with a jeweled tiara stared back at me with a strange force.

"I think it protects me somehow."

"From what?" I said. "What kind of demon is after your butt, that somebody from Tibet has to make a special trip to give you a charm?"

"I... I hadn't really thought of it that way." Curry's forehead bunched up. "Darwin?"

"What?"

"When I'm under—in a trance—I don't have any control. You won't let anyone ask the wrong kinds of questions will you?"

He looked serious, almost paranoid. I didn't want to hear his definition of 'wrong question'; it might put me in too small of a box. "You'll have to trust me."

Curry nodded. "I do. I trust you."

"Now we're getting somewhere." I tucked in the loose end of the turban cloth. "Not bad." I spoke to the mirror: "I present to you Swami Curryban. Curryban Bucklananda."

Curry looked in the mirror and shook his head. "Sheesh."

"Well, you'll have to take your glasses off."

Ms. Dozier hung a chart in the schoolhouse entry. On it, a cutout blue toad leaped from zero toward twenty-five thousand dollars. The toad hung lamely around the five thousand mark, but I knew Ms. Dozier's determination would somehow save Camp Bluetoad. The second of her Friday afternoon bazaars had been better than the first, and from all the tables and booths going up, the third promised to be a corker.

For our fortune-telling booth, Curry and I erected a circular tent we scored from the Rec Center, and furnished it with the Persian rug from Curry's bedroom and other stuff borrowed from the Twist Sisters Junque and Vintage Girdle Emporium. Paprika had drawn us a poster of a swami gazing into a crystal ball; the swami looked like a bug-eyed cannibal, but I didn't think it would hurt business too much. Curry had his sneakers off in anticipation; I filled one with sand and jabbed a couple sticks of incense in it. I had asked Keeley Uncas to sell tickets for us, but she had a table peddling medicinal herbs that she and her father grew. So I hawked tickets while Curry sat cross-legged at the tent door in his robe and turban. "Gitcha fortune read. Only five dollars.

The future is an open book to Swami Curryban Bucklananda. What do you most want to know? The last customer won an auto-mo-beel by asking the swami a simple question."

"Don't say that," Curry hissed.

"I gotta say something. It's been forty-five minutes and no takers." Lots of people had looked and made wisecracks. But nobody had laid down a fiver.

"I'm starting to cramp, sitting like this."

"Any minute now. And once we read a couple of fortunes... it's a word of mouth business."

"This is too embarrassing. Let's just fold our tent and scram."

"No, I'll light more incense. Really stink up the place." I did, and started into my pitch again. "The swami has all the answers..." Then I saw a small girl, maybe five or six years old, looking up at me. Her mom tested the stitching on a home-sewn stuffed animal at one of the more popular booths. The kid walked over to me, digging a hand into her pocket.

"How much does it cost, mister?"

"Only five dollars," I said.

"Oh." The little towhead looked into her palm. "I got a quarter." She looked longingly at Curry.

Then her mother spied her. "There you are Jenny. Would you like mommy to buy this kitty for you?"

"No!" the girl said. "I want Squeaky back."

The mom, a pinch-faced woman, looked at me as if the situation was more than she could deal with. "Jenny's kitty ran off a week ago and hasn't come home."

"We can ask the swami where he is," Jenny said. "Only it costs five dollars."

"I'll do it for a quarter," Curry said.

I opened my mouth to protest, but it was too late.

Jenny's mom leaned toward me and whispered, "Just have the swami say that Squeaky has gone to cat heaven and is very happy there."

"But what if it's not true?"

"What's truth got to do with it? I just want Jenny to get over that cat."

I only pretended to whisper the instructions in Curry's ear. I couldn't see wasting this opportunity for him to show his stuff. The four of us withdrew inside the tent and sat on cushions, except for Curry, who reclined on a divan. Curry looked uneasy until I began the drumming. He stared at a crystal we'd hung over the divan and began chanting his mantra. Finally, his eyes rolled up, his lids closed and I saw the rise and fall of breath in his chest subside.

I put aside the drum. "Can you hear me, Swami?"

"*I am here,*" came the reply, deep and melodious. Seeing Curry's lips move, with this strange voice coming out made my skin prickle.

"Swami, we have young Jenny and Missus..."

"Juniper," Jenny's mom said.

"Jenny Juniper, here, has lost her cat, Squeaky, and would like to know what happened to him. Can you help?"

"*Describe the cat.*"

I looked at Jenny. Out of my side vision, I could see her mom scowling. Jenny answered, "He's all gray, like lint that comes out of the dryer, except for one white sock."

"Tell the swami where you live," I prompted

"On Limpet Lane. Squeaky ran away last Saturday."

"*Yes, we have the entity in question.*"

Jenny's little hand tightened on her mom's fingers.

"*He was attacked by a raccoon and hid under an earth-moving machine on a trailer.*"

Jenny's face brightened. "That's Mr. DeBroeck's dozer."

Mrs. Juniper said, "And Squeaky has gone to cat heaven, isn't that right, Swami."

I tensed with irritation and was about to shush her when the swami's response came swift and sharp.

"*Madam, what you know of heaven isn't worth the twenty-five cents you paid for this consultation.*"

Mrs. Juniper's eyebrows went up so hard her whole hairdo moved. I braced for trouble, but the swami continued. "*The trailer has been moved to the area known as Glud's Pond. The driver's dog then chased the cat up a fir tree, where he has remained, 120 feet above ground, for six nights.*"

"Oh!" Jenny put both hands over her mouth then pulled on her mom's arm. "See, I told you Squeaky is all right. We have to go find him."

Mrs. Juniper had her hands full with Jenny, but took a moment to glare murderously at me for disobeying her instructions.

I turned away from her. "Swami Curryban, why does the cat stay up in the tree?"

"*The animal is injured, bitten on the right front scapular by the raccoon. Initially the cat was afraid to climb down from such a height, and now he lacks the strength because of infection and dehydration.*"

I saw the alarm on Jenny's face, and something more like fury on her mom's. "Can anything be done to save the cat's life?" I asked.

"*The cat must be rescued immediately and a poultice of monk's gravy applied to the injured—*"

Mrs. Juniper rose to her feet, yanking Jenny off the ground by her arm. "That is quite enough! I hope you've had fun tormenting this poor grieving girl. But I don't think it's amusing." She dragged her confused daughter from the tent.

"But mom!"

"These boys are just teasing you." Then she stopped, looked at me fiercely, and held out her hand. "And you can give Jenny her quarter back."

I surrendered the coin and tried to explain. "This isn't a trick. Curry really does know—"

"Haven't you done enough harm already?"

With that, they left.

I sighed and looked at Curry, then chanted OM in his right ear.

He blinked, smiled, sat up, and looked around. Seeing our customers gone, he asked eagerly, "How'd it go? Did I find the cat?"

"You found him," I said, trying to keep the bitterness out of my voice. "But Mrs. Juniper didn't buy it." I shook my head with frustration. "It's okay," he said. "I had a feeling she wouldn't. In some ways, the world gets smaller as you get older. So, where's Squeaky?"

While I regurgitated the details from my chicken-scratch notes, he stood and paced in his stocking feet, brow wrinkled with concern. When I got to the part about Squeaky being near death in the fir tree, he ripped the turban off and fumbled for his glasses.

"C'mon, Darwin, that cat needs to be rescued!"

Chapter 12
Monk's Gravy

Curry shucked his robe, tied on his shoes, and headed for the tent door. But as he approached the threshold, something strange happened. He slowed. It looked like his body wanted to keep moving, but his feet and legs seized up, each step heavier until, pulling at one leg with both arms, he managed to place one foot outside the tent, then could go no further.

"What's happening Dar?" he cried, and turned to me, eyes stretched wide.

"You can't move?" I cringed with fear that something had gone wrong with Curry.

"My feet are stuck to the ground." He instinctively patted his bird amulet, his chest heaving. Then he got a knowing look in his eyes and relaxed. He tried a step toward me, back into the tent. His foot came unstuck, and he took another step without difficulty.

"You're freaking me, Curry. What the heck's going on?"

He tugged at an ear. "I think I'm not supposed to leave."

"Not supposed to? What about rescuing the cat?"

"I can't explain it, but it's not our job. There must be some reason we're supposed to stay here."

"But... this is getting too bizarre."

I helped Curry back into his swami gear, and he took up his cross-legged position at the tent door while I fetched him a chilidog for his after-trance munch-out. Then we waited for something to happen.

And waited.

For two hours we watched lots of people buying lots of things. No shortage of curious looks in our direction, but people seemed disappointed that Curry didn't read tea leaves or palms or horoscopes, or gaze into a crystal ball, so they passed us by. Of course, most students didn't want to be seen doing business with a pair of sophomore numb-nuts like us. If only Curry would take credit for winning the Blubbermobile, we'd have a line around the block. I kept flipping the lid of the empty cigar box we used as a till. Not only had we returned the only quarter we'd made, we were in the hole a buck-fifty for the chilidog. I'd already marked through the $5 sign and drew in $2.50 beside it.

"Whatcha think, Curry—should we lower it to one bone?"

He pulled the turban off and wiped his forehead. "I still think something's going to happen."

Just then, the browsers parted to let someone through. Jenny emerged from the taller heads, leading her frantic mom straight towards us. Mrs. Juniper carried the limp, emaciated form of a cat.

Jenny ran behind my table and flung her arms around Swami Curryban and kissed him on the cheek. "We found Squeaky, just where you said. We got Mr. DeBroeck to climb the tree with spikes he put on his boots and he rescued Squeaky, but he's awfully sick, and we need to know what's that medicine you said."

I looked at Jenny's mom. She pressed her lips together as if trying to avoid tears. "I owe you two an apology," she said with a sniff, and handed me the cat, its eyes looking too big for its face. She opened her purse and laid a ten-dollar bill on the table next to the cigar box. "You mentioned a poultice," she said to Curry.

People had begun to stop, curious at the excitement.

Curry looked at me. "Did I?"

"You didn't have a chance to finish," I said. "Something about monk's gravy."

Mrs. Juniper shook her head. "I've never heard of such a thing."

"Curry—Swami Curryban—doesn't remember after he wakes up," I said. "I'll have to put him under."

I saw doubt creep into her eyes again and she paused.

"Mom!" Jenny urged.

It seemed to wake her mom up. "Whatever you have to do."

Curry withdrew into the tent and we followed. This time he slipped into trance easily and I asked about the poultice.

Compared to the excited conversation that came before, the swami's voice sounded calm, almost sterile. *"The cat's wound is infected with bacteria peculiar to the mouth of raccoons, and the monk's gravy poultice is needed to draw out the toxins. Then the wound should be dressed and a normal course of antibiotics administered. The cat is also dangerously dehydrated and should be given intravenous fluid."*

"Please describe the poultice, monk's gravy."

"In a base preparation of turpentine and peanut oil, add equal parts by dry weight of comfrey leaves and mullein, a tenth part of monk's hood, and another tenth oil of camphor."

"And where can we get all this stuff?"

This time the voice held a tinge of sarcasm. *"Look no further than the herbalist in a booth near yours."*

Herbalist? I didn't remember an herbalist. Then it struck me: Keeley Uncas.

I brought Curry out of his trance, shook his hand, promised him as many chilidogs as he could eat, and motioned Jenny and her mom to follow. We had to push our way through people gathered around our tent door. We found Keeley packing her unsold remedies in a box, as the bazaar was winding down.

"Darwin, what's going on at your tent? Is Curry charming a snake?"

"He found my lost kitty," Jenny answered.

Keeley looked at me skeptically. "Bullsockets!"

"He did," I said. "And he also said you could make a poultice called monk's gravy." I handed her the formula and held my breath, afraid that Keeley would laugh and say there's no such thing.

But she didn't laugh. She opened her mouth, said nothing, looked at the cat in Mrs. Juniper's arms and understood. "Oh, you poor thing!" She cleared a space for it and examining the wound. "I have everything except oil of camphor. Can someone get to Drack's drugstore fast?"

"Back in under ten minutes," I said.

Mrs. Juniper gave me more money and I was on my bike in seconds, pushing wind. I returned just as Keeley finished grinding the herbs in her mortar and pestle. Curry dripped water in Squeaky's mouth with an eyedropper. Keeley mixed the pungent camphor with the herbs and applied the goo to the cat's wounds as Jenny stroked his head. Then Mrs. Juniper gathered up Squeaky to rush him to the vet for the rest of the treatment, but not before saying, "Thank you so much. I don't understand it, only that it's a miracle." She gave Curry and me each a big hug, then hustled off.

Swami Curryban found himself surrounded by curious classmates who wanted to know what had happened.

Keeley and I looked at each other, still pumped from dealing with the emergency. I think we both found something new to like in each other.

"You really understand all these plants and herbs, don't you."

She nodded then asked, "What's this about a miracle?"

"I'll tell you over a chilidog."

Chapter 13
A Dark Mystery

*T*hat night, Dan Klatt scored two touchdowns while his girlfriend Paprika Buckle kicked her freckled legs at impossible angles and shook half the raffia off her blue-and-orange pompoms. Curry, in a stocking cap shaped somewhat like his turban, prowled the sidelines with his camera. And, in the bleachers, I shared a jumbo buttered popcorn with Keeley Uncas.

When I'd gone for the popcorn, I stopped at the restroom first, keeping a sharp watch for Choker Durant and his gang. At the restroom, a short freshman standing outside said, "It's busy." His eyes shifted nervously.

"I'll get in line," I said, and pushed past him, realizing too late the little ankle-biter belonged to Choker. It clicked when I recognized another of Choker's goons inside, jerking lengths of cloth from the towel machine. The towel led over the partition to where Choker fed it down the toilet bowl, his purple sneaker working the flush lever. The goon looked up when I came in. Another one edged in behind me. My breath snagged in my lungs.

"Choker, we got company!"

Choker took a step, as if to run, then relaxed when he saw me. "Darwin Bonehead." He sucked his teeth while trying to figure out what kind of welcome to give me. "Good thing you came along, smegmeister, I'm getting tired of flushing. You flush for a while."

Right, I thought, and get blamed for the whole thing.

The towel-puller gave a final yank and the end came off the roll. "That's all of it."

Choker crooked a finger at me. "C'mon, I'll show you how it's done."

"I'll pass."

He straightened his finger. "If you squeal, I'm going to flush *you* down the toilet. Got that, bicycle boy?"

"Yeah, sure." I turned. The guy blocking the doorway hesitated a second, then got out of my way. Outside the restroom, Mr. Schwartz, our geometry teacher, waited to get in. His eyes, milky as an October oyster, seemed to recognize me in a generic way. Under the circumstances, I didn't want to be recognized in any way.

"Must be room for one more now," Schwartz said to the ankle-biter.

"What took you so long?" Keeley said when I returned. "I was getting cold."

The lighted field swarmed with padded guys like enormous beetles rolling a speck of dung. We sat on the cold aluminum bleachers, my knee spread out to touch hers, and we talked, and stood when someone threw a long pass. During half time, we heard two women conversing behind us.

"Did you hear about that Buckle boy?"

"Dry Mustard?

"No, the one down there with the camera. He found little Jenny Juniper's cat—they'd given the little beastie up for dead. Louise Juniper insists the boy went into trance and spoke in a strange voice."

"No!"

"Yes!"

"Sounds like devil worship to me."

"Well, he was dressed up like a Hindu."

"Oh oh," Keeley whispered to me. "Next thing you know, the peasants will be after Curry with torches and pitchforks. Don't laugh! Look what they did to my dad."

"At least we've got a buzz going," I said. "No such thing as bad publicity. And look down there; people are actually talking to Curry. I thought I saw a kid offer him money earlier. I bet we have paying customers at the bazaar next Friday."

"I told my dad about Curry," Keeley said, then with a giggle, corrected herself, "Swami Curryban. When he heard the part about the raccoon saliva and the monk's gravy, he seemed really interested.

Dad wants to meet him."

After the game, Curry found us. He seemed tired, yet euphoric over the events of the day—pleased he'd been able to help someone.

"Bring your film around the print shop tomorrow," I said. "We'll see if dad can use any of the shots."

Keeley drove me home, though it was only five blocks. She didn't seem in any hurry for me to get out of the bug, but I wasn't sure what to do about it, so I panicked and made some lame comment about hoping she didn't get burned at the stake for making magic potions, and went into the house feeling stupid, but liking Kluge Island more than I had since moving there.

Dad printed one of Curry's pictures in the following Thursday's paper. Someone catching a pass. At my suggestion, he also ran a paragraph in his Hearsay column:

Cat-astrophe Averted

Jenny Juniper (age 6), happy owner of Squeaky the cat, credits her pet's life to local hero, Curry Buckle, Kluge High sophomore. Squeaky had been missing a full week and was feared dead. Buckle, posing as a fortune-teller at the school bazaar, specified Squeaky's location, high in a fir tree, miles from home. Also, according to Louise Juniper, Jenny's mother, he correctly guessed the nature of Squeaky's injury (animal bite). Squeaky has been treated at Island Veterinary, and is expected to recover fully. When asked about his role in this drama, Curry, like any good stage magician, refused to divulge his trade secrets. "I don't know how it works," he said. "The answers just come to me."

Dad didn't exactly word it right—he made it sound like a trick—but at least Curry got some well-deserved credit. And when Swami

Curryban Bucklananda's tent opened for business the following Friday afternoon, we had a short line. I hastily changed our sign back to five bucks. Besides the *Whalebone* article about Squeaky, word had spread of Curry's performances in biology class. So we had some takers willing to risk five clams.

The first was Ted Griswald, a tenth grader I'd seen smoking behind the school and bouncing a tennis ball against the wall. Gangly, thick lips, and dandruff. He had a straightforward problem. "My granddad gave me a twenty-dollar bill for my birthday and I hid it good, only now I can't remember where. I'll pay the fi'dollars after I get the twenty back."

I didn't like the arrangement, but Curry looked him over, then said okay. While Ted waited outside, I put Curry into his trance. When I let Ted in, the others in line inched forward to eavesdrop. I repeated the situation to the swami then asked Ted, "Did you hide the money at home?"

"Yeah. Or somewhere close by. I've checked all my usual places."

"Then tell the swami where you live."

"Razewoods Apartments, number 8."

Curry didn't respond, so I asked, "When was your birthday?"

"April 16th."

The swami spoke, his *voice* from Curry's lips sounding as if it had come a great distance. "*Yes, the location is clear. The subject is rolling the money up and sliding it inside the pipe from which clothes are hung in his bedroom.*"

Ted Griswald's face brightened. "That's it! I remember now."

He stood up to leave, but Swami continued. "*However, the money is being removed by a man with long side whiskers, yellow shirt, and a faded tattoo.*"

Ted clenched his fists and grimaced. "Jim!"

"Who is Jim?" I asked Ted.

"My stepfather. The son-of-a..." He muttered a string of curses.

I followed up. "Swami Curryban, what happened to the money?"

A pause. "*The money is spent on lottery tickets. None of the tickets won.*"

Ted Griswald looked as if something vile had backed up in his throat. "Slug-eyed scumbag!" he muttered.

Sadly, he seemed all too ready to believe Curry's vision of robbery. "I'm sorry," I said.

He stood, scowling. "You should be. You won't be getting your fi'dollars now, will ya." He pushed through the onlookers and vanished.

Ted may not have been impressed with Curry's answers, but those listening outside the tent were. Even more people had gathered, curious about the fuss, and word circulated that Curry got it right again.

"Next," I said, and a buxom girl with worried eyes and bite marks on her lower lip stepped forth. She had folded her fiver into a wad the size of a Blubbergum ball, and it took her a while to get it smoothed out. She handed me the bill while glancing at Curry, who remained in his trance, then at the people, just outside the tent, straining to hear. "Would you like some privacy?"

She nodded. I appointed the guy next in line to keep everyone back.

We sat. "Okay, what would you like to ask the swami?"

"I don't see how he can possibly help," she said, almost quivering. She had a cute face but being upset made it red and bulgy.

"If he can't answer your question, you can have your money back." I wasn't doing a very good job of making this operation pay.

"I don't care about the money. I just need to know something, and nobody will tell me, and I'll try anything."

"Okay. Your name is Gretchen, isn't it?"

"Yes." She seemed surprised I knew. But I'd learned most of the girls' names at school, starting with the buxom ones.

"Go ahead. State your full name and where you live."

She did, then said timidly, "Two years ago, on my thirteenth birthday, I got a card in the mail and it said, 'My Daughter Gretchen.' But it wasn't from my mom, and my dad died in a fishing accident before I was born." She pressed a tissue to her eyes and blotted up some soggy make-up along with her tears. "Or so that's what my mom told me."

"Do you have the card with you?"

"Mom took it. She must have destroyed it because I've looked everywhere."

"Have there been other mysterious attempts to contact you?"

"No, but the card really freaked mom. She doesn't let me pick up the mail anymore."

"So, you want to know who sent the card?"

Gretchen nodded five or six times, then unwadded her tissue and tried using it again. I searched my pockets for a fresh one, but no luck. "I *need* to know. Do you understand? I'm not stupid. I know something's going on and it's driving me crazy."

I hesitated. Maybe her mom had a good reason for holding back. But playing it safe is not my style. "Swami, can you shed any light on this dark mystery?"

The light he shed sent chills through me.

"*The situation is troubling for all concerned. The subject's father is alive, and the birthday communication was indeed from him. He left his marriage shortly before his daughter's birth after realizing he was ill-suited for a male-female relationship. He is now living with a partner in a coastal town in Oregon.*"

"Oh, God!" Gretchen said. She closed her eyes and bit her lip so hard, I thought she might draw blood. Tears literally squirted out, and through her sobs she demanded, "Then why did he send the card two years ago, and why haven't I heard from him since?"

"*Shortly before sending that card, he'd received a preliminary diagnosis that he'd contracted an incurable disease. He didn't want the truth to die with him. Later, the diagnosis was found to be in error, and he reconsidered trying to make contact with his only child. He doesn't want to cause any grief in her life.*"

Gretchen sat stunned and sniffling for a long time. Cool beads of sweat tracked down from my underarms. Finally, she made two hard fists, looked at Curry, and asked for her father's name, and the town in which he lived.

Swami answered precisely.

Gretchen did some deep breathing. I realized her choice would change several people's lives. "Are you going to track him down?"

"I don't know." She got up to leave, then said, "But I feel so much better just knowing that I can."

Chapter 14
The Realm of The Future

I left Curry reposed peacefully in his trance and escorted Gretchen past the people lined up outside. Then Dan Klatt muscled aside the lesser customers. "Hey Darwin, how ya doin' good buddy?"

It both flattered me, and made me suspicious, that he remembered my name. Me, a toady underclassman, an insect, one of the masses evolved from slime for the sole purpose of worshipping football heroes. Dan put an arm around my shoulder. I'm tall for my age and we were about the same height, but I'd have to GooeyGlue a pair of Virginia hams to my chest to match his bulk. He already had the face of a man. I'd probably have to wait ten years to find out what I'd look like as an adult.

"What gives?" he said confidentially. "Curry's telling fortunes for these maggots, but he refuses his dear old mom and dad?"

"It's for Camp Bluetoad."

"Oh, that's right. I could see where Mr. Buckle might not understand, but I would never bring it up to him—provided a friend of the family gets line-cutting privileges." Klatt stuffed a fiver in my shirt pocket.

I looked around anxiously, hoping something would come along to change the situation. It didn't. "Ah, what question do you want to ask?"

"That's between me and the swami."

I had to block his path to keep him from barging into the tent.

"He's had a couple rough cases and needs a rest."

For a moment, Klatt looked at me as if I were a tackler in the open field, someone to be ground into hamburger under his cleats. Then he relented. "Well, am I first in line, or what?"

"Yeah, sure Dan."

He checked his watch. "I'll be back in ten."

"Better make it a half-hour. He'll be needing a snack."

"Thirty," he said, and clapped me on the back hard enough to knock my breath out.

I apologized to the other customers and went back in the tent. As I stood before Curry, I felt bad for making him wear the cheesy cape and turban. But no sooner had I thought it, when the costume seemed to take on a richer quality, an aura of authenticity. Perhaps the sun had burned through the clouds a little. Curry's eyes remained closed, but he didn't look asleep. He had the faint smile of a contented daydreamer. Before I roused him from the daydream, I had to check on some things that were troubling me. "Curry, about the girl who just left—Gretchen—I'm not sure the information about her father is going to help things, or make them worse."

"*What is your question?*"

"Can information from your readings be harmful?"

"*If the heart is filled with greed or revenge or other dark motives, then information may be used harmfully.*"

I wrote down the answer. "I think Dan Klatt is going to ask you to pick the winning lottery numbers or something. Is this within your power?"

"*No. Lottery numbers are determined by future random events and the karma of the players. Nevertheless, it would be possible to amass wealth by knowing what is foreseeable.*"

"So what kinds of things can you predict?"

"*Events stemming from existing forces or tendencies, sometimes to a high degree of probability.*"

"Give examples of these, please."

"*A body that violates laws of health, or that is subjected to much negative emotion, will develop illness. The pathways of that illness are apparent in the ethereal body long before manifesting in the physical. Another example would be stresses building within the planet which will be released in the form of natural catastrophes.*"

"Wow! Swami, can you foretell the events of a person's life?"

"*To the extent they are in the grip of karmic tendencies.*"

"What do you mean?"

"What is sown, is reaped. The implications run deeper than most people can imagine. This does not imply that a person's future is fixed and that they merely live out a scripted life. Tendencies may be overcome by self discipline and exercise of free will." I wanted to ask more, but was concerned about Curry. He'd been in trance for over an hour. But I couldn't help asking one more question. "Then would it be possible in my life, for instance, to say what job I'll have? Or... um... when... er... I mean with who... ah... never mind."

Instead of the usual flat tone, the *voice* sounded slightly amused. *"Your jobs will be many and varied, and your first intimacy will occur in a foreign land. Indeed, it is more likely the earth will change its orbit than will the two of you fail to love. Would you like to know her name?"*

I almost said *sure*. But something stopped me. It would be like skipping ahead to the last page of a mystery novel. "No. I think I'd rather be surprised."

Now the swami actually laughed—well, more of a chuckle. *"A wise choice, Darwin Bownes."*

I sat for a moment before waking Curry, the chance of a lifetime to ask any question. To thumb through the cosmic book of knowledge. But my brain seized up, and couldn't think of anything important enough to ask. I'd be better prepared next time.

"Curry, when you wake, you will feel refreshed, and," I added with a grin, "you will have an incredible yearning for a dill pickle." When I chanted OM in his ear, Curry opened his eyes, stretched, checked his watch. "Jeez, I've been out forever. Did I say anything?" He shed the turban and robe. "How about a snack."

He pawed through a shopping bag full of goodies, which—I happened to know—included a large piece of his mom's spice cake. When he couldn't seem to find just the right thing, I upended my lunch bag and out tumbled a dill pickle wrapped in plastic—the only thing I hadn't eaten at lunch.

"I'd be willing to trade this for something," I said. "Maybe that cake."

"Done," Curry said, snatching the pickle.

After we made short work of our snacks, I reviewed what had happened with Ted Griswald and Gretchen. Curry shook his head, as much in awe of his own powers as I'd been. When I got to the part about Dan Klatt, a flicker of panic crossed his eyes.

"But he'll want..."

"I know. And you told me in private that it is possible to predict things that could make you rich. But don't worry. I've got a plan."

His brow wrinkled. "I can predict the future?"

"Certain things." As I read from my notes about karma and stresses within the earth, Curry's face became colorless and anguished. "What's the matter?" I asked.

"Earthquakes? What about floods... and wars?" He took a deep breath. "I don't know... it's too much responsibility, Dar."

"Don't worry about it."

"Why shouldn't I worry about it?"

I laughed. "Who's going to believe a tenth-grader, anyway?"

Chapter 15

Breaking Klatt From Sucking Eggs

I checked my watch. "Get your brain diaper on, Swami. Klatt's due and I need to tell you the plan."

"Plan?"

Just then the tent flap opened and Dan Klatt's broad shoulders filled the entrance. "Let's do it. I've got a full life."

"If you can just give us three minutes—alone—so I can put Curry into his trance."

Klatt scowled. "Three minutes counting from right now." The tent darkened as he released the door flap.

"But Darwin—"

"Shhhh. This guy thinks the world owes him everything. He needs to be broke from sucking eggs." I'd first heard the expression from Curry's dad, so Curry knew what it meant. I didn't give him a chance to argue, just told him how to play it.

"But we can't—"

"You want to go into a real trance and let him exploit you?"

Curry frowned. "No."

"Then let's give him his five bucks worth."

When Dan Klatt returned in exactly three minutes, he found Swami Curryban Bucklananda in repose, though breathing a bit jerkily. I had a groove running on the drums, but not the mantra beat. This one had a thudding heart with a nervous fill.

Klatt had a notebook and pencil in hand. "All right, Swami, let's start with who's going to win the World Series, then we'll move on to lottery numbers."

I put a finger to my lips and motioned for him to sit. "These things are not so easy."

"What do you mean?"

"Patience," I said. "Sit."

Grudgingly, he sat.

"Now, I must ask the questions. He can't hear anyone else." Dan Klatt nodded. I asked, "Swami, are you with us?"

"Yes." Curry's voice sounded thin and deliberately mysterious. But Dan Klatt had never heard the swami's real voice.

"Swami, are you able to predict winning lottery numbers?"

"How can one know what hasn't been determined?"

I whispered to Klatt. "I was afraid of that. But don't give up hope—we'll try something else. I know, we'll ask what career you'll have."

"Why?" he challenged.

"If we find out you don't have to work because you're rich, we'll know you're going to win the lottery, which means there's a way to find the numbers."

Dan rubbed his chin. "He just said he couldn't predict the future."

"Some things are already locked in by karma. That means stuff that you deserve, that just hasn't happened yet."

"I know what it means. Get on with it."

"Swami Curryban, Dan Klatt is here and would like to know what his profession will be at age, say, twenty-five."

"The subject will be employed by a large international business."

"What kind of business, Swami?"

"The restaurant industry."

"In what capacity will he be employed?"

"Preparation."

Dan Klatt shifted on his cushion and leaned forward. I could see the first inkling of concern in his steely eyes.

"Where will he live?"

"Bremerton, Washington."

"That can't be right!" Klatt said.

"Shhhh! You'll wake him and never find out the details."

Klatt gave a backhand swat in Curry's direction. "Ah, he doesn't know nothing."

"He got the Blubbergum right," I said. "Swami, could you be more specific about what is meant by 'preparation'? And how much money will the subject be making?"

"Flipping hamburgers for minimum wage."

Dan Klatt stood up, his face scarlet. "What!"

"Just a minute," I said. "There's still hope. Swami, will there ever be a time when the subject has enough money that he no longer needs to work?"

Dan froze, and listened carefully for the answer.

"Yes."

Dan relaxed and waited for the rest of it.

Curry continued. His jaw muscles tightened as he tried to keep straight face. "The subject at age twenty-six will receive a medical retirement because of a disfiguring injury to his face, caused by boiling grease."

I don't know how Curry kept from laughing, but with closed eyes, he couldn't see how Klatt's face had lost its tan, and how his mouth sagged like one of those sad masks on theater doors. I kept my face straight only by thinking of the pounding I'd get if Klatt caught us messing with his head.

Curry started pouring it on—"Your wife will leave you and your children will be afraid because their father looks like a monster"—but I stopped him, fearing that our chump would catch on. "Swami Curryban, is there any way the subject can avoid this terrible fate?"

Curry thought for a moment. We hadn't gotten this far in our planning. Then he said, "There is a chance—a slim one. Fate will serve Dan Klatt only if he stops expecting other people to serve him. In fact, only by continuous serving of other people who are in need can he avoid a life of loneliness and shame."

Silence hung like a stopped clock. I gave Klatt a full minute to think on what he'd heard, and he seemed to be thinking hard on it. Curry's words vibrated in the air like the ringing of a gong. Finally, I brought Curry from his 'trance' in the usual way, nearly forgetting that he'd only pretended sleep.

Dan Klatt rose and left. His dazed expression made great advertising for business. I turned back to the swami, who was all grins, and I snapped the fiver in front of him. "You're *good*," I said.

"Yeah?" Curry giggled behind his hand. "And if he finds out, we're going to be buzzard bait."

Chapter 16
Ms. Dozier's Little Inconvenience

"Yoo hoo, Swami," a woman's voice bugled. I stepped out of the tent. Among the onlookers stood our English comp teacher, Ms. Dozier.

"Business is booming," she said cheerfully.

"I don't think we'll save Camp Bluetoad single-handedly," I said.

"Every dollar helps." She reached for a coin purse slung from a chain around a neck wrinkled as an elephant's leg. Out came a wad of dollars. "I should contribute my bit, don't you think? Or is someone else in line?"

The line deferred to Ms. Dozier—in fact, urged her on. Three weeks ago, she'd been dissed as a fruity old woman who wore the same Hawaiian muumuu every day. But since standing up to Mr. Krogstrand, and organizing the bazaar, she'd become something of a hero. With line-cutting privileges.

"Then make it good. I want the swami to foresee plenty of romance in my life." She chuckled for too long.

I didn't like others watching as Curry went into his trance, but Ms. Dozier seemed to be making light of the whole thing as if we were play-acting, and I wanted her to understand. I seated her cross-legged on a pile of cushions in the tent. I wondered if she'd been working too hard on the Bluetoad campaign because she'd lost some bulk, and her skin had a grayish pallor. Curry composed himself, traced a finger over the weird bird on his amulet, and began chanting his mantra. "*Tat Savitur Varenyam Om. Tat Savitur Varenyam Om...*"

I heard the proper beat in my head then let it flow through my fingers on the drum, fitting the cadence of Curry's chant.

But it wasn't working. After several minutes, Curry's eyes remained half-opened and his lips still moved with the mantra. Ms. Dozier had begun picking at her nail polish. She noticed my glance and smiled as if to assure me she found our show amusing. I closed my eyes and focused on the sound, wondering if I had the beat perfectly right. No sooner had I wondered when a peculiar phrase lighted on me like a thought-butterfly: *dump the lump, Swami, dump the lump.* The phrase had a rhythm of its own and I wove it into the groove, adding a level of complexity that had my body swaying in several directions at once. When I cracked an eye to see if this had helped Curry, a beam of low sunlight had slanted through a mesh window, casting a golden halo about him. His eyes were closed, lips still, breath nearly stopped. I faded the drums out.

The effect hadn't escaped Ms. Dozier. She whispered, "Heavens, I feel like I've got my money's worth already."

"You may ask Swami Curryban your question now."

"Okay, Swami." She screwed up a smile to indicate she'd play along with the make-believe. "What will the weather be tomorrow? Will it rain?"

I sighed and watched Curry to see how he'd react.

"*The weather is of no concern to you. Ask your question.*"

Ms. Dozier tightened at the tone and authority of the swami's voice. She began fiddling with the catch on her coin purse. "Oh," she said. "Um, ah... okay. My grandchild in San Diego, is he doing well?"

"*Your grandson, Timothy, is doing as well as can be expected. Stop wasting time and ask the question that weighs on your mind.*"

"You... you knew his name!"

The effect on Ms. Dozier, always a strong, confident woman, gave me shivers. She looked at me with astonishment then began wringing her hands. Her face became rubbery and she fished a handkerchief from her sleeve and dabbed the corners of her eyes. Then she cupped her hand to a spot just below her right breast.

"Well... I do have a question. What I'd like to know is..." her breathing became labored as if the oxygen in the tent had been used up.

I had the tingling feeling of swimming in deep water. I took a breath and urged, "Go ahead."

She sniffed, looked at me, then mustered her nerve. "I have a little inconvenience that's been troubling me. I wonder, dear Swami, can you tell me... what I can expect?"

The Swami's answer came quickly. *"You will pass from the physical sphere within six months unless there is immediate intervention."*

"Oh my."

Something happened to my sense of equilibrium. I thought I might be falling over, and braced my hands against the Persian rug. Ms. Dozier looked wobbly, too, so I took a knee beside her. She clutched at my hand and held on. She'd always seemed such a robust woman; I wouldn't have believed Curry's prediction if not for her reaction. She seemed unable to continue—again she rubbed the area below her rib cage—so I asked, "Swami, what's wrong with Ms. Dozier?"

"This body has long been afflicted by a metastatic tumor. The body's natural healing forces are strong and have at times gained on the condition, but have now been overwhelmed because of poor diet and stress, among other things, and the morbidity has spread into the surrounding lymph and into the blood."

I shook my head, not wanting to believe it. Curry had devised a treatment for my wart, but this? I didn't know much about tumors except that you attacked them with knives and poison and radiation. And prayer. But Curry's comment about intervention gave me hope. "What treatment is required?" I asked, reaching for my notebook.

"The body's defenses must be assisted—the circulation improved and the eliminative forces stimulated. Blockages are inhibiting healing energies emanating from the spinal plexuses, and must be cleared."

As I scribbled to get it all down, the swami described a device used to administer a mild electrical charge to the cancerous areas, and a solution containing atropine to be absorbed through the skin while using the electrical cell. *"Increase the atropine concentration weekly until maximum dosage is reached—as much as the body can tolerate."* Then he prescribed a mixture of cleansing herbs to be taken internally, along with elimination of meats from the diet. *"The condition arose originally from infectious forces present in meats, in combination with genetic predisposition."* As he continued, I had to guess at spelling some of the terms Curry used, as I'd never heard them.

Ms. Dozier, who had been breathing heavily with open mouth, asked, "Is there hope then?"

"There are no incurable diseases, provided they are not so advanced as to overwhelm the restorative energies that may be brought to bear. The present sarcoma is very near that point, but might be pushed back, and eventually defeated, if the prescribed regimen is followed exactly, along with prudent treatment from a physician."

"But my doctor is recommending massive surgery. I'm afraid of knives and I've refused chemotherapy. I'd rather die with all my parts and all my hair."

"Surgery will not prolong your life."

"I knew it!" Ms. Dozier's manner had some of her usual stubbornness in it. "Thank you, Swami. I'll do as you say, if I can only find a doctor to help."

"There is one who will understand the treatment. You know him by the name of Doctor Wesley Uncas."

Chapter 17
Chicken Run

I t seemed eerie. Curry's breath had all but stopped, but a fitful wind worked the tent walls in and out like a bellows. I imagined Curry filling every particle of space in the tent; I imagined him riding freely on the wind. I bent to his right ear and chanted OM to summon him back. When he woke and found Ms. Dozier weeping into her hands, he sat up stiff with alarm. "What happened?"

She reached for his hand and cradled it to her soggy cheek. "Dear boy."

When Curry looked at me, I motioned my head toward the tent door. Ms. Dozier would want some time to compose herself. I asked her, "Okay if we talk to Keeley Uncas about this?"

She nodded and began repairing her face with a handkerchief and small mirror.

"Lose the swami gear," I said softly to Curry. He looked blankly from me to Ms. Dozier and back again. "I need to write up my notes while everything's fresh, and Keeley can help with some of the gnarly words."

Outside the tent, I apologized to the people waiting in line and said we were done for the day. We pressed through the crowd toward Keeley's herb booth, Curry badgering me for information all the while, but I wanted to explain to both of them at once.

Keeley looked boyishly thin in a white turtleneck and purple vest. "Can you close shop?" I asked. "It's important." She must have seen the gravity in my eyes because she didn't hesitate, writing out a card in her neat hand:

Self-Service
Put Money in Box
Back Soon

I led her and Curry to the schoolhouse to look for some privacy. I tried the door to Ms. Dozier's empty classroom and found it unlocked, like everything else on the island. I laid it all out, my voice thickening when I looked at Ms. Dozier's desk knowing it might soon be vacant. Keeley listened, her mouth twisted into a skeptical grimace. But she knew about the monk's gravy, and I'd told her about my cured plantar wart. As I went through my notes, her dark-chocolate eyes kept widening, and she stole frequent glances at Curry. His face had a numb, inward stare, his pupils shrinking with a kind of fear. Though Keeley supplied the correct medical terms in several cases from my crude phonetic spelling, there were some details that stumped her.

"We need to ask dad about this."

"Will he believe it?" I asked.

Keeley turned her palms up.

"Let's find out." Though Ms. Dozier might have six months, I felt every second counted. But I did take a minute to run upstairs to ask Mrs. Muldoon to photocopy my notes. I rushed in, finding her already at the copy machine. She jerked around, startled, and positioned her body as if to hide something.

"Bad timing," I said. "I wanted to burn copies of some notes."

A light of recognition went on in her eyes: the kid who'd burst into her boss's office a few weeks ago to stick up for Curry Buckle. I thought my chances at that point were somewhere between zilch and nonexistent, but she took my pages and zipped off the two copies I asked for.   I rolled the warm paper, thanked Mrs. Muldoon, and hustled downstairs.

We returned to Keeley's booth. Curry helped her pack up while I retrieved my drum for safekeeping. A trace of Ms. Dozier's fruity perfume lingered in the swami tent; she must have spritzed herself before leaving. When I got back to the herb booth, I noticed Curry glancing toward the food court.

"Jeez, Curry, I forgot." I fished Dan Klatt's five-spot from my pocket. We'd come by it fraudulently so I didn't feel guilty using it to cover expenses. While Curry grazed, I found Ms. Dozier walking among the booths, acting every bit her old jovial self. It made me ache knowing how much effort it must have cost her. I gave her a copy of my notes. For an instant, the facade cracked and I saw her lip tremble as she tucked the notes in her sweater pocket, buttoned over her cancered torso. "Curry and I are going to see Doc Uncas now," I said. "We'll phone tonight."

Keeley pushed the envelope, raising boils of dust behind her speeding V-Dub Bug. Curry, seated in back, oblivious to the blurred landscape, fed his second foot-long chilidog into his eating hole. I hoped he wouldn't gork it all up when Keeley hit zero-G over the little bridge. He didn't; life wasn't *all* bad.

At the Uncas house, on the lonely cliffs overlooking Octopus Rocks, we found Doc Uncas in the living room trying to catch a live chicken. His bent, deliberate manner worked well for stalking, but he lacked the burst for the catch. Keeley, however, simply threw a coverlet over the bird and was soon holding it upside down by the feet. "So Mrs. Mudge has been over for a consult."

Doc bunched his brows over deep-set eyes. "Every time the Readers' Digest prints a story about a disease, she thinks she'll be dead of it in a week." He explained to Curry and me, "So she wastes my time and pays me in chickens." He said *chickens* as if they were some gross mistake of nature. "Offer that beady-eyed thing to the fox gods, will you?" Then he recognized me from the stitched eye. His neck craned forward to inspect his work. "Hm. Bit out of practice, I'm afraid."

When Keeley had disposed of the chicken, she said, "Daddy, you remember Darwin Bownes. And this is Curry Buckle—I've mentioned him?"

"The one who cheats on his biology quizzes?"

Keeley swallowed and turned pink. "Ah, he's the one who found the Juniper's cat and said to treat it with monk's gravy."

Doc scrutinized Curry more closely, frowned, then pressed three bony fingers into Curry's belly.

"Ow!" Curry took a step back and covered his chilidog-distended middle.

"Not exactly a prime specimen," Doc Uncas muttered.

"Daddy, we have something terribly important to tell you."

"So did Mrs. Mudge, and all it got me was ten laps around the sofa after a brainless chicken."

Keeley ushered her father into his study, which, as I learned when he stitched my brow, doubled as his consulting room and surgery. He kept his medical instruments discretely out of view, but the room smelled faintly antiseptic.

"It's one of our teachers," Keeley said when we'd taken seats. "Ms. Dozier."

"Bull Dozier?" Doc said, giving me a wink.

But I'd never be able to joke about her again. "Curry did a reading this afternoon," I said.

"Reading?"

Keeley said, "Remember, I told you? He goes into a meditation trance and, well, he can know things."

Doc stared intently at Curry. "Hmm."

"You're always saying that healing is more magic than medicine," Keeley said.

"Don't always say it," Doc grumbled. "May have said it once or twice."

"Well, Ms. Dozier came in for a reading and she has a tumor. It sounds bad. Darwin, let father read your notes."

I unrolled the pages. Odd, I had only the photocopies, and not my originals. I shrugged it off, and watched Doc's face. He read through the pages once, then again, this time with glasses, and a third time while chewing on the earhook of his glasses.

Then he crumpled the notes and threw them into his waste can.

I closed my eyes for a moment in disappointment. I'd half-expected this.

"Clever," he said, scowling. "A jolly good hoax. But I don't much appreciate this bit in here about me. Bad enough trying to fool your old man, Keeley, but to make fun of him.... Why don't you all go..." he waved his hand, "go play with the chicken or something."

Keeley looked puzzled. "But it's not a hoax." Her gaze narrowed on me. "Is it Darwin?"

"No."

Doc stood and walked brusquely from the study. I exchanged helpless looks with Curry. I remembered the hopeful expression on Ms. Dozier's face when I told her we were going to see Doc Uncas, and my heart felt like a brick. The words I'd used to reassure Curry now haunted me. *Who's going to believe a tenth-grader?*

The phone rang.

Keeley answered. "Yes? Oh, hi Ms. Dozier. Just a minute." She called her dad back to the study. We listened as he took the call.

"Yes... yes... okay. So he really did? Yes, I've read them. Doctor Slather? No one else knew, you say?" Doc sank into his chair and pressed a hand to his forehead. "No... I mean... well, where's the harm? Of course it will take time to construct the, ah, instrument. Tomorrow? I suppose. Why not come at three. And, Ms. Dozier, kindly don't mention this matter to Dr. Slather... She's what? Given up, you say? Well, ha ha, I always say healing is more magic than medicine. Yes, that would be fine, but no live animals please."

Doc Uncas hung up, propped his chin in his hand, and took a long look at Curry. Curry looked almost dwarfish, sitting in a high-backed chair, feet barely grazing the carpet, his broad face and chest slightly out of proportion to his limbs. Curry returned Doc's scrutiny in full. I sensed they saw things in each other that were beyond my notice. I hoped they'd decide to give each other a chance.

Then Doc reached into the trash for my notes, smoothed them on his desk, and consulted them more closely through the glasses on his nose. He put his finger at a spot on the second page. "I understand the concept of the wet cell appliance, but the details of making one... the wattage for example..." He read more, then shook his head in frustration. "There simply isn't enough information here."

"I'm sure Curry can give the details," I said. "My drum's in the car."

Chapter 18
Put to the Test

"**You** look trashed," I said to Curry. He sat on a stuffed chair, fat-fingering his shoelace. His trance sessions that afternoon had sapped something that two foot-long chilidogs hadn't been able to restore. I helped Curry pull off his shoe. He didn't seem to have the energy.

Curry blinked twice. "If Ms. Dozier can carry on, half-dead with cancer, then I can do one more reading for her."

So I wedged a pillow behind the small of his back, propped his feet on a hassock, and removed his other shoe. The tip of a big toe showed through a hole in his sock. I sat cross-legged on the carpet and struck up the hypnotic rhythm while he chanted *Tat Savitur Varenyam Om... Tat Savitur Varenyam Om.* The sounds resonated from the wood paneling in Doc's study and seemed to be coming from all around us. Curry's chanting gradually became a whisper, then only a faint movement of his lips. In another minute, his eyelids quivered and, his breathing appeared to stop. He had dumped his lump, becoming our search engine to the cosmic internet.

I set the drum aside and nodded to Doc Uncas and Keeley. I think their breathing, too, had all but stopped.

"Can you hear me, Swami?" I asked.

A pause, then the voice that seemed to flow from some craggy mountain. *"I am with you."*

"Doctor Uncas needs to clear up some things about the treatment for Ms. Dozier."

"He may state his query."

The Doc looked for something in his desk drawer, then approached slowly, hands clasped behind his back, to where Curry reclined. Doc waved his left hand before Curry's face, and when Curry didn't react, he drew his right hand from behind his back. It held a pair of pliers.

Before I could react, Doc Uncas had gripped Curry's protruding toe with the pliers and gave it a nasty tweak.

Curry didn't so much as twitch. But I did. I leapt to my feet and ripped the pliers from Doc's hand and brandished them in his face, hot anger spreading through my blood. "Nobody does that to Curry," I said. "Can't you see he's helpless? We're done here. I'm waking him up. He trusted you."

Doc held up his palms. "Sorry. But I had to be sure. I'm being asked to administer an unknown and untested cancer treatment involving electric shock and a toxic drug. I think you know why I can't take foolish chances."

I remembered Governor Bigelow's dead daughter and what Keeley had said about her father risking prison if he continued practicing medicine. I understood, but still didn't like it. After Doc examined the tool marks on Curry's toe, I said, "Satisfied... doctor?" I loaded it with sarcasm.

He nodded, and bit at a hangnail while staring at Curry's peaceful face. "If you can hear me, Curry, I apologize for what I just did."

"Did you not repeat the Hippocratic oath upon becoming a physician?"

Doc Uncas flinched. "Why, of course."

"Your license to practice medicine may have been revoked, but not your oath to do no harm."

Doc Uncas pulled himself upright and lowered his gaze to the floor. "I know that."

"Then let us proceed to the matter at hand."

For fifteen minutes, Doc Uncas asked technical questions about Ms. Dozier's condition and construction of the wet cell device. His chin whiskers twitched as he concentrated on the answers, which Curry gave in precise medical terms.

When satisfied about the treatment, Doc Uncas had one more question. "The information you've given is clearly beyond anything Curry Buckle could have known." Doc's eyes shone from their deep caves. "So I want to know, who are you?"

I glanced at Keeley to make sure she was still taking notes.

"I am that which Curry will become. Neither existent nor non-existent. I am all that is he, but he knows me not."

"That helps a lot," Doc muttered, shaking his head. "What should we call you?"

"I have been addressed as Swami. This is satisfactory."

"Swami then, explain why Curry has the power to contact his... higher self, if we may refer to you in those terms."

"As humankind enters an age of higher consciousness, the understanding of subtle forces expands. Only in the last hundred years have electromagnetic waves and atomic energy been discovered. Other forces which cannot be detected by physical instruments will soon be known. But spiritual advancement must keep pace with technological progress. Advancement relies on attunement with the Source. The children of your generation will understand this better than you. Many lamas murdered in Tibet by the Chinese will come again in this generation, to diverse nations."

While Doc chewed on that, I brought Curry back to his normal consciousness by whispering OM in his ear. The Swami's last answer had my brain chasing its tail. It all sounded too big for me to grasp. Curry sat up and knuckled the sleep from his eyes. Doc stood and extended his hand. Cautiously, Curry shook the hand, glancing at me for some clue as to what had happened.

"Young man," Doc said, "I've traveled a great many places, lived with unknown tribes in the Amazon basin, experienced things that most western doctors and scientists couldn't begin to fathom. Had I not seen these things, maybe I'd try to explain away what's just happened." He sighed. "But I know better." He clapped his hands on Curry's shoulders as if sizing them up. "I just pray you can bear the load you've been measured for."

Chapter 19
Mr. Buckle's Drift

Curry invited me to spend the night at his house, so I called for mom's okay. Nobody spoke as Keeley drove us to the Buckle farm. In fact, Curry fell asleep—the usual kind—after chowing a sandwich. Keeley turned her jazz station off and drove under the speed limit, her mind elsewhere. Mine too. What kind of miraculous thing had I become involved in? What kind of human being was this gentle, withdrawn kid curled in the back seat? My new friend. I felt jealous at sharing Curry's secret with others, but also relieved at not having to bear the full weight of his trust.

When Keeley let us off, I looked at her before waking Curry. Her wide-set eyes had a depth to them that gave me vertigo, like standing on a cliff before jumping into a deep pool. Something was troubling them.

"Darwin."

"Yeah?"

"This can't get out. You understand?"

"About your dad treating Ms. Dozier?"

"Nobody—not even your parents. Not the Buckles either."

"I know. His fanny's really hanging out."

"He's all I've got."

"I promise."

She nodded.

I woke Curry. We climbed the front stairs as Keeley drove off.

On the porch, same bottle of amontillado, same three wicker rockers. But, this time, only two sisters—Aunt Iris and Curry's mom— and nothing felt the same. No banter or wisecracks, just the creak of rockers. Though bundled in thick sweaters and lap blankets, they looked cold. The horizon held a pillow of clouds over the sun's face.

Pansy murdered. Stubby old Pansy with the simple expression, chortling at her own moldy puns, gone. Case unsolved despite the reward. Conversation came in low tones, with handkerchiefs at the ready. Iris seemed to have aged markedly, and had developed a tic under one eye. Curry and I said hello and tried to rush past, but his mom's arm shot out and snagged him. I'd bet on her in any chicken-catching contest.

"What do you know about holes on your aunt's property?" Her stern look dared him to lie, though he'd probably never lied in his life.

"Holes?"

"Someone's still digging holes, and she's worried sick about it."

"Not me, auntie."

"Oh dear," Aunt Iris said. "Now that I'm alone, I let things get to me." She gave a little laugh. "After Pansy turned seventy, she'd say it unnerved her to see someone digging a hole, because it might be for her."

I asked, "Could there be a connection between the holes and... what happened to Pansy?"

"The sheriff and I don't see eye to eye on that," Iris said. "He thinks there might be, just because he can't find any other clues. To me it looks like robbery, plain and simple. But I'm not as brave, now that I'm alone, and I wish the holes would stop. It looks like a giant gopher moved in."

Curry and I promised we'd stop over for a look, and then went inside.

The sight of Dan Klatt, sitting on the couch with Paprika, jolted me. I'd forgotten he might be there, and hadn't noticed his truck in the driveway. This was why Curry wanted me to spend the night: so he wouldn't have to face Klatt alone after we'd suckered him at the swami booth. Klatt sat apart from Paprika, hugging a knee, looking sober and tense.

Mr. Buckle piloted his recliner before the TV, remote control in each hand and a beer between his knees. On the tube, bulge-mouth boxers knocked sprays of sweat and blood off each other, but he'd muted the sound. Mr. Buckle listened instead to Paprika's school gossip. And the gossip was about Curry. Swami Curryban Bucklananda.

"Here's the celebrity, now," Mr. Buckle said. "Sit down. Tell your papa what's going on in your life."

Curry looked at me and rolled his eyes. I had the feeling his life didn't often take priority over two steroid-sculpted brutes inflicting brain damage on each other.

"Your sister says people have been paying good money for you to tell their fortunes." He pronounced it FORE-toons. "You know, when I was a young buck, and started working for cash money, why that's when my pa expected me to pitch in toward the rent. I was young, but things were tight so I did my share. You unnerstand what I'm saying?"

Curry might have been too exhausted, but I understood well enough. By reflex, my hand felt for the faint outline of folded money in my shirt pocket. The day's proceeds from the booth, minus expenses for chilidogs.

"We really don't take much in," I said. "And what we do, goes to save Camp Bluetoad. We don't keep any of it."

Mr. Buckle glared at me, breathing through his mouth. "Point is, it's been proved people will pay money to have their fortunes told. Am I right?"

I conceded the point, trying not to look at Dan Klatt.

"That's all I'm saying. And that a workingman ought to shoulder his percentage. That's the way the world operates."

"I think we'll go upstairs," Curry said.

Mr. Buckle held up a hand. "We're not quite done yet. Until we get you set up making regular money, I'm thinking there's a way you can contribute right now."

Curry said nothing. He looked wobbly on his feet. I felt heat escaping up my collar.

When Mr. Buckle scratched his two-day growth of beard, it sounded like cards being shuffled. "You know the sheriff's spinning his wheels trying to find your aunt Pansy's killer. So the reward still stands for the first legitimate tip. You get my drift?"

Curry's tired eyes stretched open. "But dad, it's Aunt Iris who's offering the reward. We couldn't claim it, being family." Curry looked at me to see if I agreed. I could have made a case either way, but I didn't like Mr. Buckle's drift, so I nodded my support.

Mr. Buckle said, "It don't make no difference. Your Aunt Iris is sick at the heart, and just wants the murderer locked up." He flicked a glance toward the porch and lowered his voice. "She's got enough beans salted away, she'd barely miss ten thousand."

Curry's mouth opened, but nothing came out. But I knew then why he'd refused when I'd suggested using his powers to identify the perp. Mr. Buckle would have claimed the reward and, for whatever reason, Curry didn't like the idea. Spooked by the monkey's paw probably.

"Mr. Buckle," I said, "Curry's going to spend the night over at my place. Okay?"

"We ought to take care of business. Wouldn't want someone else claiming that reward, eh?"

"He can only do a couple of sessions in a day, and right now he's all used up."

Curry really did look used up. Mr. Buckle glanced between him and the fighter getting seriously jacked in the ring. "Well," he said, "first thing in the morning then."

Chapter 20
Holes

I phoned my mom about having Curry over. No problem. Curry's dad hadn't said no, so we hauled butt before things changed. Curry kick-started his motorbike and we strapped on our brain buckets. With Curry still dazed from his psychic readings, I drove.

Friends who meet my mom think she's a hoot. She has more energy than the entire Buckle family combined, and tries to make everything fun. She's small, and reminds me of a kitten who likes to bat things around and make friends with the neighborhood dogs. Dad and I get along, but he works ridiculous hours. Mom works at the newspaper, too, doing some layout, but she's the one who taught me how to escape a half-nelson, shoot a fade-away jumper, locate the pole star, and finger my first chords on the guitar. She can cook an entire Thanksgiving meal in the microwave and has discovered dozens of uses for GooeyGlue, including darning socks, pulling ticks, hanging Christmas ornaments, and closing wounds. She'd even tried to cure my plantar wart with it during the summer, but it didn't work.

Curry got a hug, a kiss to the forehead, and a microwave brownie all in the first minute of walking in the door.

Dad was home, too. He liked to unwind by hitting the treadmill in the basement and listening to loud, narcotic music from his past. We could feel early Eric Clapton chops through the soles of our feet. Other than his taste in music, he's a complete embarrassment. When he came upstairs, sweating, head still bobbing to the bass line, he said to Curry, "Hey dude, did you catch your act in the *Whalebone*?"

I thought about how young my parents were compared to Curry's, and figured his had burned out by the time Curry came along.

Curry looked confused.

"Forgot to tell you," I said. Dad ran one of your pictures from last week's game."

"Yeah?"

I opened a paper and showed him. Curry beamed.

Dad found his pants and took out his wallet.

"Ten bones per shot. That was our deal?"

Curry nodded shyly. Ten bones: twice what Swami Curryban got for his schtick.

Dad thumbed a bill from his wallet. "Good work, my man."

Curry accepted the cash and looked at it. Then his shoulders slumped. "I guess this should go toward my room and board."

"No way," I said. "You've got expenses. Film. Maybe a new lens or something, right?"

Curry smiled crookedly at me. "Dar, you could talk fleas off a dog."

The next morning, Saturday, we walked downtown. Dad had offered Curry use of the darkroom at the print shop, and Curry wanted to look it over. On the way he asked, "What should I tell dad about trying to find out who killed Aunt Pansy?"

"I don't know," I said. But I did know. Ever since he told Ted Griswald how his birthday money got ripped off, I figured Curry could solve the Twist case too. I just didn't see any way to snag the reward. For one thing, Sheriff Biggs wouldn't believe us. Also, the idea of Mr. Buckle cashing in on Curry twisted my skivvies. "Let's ask Swami for advice. Did I mention? —he says it's cool to call him that."

Curry shook his head in quick jerks. "I could hardly think straight last night—felt drained. I don't know who this Swami is, and it's weirding me out. "

"Oh, that's the other thing." I got out the excerpts I'd copied from Keeley's notes and read them aloud. "I am that which Curry will become. I am all that is he, but he knows me not."

"That's supposed to help?"

"Sounded better coming from Swami. Anyway, he isn't someone else. He's you, but you don't know it." I looked at the notes. "He made it sound like you were a Tibetan lama in your last life, until the

Commies snuffed you. He said mankind was entering a higher age and it was up to our generation to help."

Curry looked unconvinced.

"Plus, your amulet protects you. Right?"

A whirlwind swept leaves from the gutter and rattled them into the street. Curry said, "I like being able to help people, but why does it have to be so complicated. Shouldn't things get easier in a higher age?"

We peered in the drug store window. There were guys from our class at the video machines, and Curry had ten bucks in his pocket, but we still had more to talk about. We moved on and Curry said, "I really don't want my dad involved in this."

"You're afraid if he gets the reward, he'll just want more?"

Curry stopped abruptly. "Exactly! Nobody should be in control of me. This thing that's happening, I'm responsible for it. I trust you, Darwin, because you never try to make me do something I don't want to do."

"Except wear a turban?"

He laughed. "Well, there's that."

"Check this out. What if I ask Swami to name the murderer, and we feed it to the cops anonymously. Then no one gets the reward and justice is done—and your dad gets off your case."

"But if dad found out somehow... he knows Sheriff Biggs pretty well." We crossed over to the Junque and Vintage Girdle Emporium. Curry didn't even look for traffic; there weren't many moving vehicles in town, except when the ferry came at noon. "I'll think about it." He paused at the shop door. "You know, Darwin, somehow I've always known there was something missing from my parent's lives. Almost like they were pretending not to be aware of some big secret."

His eyes shone with an intensity that sent a wave of disorienting energy through my body.

"Now it feels like the big secret is trying to bust out from inside me."

*   *   *

We found Aunt Iris on a step stool reaching for old hats. She looked like a grazing giraffe.

"These dusty old things." She held at arms length a contorted felt monstrosity, complete with ostrich plume. "Pansy would throw a fit every time I tried getting rid of them. 'They'll be back in style next year, I'll bet my eyeteeth,' she'd say." Iris dropped it into a cardboard box half full of other church hats. "She didn't have a real tooth left in her head, and only the one eye." Iris surveyed the shop with hands on hips. "Finally, I'll be able to get rid of this clutter."

The shop did look more organized than when I'd been in to select props for our swami tent. Was she truly glad to have her way, or did she just need to keep busy out of loneliness? At least she seemed functional again.

"Aunt Iris," Curry said, "we thought we'd check out those holes at your place."

She took an indignant breath and raised a finger. "They were back again last night. I saw their lights through the poplar trees. What *can* they be looking for?"

Curry assured Iris we'd check on it then we boogied down the street to the print shop. Dad could have had the newspaper printed off-island for the same cost, but he liked the greasy old printing press, and the greasy old guy, Leonard, who took care of the press, crawling through its innards, talking to it, tuning it constantly like a cheap piano. Dad showed Curry the darkroom. While I hung around the shop breathing the glandular smell of printing ink, they turned on the red light and sealed themselves in to make a couple strips of contact prints. We didn't have a football game that week, but dad had told Curry he wanted some photos of next Friday's school bazaar.

Dad tried to give us lunch money, but Curry remembered he had ten dollars. "I'm buying, Mr. Bownes." I made a mental note to talk to Curry about turning down money. Around noon, Curry and I headed to Troutigan's lunch wagon. I took a chance on the special: Vietnamese Napalmed Noodles. Curry scarfed a murderburger, and we scored a bag of Ho Chi Minh Trail Mix to snack on later.

Iris's weathered mansion stood at the edge of town, in one corner of her sprawling property. The gingerbread woodwork under the gables had begun to crumble, and the windows of the lighthouse turret were boarded-up. As we tromped through her thistle-infested field toward a poplar windbreak, planted maybe a century ago, Curry explained that Iris's acreage ran across the street to Treachery Bay and north toward the old limeworks. The poplar leaves had changed to chromium yellow, and when a breeze shook loose a drift of them, distracting our attention, Curry quite suddenly dropped out of sight with an "Oomph!"

I laughed at him standing chest-deep in a hole. "Did you, by chance, see a white rabbit? Waistcoat, pocket watch?"

"Yuk yuk. Get me out of here."

I gave him a hand up. It took time to find the other holes because of the tall weeds, but beyond the poplars we found plenty of them, mostly three to four feet deep, less where shovel had struck rock or hardpan. Curry also found a magnetic compass on the ground. It still worked. We counted a dozen holes before crossing a collapsed fence—strands of rusted wire on the ground and a few rotting posts still upright.

"Is this your aunt's property line?"

"Search me," Curry said. "There used to be lime kilns just over there."

"Who owns the old limeworks now?"

He shrugged. "It's not used for anything, not even grazing."

"I'm not surprised. Check out all these holes!" There were more the farther we explored, dozens of them, along with the odd piece of rusted farm equipment bound in blackberry vines.

"There's sort of a pattern," I said, though I hadn't been able to put my finger on it. Many of the holes seemed to line up with each other. "Maybe if we map them out..."

"What if they were dug according to a map," Curry said. "That would explain the compass."

I agreed, and we began diagramming the holes, pacing off the distances, entering data in the pocket notebook I carried for recording Curry's readings. An hour later, we'd found some eighty holes in all, and my notes were hopelessly cluttered. I'd draw them to scale later on a piece of graph paper. We could tell the older holes because weeds had germinated in the dirt piles. The freshest holes—soil still damp around them—were those closest to the poplars.

In the damp soil, we found footprints. At least two sets. Lug-soled boots, size extra-large, and another print the size of my foot. Curry said, "Look, a lightning bolt design! Unusual. Wonder if they'll come back tonight."

That gave me an idea. "Maybe we should be here, waiting."

Curry swallowed, looking like he wished he'd kept his mouth shut. "But... it'll be cold. And dark."

"If they can handle it, we can too. You want your aunt to worry herself to death?"

Curry's cheek bulged where his tongue stiffened, and he shook his head.

"You got a flash for your camera?"

"Yeah."

"Good! Meet me at your auntie's house at sundown. I'll bring the hot chocolate and sandwiches."

Curry looked around as if someone might hear. "Have you considered that whoever's doing this might have shot my Aunt Pansy?"

"Of course." I'd also considered the possibility we'd get a picture of them and maybe wind up with the reward. We could always ask the swami, of course, but Curry was getting hypersensitive about what he used his special talent for, and Sheriff Biggs would pay more attention to a photo.

"Well? What if they're murderers?"

"No way. The holes are always dug at night; the shooting happened during the day. Where's the connection?"

Curry just stood there, licking the fuzz on his upper lip as he tried to make up his mind.

"What?" I asked. "You'd rather spend the evening having your dad browbeat you over reward money?"

Curry squirmed. "Well... if we want pictures, I'd have to load some super-fast film."

Chapter 21
Mercury Madness

Curry had chores that afternoon, so I went to my room and plotted holes on graph paper. A straight-line row of holes became clear, with shorter spurs branching off it. The spacing between the holes usually ran about five paces, but, strangely, there were two gaps of twenty paces in the main row with no holes at all. I connected the dots, and only then did something click into place. After the first twenty-pace gap, the pattern of the oldest holes repeated precisely, then began to duplicate on Aunt Iris's property. But why?

I went looking for mom and found her 'ironing' clothes. Her idea of ironing was to give the shirts and pants a violent shake to snap the wrinkles out. Then they went on hangers. Dad and I generally wore knits or sweatshirts that didn't show wrinkles.

"Where can I get a map of who owns what property?" I asked.

"The courthouse."

I thought. "I don't remember seeing a courthouse."

"That's because it's on Tugboat Island. It's the county seat."

"But I need it now." I knew dad could really use the reward because the newspaper was losing money. I could find out the information from Swami, but Curry didn't want to ask about anything connected with the murder because of his thing about a monkey's paw curse. Wishing for money got you a chopped-up uncle, or something equally bad. Also, I figured Mr. Buckle would claim the whole reward if Swami Curryban played any part in solving the case.

Mom pulled one of my sweaters out of the pile and frowned. "You've got a snag here, snagglepuss. Never mind, a dab of GooeyGlue and she'll be good as new." She reached for one of the tubes she kept in strategic locations throughout the house, and began gyrating her hips to a finger-snapping beat. "Dab of glue. Good as new. Dab of glue..." As she made the repair, her hips kept shaking as if they had a mind of their own. She admired her work then said, "You need the map now? Try Tuba Lord."

A lot of businesses in town treated my family as if we had leprosy. We got looked at crosswise when we went to buy something. And voices dropped to whispers. Worst of all, dad had to cut back the newspaper to eight pages because there was hardly any advertising. But Tuba Lord, the real-estate agent who'd sold us our house, always bought an ad. Blubbery as a sea lion, and proud of it. When you saw her, it usually went something like: *How you doing today, Tuba?* And she'd say: *Like three hundred pounds of pure wonderful!*

When I walked in her office, she had the phone wedged to her ear with a little crutch, and a fan blowing air on her face, though it wasn't hot. When she finished her call, I said, "How ya doin', Tuba?"

"Like a prize punkin in the sunshine, Darwin."

I thought of Mr. Buckle's Big McGillicuddy, and could envision Tuba's broad smile carved in it.

"Mom said you could get me a map of Iris Twist's place—and the property next to it. Her fence is down and Curry Buckle and I are trying to figure out the property line."

"Oh, will she be selling?" Tuba Lord said in a sugary voice.

"No, no. Probably just fixing her fence."

She sighed and popped a chocolate turtle in her mouth. "Just as well, that old place is almost beyond repair." She settled back, filling her chair that she rarely got out of. "The Twist House used to be the grandest on the island. Iris's great-uncle, Cyrus, came back from prospecting in the Yukon and built it for his bride. Had forty acres originally, but it got broke up between his boys."

"Cyrus must have struck it rich."

Tuba made a peculiar whistling sound through her teeth. "For sure, he never worked a day after coming back. Off he'd go to Seattle every so often, probably to sell a few nuggets, because he'd come back with cash money to deposit in the local bank. Tight-lipped old badger, they say. Nobody ever knew where he struck pay dirt, or how much he squirreled away. Went mad at the end, you know. Died in an asylum." The superstitious wariness in her voice made me uneasy.

"Strange, his boys never found out what business he did in Seattle."

"Strange," I repeated. "Speaking of strange, why'd he build that tower on his house?"

"He had a wild hair about keeping a lighthouse. Sort of a hobby." Her chair creaked as she leaned forward to confide. "Sadly, that's what put him in a strait jacket."

"The lighthouse?" I leaned forward too, as Tuba's voice had dropped toward a whisper.

She nodded. "In those days, many light keepers went insane. Everyone thought the loneliness brought it on."

"But it couldn't have been loneliness. He was in town."

Tuba's mouth curled up in a lopsided smile. "Indeed. Mercury poisoning. In those days they used to float the rotating light in a pool of mercury. He went mad as a hatter."

I felt a chill—as much from her hushed tone as from the tragedy of Cyrus Twist.

"Yes, there is ill-fortune in that house. I shouldn't be surprised if it's thoroughly haunted, and if Iris were to sell, I would insist that any ghouls be disclosed." Then she pressed her lips together in thought. "Some bed-and-breakfasts *do* advertise ghosts, so I'm not saying the property can't be turned. For every seller, there's a buyer, and Tuba Lord is just the one to match them up. Yes?"

"Who else?" I gave her my Colgate smile.

"See that you tell Iris, then: ghost or no ghost, Tuba Lord can turn it."

"I'll tell her."

"Good. Now, that plat map. She wheeled her chair across the floor to a filing cabinet. When mom and dad were buying our house, we'd been in to see Tuba several times, yet I'd never seen her out of her chair. She just glided around the office in it. "Yes, here it is." She turned her chair and padded backwards to the copy machine. She zapped a copy and handed it to me. "Of course, this doesn't say who owns the land. That adjoining parcel was on the market two years ago, but I never heard who bought it."

"I need to find out," I said. "If we're going to rebuild that fence, we'll want to call."

Tuba tilted her head at me. "Dear heart, there hasn't been so much as a coat of paint put on that house in fifty years. Don't ask me to believe she's going to build a fence."

I looked away, my ears heating. "I... ah..."

She smiled and covered my hand with hers, the back of it spotted as an overripe banana. "You wouldn't be asking without a good reason, Darwin. Tuba knows that. Monday, I'll get the title company to fax me what you want."

"That would be great," I said, gazing sheepishly into her knowing eyes.

Chapter 22
Nightcrawlers

At sundown, Curry and I stepped up to Aunt Iris's creaky porch and rang the ship's bell hung beside the door. After a long wait, Iris, wearing a quilted housecoat and molting slippers, let us in. Without greeting, she led us to the living room where we explained our plan. She nodded at the right places, but said nothing, then blinked and turned away. In the fancy wall mirror, I saw her pinch the bridge of her nose to hold back tears. Still shook over the death of her sister. The old house groaned as if relieved to have survived another day. "So this is what it's like to have men around the house. Things get done!" Her composure restored, she said, "They only start digging after I've turned my lights out—the sneaky rascals—so I'll douse them in about an hour. If they show up, blink your flashlight toward the house and I'll call Sheriff Biggs."

"Maybe we should black our faces," Curry said. I could tell by the way he'd been fidgeting with his camera bag that he still felt shaky about the scheme.

I agreed, and he headed to the fireplace for some soot, and was about to reach up the flue when Iris scolded, "Don't! You'll get fingerprints everywhere. There's something better, anyway." She fetched a kerosene lamp with a sooted-up glass chimney. "Just the thing." She smeared our faces with lamp black, and Curry and I looked at each other and laughed. It loosened us up some, until we looked out the kitchen window at the dusk raising fog from the fields, dank and malignant. Perhaps the murderer awaited the coming of darkness, too. But we couldn't back out with Aunt Iris counting on us, so I hoisted my pack, heavy with sausage, cheese, and a flask of hot chocolate, and Curry gamely shouldered his camera bag.

As the last drab light drained from the sky, we settled at the base of the poplars and waited. The ground still felt warm from the day, and fallen leaves released a spicy fragrance. As bats swooped, I retold Tuba Lord's account of Iris's great-uncle, Cyrus Twist. How he went bughouse from mercury poisoning. When I mentioned ghosts, Curry said, "Aunt Pansy used to claim she heard insane shrieking coming from the lighthouse tower, and she'd demonstrate just to scare the snot out of us."

"Such strong language," I reprimanded. As I did, the upstairs light went out, and the house became a sharply gabled shadow. We didn't speak, just listened to the crickets: one for each star that came out: five, twenty, then a whole universe of them. As the air chilled, more pockets of mist formed over the fields. The poplars loomed over us, gnarly with age, taking on malevolent shapes. I wished I hadn't brought up the subject of insane ghosts. More than once I thought about having Swami Curryban tell us everything we wanted to know about the hole diggers—in the comfort of my bedroom. But without pictures, or at least eyewitness evidence, we couldn't prove anything. Keeley and her dad might be willing to listen to a voice from the ether, but the sheriff wouldn't. Minutes stretched to an hour and chill seeped through my jacket. I took out a fat sausage and traded bites with Curry.

Then he clamped a hand on my elbow. "What?" I whispered, suddenly alert.

"Shh." He cupped his other hand to his ear.

I listened too, then understood. The cricket chirping no longer surrounded us. Directly ahead it had stopped. Maybe something, or someone, had passed near them. I crouched on one knee and listened so hard I could hear the blood in my veins and the creak of my tensed sinews.

Then a sudden movement!

Swishing of dried grass, weed stalks breaking, drumming of feet on packed earth, closer, ever closer. I crouched behind a patch of weeds, ready with my flashlight, every muscle coiled for action. Curry hunkered beside me, cradling his camera. Then a black shape bounded above the thigh-high grasses, coming directly at us, jingling as if wearing tiny bells. I barely had time to raise a forearm to protect my face when the huge hound burst into our hiding place, landing squarely on Curry and knocking him backwards.

Curry made a croaking noise that sounded like fear, and the dog whined with excitement, its stump of tail flogging my face. It straddled Curry, its great muzzle lunging toward his face, and I raised my flashlight to crunch the monster's skull.

Then came a little giggle of laughter from Curry, and I relaxed, remembering the pack of mutts at his house and how he loved them enough to nurse one through the night. Curry sat up and I saw a patch of white where the dog had licked the lamp black from his face.

A shouted whisper came from the far side of the field. "Spike, piss on ye, ye blooming beastie. Get back here, or I'll wring your hairy neck."

The powerful dog raised its head, sniffed, ripped the sausage from my hand—nearly taking some fingers with it—and bolted the entire ten-inch length of meat in one great head-jerk. He briefly inspected me for more, then sprung away toward its master.

As Curry blotted drool off his face with a snot rag, we retreated to the shelter of the nearest poplar. I made out two, no, three flashlight beams, sweeping and crossing. When one of the beams combed the line of poplars, we froze, hoping to blend with the tree trunks. The light passed and didn't return. I breathed again. When the ovals of light settled in an area near the old fence line, I whispered to Curry, "C'mon, let's get closer."

"Do we have to?" Curry asked. In the meager moonlight, the smeared carbon on his face and mussed hair made him look like an Amazonian savage. He followed as I led through a swale of tall grasses toward the lights and the scraping of a shovel. I paused when I heard a repeated thumping. Someone held a light on a wooden stake while a burley figure pounded it with a field rock. A third person dug nearby, while the dog seemed content to watch and digest my sausage. We crept to within twenty yards and listened.

"I don't get it," came a muffled voice from behind the flashlight. "Why do we keep digging when we already found the place?"

"Are ye daft? Were ye drapped on yer head as a wee baby?"

"That's Mr. Angostura," Curry said.

I didn't know any Mr. Angostura, but could ask later.

"He pays us for making holes, and if we stops making holes... you see, holes is money."

"I know that. It's just, since we found the place, why don't *we* look for what *he's* looking for? Keep it for ourselves."

The voice sounded husky, but unclear.

"Greedy, eh laddie?"

"I've got my reasons."

"Maybe ye ain't so daft. We'll be after the prize soon enough. But if we make no more holes, the squire knows something's up."

"Oh, I get it now," said the second voice, and he laughed coarsely.

Curry fumbled with his camera and switched on the strobe attachment. It made a thin whine as it powered up, almost above the range of my hearing. But not above a dog's. The beast alerted, pointing in our direction, a growl gurgling in his throat.

Mr. Angostura looked in our direction. "Something's there. Give me that torch." Taking the flashlight, and palming the stone in his other hand, he thrashed through the weeds directly toward Curry and me, the dog cautiously showing the way. The strange whine had made the massive dog nervous.

When they'd come within ten yards of us, I made ready to burst from my crouch and run, but Curry had another thought. He popped out of the brush, directly into the beam of the flashlight.

The sudden appearance of his soot-streaked face stopped Mr. Angostura cold.

"Mother, Mary, and Joseph!"

"Say cheese," Curry said, and snapped off a picture. The flash left spots swimming before my eyes, along with the afterimage of a startled man, mouth gaping from an unkempt tangle of red beard.

"To the hills!" Angostura called, and though he must have been more blinded than I was, he and his comrades scattered. I'd dropped my flashlight in the excitement; by the time I recovered it, and aimed a beam over the field, the three night-stalkers had simply vanished. Perhaps they were still out there, crouched in holes, but we didn't care to find out.

Chapter 23
G is for...?

Curry and I leaned over Aunt Iris's sink, scrubbing soot from our faces. "Who's Mr. Angostura?" I asked.

"You mean that mutton-faced, addle-pated Scot?" she said. "The sheriff will be wanting a word with him, I can promise you."

"He does odd jobs around the school. Not the regular maintenance guy." Curry laughed. He had a natural, skipping giggle. "Kids used to roll toilet paper down the hall just to hear him say, 'Piss on ye, piss on ye laddie.'"

"Did you get a look at the other two?" I said.

"I think they had masks. The voices sounded muffled."

"Well, we can develop your picture at the shop tomorrow, and give it to the sheriff."

Aunt Iris didn't seem frightened at being left alone, so Curry and I returned to my house. We found mom playing flute along with a jazz record. She used to play with the San Francisco Symphony until she got pregnant with me and lost her wind. Curry seemed entranced by the sight, and used up his remaining film on shots of mom dipping and arching with the music, her unpinned hair swirling around her shoulders.

I set up a cot in my room for Curry and we crashed, telling each other the story of Crazy Charlie Angostura, how he must have crapped a crab when Curry popped out of the weeds looking like a headhunter, telling it until we could stay awake no longer.

*   *   *

Mom did her Sunday morning waffles with fresh jiggleberries. They were really blueberries, but she called them jiggleberries because she didn't have the patience to pick them one by one. She put a cloth down and jiggled the bush. For dad, the Sunday break in routine meant he dashed off a few thousand words on the computer at home in his pajamas instead of opening up the office. But, after breakfast, us three guys headed to the print shop.

While Curry worked in the darkroom, I tried to tell dad the miraculous things Curry had revealed in our swami booth.

He cut me off before I finished. "You have to understand, Dar, that fortune tellers pick up clues from people's behavior. It's all educated guesses based on age and background and feedback they're picking up. Curry just has the knack."

"But dad," I said, trying not to sound too whiny, "Curry has his eyes closed. He's in a trance. And he's said things no one could have guessed."

"I know it seems that way. You watch a magician and he does the impossible. But if he explains the trick, it seems ridiculously easy. The illusion is gone."

"If you could just see him, dad. He diagnosed Ms. Dozier's cancer and said how to cure it."

"Cancer, huh? And you've seen a doctor's report? Has she been cured?"

I shook my head in frustration. "She said afterwards it was true."

"Maybe Curry heard a rumor about her being sick. You can't keep anything secret on this island. Or maybe she wasn't looking well."

I wanted to tell about Doc Uncas, but remembered my promise to Keeley. "You'd just have to be there, dad."

Dad gave a half-hearted smile. The light slanting through his office blinds brought out lines of fatigue on his face. "We could sure use some magic around here."

"Advertising still kinda bleak?"

He thumped a pencil on the edge of his desk. "We lost another account yesterday. The feed store. And Highly's Hardware is past due on their account. I don't know whether to run more ads for them or not, because we might never get paid. Probably better to take the chance. At least it looks good. People don't want to do business with losers."

I crossed my arms and thought. I couldn't blame him for not paying attention to what I'd said about Curry. I wanted to help but couldn't think how.

Then Curry called us to look at the wet prints he'd clipped to a wire. They were black and white, and grainy because of the fast film, but now I understood what had entranced Curry about mom. He'd been seeing her with quite different eyes. The best shots were longer exposures with smears of movement, zoomed in close, filling the frame. Because there wasn't much detail, the pictures didn't even look like mom; rather, an ethereal creature come to this world from a fairyland, to bring music and show us how to be joyful.

Even dad seemed breathless. Finally he said, "These are wonderful, Curry. Treasures."

Curry himself seemed amazed at what had materialized in the developing pan, but shuffled with embarrassment at the praise. Then he pulled another print from the fixer and hung it. Amid a jumble of out-of-focus weeds in the foreground was the contorted face of Charlie Angostura.

Dad examined it with interest. "I think the sheriff needs to see this, and I don't want you boys messing around there after dark any more."

"I can't imagine Charlie hurting anyone," Curry said. "He's gruff, but pretty harmless."

"Well, somebody killed your Aunt Pansy."

Curry nodded grimly. "I suppose they might have broken into the house. She came home early that day."

Something caught my interest on the print. I looked closely, squinting through the sharp fumes at a line in the background next to a flashlight beam. "That smudge: could it be a face?"

Curry looked. "I'll print it again and burn that part in, try to bring out some detail."

While he worked, I sat at the reception desk and, to kill time, made a list of questions. Questions I wanted to ask the swami. Presently Curry yelled, "Think we got something here!"

He pointed with the nail of his little finger to something on the wet print. I could make out the light-toned streak of a shovel handle and the face of the digger half-covered with something like a bandanna."

"Doesn't help much," I said. "Oh well, nice try."

"What about this?" Curry pointed below the face to a light-toned area shaped like the letter 'G'.

"A letter jacket?" I said.

Curry nodded. "Kluge Island Gooeyducks. But there must be hundreds of those jackets around."

When dad left, I said to Curry, "Remember what Charlie Angostura said about already finding something?"

Curry stared at his photo of Angostura. "Yeah, something about keeping it for themselves."

"Okay, that means they're working for someone, right? But who? And what are they looking for?" Two of the questions I'd written on my list. "What do you say, Curry, shouldn't we do a reading and get some answers?" If the answers led to the murderer, and Aunt Iris insisted on paying us the reward, well....

Curry grimaced. Ever since Mr. Buckle tried to use him to horn in on the murder reward, he'd tensed up any time I'd suggested asking the swami anything. Were *my* thoughts about the reward money any different from Mr. Buckle's? My half—five-thousand bucks—might tide dad through until the newspaper began making money. I admit there'd been days when I wouldn't have minded dad selling the business and moving back to civilization. But things had changed. Now I wanted us to survive on Kluge Island. The determination felt like the powerful, mindless instinct of a wild animal.

"We could at least find out about Angostura," I said, "see if he's the culprit before we turn this picture over to the sheriff."

I thought Curry would understand, but something snapped in him, and he turned sharply away and stiff-armed his way out the shop door.

I scratched my neck for a moment, then decided not to let him off so easy. I hustled out to the street and caught him within a block. "I don't get it. Did I say something wrong?"

He kept walking. I gritted my teeth and followed.

"Are you too chicken to use your own talent?"

Curry didn't look at me. "Yeah, I'm your basic coward."

"Right. Only a coward would pop up in front of crazy Angostura and snap a picture."

He stopped, took a deep breath, and spoke more calmly than I had. "I've been thinking about it a lot. Almost constantly, if you want to know. This bizarre thing is happening with me, but I don't know why, or what to do with it. It's like there's an inner voice trying to guide me, but I can't quite hear."

"Duh! The swami *is* your inner voice. Ask him what to do."

"What if he's not? How can I trust him? You forget, I've never even heard his voice."

"Has he ever been wrong? Has he ever forced you to do anything? We can tape-record the doggoned sessions."

No response.

"You've helped lots of people. Doesn't it make you feel good?"

"Sometimes, like helping Jenny find her cat."

"What about diagnosing life-threatening illnesses? Coming up with treatments? You don't think solving a murder would qualify as helping people?"

"I..." He blew out a breath. "I don't want that kind of responsibility."

"Great, so we'll specialize in cats and warts. We'll just let people die of cancer and let new sources of energy go undiscovered and wait a few thousand years to find out if there's other intelligent life in the universe. What the heck. And we can wonder for the rest of our lives if there really is a God." More questions from my list.

"Jeez, Darwin! We're tenth-graders. Is it okay to start small?"

I leaned towards him, my chest constricted with frustration. "No! Has your curiosity been surgically removed, or what?"

Curry started walking again. I dogged his every step, wondering what I could say to turn the lights on for him. Small houses lined the road, yards decorated with driftwood and whalebones and fishing net floats. Almost every house had some kind of boat in the yard. We walked a little easier after a couple of blocks, and I gave it another shot. "Look, what if your swami connection is a use-it-or-lose-it deal? It could fade away, and you'll always kick yourself for not taking advantage. Think of it this way: you're at this cosmic all-you-can-eat joint, right? I say don't screw around at the salad bar; head straight for the meat."

He stopped, stuck out his lower lip and blew so hard, his hair fluttered.

I laughed. A crack had appeared in Curry's resolve, so I backed off a little to see if it would open up. "Hey, we'll do whatever you're comfortable with. But here's my wish list." I handed him the folded sheet of paper.

We sat on a retaining wall and he read it, then he took a pen and crossed out several things. He said, "You stuck up for me in the principal's office, Dar. I owe you something. One reading, tape recorded, stick to the questions on the list."

"Whatever you say."

We were back in business.

Then he added a question of his own to the page.

Chapter 24
Going for the Meat

urry said he knew a private place for the reading. We borrowed a tape recorder from the newspaper office, walked the three blocks back to my house for Curry's scooter, lashed my drum behind the seat, and putt-farted down the lonely coast road, past cliffs, a small cove with a B&B, an emu ranch, a mushroom-shaped artist's house like something out of Dr. Seuss. A side road veered right and we took it a few hundred yards to a barricade. A sign said *keep out.* We were near the peninsula that looked like a witch's chin if you were looking at a map of the island.

"The land out here was donated for a park," Curry said. "But people can't get to it because old man Sturgis won't let them through his land. But he's going blind and can't shoot straight anymore."

"Shoot?"

Curry ignored me, hid the scooter in the salal, and climbed the barricade.

I hesitated. "You've done this before, right?"

"If you keep quiet, he doesn't know where to aim."

Not exactly reassured, I handed the drum over, climbed the gate, and dropped down the other side. The parallel ruts, once a road, curved past a pond fringed with rushes. A type of duck I didn't recognize paddled through the lime-green scum. An adjacent cornfield had gone to waste and geese pecked at the dried cobs. A few more steps down the road we came to a run-down shack, yard littered with tires and rusted engines, a half-toppled windmill loomed over a tar-papered shed with door sagging from one hinge. A sheet of tin roofing lifted and banged in the breeze. The place set my teeth on edge. Just when I thought we'd skulked by unnoticed, a huge white bird came running from the side yard, making a blaring honk that sounded like

GO-home, GO-home. Its wings were half-spread, neck extended, bigger than any goose I'd ever seen.

Curry motioned for me to get behind him. I didn't waste any time. The bird got to within arm's reach of Curry then pulled up, and through its long black bill, issued a sinister hiss. By now I knew we were dealing with an attack swan.

"Get low," Curry told me, patting the air. I crouched but remained ready to run—especially if some old guy stepped from the shack with a gun.

Curry put his arms behind his back and began making soothing noises to the bird. "Yo Gertrude. You're looking pretty today. Don't you know your old friend Curry? Pay no attention to this tall snarky-looking guy. He won't hurt you."

Gertrude stopped hissing and looked us over. As Curry continued his mush talk, she folded up her wings and relaxed. Then Curry did something that amazed me. He leaned forward within striking range of the irascible swan, and the two of them began rubbing their necks together in some kind of ritual swan greeting. Awkward, considering Gertrude had a foot of neck for every inch that Curry had. I gawked, failing to notice the screen door swing open.

"Is that you, Curry?" came a raspy shout. The old man looked stiff as a bent coat hanger. He, indeed, cradled a shotgun in the crook of his arm.

"Hi Sturgis."

"Who ya got with you? Did you finally find me a girlfriend?" Sturgis chuckled until a wad of phlegm dislodged and blocked his windpipe. He hawked it into the wasteland of his yard.

"Just my buddy, Darwin. He's new on the island."

"Thought you'd introduce him to Gertrude, eh?" He cackled. "Ever seen a trumpeter swan up close, there, Darwin?"

I straightened up and relaxed. "Not really."

"There ain't many of them left, I can tell you. Why, before I was Curry's age, we'd go out and blast them. Plenty of birds then, all kinds. Then they started disappearing and, for an old bird hunter, the air sounded too danged empty. So I turned my land over to make a safe place for 'em to come. The only things I shoot now are trespassers."

He was a spiny old cactus, and I took an instant liking to him.

"How's the peepers?" Curry asked.

"The peepers have just about pooped out. Can't hardly count my fingers any more. But I can hear the loons and the wood ducks, and the wind rushing through the wings of the osprey."

"Can I bring you anything from town?"

"Naw. Bertie comes out regular. My old hunting chum. He just likes looking at 'em now, too. It's Bertie who puts in the corn for the migrants."

"Well, we're going to walk out to the point, if that's all right with you."

"You and your friend have a good walk, and keep your ears open for the winter wren."

We moved on to a sprawling headland overlooking the Strait of Juan de Fuca. Tugboat Island to the west floated like a greenish haze over the sea. We took a faint trail through the windswept grasses, stunted junipers, and wild roses studded with hips. Curry showed me a line of old concrete bunkers and artillery mounts from the days when the Puget Sound worried about foreign navies. On the hillside below the bunkers, we settled into a grassy niche protected from the wind.

While I tested the recorder, Curry pulled his knees up to his chin and looked out to where seals bobbed in the kelp. Then he removed his shoes, rolled his jacket into a pillow, and got comfortable on a bed of thick, dry moss. Before we started, he said, "Something else. Ask if anything can be done for Sturgis's eyes."

I nodded then began drumming. It felt jittery and forced at first, but then Curry's mantra—*Tat Savitur Varenyam Om*—formed a continuous loop in my mind and I calmed down. I watched for the little twitch in Curry's eyelids that indicated he'd fled his body, dumped the lump. The ripples of my own thoughts melted away.

By the time Curry slipped into trance, I felt so peaceful I could hardly make myself move. But we had a purpose, so I unfolded the list of questions and read them over. I'd been wondering a lot about the *voice's* identity. Doc Uncas had asked, and got mumbo-jumbo for his trouble. *I am that which Curry will become. Neither existent nor non-existent. I am all that is he, but he knows me not.* I didn't know what it meant, but it gave me a chalky stomach to think about it. We were ants at Einstein's door. No wonder Curry had grown reluctant to ring the doorbell. For one thing, how do you hide anything? If the swami can see the past, present, and sometimes the future, then what about all my embarrassing thoughts? *All* my flaws. The magazines under the mattress. I rubbed my hands together until they were warm. The best answer I could come up with was that Swami had seen it all before, and wouldn't hold it against me. I could only hope.

My finger paused over the record button on the tape machine while I fought off a final wave of doubt. But if people didn't try crazy stuff occasionally, we'd still be knuckle-walking around the Serengeti. I pushed the button.

"Can you hear me, Swami?"

"I am with you."

Strangely, my apprehensions vanished. Something about the *voice* made me feel that he was on my side, never mind my dirt. From the list I asked, "You said you're neither existent nor non-existent, and some other things we don't understand. Are you Curry's soul, or a ghost, or what?"

"All entities, Darwin, are threefold in nature. There is the physical body. Then a finer, astral body, invisible to physical eyes. And beyond the astral body is the spirit. The trinity spoken of in scripture. You might think of the spirit body as the blueprint upon which the astral and physical bodies are built. I have served in a physical body countless times, and have come now as Curry."

I looked out over the glimmering sea and chewed on this a moment before asking, "Why doesn't everyone's spirit speak through them, like you do through Curry?"

"Each has a role, according to their level of development."

"So Curry is—you are—highly developed, compared with me for

example?"

"Comparisons of this nature serve no purpose."

"But if Curry is so highly evolved, how come he doesn't understand this any more than I do?" I was already freelancing from the list, but Curry didn't say not to ask follow-up questions.

"Though he has come far, there remains much to do before final liberation."

"Liberation from what?"

"From delusion."

"When you say he's come far, what do you mean?"

"Through many lives, he has become dissatisfied with things of the ego and the material world. He yearns for something more deeply satisfying."

"So there is really such a thing as reincarnation?"

"Do you imagine perfection can be achieved in a single lifetime? A hundred lifetimes?"

Perfection! Talk about a steep ticket. To my astonishment, Swami read my thoughts as if I'd spoken them aloud.

"Ah, but the reward is worth it. Ever-expanding, ever-new bliss."

This was getting too deep, so I went back to the list. "Do these readings pose any danger to Curry's body or mind?"

"All actions have reactions; everything sown must be reaped. To the extent the motives remain pure, there is no danger."

This led to the question Curry added to the list. "How is Curry to know when it is proper to seek knowledge through you?"

"All people know when they are doing wrong. Their whole being is shaken, surrounded with the voice of conscience. If you do not listen to the voice, it becomes quiet; but when you spiritually awaken, it guides you."

A gull rode a current of ripe, salty air up the cliff face and hovered mere feet from me, its eyes staring as if they wanted to tell me something. How many times had my conscience come with a message; how many times had I blown that little voice off? The gull veered and I turned back to Curry. "Can Sturgis do anything to improve his eyesight?"

Curry seemed to go completely inert, as if he'd flown his body. A half-minute later he drew a slight breath and answered. *"Yes. The subject is afflicted with optic neuritis. A deviation in the upper spine is reducing circulation to the optic nerve. Additionally, his system is starved of vitamin A and other nutrients because of lack of fresh, unprocessed foods. Everything he eats comes from a can. Improved diet, chiropractic neck adjustment, and regular neck exercises should gradually restore his vision."* He described a series of neck rolls in detail. *"As in any healing, right attitude is important. All stubborn diseases have deep roots in the subconscious mind. The subject must remember what it was to be healthy, and visualize returning to his original state of perfection. Then the Universe will once more regard him as whole."*

"Thank you, Swami." I looked over my list. Some of the questions now seemed trivial, but there was still the Meat. The cassette reels turned. I didn't hear my inner voice telling me not to ask.

I would have asked anyway.

"Swami, is there some kind of supreme somebody? A master of the universe? Extreme brain? You know, the ultimate egghead? The Grand Wazoo? And, if so, what's he, she, or it hiding for?"

"Whence comes the wisdom, talent, and intelligence of great men and women on this Earth? Not evolved for the survival of a little bundle of genes, be assured. If the audience does not applaud the play, why should the Author take a bow?"

Chapter 25
Cast a Blind Eye

$\mathcal{I}$ woke Curry, fed him a can of mustard sardines, and rewound the tape. The south wind rustled the salal and manzanita growing around the old bunkers.

"Ready?" I asked.

Curry nodded. I ran the tape.

When he heard, for the first time, the *voice* that had come from his own throat, he melted into silent amazement. He kept looking at the machine as if listening to someone else. Then, part way through, he shook his head and hit the stop button.

"But I don't believe in reincarnation. My church doesn't believe in it. This can't be right."

"Hasn't been wrong yet," I said. When it came to weird ideas, like reincarnation, I hadn't ruled out much of anything. Didn't seem any weirder than resurrection.

"We're not sure about some of it," Curry said. "Gretchen's missing father for instance, or even Ted Griswald's money. Maybe the Blubbergum contest was a lucky guess, and maybe I just... I don't know." Then his eyes puckered with suspicion. "This isn't some elaborate hoax you're playing on me, is it?"

"C'mon Curry, is that any way for a highly developed human being to think?"

"Don't call me that."

"Okay, but get a grip."

He sighed. "I don't want to be like some nut case who thinks he's been abducted by aliens."

"Curry, the tape doesn't lie. Listen." I hit the play button again. After the bits about conscience, eye treatment for Sturgis, and the Meat, I asked, "You still think someone's scamming you?"

Curry shook his head. He looked shaky and I offered him a candy bar. He took it mechanically, but didn't peel it; just looked out over the ruffled sea. "Dar, I used to think life was full of amazing secrets. But as I've gotten older, that feeling gradually went away. Until now."

It struck a chord in me from long ago. From a world of unlimited wonders, it seemed like the best parts had got narrowed down to girls, facial hair, unlimited pizza, and playing rip-your-head-off guitar solos. The bummers included going blind. "How do you want to handle the stuff about Sturgis anyway?"

"What do you mean?"

"Okay, you go up to him. Hey, Sturgis, this cosmic voice said if you ate your spinach and rolled your neck twice a day, you could throw away the cane and the dark glasses. He'd think you were on drugs."

Curry nodded. "I suppose you're right."

"Of course I'm right. And as far as being normal, you're not—so get used to it."

When we got back to town, I phoned Keeley. "Can you meet us at my place? I've got an idea."

"What kind of idea?" she asked cautiously.

Why are people always suspicious of my ideas? "Tell you when I see you."

"Bullgoobers! Well, I'm just leaving to give Ms. Dozier a ride home..."

"Oh?" I asked. "How'd it go? Did she get the atropine treatment?"

"Uh huh."

"And?"

"Too soon to tell. But she has a positive outlook, so that's worth something. I'll be at your place in a half-hour."

Keeley arrived and joined Curry and me for chips and soda at the kitchen bar. I found the part about Sturgis on the tape and played it for her. She listened carefully, but said afterward, "Darwin Bownes, if this turns out to be phony, so help me, I'll..."

"You'll what?"

"I'll put squaw root in your Coke." Her eyes glinted.

"Yeah, what'll that do?"

"It's loaded with estrogen. In a few months you'd be able to try out for cheerleader."

Curry cracked such a big smile he could have eaten a banana sideways.

"Gulp!" I said, then got serious. "Keeley, it's no hoax."

"Well, I don't believe in miracles."

"I wouldn't exactly call it a miracle," Curry said. "Just something special I was born with, like how Johnny Rottler was born with two thumbs on one hand."

"Oh, so it's not a miracle—it's a birth defect," Keeley said. "Thanks for clarifying that. Must have been all that DDT your dad used to spray on the pumpkins."

Curry gave a defeated shrug.

"Keeley," I said, "he just wants to help people. But the thing about Sturgis—it's better coming from a doctor. If we can get him to see your dad, then he'll believe it and follow the treatment. What do you say?"

Keeley's wry smile changed abruptly into a withering look and I felt our friendship shrink into a mere particle. "My father isn't going to get involved. I thought I made it clear what could happen to him."

The aluminum can crinkled in my grip. "You'd let an old man go blind?"

Keeley set her jaw and her eyes flashed. "Yes!"

Chapter 26
Cyrus Twist's Dangerous Secret

*M*onday. Social studies. Mr. Lingam, the prude, tried to rush through the chapter about customs and taboos surrounding puberty. He stammered and looked out the window a lot. Of course, he was a language teacher doubling as a social studies teacher to collect full pay; I heard he used to teach Latin at a Catholic school. Most students liked him because he gave multiple guess tests and was an easy 'A', but we tended to zone him out or crack rude jokes. I belonged to the rude joke camp, and had just made a snide comment about him getting his children at the Take It Or Leave It, when a finger jabbed me in the back. The girl attached to the finger, Sqyrl Marx, was one of those people with a dangerous amount of energy. A nuclear reactor with knockers. Her brassy laugh could scatter crows. She whispered, "You and Curry Buckle are friends, right?"

"Sure." Funny, two weeks before, I would have been embarrassed to admit it.

Sqyrl was a tanned, horsey-faced jock. I focused on her plump lips because I could barely hear what she said. "I've heard stories... he's helped people, right?   With information, I mean." Her lower teeth raked her upper lip.

I'd never known Sqyrl Marx to have so much trouble getting words out. "Do you need to ask him something?"

She nodded rapidly and blinked her teardrop-shaped eyes.

"Come to the bazaar Friday."

She leaned to within two inches of my face. "It can't wait!" She reminded me of Gertrude the swan, and I would have been just as frightened to rub necks with Sqyrl Marx.

Mr. Lingam stopped talking. A runner from the principal's office had handed him a pink note. I turned back to Sqyrl. "Curry is only going to handle certain kinds of cases. What's it about?"

She glanced to either side. "Not here. Tell him to meet me by the backstop before lunch. Okay?"

Before I could say anything, Mr. Lingam called out, "Darwin Bownes?" I stiffened at the sound of my name and at the sight of him waving the pink slip at me. "You're wanted upstairs."

I rushed out the door, down the wooden floor to the narrow staircase, heart thumping. Had something happened to one of my parents? I took the stairs by twos up the old bell tower. Mrs. Muldoon looked up from her work when I bounded in. Worry creased her forehead and she mouthed the words, "I'm sorry." She motioned me to sit, then averted her eyes.

"Is someone hurt?"

Her quick smile went a long way toward calming me. "Oh no, no. I didn't mean to alarm you. Just have a seat for a moment."

"Well, did I do something wrong?"

"You'll just have to wait."

But I felt too agitated to sit. Must be bad news or Mrs. Muldoon wouldn't have apologized. Her office had no windows and the walls pressed in on me. Then two sets of footsteps clumped up the stairs and the runner led Curry in. At least I'd have company.

Mrs. Muldoon spoke into the intercom, "The boys are here, Mr. Krogstrand,"

"Send them up."

When Curry and I started up the winding iron stairs, Mrs. Muldoon pigeon-stepped over to us and whispered, "It's all my fault."

I felt more mystified than scared. My family was okay and I didn't think we'd done anything wrong. We climbed the steps and found the principal standing with his back to us, hands clasped behind him, taking in the view from his tower. Silhouetted against the window, his head had the shape of a light bulb, but it seemed to suck light instead of giving it off.

"Sit down, boys. Thanks for coming."

This was different. The last time we had to stand at attention. But, settling into the low sofa, with Krogstrand looming over us, I felt even smaller. Curry looked at me like *what did we do?* I began to understand why Mrs. Muldoon said it was her fault when Krogstrand picked up some papers from the corner of his tidy desk.

"Recognize those?"

"My notes." From Ms. Dozier's session with the swami. I reached, but he drew them away.

"Notes pertaining to what?"

I thought fast. "Um, a composition I'm doing for Ms. Dozier. Sort of sci-fi." I tried to put just enough truth in it to make it sound plausible.

"Notes for a composition." Krogstrand smiled thinly. "Then why ask Mrs. Muldoon to make copies? Do you generally photocopy your notes?"

Mrs. Muldoon had handed me the copies, but forgot the originals. She must have left them on the machine, where Krogstrand found them.

"No sir. I just wanted Keeley's help with the medical stuff."

Krogstrand gripped the pages tightly and shook them in my face. "Cut the games. I've already had Ms. Dozier up here, and she's admitted everything. She's dying of cancer. But that's not all she said."

Again, Curry and I exchanged glances.

"Ms. Dozier is of the firm opinion that you, Curry Buckle, are a bona-fide psychic."

So that was it. Krogstrand had heard about our swami booth. I hoped Ms. Dozier hadn't mentioned Doc Uncas.

Curry looked Mr. Krogstrand in the eye. "I don't think we did any harm."

"Did I say anything about harm?" Krogstrand tried to look friendly, but he couldn't change his reptilian eyes. "In fact, Ms. Dozier is convinced you've done her a great deal of good. And there's the lost cat. No harm in finding a cat. I've spoken with the girl's mother—she happens to be on the school board." The lanky principal returned to the same window he'd been gazing out. "I think it's just possible, Curry, that a mistake was made when we last spoke. You stood accused of cheating. I am not too proud a man," he turned toward us, standing erect, "to acknowledge a premature judgment—though at the time, I submit, it was a perfectly sensible judgment based on available facts."

I knew a suck-up when I heard one, but it got worse.

"And Darwin," he gave me a sharp sideways glance, "it may even be possible to excuse your intrusion into the matter."

Here it came.

"On the other hand, I've warned you against certain things." Now he began pacing as if struggling with a difficult decision. "Specifically against claiming supernatural powers. Do you recall me mentioning expulsion?"

It felt like a trap. We returned his questioning stare with blank faces.

"You don't deny it. Yet, shortly after we reached this understanding, you, Curry, dressed up like a yogi and began telling fortunes on school grounds. For money."

"For Camp Bluetoad," I said.

Krogstrand's light bulb head turned the color of raw beef, and his voice raised a notch. "Mr. Bownes, if you are extracting money from schoolmates under false pretenses, there is no justification."

Curry listened without expression, but my whole body seethed. "It wasn't false pretenses!"

Krogstrand smiled, and I knew I'd said exactly what he wanted me to say. "*That* is what we are here to determine." He examined us for a long moment, until it became clear he expected Curry or me to say something.

I didn't like him pulling my strings, so I waited, but Curry finally asked, "How?"

"A test. A simple test of your alleged powers. If you prove I've been wrong about you, then all sanctions are withdrawn."

"Do you mean Darwin and I get our grades back?"

"Precisely."

"What kind of test?"

"You will perform a séance, or whatever you call it, and answer a few simple questions. If I'm satisfied, I'll instruct Mrs. Muldoon to expunge all derogatory notations from your files."

Curry looked at me for help. I asked Krogstrand, "And if Curry doesn't want to do it?"

"Then you leave me no choice but to assume you have violated my instructions and impose further sanctions."

"Such as?"

I could tell by his flaring nostrils that I'd become an irritant, a speck in his eye. "How about loss of privileges for a start? A ban from extracurricular events." He raised an eyebrow at me.

On this little island, there were precious few activities or events, other than what the school sponsored. Football and basketball games, dances, plays, a talent show, clubs. I wanted to participate in things. Make friends. Maybe try out for drama and track. I could live with giving up a grade, but...

I couldn't look at Curry. He'd already refused a demonstration to Krogstrand once, and didn't need to prove anything now. Curry wasn't a joiner anyway and losing privileges wouldn't mean so much to him.

"This wouldn't include attending Camp Bluetoad, right?" Curry asked.

Krogstrand tilted his eyebrow a notch further. "Huh? Of course it does—in the unlikely case it hasn't been sold."

Curry and I searched each other's eyes. I could imagine his conscience tearing him in different directions. He'd never willingly do what Krogstrand had asked, but had to consider the impact on me. As I watched, his face became stony and determined. "I'll do it," he said

I didn't have the guts or the good sense to talk him out of it. "I'll need a drum from the band room," I said. Mrs. Muldoon wrote me a note for it and I was back in minutes with a set of bongos. Curry had slipped off his shoes and was doing a deep breathing exercise. Krogstrand stood close as I began finding the printing press shuffle on the drums. The window light seemed eclipsed by a cold, misshapen moon.

"You should stand back, sir," I said. "Sometimes he vomits wildly."

Curry kept a straight face. Krogstrand bought it, and retreated behind his desk. I tried to sharpen my focus on the beat. If Curry had half my jitters, he'd never be able to meditate. Yet we continued, Curry chanting softly, his droning cadence riding the drums like a surfer, and perhaps because we'd done it often enough, that special cocoon of warm yarn began to spin around us, and before long, I detected the trance coming over Curry, and felt that special feeling of becoming a wave rolling over the ocean. His chanting faded and a knowing smile flickered on his lips. An invisible band of honeyed energy bound us together.

"Swami?" I said.

"Yes."

"We have with us Mr. William E. Krogstrand," I said, reading from the fancy nameplate on his desk. "He'd like to ask some questions."

"He may approach without concern: the stomach is not presently unsettled."

So the swami had a sense of humor. I took it as a sign we'd done no wrong by summoning him.

Krogstrand approached as one might creep to the edge of a cliff. "Tell me my social security number."

Without hesitation, the *voice* recited a string of numbers.

Krogstrand swallowed.

"What's my mother's maiden name?"

"Zacher. How many of your tests must I pass? Perhaps you could move on to the real question in your heart."

Krogstrand looked rattled by the backtalk. He regrouped and said. "The purpose of this interview is to establish whether you—Curry Buckle, that is—has genuine psychic ability. So I do have a final test in mind. There was a man, Cyrus Twist, a prospector who made his fortune in the Yukon and settled on Kluge Island."

"Yes... what is the question?"

"Ahem. I want to know if anything remains of his gold."

"There is no gold. There never was any gold."

Krogstrand scowled. "Of course there was. He joined the gold rush and came back rich."

"*Cyrus Twist derived his wealth from discovery of a diamond field in Northern British Colombia.*"

Krogstrand's jaw dropped, then he slowly pulled it shut in a crocodilian smile. "Is that so? Now we're getting somewhere. Did he hide some diamonds here on the island?"

"*There is a quantity, some twenty-seven thousand carats.*"

My eyes closed and I felt cold. I knew Curry wouldn't like it either. I'd lost control of the reading—but the swami had invited Krogstrand to ask questions directly. I didn't know if I should cut if off.

Krogstrand leaned in. "Precisely where did he conceal the diamonds?" Breath whistled through his teeth when he said *precisely* and *conceal.* I wanted to wake Curry and blast out of there, but somehow couldn't.

"*They present much danger to the body, and the soul.*"

Krogstrand leaned closer. "Details. Give details."

"*The objects are in a place subject to periodic flooding. The flooding has made the subterranean chamber inaccessible and measures have been taken to protect the gems.*"

Krogstrand snapped his fingers as if something clicked into place.

My guts twisted with indecision. Curry was doing this reading for my sake, but Krogstrand had crossed the line into greed. Curry's plea of a few days ago rang in my ears: *You won't let them ask the wrong kinds of questions, will you?* Before Krogstrand could follow up, I interrupted, stalling for time to decide what to do. "Swami, describe the danger to the soul."

"*This is the greater danger, for its effects carry beyond the physical lifetime. The diamonds are not to be found on the property of he who seeks them. Hence, they rightfully belong to another. To claim them under these circumstances, driven by avarice, would cast a shroud of darkness over the soul.*"

Krogstrand flinched as if a shock traveled through him, but then a slow grin invaded his face. "I'll weigh the risks for myself. Just tell me the location."

The wrong kind of question... the wrong kind... won't let them ask... wrong... will you? Will you? Curry's plea echoed in my head, along with my promise. I somehow knew the swami would answer if I didn't do something. He was testing me. Testing the worth of my word.

I lunged to Curry's side and covered his mouth and began to chant OM in his ear.

"What are you doing?" Krogstrand demanded.

"Bringing him out of it."

Krogstrand pulled me away by the collar. "We're not done yet."

"The heck we're not!" I hit an instant boil, the peace I'd felt vanished.

Krogstrand looked like he wanted to twist my collar, but held off, and glared at me with pure venom.

"Curry proved he's psychic, and that was our deal."

Krogstrand growled from low in his throat, "He's proved nothing unless the diamonds are found."

Then I hit on an angle. "As of right now, sir, the secret about the diamonds is between the two of us. If you honor your end of the bargain—"

Krogstrand turned eggplant purple. "Don't try to bargain with me, Bownes. If you so much as breathe a word, you and your whole family will wish you'd never set foot on Kluge Island."

The breath squeezed from my chest. I looked into Mr. Krogstrand's face, and saw things I didn't understand because I'd never seen them in a human face before. Things that made me feel dirty. Things that made my skin crawl. But I'd made a promise to Curry. I wrenched free from Krogstrand and chanted in Curry's ear *"AAUUUMMM."*

Chapter 27
Sqyrl Marx

From the principal's control tower, Curry and I descended into a confusion of students rushing for class.

"What's the matter?" Curry asked. "You're all jittery. Something's wrong."

"Just an extreme level of adrenaline from being massively bent out of shape." I checked my watch. "I'll tell you what happened at lunch. Reminds me—we have an appointment at lunchtime with Sqyrl Marx. Gotta go."

During geometry, I ignored Mr. Schwartz's eye-glazingly dull spiel about isosceles triangles, and made notes of what the swami had told Krogstrand about Cyrus Twist's diamonds. Then I fretted about whether Krogstrand might really revoke our extracurricular privileges and I began getting torked-off all over again. Just when I was tight as a bowstring, Swartzie blindsided me with a question. I'd called him on some brain farts earlier in the year; this was payback. I just sat there and endured his smug, limp-witted smile. When the lunch bell rang, I stashed my books and grabbed a tuna sandwich. I found Curry elbow-deep in his lunch sack near the rear exit. We started walking outside.

"Well, did we get our grades back?"

It wouldn't have taken a clairvoyant to read my expression. "Not exactly." I gave him the nutshell version.

"So old Krogstrand was using us to find Cyrus Twist's treasure. The rest was all an act." Curry stared hard at nothing in particular.

"At least you didn't tell him what he wanted to know."

He paused and glanced up at the bell tower. "What if I had? What if you hadn't stopped him? And what if he used the information to take something that doesn't belong to him? I don't like it—not being able to control the words that come from my own mouth."

"You didn't exactly spill your guts."

"Wish I hadn't told him anything at all. About the diamonds, I mean. I knew this would happen. People are just too doggoned greedy."

I wanted to reassure him. I liked being part of something mysterious and wonderful. I liked the notice we'd been getting around school. But I knew Curry didn't like being pushed, especially where his principles were involved.

Then I remembered Sqyrl.

"What does she want?" Curry asked as I led him past the gym toward the ball field.

"Beat's me. Sounded urgent."

"I'm not going to do any more readings." His voice had a slammed-door certainty to it.

"Fine," I said. I'd talk sense into him later. "But we can't leave Sqyrl standing by the backstop all afternoon."

"I suppose not."

Sqyrl Marx jogged around the infield in her orange gym shorts and black jersey, headband keeping her amber hair out of her eyes. She flagged a hand at us and headed over. With cheeks reddened and chest heaving, she looked the picture of vitality. But she had the same worried droop to her mouth and shoulders I'd seen earlier.

"Hi Curry." She sounding almost shy—probably for the first time in her life. She wiped sweat off her neck with a fuzzy wristband. Her teardrop-shaped eyes, flaring nostrils, big teeth, and thin face somehow all went together. A thoroughbred born to race.

"Sqyrl," Curry answered, jamming his hands into his pockets.

"I... um... I have to make the most important decision of my life. And I only have until Friday." While talking, she pushed against a post to stretch her Achilles. "Will you help me?"

"I don't know if I can," Curry said. The words seemed to stick in his throat. They'd probably known each other for years, but their shy little glances told me they were on new ground.

She continued stretching, the body going through its habits even as her emotions approached meltdown. "My grandmother in West

Seattle said I can come live with her, because their school has a world-class swimming program, and a coach who's handled Olympic swimmers, and we only have this dumb little pool here, and Coach Flatski doesn't know the difference between a butterfly and a horsefly, and the deadline for joining the team in West Seattle is Friday, but all my friends are here and everything is here..." She looked up at Curry and the tears gushed. "But I'll never have any chance of making it to the Olympics if I stay here. I'll be a nothing! And if I try, who knows, maybe I'll go all the way. But if I try, and don't go all the way, maybe it's not worth it, giving up my friends and my life on Kluge Island and my parents and my brothers and my dog, Roust."

As Sqyrl began hyperventilating, Curry put out a comforting arm, but couldn't bring himself to touch her. "You want help making the decision."

Sqyrl stopped stretching and draped herself around Curry, though he tried to take a step back before she captured him. "Oh yes!"

Curry held his hands out awkwardly, not knowing what to do with them. Then he cautiously patted Sqyrl on the back. It helped. She dried up and stopped whimpering. "You see, I know I'm a good athlete. I can out swim any man, woman, or fish on this island. But I don't know how tough the competition will be in the city, and whether I have what it takes. Can't you look into the future and tell me if you see gold medals? Or would I be wasting my time?"

Curry raked at his hair, then shook his head. "No, Sqyrl, I'm not going to look into the future. I don't have to, because I've known you for a long time, and I *know* you can do it. And even if you give it your best, and somebody else does better, you still win. And if somebody else is going to do better, I wouldn't dream of telling you and making you give up."

I just faded into the background. I remembered how the swami had given me the opportunity to know about my future love life, and I hadn't regretted saying no. So I knew Curry had given Sqyrl the right answer. How dreary life would be if we knew these things in advance.

Sqyrl listened with shiny eyes and scuffed dirt with her toe. "So you think I should go?"

"You've got more vinegar than anyone I know. I'm betting on you. And you can always come back if things don't work out."

Sqyrl sniffed, wiped her eyes, and gave Curry another hug, this one quick and embarrassed. As we started to walk off, she said, "When I get on the ferry, will you come see me off? You too, Darwin, if you want." But she scarcely looked at me.

When we were beyond range of her hearing, I asked, "Well, hunk, what do you have to say for yourself?"

He looked solemnly at me and said, "If you're not going to finish your lunch, can I have it?"

Chapter 28
The Bottom Falls Out

*A*fter our last class, I waited for Curry by his motorbike. The rush of students thinned before I spotted his thick-chested, large-headed shape coming my way. "C'mon, we've got things to do," I said. "What kept you?"

"Just talking to Sqyrl Marx a little."

"She's sweet on you. You know that, don't you?"

"Oh, sure," Curry said. "Killer jock falls for dweeb with marshmallow filling."

"Strange world. You're going to see her off at the ferry, aren't you?"

"She mentioned it again. Lot of good it would do me—she's moving away."

"Find out if she's coming back on weekends and holidays."

"She'll make new friends, and forget all about us."

"Curry, it's a good thing you have me for advice, 'cause you can be a real bozo. Just ask her, will you?"

"I bow to you, O studly one." He said it with just enough sarcasm to sting a little. "So what things do we have to do?"

"Just get on your scooter and follow me to the real estate office. Then I'll tell you."

I covered the half-mile on my road bike before Curry did. As I leaned the bike against the building, I could see Tuba Lord through the window, phone lodged in the flab between shoulder and ear, fingers tapping away on her keyboard.

Curry and I went in. Tuba finished her call, but left the receiver in place. Someday her neck would engulf the phone like a feeding ameba, and it would have to be surgically removed.

"How you doing this wonderful day, Tuba?" I asked.

"Like a washtub full of sunshine."

Every thing about her was round, even her laugh. "That's a lot of sunshine," I said.

"The only thing that could make me sunnier is a new listing. Curry, is that aunt of yours ready to sell that dilapidated place?"

"I don't think so, Tuba."

"Well, I won't let it ruin my day entirely. But you be sure and tell her: Tuba can turn it."

I couldn't help but smile. Tuba Lord had no competition on the island probably because she made people feel so doggoned good, nobody wanted to disappoint her.

"Oh, Darwin, dear, you're here for that map." She extracted the phone from her neck, swiveled her chair to aim it at the fax machine and set sail for it. The chair and cargo coasted to a stop precisely at its destination. "I phoned the title company this morning," she said, thumbing through the day's faxes. "Ah, here it is." She put a sausage-like finger under a numbered land parcel labeled *Twist.*

I searched for the owner's name on the property adjoining to the west. My stomach tightened when I found it. "Krogstrand," I said. Of course! Cyrus Twist's treasure. Holes. Charlie Angostura, school handyman. I should have known.

"Hmm. Emil Krogstrand," Tuba Lord said. "Our illustrious principal. I didn't realize he'd bought that piece, and believe me, very few properties turn on Kluge Island that I don't have a finger in."

I studied the map more closely. "What's this big chunk of land to the north? It says *Limeworks.*"

"Oh golly, that lime kiln closed down after World War II. They used the lime to make cement, you know. A lot of the cement that rebuilt San Francisco after the '06 quake came from those kilns."

I thanked Tuba for the map. We left our transportation behind—it still bugged me to leave my bike unlocked, but no one else locked anything, and I didn't want to look paranoid—and I steered Curry toward the Junque and Vintage Girdle Emporium.

On the way, I gave him the details of the swami's answers in the principal's office.

"You mean Krogstrand is responsible for those holes?" Curry asked.

"Who else?"

"And there're diamonds buried out there?"

"Yup."

Curry scratched his head. "But Mr. Angostura and those other guys were talking like they already found the place."

"Yup."

"So what gives?"

"I'm hoping your Aunt Iris can help."

The Emporium had taken on a more austere look since I'd last seen it. More orderly and less stuff. The cheesier junque had vanished, the gaudy ceramics and pictures of poker-playing dogs. I wondered how the two sisters, being so different, managed to keep their partnership together. Being old maids gave them plenty in common, I supposed.

"Closing time, isn't it auntie?" Curry said.

"What for?" Aunt Iris sighed. "Just an empty house to go home to."

"We found out who owns the land with the holes. Mr. Krogstrand."

Her face curdled. "I have no use for that man. He outbid Pansy at an estate auction this summer. Oh, she had a hissy fit and rolled in it. The lot she wanted, you see, included our Uncle Cyrus's sea chest."

My pulse quickened. "Sea chest? What was in it?"

"All his books and papers and lots of navigational instruments and old clocks—he loved mechanical things. His stepdaughter took the chest after they put Cyrus away. She had no right, but the family didn't know where it had gone to, and it wasn't worth a lawsuit once the stuff surfaced at the auction. We expected to buy it, but got outbid."

I asked, "Were you around when the limeworks were still open?"

"Just how old do you think I am?" She put her knuckles on her bony hips and leaned like a heron about to strike a minnow.

"Not nearly old enough to remember." Sometimes a person needs a loose concept of truth.

She straightened and dusted her palms as if just completing a tough piece of business. "That's the right answer. But I might know a thing or two about it—from what the old-timers have said. So, what do you want to know?"

"Just if they did any tunneling."

"Oh my, yes. All over. I remember when Buster Henry's milking shed just disappeared one day. One minute standing there big as life; the next minute, wiped clean from the earth, along with Daisy, his prize milk cow, and his wife in the bargain."

"What happened?" Curry asked.

"What happened is one of those tunnels busted through and swallowed up the whole kit-and-caboodle. Daisy panicked and ran down the tunnel and old Buster refused to pull his wife out until she'd found the poor beast. It seemed for a while both of them were goners, but then Daisy wandered back and Buster yarded her out with his pickup truck. The wife never did show up but Buster seemed pleased enough just to get Daisy back."

I gave Aunt Iris a sideways look to show her I wasn't necessarily buying the story. "Anyway, I think that's what all the digging is about," I said.

"Looking for Buster Henry's wife?" Iris asked.

"No. The tunnels."

"Can't see why. They've probably caved in by now. They dug them just to find out how far the best limestone deposits ran."

"Auntie, did you call the sheriff about Mr. Angostura? The picture I took of him turned out okay if he needs proof."

"I called him all right, for what good it'll do. He couldn't find his butt with both hands on a clear day."

"What did he say?" I asked.

Iris smiled at herself in a mirror and picked a fleck of something off her teeth. "Sheriff called back later and said that Angostura had an airtight alibi for when... when Pansy got shot." Iris deflated. Her old spunk had started to return, but the thought of Pansy set her back.

I felt let down too, partly because the alibi snuffed any hope I had of earning the reward.

She said, "Angostura claimed he had permission to dig on the adjoining land, and strayed on to my land by mistake, the fence being down."

"Sure," I said. "So tell us about Cyrus. I heard he came back from the Yukon with a fortune. Was there anything left when he died?"

Iris kept polishing her tooth with a thumbnail. "Now there's a sore subject. He went batty before making a will. By the time the estate settled, my sisters and I were the closest living relatives, so we got his land. His money would have been ours, too, if we knew where to find it."

"You think he might have stashed it?"

"Possibly. Then again, he might of spent it."

"That chest you mentioned—the one Krogstrand bought at auction—do you suppose Cyrus might have left something showing where he'd hidden the loot? A map?"

Iris's gaze floated for a moment, then she shook her head. "The step-daughter would have gone through the papers with a flea-comb."

I considered telling her about the diamonds, but decided against it. The swami said they were inaccessible, and someone might get hurt trying to find them. Besides, I had a brainstorm. Curry, after all, was a blood relative of Cyrus Twist. Suddenly I couldn't wait to get out of there. "Are there some tools at your house? Shovels and things?"

"The old garden shed out back. It's probably full of black widows. You're not going treasure hunting, are you?"

We had a few minutes of daylight so we headed to the Twist House, shuffled through leaves below the enormous copper beeches in the front yard, back to the shed. Sure enough, cobwebs stretched when I opened the door. Curry used a stick to clear them so we could get to the tools. I handed him a shovel and found an eight-foot length of galvanized water pipe for myself, and we scattered grasshoppers out past the poplars to the holes.

"Your dad said not to come here in the dark," Curry reminded.

"My definition of dark is you can't see. We'll be done by then. Angostura and his grunts must have been looking for an entrance to the tunnels. The limeworks probably sealed the main entrances when they shut down. Angostura must have found a way in, then hid it so they could keep drawing pay for digging new holes."

"From Krogstrand," Curry said.

"Yeah. But Angostura is trying to cross him by looking for the stash on his own."

"But does he know what he's looking for?"

"Sounds like everyone's heard the stories about a buried fortune. But Krogstrand isn't stupid. He wouldn't tell Angostura anything more than where to dig. Krogstrand himself thought he was looking for gold, not diamonds, until you told him this morning."

"How does Krogstrand know where to dig? Oh, that's why you think there was a map in Cyrus's trunk."

"Uh huh. Remember how I plotted the holes on graph paper? They aren't random. There's a plan. But even with a map, the landmarks might have changed over the years. Like what if the map said *thirty paces west of the giant oak* and five years later the giant oak is struck by lightning, and fifty years later, you can't even tell there ever was a giant oak. Or a stone wall gets torn down, or an old building gets bulldozed. Or maybe the writing on the map got smeared and he can't tell if it's thirty paces or eighty paces."

"That's why the pattern of holes is being repeated on Aunt Iris's land," Curry said.

"Could be. Anyway, I figured Angostura must have found the entrance, then covered it, maybe with a piece of plywood and a couple inches of dirt. That's what the pipe's for—to thump around for something hollow."

"You don't mean we're going in the tunnel if we find it?"

"One step at a time," I said. No sense alarming Curry prematurely. We reached the holes and split up. We probed and thumped until we could no longer see well enough to avoid falling in a hole.

"I don't know how we missed it," I said.

"Maybe we're on the wrong track."

"We could save ourselves the trouble if you'd just let me put you in a trance and ask."

Curry paused. "That's not—"

"I know. Doesn't fit your code of ethics, which are beyond me because I'm spiritually stunted."

Curry's glasses glinted as he scanned the field. "Let's scram in case Angostura comes back. I thought I saw something move over there."

I looked but didn't see anything. "Yeah, okay." I thought about hanging around to spy on Angostura but didn't really want to find out what he'd do if he caught us. So, in silence, we headed to the house. Curry kept checking behind, but the details in the field were becoming lost in the thickening dusk. By the time we reached the shed to return our tools, I could barely see inside. Then Curry banged the doorjamb with the blade of his shovel and I practically jumped off the ground.

"What are you doing?"

"There might be rats," he said. "Just trying to scare them away."

"Rats, huh." I gave the ground a couple good pokes with my pipe in case the rats hadn't got the message—and heard something that made me forget all about rats.

"Curry!"

"What. I didn't hear anything."

"You did too. It sounds hollow."

We both chunked our tools against the packed earth floor.

"I wouldn't exactly say hollow."

I tested the sound again. "Definitely hollow."

"Probably a rats' nest."

The thought of it made my skin quiver, though I knew he was just saying it to get out of there. "Stand back," I said. When Curry gave me room, I raised a leg and stamped, feeling a definite reverberation. Then tried it again, harder, but nothing gave way. I cleared away some junk on the workbench and clambered up.

"What now?" Curry asked.

"You'll see."

Then when he saw me stand, facing the floor, he said, "Darwin, that's stupid—"

Too late. I sprang off, coming down with all the force I could muster, driving my legs like pistons.

I felt a crack as something gave and the next thing I knew, I was tumbling into a black void, an odd thought flashing in my mind as I plummeted along with a hail of debris: a mental image of Daisy—Buster Henry's cow—and her terrified eyes.

Chapter 29
The Monkey's Paw

A s I came to my senses, I heard Curry shouting. I lay in darkness, crumpled on a rubble heap, trying to find the breath to answer, wondering how many bones were broken. When my wind did return, it came in a sharp gasp that vacuumed in a load of dust. The sound of my coughing took some of the anxiety out of Curry's shouts.

"You're alive! Are you hurt?"

His voice sounded distant and my coughs echoed strangely. Hurt? Maybe. I'd have to find out eventually, so tried moving an arm. When it worked properly, I tried the other. My luck held, but it seemed too much to hope that the legs were okay. One of my ankles hurt, but nothing seemed broken. I got to my knees and looked around. Nothing but blackness.

"Think I'm okay," I said. "Can you find a flashlight?"

"Like I tried to say, that was stupid!"

I didn't argue.

"That's auntie's car pulling in the driveway," he said. "Hold tight."

I held tight, mostly thinking about spiders and rats. Soon a light beam cut through the sifting dust. I shaded my eyes and looked around at the mound of dirt and rotten wood fragments I'd fallen on. There were rock walls on three sides, and the remains of a wooden ladder. I'd probably smashed it in my fall. On the fourth side, an opening.

"Goodness gracious," Aunt Iris' voice came from above. "I never would have believed..."

"We found the tunnel," I shouted and dusted myself off. I figured I'd survived a drop of almost twenty feet.

"We'll need the extension ladder," Iris said, sounding like a person who kept her head in a crisis.

"Send the flashlight down. While you're getting the ladder, I'll snoop around a bit."

"The whole thing might be ready to cave in," Curry said.

"I'll be careful." Curry lowered the light on some twine and I had my first look down the passage hewn from bedrock, built for men slightly shorter than I, and narrow—two men would have to turn sideways to pass. I ventured at most twenty yards down its length before the idea of being enclosed in rock weirded me out and my bowels tightened, and I turned back. Curry and Aunt Iris had the ladder in place and I climbed out into the sweet dewy air.

"How far does it go?" Curry asked.

"Forever. Couldn't see the end. Let's leave the ladder so we can explore it properly, later."

"I don't suppose you can be talked out of it," Curry said.

"Nope. I can be non-negotiable too."

We got Aunt Iris settled, and I limped beside Curry downtown to get my bike and his scooter.

"We'll need two strong flashlights, extra batteries, that compass you found, maybe some rope just in case, and a surveyor's tape so we can map the tunnel. Think of anything else?"

"Yeah," Curry said. "Let's forget we ever found that stupid thing."

"Where's your sense of adventure? Cyrus must have used that tunnel for his secret purposes."

"To hide his diamonds I suppose."

"Sure. And who knows what else. We gotta explore it. In fact, we might as well do it tonight."

"Tonight? It's dark out!"

"Curry, it's always dark in a tunnel."

Just then a siren powered up, and the sheriff's car zoomed past us with lights flashing. A minute later, the meat wagon followed. I turned and watched the lights until they were out of sight. We hadn't taken but a few steps more when I saw my dad's car giving chase. I waved my arms and he put on the brakes and zipped down the window.

"There's an accident. You boys want to ride along?"

We piled in and dad took off before we had the doors closed, headed up the north road toward the ferry landing. Hilly country, and we didn't see the emergency lights until cresting a hill. Below, where the road veered left we saw the accident scene bathed in harsh headlights—the wheels and undercarriage of a car rolled in the ditch. Dad pulled over and grabbed his camera and told me to run a couple of emergency flares up to the hilltop. My ankle gave me some grief, but I didn't want dad asking about it so I went. Meanwhile he and Curry hustled toward the wreck.

I struck the flares and hobbled back, hearing men shouting, and seeing five or six of them pushing on the side of the car and tipping it on edge. The top of the car had been sheared off level with its crumpled hood. While some of the men, including my dad, stabilized the car, others worked at getting the driver out.

It didn't start sinking in until I saw Curry walking toward me, weaving, one hand over his forehead, cheeks awash with tears, glasses reflecting the blue and red flashing lights.

"What is it?" I demanded, rushing to him and shaking him by the shoulders.

He looked at me with stunned eyes. "It's my sister. It's Paprika."

Chapter 30

Lightning Strikes

*K*luge Island's aid car had seen all kinds of trouble, most of it in some other town whose name was spray-painted over. Maybe a coastal town, by the rust. When dad and I followed it back to the village, and it's muffler scraped on the dips, I felt it on my raw nerves. Felt it mostly for Paprika, who'd been loaded into the back, strapped to a spine board. Curry rode with her along with the EMT. Paprika's girlfriend, Elise, who'd landed clear of the car, took the passenger seat. Elise had blubbered something to Sheriff Biggs about a deer jumping in front of them.

Dad and I drove in silence, the road back to town endlessly long, our tires sounding harsh on the pavement. I imagined rolling a convertible and having my face scoured off by asphalt. I hadn't got close enough to see Paprika so I kept imagining the worst.

"Dad, where's the nearest hospital?"

"Tugboat Island. If it's bad they'll send a chopper. Otherwise we have our clinic and a couple docs."

A wrecker passed, heading the other way.

At the clinic, a doctor met the aid car and asked some questions as the men slid the gurney out. I ventured near and, to my relief, heard Paprika responding, although feebly. I found Curry still huddled in the car. He stared like a zombie when I tried talking, so I left him alone. Then Mr. and Mrs. Buckle drove up, and the doctor reassured them. The other doc arrived, and an hour later they told us to go home. They'd treat the abrasions, observe her overnight, shoot a few X-rays, and maybe even release her tomorrow.

Having seen the car, it seemed a miracle.

Curry came out of his funk a little, and I patted him on the back as we watched Elise get into her parent's car, a bandage above one eye and a soft cast on one wrist. Everyone looked sickly under the clinic's vapor light.

"You knew this would happen, didn't you?" I said.

The chill air frosted Curry's breath. I counted three breaths before he answered. "I knew *something* would happen. I saw a black haze around her. I didn't really know what it meant. If only I'd made her give it up."

"You and who's army?"

"I should have tried."

"Looks like she's going to be okay."

He turned away.

"What?" A weird energy went off like an alarm in my chest.

"I saw the black mist still swirling around her."

I waited for Curry at his locker the next morning, but he didn't show up. I walked into English comp just as Ms. Dozier announced this would be Sqyrl Marx's last week, as she was moving to Seattle. Sqyrl watched me all the way to my seat, then whispered, "How's Curry's sister? Did Curry come in today?"

"Don't know."

I didn't hear a word Ms. Dozier said about O. Henry, and she must have noticed because she didn't call on me. Words didn't penetrate the strange, detached space I was in. I saw how Ms. Dozier paced herself, as if trying to conserve limited energy. And it brought me down. I understood then that Curry's gift of knowledge had a dark underside. That knowing everything could be perfectly hellish.

"Hey smeghead!" Choker called after the dismissal bell.

Even Choker couldn't bust through my mood. I ignored him.

In gym class the next period, I suited up, stood for roll call and jockstrap check, and trotted out to the field to play football. Even though I had some aches from falling into the tunnel shaft, I felt uncaged and ready for something physical. I got more than I bargained for.

On offense, I played running back because of my speed. But since our quarterback liked to pass the ball all the time, I usually just blocked. Choker Durant played on the other team, whatever position pleased him. Today it pleased him to blitz the passer on every down. The first time he blitzed, I blocked him, and after the ball had been passed, and all eyes were tracking it upfield, Choker sank a fist in my belly.

"That's for ignoring me," he said, as I sat on my bum, trying to breathe.

On the next play, still feeling weak from the gut-shot, I let Choker through, thinking I'd feed him the quarterback and maybe his mood would improve. But Choker wasn't hungry for quarterback. He followed me around, pretending to be blocked. The QB threw long, and Choker threw short. He knew just where to land a punch to drive the wind out of a person.

"That one's for sticking your gob where it don't belong."

I wondered what bug had crawled up his behind, but didn't have the breath to ask. In the huddle, our illustrious quarterback called for another pass. With any luck it would be intercepted. Again, the second the quarterback let fly, Choker aimed an uppercut at my breakfast. I caught most of the force on my arms, but right on one of my bruises.

"What was that one for?" I asked, rubbing my forearm.

He showed me his crooked teeth. "For your friend sticking his gob where it don't belong." Choker polished his fist in his left palm. "Since he's not here... what are friends for, anyway?"

"I don't know what the heck you're talking about," I said between gasps.

"Then have your rag-headed buddy gaze in his crystal ball."

Luckily, the pass *was* intercepted and our team went on defense.

"Bownes, you rush the quarterback," our team captain ordered.

I could hardly hear him over the thumping of my heart. Dizzy with adrenaline, I said, "You rush him. I'm covering Choker."

Before he could react to my backtalk, the play started and Choker went deep. I knew he'd go deep because he always went deep. And if his buddy, the quarterback, didn't throw it deep, Choker would be on his case. So when Choker went deep, half our team went with him, hoping the ball would be underthrown and they could pick it off. Not much strategy involved here. So, one more person covering Choker didn't matter, except with no one rushing the quarterback, he had all day to throw, and Choker went deeper than usual, with me right behind, trying to keep up on a bad ankle and a very sore gut. My focus became a tunnel with only Choker in it, only the soles of his super-purple high-top air-pump cross-trainers as they flashed up behind him, left, right. When I had the timing down, I slapped his right heel, causing it to catch behind his left leg, and he did a nasty face plant on the dirt part of the field. The ball came down and plunked him on the back. He got up fuming, looking for someone to retaliate at, but not knowing who.

Not knowing, that is, until coach blew his whistle and pointed directly at me. "Pass interference—tripping against Bownes."

Fine with me. I wanted him to know.

Choker seethed with fury and took a few steps toward me. But the coach was watching.

"That's to teach you some manners," I said.

"You're a dead man, Bownes."

Then the team captain got in my face. "Now look what you did. I told you to rush the passer."

"Yeah, okay." I lined up for the next snap, but I wasn't thinking about the passer. I was thinking about those purple sneakers— probably a hundred bucks a copy. Choker didn't dress in trendy duds and didn't seem to have money of his own. He always strong-armed guys into buying him sodas.

Choker's team huddled (I didn't know why—they almost always ran the same play) then lined up and snapped the ball and everyone took off leaving me the only one standing still. Me and the guy blocking me. He braced for a battle, but I had no interest in giving him one. Instead, I went to the place in the dirt where Choker had lined up, got down on one knee and looked for a print.

And there it was. Faint, but certain.

A lightning-bolt.

Chapter 31
The Voodoo Button

$\mathcal{I}$ rode out to the Buckle farm after school. Paprika had come home that day with orders to stay down for twenty-four hours. As I threw a tennis ball for the mutts, Curry described how she cried about her red convertible most of the day, then, to get her mind off it, tried walking through her cheerleader routines. "I keep telling her to rest, but she's bent on making the big game this weekend."

"You still see the black mist?"

"No."

"Well then..."

"It's not like I have X-ray vision. Sometimes I sense things, but don't know what they mean. I ignored it last time and look what happened."

"Stop beating yourself up about that wreck."

"But, in a way, I caused it. Giving her the winning number of Blubbergum balls."

"So the car's junked. If Paprika is doing cheers, that means she's okay, right?" Then I asked something I'd been putting off since the accident. "Tomorrow's Friday—we're still doing Swami Curryban at the bazaar, aren't we?"

Curry shook his head. "I can't."

"Why not?"

"I... I don't understand what's going on."

"Not a good reason." The dogs were starting to annoy me so I threw the slobbery ball deep into the pumpkin patch.

"Dar," Curry said. He blinked a couple times then looked directly at me. "What if terrible things keep happening to people I give answers to?"

"You make it sound like Pandora's box. Look," I counted off my fingers, "my plantar wart is cured. You saved Jennifer's cat. You helped

Gretchen find her dad. Ms. Dozier is getting treatment from Doc Uncas, thanks to you. All kinds of good stuff. So knock it off, and let's go back to work."

"It's... confusing. There must be a reason, but I just need time. I don't want anyone else to get hurt."

When I saw him Friday morning at school, he looked gray and gaunt, almost in a mist of his own. "She's worse," he said. "I told Dr. Slather that Rika needs to go to the hospital for more tests, but she says it's a temporary setback, delayed shock."

"We should do a reading, and find out if they've missed anything."

He glared at me with a surprising ferocity. "No!" Then he softened his tone. "That's what got her in this predicament in the first place. It's a curse."

"Curse? Who's been feeding you that baloney?"

"I had a talk with Pastor Fern."

"Curry, it's not a curse to help people. What'd the old foghorn say exactly?"

"Well, he said the voice that comes through me must be the devil because it surely isn't Jesus."

"So there's only two options, huh?"

"And that Jesus doesn't talk to fifteen-year-olds."

"Yeah, what good is he then?"

"And that I need to shut off the voice and not listen."

"Who elected Pastor Fern the expert, anyway? Did you ask him how he knows all there is to know in the universe?"

"No."

"Did Jesus sign off on his diploma or something? He's God-certified to say what's what? Somehow I doubt it."

"I don't want to talk about it Dar." Calm. Too calm. Almost zombie-like.

"Right," I said, and stuffed my hands into my pockets.

"You shouldn't grind your teeth like that."

I let some of the tension go. "Can't have you feeling responsible for wrecking my molars." He gave a forced smile. "See ya later then," I said. "Remember your promise to Sqyrl—to see her off at the ferry tomorrow."

Curry's face remained blank. "Why don't you go without me."

"Am I really hearing this?" I said, a little too loud, and with a little too much arm-flinging. "Were you formed in a uterus or in a gelatin mold? The point is, Sqyrl Marx doesn't care if I'm there or on Jupiter. She cares if *you* are there." I passed my hand before his eyes. "Earth to Curry."

He lowered his gaze. "Not sure I can make it."

"No wonder you don't have any friends."

The instant I said it, I wanted to take it back. But the best I could do was add, "Except me." He still didn't look up, and I couldn't tell if the remark had stung. Then I remembered something. "I took a punch to the guts the other day just for hanging around with you. Choker wanted to send us both a message not to stick our gobs where they don't belong."

Curry furrowed his brow with puzzlement.

"He didn't go into detail. But I figured it out—Choker was one of the guys helping Angostura dig those holes. The lightning bolt footprint? It's Choker's."

"Holy buckets!"

"What?"

"The letter jacket..."

"Yeah, what?"

"It's Dan Klatt. Paprika's boyfriend."

"Klatt? How do you figure?"

"Don't you know?"

"I've only lived here three months."

"Choker is Dan Klatt's cousin."

Curry became even moodier the next few days as Paprika slid deeper into lethargy, fever, even delusion. Dr. Slather finally had her patient transported to the hospital, but even there, they found nothing to explain Paprika's decline. So they returned her home to be dosed with a variety of colored tablets, and to be prayed over by Pastor Fern and the Buckle family.

I rode my bike over on a Saturday morning to check on things. Curry led me upstairs to his sister's room, where we found Dan Klatt holding her thin, bluish hand, and talking to her. Paprika's eyes would flutter open sometimes but her comprehension seemed feeble at best. Dan had his back to us and didn't hear our approach. I touched a finger to my lips so Curry wouldn't say anything. I thought I'd heard Klatt say a name that caught my interest. It sounded like 'Cyrus'.

"Danny Klatt's a winner, and nothing's going to change that, babe. Winners make things happen. Just like old Cyrus made things happen. He made his fortune, and he's going to help make our fortune, too. You might say he's on the team, and I'm on the team, and you're on the team, too, Rika. And the team's on the two yard line, ready to punch it home, and none of us will ever have to flip burgers for a living, or have our faces burnt off, so you need to get better, sweetheart, if you want to hang with the champions."

Klatt babbled on, but I'd heard enough, and motioned Curry back into his room.

"You're right about him," I said. "He thinks he's on to Cyrus Twist's treasure."

"I think he's coming unhinged because of that joke we played on him."

"It's good for him."

"I don't know, I've been thinking—"

The doorbell rang. He hurried to answer because his mom had gone to visit Iris, and his dad had the game on, and his brother Basil was outside resuscitating chickens or something. Before Curry got to the head of the stairs though, the door opened and a woman announced herself in a brusque voice. "'Lo there, it's Dr. Slather." In walked a stout, bow-legged woman in a short skirt and short jacket she must have bought fifty pounds ago. If we ever had tryouts for a Gooeyduck mascot, she'd get my vote.

The TV went mute. Curry and I hung out on the landing above the stairs to listen.

"How's your prize this morning, Mr. Buckle?"

"Not so well, doctor. Did you bring them other pills you were talking about?"

"You bet. We're going to keep pushing buttons until... bingo."

Mr. Buckle brightened and pretended to push some of the buttons on his TV remote. "That's the spirit. 'Cuz you might say Paprika's the last hope for this Buckle clan, now that Curry's been touched by a demon. You need to get her snapped out of this thing."

I shook my head with disgust. To Dr. Slather's credit, she said, "There're no demons involved, Mr. Buckle. I don't want to hear any more talk... cripe sakes."

They climbed the stairs. We all crowded into Paprika's room as Dr. Slather poked and prodded and used her bag of doctor gizmos and wrote on the chart. Then she just stared at Paprika with concerned eyes. I expected somebody to give me the goodbye look, but nobody did so I stayed.

"It's not good, is it?" Curry said.

Dr. Slather shook her head. "I hoped we'd be seeing improvement."

Curry turned away and looked ready to fold up. I'd been thinking about something for quite a while and finally raked up my nerve to ask Dr. Slather, "What about calling in Doc Uncas? I heard he can sometimes do things with hopeless cases."

I knew I'd stepped into it by Dr. Slather's monkey-like expression of disbelief. "Who is this *boy*? First of all, who said anything about this case being hopeless? Can you believe? Second of all, the last time Wesley Uncas practiced voodoo on a young girl, he killed her. So he jolly-well better not be treating cases, hopeless or otherwise, or I'll report him to licensing in a heartbeat."

Drat! Double-drat! I tried to think of a way to get Doc Uncas out of the mess I'd made, then noticed Curry had taken an interest. "It might be something to think about," he said. "Of course, he'd just be consulting with you, doctor, and not doing the actual treating."

Dr. Slather mouthed the word NO! and stood before Paprika as if expecting incoming hockey pucks.

We all turned to Mr. Buckle. He tugged at his belt and shifted his weight from one foot to the other, trying to decide whether to push the voodoo button.

Chapter 32
A Ghost Laughs

W hile Mr. Buckle went outside to talk it over with The Big McGillicuddy, I followed Curry on his rounds to feed the animals. In the barn, I spied a coil of rope and a lantern. I hadn't been able to get that tunnel out of my mind.

Curry stiffened when I suggested it. "Ah, I've got lots of homework."

"I'll help you with it later. And exploring will take your mind off things."

"I don't like dark places."

"That's what the lantern is for."

"It might cave in."

"Those tunnels have held up for a hundred years; they'll hold up another hour or two. If it looks dangerous, we'll turn back. I promise."

"But the *voice* said the diamonds were in a treacherous place."

"We're not necessarily going after diamonds. Just exploring for the fun of it. Besides, maybe old Cyrus Twist stashed other stuff down there."

"Like what?"

I tried to think of something that would appeal to him. "Like old documents. Photographs. Inventions. Coins."

Curry's eyebrows rose. "Do you suppose there might be blue toads down there?"

"Why not? Are there really such things as blue toads?"

"Used to be. Only on Kluge island. But nobody has seen one for fifty years. They had a certain chemical on their skin that could heal stuff. The Indians used them in sacred rituals. But when the fur traders came, they captured too many blue toads and they got scarcer and finally disappeared altogether."

"And you'd like to find one?"

"It would be the highlight of my life—so far."

I nodded earnestly. "I'd say if there're any blue toads left in the world, they've got to be in those tunnels."

"Nah, it's just a story."

I took the rope down from its nail. "Look Curry, I'm going exploring with or without you. I'd feel a lot safer with company, but what the heck."

He shook his head. "Sheesh, Darwin. Life was a lot more normal before you came along."

"You dreamed me up, remember?"

I whistled like a dwarf as I descended the ladder into the dank blackness. Curry followed like Grumpy. But my mouth dried up as we ventured into the passage, and soon the lantern's hiss drowned out my whistling. Because I had to stoop slightly, it felt like the rock was pressing around me, ready to mash me into grease. If Curry had lost his nerve, I'd have gone back with him without serious argument. The lantern cast exaggerated shadows of my legs as I paced off the distances. I called the numbers back to Curry, who noted them down, along with a compass heading every time the tunnel angled in a different direction. Having something to do kept my claustrophobia under control, and it seemed to be helping Curry, too. Taking his mind off Paprika.

After 120 of my long paces, our tunnel intersected with another, so we had a choice of three directions, not including retreat. Straight ahead seemed to be leading toward the field of holes, so we kept on in that direction. I expected to find another tunnel entrance there, because of what we'd overheard Charlie Angostura say to Choker and Dan, his grunts. And perhaps we would have except for one thing: after another sixty paces, the tunnel had caved in. I looked at a snapped timber pinned under tons of rock.

"That's that," Curry said, whispering as if afraid the sound of his voice might bring down more of the ceiling.

"We've got two other tunnels to explore," I said, trying to sound like the cave-in was no big deal.

"There's nothing down here."

"C'mon, you'll never find any mutant blue toads with that attitude."

"You made me think there were blue toads just to get me down here. And what if we run into Angostura?"

I admit, it hadn't occurred to me, and my heart thumped harder at the thought of his wild face lurching out of the darkness. We hurried back to the intersection.

"Left or right?" I asked, not giving Curry the option of heading straight for the ladder. By my reckoning, the left passage headed inland, while the right led toward the shore. "Left," I said before Curry could answer, and since I had the only lantern, he had to follow.

This tunnel soon became even narrower than the others, with many twists and turns, and side passages, most of which petered out after a few yards. We explored every dank hollow, looking for possible hiding places Cyrus Twist might have used, or for another exit from the tunnel system. We found nothing but bare, dry rock—occasionally a seep fed a growth of slime—and one worn-out iron chisel. We continued taking measurements so I could map it later. It was while pacing off a long straightaway that we made a horrific discovery.

Curry kept the lantern so he could read the compass and make notes. My shadow and I paced into the dimming passageway, counting aloud, "... twenty-three, twenty-four, twent—UNGH!" I tripped over something and sprawled on the rough floor, my hands absorbing most of the damage. I scrambled to one knee and caught my breath, feeling lucky I hadn't stepped into a bottomless pit. The thing I'd stumbled over felt like a bag of loose kindling when I'd kicked it, and it raised a sickly-smelling dust. The lantern bobbed as Curry hustled down the passage toward me.

"Darwin! You okay?"

"Yeah, except somebody left their firewood in the path." But as the light got stronger, the obstacle took on more detail, a scrawny frame covered with a shriveled brown membrane and patches of cloth. But it wasn't until Curry's lantern spilled light over the thing, that I recoiled with horror.

A human skull looked directly at me, shrink-wrapped in dried brown skin, hollow eye sockets, and big teeth bared in a hideous grin.

"Ahhhhhh!" Curry shouted, almost dropping the lantern.

I kept my distance from the mummified corpse, the hollow rock amplifying my heartbeat. Curry recovered his composure more quickly, and crouched near the awful thing that used to be a human being.

"It's a woman," he said. "In a flannel dress. Look at those clunky old work boots. She must have died a long time ago."

We both figured it out at the same time.

"Buster Henry's wife!"

The woman who'd fallen in the sinkhole with Daisy the cow, and got lost in the maze.

"Look, she's got a bit of candle in her hand," Curry said, sadness in his voice as if the calamity had touched him personally. But that was Curry. He felt everyone's pain.

"How could they not have found her?" Then I took the lantern and looked around and got my answer. There were at least a half-dozen black arches leading in all directions. Spokes from a hub. "This whole section of the island must be honeycombed," I said.

Suddenly Curry's eyes turned up and he leaned against the tunnel wall for support. "Oh! So much fear. I can still feel it around her like... like it's still happening."

His voice was a breathless whisper and the tremor in it made cold beads of moisture form on my forehead. "What do you mean, Curry? What's still—you're having a vision?"

"There was a cave-in and she got cut off from where she fell in, and kept trying to find another way back. Then she stumbled and the candle went out and her matches didn't work." Curry shuddered. His hands went out like antennae receiving pictures from the air. "Kept trying different tunnels in the dark. Heard voices but didn't know if they were real and couldn't tell where they were coming from, thought she was headed for the kilns, but must have got turned around. Frantic and paralyzed with confusion." Curry panted for breath. "The voices faded. Were they ever there at all? Or just echoes of her own insane screaming. After what must have been days, she just gave up. Curled into a ball and waited."

I held the lantern close for warmth. I realized that if Curry had dropped it, we might now be in the same predicament as this poor soul at our feet. Lost in the subterranean darkness. Curry held his hands over his eyes as if trying to shield them. "You've had this kind of vision before?" I asked.

"Not like this. Once in a while, I get strong feelings about things, but not this vivid."

"You could see her face and everything?"

"More her heart—her panic."

"Dang, Curry, I don't know what to think of you."

"I don't know what to think of me either."

He took a couple of deep breaths then knelt to ease a locket from the mummy's neck. I stepped over the remains and we returned to the first intersection. There, Curry wanted to head for daylight, but I blocked the way and pointed down the remaining unexplored passage.

"C'mon, Dar, we've got to report the body."

"We can't. Not yet anyway."

"We have to."

"Then everyone would know about the tunnel, and the secret entrance."

"So?"

"We need to explore it first."

"Who do you think you are, Indiana Bownes?"

"This other passage, it's got to be where Cyrus kept his loot, because we've already checked the other ways."

"But the *voice* said—"

"It's dangerous. Yeah, but if we know it's dangerous, then maybe we can do something about it, right?"

"Darwin, I don't want the diamonds. They can stay down here

forever—oh jeez!"

"What?" I followed his gaze. There, scratched into the stone, was a symbol, small, almost lost in the tool marks left by those who'd hollowed the rock. The same mark we'd seen engraved on Cyrus Twist's planet contraption. The looping 'T'.

"That does it," I said. "We're hot on his trail."

Curry sighed, and we inched ahead, eyes peeled for any other signs Cyrus might have inscribed. We didn't even bother to measure the passage, just pushed deeper into the cold rock. In a few minutes, the tunnel forked. After searching the walls, we found the Twist mark on the left branch and took it. Then another fork, and this time, the mark indicated the right tunnel.

"Does it seem like we're going downhill?" I asked.

"A little. It smells funky."

I sniffed the ripe air. "Like a Vietnamese restaurant. Fermented seaweed or something."

We rounded a bend and I stepped into a pool, taking cold water over the top of my shoe. The pool had been so perfectly reflective, I hadn't seen it. The splash sounded alive compared with the stony tube we'd been traveling through. With the water's surface providing a flat point of reference, we could easily see how the tunnel sloped deeper into the earth. However, we wouldn't be going any further, as thirty yards ahead, the roof of the tunnel angled under the water. Curry crouched by the edge of the pool, dipped a finger, and tasted it.

"Salty."

As ripples spread out over the pool, I thought I saw the shape of a man in the water. A man with a twisted, mercury-mad face. I shuddered and blinked, and when I looked again, the image was gone.

Chapter 33
The Big McGillicuddy

*W*hen I arrived at school Monday, Ms. Dozier stood on a chair in the foyer, moving the cut-out blue toad to account for money raised during Friday's bazaar. Early on in the campaign, the toad had quickly jumped past the five-thousand dollar hurdle, but he'd lost momentum lately. Now, Ms. Dozier moved him barely a body length. Still under ten thousand and we needed twenty-five. Curry and I had contributed nothing for two weeks, Swami Curryban being on strike.

Several glum faces stared at the chart. I even heard a mocking laugh that raised my hackles. I gave the guy who did it a dirty look, then held out a hand to steady Ms. Dozier as she stepped off the chair. Deep lines scored her face, and her muumuu needed ironing. She smelled garlicky too, maybe because of the liniment Curry had prescribed.

"Maybe ten grand is enough to fix the important stuff at the camp," I said.

"I'm afraid not, Darwin." As I walked her to her classroom, she said, "I thought we'd be farther along by now. The students have worked so hard."

Her feet shuffled along the floor. "Why don't you take a sick day and get some rest," I said.

"That's kind of you, but whatever strength I have comes from doing my job. I don't think I'd last long at home."

"But the treatment?" I asked, alarmed.

"It's not doing any harm. Don't worry about me. I'm just down about this Camp Bluetoad thing. We had such fun there when I was a student, and it's such a tradition. But I'll get over it."

"I wish I could do something."

Her face clouded, and she leaned toward me to whisper, "You can send Mr. Krogstrand to the Wizard of Oz for a heart." Then she waved it off. "Just kidding."

   I walked to biology, oblivious to the students jostling around me, until a certain remark caught my ear. "Did you hear Choker ran away from home?" I didn't pay much attention to the comment or who said it, and turned my thoughts to saving Camp Bluetoad.
   Then I had another of my brainstorms.
   I stared blankly into my locker, working on the details. One big detail would be getting Curry's help.
   On the way to class, I had another idea, and paused by the bulletin board to study the tide tables. Island people knew ferry schedules by heart, and kept track of the tides. These were the clocks that things ran by. I put my finger beneath yesterday's numbers, and nodded with satisfaction.
   In the science theater, I found Curry talking with Keeley Uncas. He looked nearly as haggard and bummed as Ms. Dozier had been. Keeley, on the other hand, looked mad.
   "How's Rika?"
   Curry shook his head. "Not good."
   My insides riled at the way Keeley turned her shoulder to me. I wondered what Curry had told her. "What did your folks decide?" I asked Curry.
   "About calling Doc Uncas? I was just asking Keeley. Dad wants to try, but..."
   Keeley finished the sentence for him. "But Dr. Slather says my dad's a witch doctor. You don't have to spare my feelings. We've heard it before."
   "What about your mom?" I asked Curry.
   He squirmed. "Um, well..."
   "Curry's mom thinks my dad is a murderer and belongs in jail. Correct?" Keeley's dark eyes flashed and her lips looked rigid. "We've heard that one, too."
   I admired the way she stuck up for her dad. I remembered Curry

thinking she wanted to be top student, not so much for the glory, but as a way to make her father look good. Polishing his reputation the only way she could: *if Keeley is that brilliant, then the Doc must be brilliant, too.*

I felt the slight ridge of scar over my eye where Doc had stitched me. "Keeley," I said, "they're treating Paprika like a lab rat. We know how risky it would be for your dad, but... it's Curry's sister at stake." I asked him, "Who usually gets their way at your house?"

"Besides Paprika, you mean? That would be mom. Except Rika is dad's prize and he'd do anything for her."

Old Flattop Flatski cleared his throat. From their seats, everyone stared at us, and we scurried to ours. One seat remained empty: Choker's. Made me wonder how a person runs away if they live on an island.

After school, Curry and I helped his dad load The Big McGillicuddy in his pickup. First, Mr. Buckle used a tractor to lift the pumpkin and weigh it on a freight scale. Curry moved the weights and shouted out, "Nine-hundred and twenty-seven pounds!" Mr. Buckle's mouth curved up in a satisfied smile. Then he revved the tractor and hoisted the pumpkin over to his pick-up. Curry and I had arranged a thick sheet of plywood over some rollers in the bed of the pickup. The springs sagged as the grotesque pumpkin filled the truck bed. Then we loaded some planks, a straw bale, a shock of cornstalks, and the three of us climbed in the old Dodge. It backfired every time Mr. Buckle shifted on the way to Keeley's house.

Doc Uncas and Keeley watched from their porch as we rolled the bulging monstrosity down the planks to a bed of straw Mr. Buckle had laid near the steps. While the doc wore an expression of amused curiosity, Keeley looked grumpy, probably wondering what she'd do with The Big McGillicuddy when it decayed into nine hundred pounds of mush. Mr. Buckle placed it just so, stepping back to frame it from various angles before garnishing with cornstalks. He rubbed his hands together at the overall effect, then greeted the proud new owner of

The Big McGillicuddy with a vigorous handshake. Doc Uncas accepted it with grace. He couldn't have known that, besides Paprika, and possibly his vibrating recliner, the Big McGillicuddy meant as much to Mr. Buckle as anything. But Doc acted like he did know.

"Thank you, Mr. Buckle. Shall we go in?"

We did, but not before Mr. Buckle remembered his camera and got a snapshot of his greatest pumpkin.

"Sit here, my young shaman," Doc said to Curry, steering him by the shoulders to the chair next to his. Mr. Buckle and I took opposite ends of the sofa. Keeley looked at the vacancy between, but chose the floor. She drew a slender knee up and rested her chin on it. I studied the line of scalp where her black hair parted. She hadn't even said hello to me.

Doc surprised me by sitting cross-legged in his chair. He fixed his gaze across the coffee table at Mr. Buckle. "Now, tell me about your daughter." Mr. Buckle eyed the doctor warily, then explained the situation in halting phrases. Doc peered through reading glasses at the prescription bottles Mr. Buckle produced from various pockets. He made some slight reaction to each: a pursing of lips, exasperated nod, a rolling of eyes. Finally, he removed his glasses and frowned.

"Mr. Buckle, when you grow a prize pumpkin, do you feed it gasoline?"

Curry's dad straightened. "Why, I feed it goat manure."

"Exactly! And when the human body heals, it needs certain nutrients. Sometimes drugs are helpful, but often they throw the glands and organs out of equilibrium, creating new problems." He handed back the pill bottles as if he never wanted to see them again.

Mr. Buckle squirmed in his seat. "Will you come and see her then?"

Doc Uncas stroked his chin whiskers, groomed to a point.

"Please. She's my special girl, and I think I'm losing her." Mr. Buckle laced his thick farmer's fingers as if in prayer.

Doc nodded. "I'm not a miracle worker, but yes, I'll have a look. Just a consultation, you understand. No treatment. We'd better do it now before any more harm is done."

I looked to Keeley for her reaction. Her eyes were closed and she massaged her temples as if trying to make a headache go away.

* * *

When I saw Dr. Slather's Volvo parked in front of Curry's house, I knew there'd be trouble. Keeley parked the Bug next to it. Her father got out and hesitated at the Volvo, probably not to admire the paint job. Basil was trying to learn banjo on the porch. Sounded like he had baling wire for strings, but the dogs seemed to enjoy it. Inside, Mr. Buckle and Curry led us upstairs to the sickroom.

Seeing Doc Uncas, Mrs. Buckle stepped between him and her helpless daughter. Dr. Slather locked arms with Mrs. Buckle, making a barricade. With her free hand, Dr. Slather held up a cautionary finger. "I can't stop you from examining her, but so help me, if you..."

"Spare me the threats, Melanie."

"It's Doctor Slather to you."

"And how are you going to address me?"

She worked her jaw in agitation. "There's plenty of things I could call you."

"But *doctor* isn't one of them."

She avoided his stare.

Doc breathed on the lens of his half-glasses—more of a sigh—and polished it with a pressed handkerchief. "You're entitled to your opinion... doctor."

Standing in the doorway beside me, Keeley's little fists were vibrating with tension. Meanwhile Curry had crouched over his sister. With Paprika's freckled hand in his, he pinched his eyes shut and his lips moved as if praying.

Doc Uncas said, "May I ask what your diagnosis is?"

"My diagnosis?" Doctor Slather sounded put out, as if asked to reveal her weight.

"Surely you must have one," Doc Uncas said. "Your name is on eight different prescription bottles for this patient."

Her gaze shifted aside. "She's being treated for general bodily and emotional trauma. Clinical tests didn't indicate... why am I telling you?"

"Emotional trauma?"

Dr. Slather stood as tall as her bowed legs would permit. "In my professional view, the young lady was excessively attached to her new car, and now that it's wrecked, she's internalizing."

Doc Uncas nodded. "Internalizing. I see. It's all in her head. And your hope—as a professional—is to drug her to the mental level of a mollusk, hoping she'll snap out of it?"

Mr. Buckle, who'd been scratching his arms, said, "That's what she needs, by golly—to be snapped out of it!"

"For goodness sakes, Neil," Mrs. Buckle said.

Doc Uncas muttered something about chickens and pumpkins.

"Chickens?" Dr. Slather said. "I suppose your idea is to wave a dead chicken over her, or drill holes in her skull to let the devils out."

Mr. Buckle held up both palms like a traffic cop. "There will be no hole drilling. That is where we draw the line."

Doc Uncas and Dr. Slather looked at each other, and seemed to reach some kind of truce. Doc said, "I want the room cleared, except for Dr. Slather, the patient, and myself."

As we went down the creaking stairs, I had a thought. Keeley was already torked at me, so I didn't have much to lose. I told Curry I needed to use the john, but slipped out the back door and circled around to the cars. I opened the door of the Bug, slid a cassette into the tape player, turned the knob on, then returned to the house.

I found Keeley standing alone, arms crossed, at the front picture window.

"Whatcha looking at?"

She eyed me accusingly. "I don't miss much."

I smiled guiltily. "You sure don't."

"So what were you doing in my car?"

"Just looking. Been thinking of getting one someday."

"Liar."

I shrugged. Keeley might not trust me, but I was one of the few people she took any notice of at all. "How are things coming with Ms. Dozier?" I asked. "She seemed to be dragging fanny this morning."

Keeley sighed. "Dad thinks the treatment is helping, but the Camp Bluetoad thing is wearing her down."

I shook my head. "She needs to let go of it."

"You don't understand all the tradition, Darwin. It's very important to her, and to the students, and to lots of people. But times are hard and people don't have much money to donate."

"Keeley, are you saying that if Camp Bluetoad dies, then Ms. Dozier...?" I couldn't finish the question. I noticed Curry was suddenly paying attention.

Keeley nodded. "Dad thinks it's a matter of will to live."

I leaned against the wall, and remembered how Ms. Dozier stood up to Mr. Krogstrand, and how she'd always treated me like... like there was something special in me. "Keeley, I had one of my crazy ideas this morning. A way to raise some serious money." Just then, the two physicians came downstairs, expressions glum.

Doc Uncas told Mr. Buckle, "This is a very puzzling case. I'll have to give it some reflection."

Mr. Buckle shook Doc's hand vigorously. "Last week, when I got stumped about how to mount a radiator from a Jimmy truck on to the tractor, why I just talked it over with The Big McGillicuddy, and it came to me," he snapped his fingers, "just like that."

Doc Uncas smiled. "I'll give it a shot, Mr. Buckle. I truly will."

Chapter 34
The Little McGillicuddy

*W*ith Curry's mom entrenched at Paprika's bedside, it didn't seem likely we'd get fed that evening, so I offered to buy Curry dinner in town. As usual, I pedaled my bike and Curry rode his scooter. Dinner doesn't come any cheaper than murderburgers at Troutigan's food stand, and as the old hippie-freak sizzled the clam patties, we listened to him rant about the Pansy Twist case. He seemed obsessed to the point of paranoia. Another day in the life of Troutigan.

"I've been having these weird rushes, man, ever since those nuns started up the convent at the old holly farm. You never see them praying or anything, do you? And you don't really know how many of them there are, because they dress in tablecloths and you can't tell one from the other unless you're close enough to count the warts on their noses. In fact, I'd like to see a chromosome count on some of them. But there's more of them than you think, and, you know what?" He leaned forward and strained his voice through the huge moustache that overhung his mouth. "I don't think they're really nuns at all. They're an advance guard sent here to buy up the island. They try to recruit widows and old maids to join and sign over their property. Well, I think they went after Pansy, but she wised on to them, so they had to eliminate her. Iris knows the truth, but she's afraid to talk now, and who could blame her, after what happened to Pansy."

Then our local genius—the guy who invented GooeyGlue—came along for a dish of napalmed noodles, and Troutigan encouraged him to invent a weapon the whales could wield against the Norwegians.

Curry and I retreated to our usual bench. While I chowed, Curry stared at a slash of white sail on the horizon, his burger scarcely nibbled. "Murderburger for your thoughts?" I said.

Worry shadows made his eyes look old. "Lots of stuff."

"Stuff. Stuff means problems, right? So let's start with the easiest stuff and work up to the gnarly stuff, okay?"

Curry nodded. He fished the heart-shaped locket from his shirt pocket—the one he'd taken from the mummy's neck. "What do I do with this? Shouldn't we report it? There's probably some family that would want to know."

"Curry, she's been dead longer than Elvis. What's the rush? Anyway, she's not going anywhere."

"But why not report it?"

"Do you really want the whole island crawling through those tunnels before we've done exploring them?"

"What do you mean, *done?* What more can we do? The tunnel's flooded, for crying out loud."

"I've been wondering," I said. "Is it flooded only at high tide? I checked the tables this morning. It would have been a ten-footer when we were in there."

Curry thought. "But why would anyone dig a tunnel that would flood?"

"Maybe it was dry once, then the ocean found a way in. Maybe an earthquake made a crack. Or they dynamited too close to an underwater cave."

"Sounds way dangerous."

"Sounds like the perfect environment for blue toads."

Curry huffed. "I'm not falling for that rap again."

I put up my hands to say *okay.* "But if there's even one chance in a million, do you want mobs of people stomping around down there?"

Curry took one more look at the locket and put it away.

"Next problem?" I asked. Curry, in his natural state, could seem contented as a freshly watered begonia. But he could also be a worrywart.

"There's something I don't understand. Why would the swami give Paprika the winning Blubbergum number? He must have known she'd wreck the car. And he warned Krogstrand about the physical and spiritual danger of Cyrus Twist's diamonds. Why didn't he warn

Rika about the car?"

"Good question, Curry. Only one way to find out." I'd wanted to do another reading, but Curry had been so sour on the idea that I hadn't dared ask.

"I don't know, Dar."

Then, while I tried to think of an angle, something happened.

Old man Sturgis came from the grocery store, a brown bag in the crook of each arm. Another old guy in a plaid hunting cap, hefting a humungous bag of dog food on his shoulder, held the door for him, and they began walking our direction. Though Sturgis shuffled his feet a bit, he carried on so normally that I wondered if his eyesight was as bad as Curry thought. Then I saw it coming, but not in time to warn him. Some kid's bike had fallen off its kickstand, partially blocking the walk. Sturgis's friend couldn't see the bike because of the bag on his shoulder, and, sure enough, Sturgis got tangled up in the handlebars and went sprawling, flinging groceries before him. An orange rolled all the way to the bench Curry and I sat on.

Curry rushed to help Sturgis while I shagged oranges.

But Sturgis didn't want help. He cleared Curry and the other guy away with a hard swing of his arm. "Leave me alone!"

One of the grocery bags had ripped, and a pool of milk spread from a ruptured jug. Most of the stuff was in cans, though.

"Loan me three bucks," Curry whispered, so low I had to read his lips.

I handed him the money and he headed to the store. Mr. DuToit, the grocer, had heard the commotion and rushed outside in his apron. Curry thrust the money toward him, pointing to the mess on the sidewalk. Mr. DuToit pushed the money back, ducked into the store and returned with a jug of milk and a fresh paper bag.

Curry returned the three bucks to me and we quickly had the groceries tucked back in the crooks of the old man's arms. He didn't even recognize us, and Curry didn't say anything.

When Sturgis made it to his friend's jeep, we settled back on our bench. Curry found another orange, but the jeep had already pulled

away. He sat down and turned it over in his hands, as if he were the
Creator of the universe admiring a new sun. Perhaps a world where
people's eyes didn't fail. Which reminded me: had Keeley Uncas tried
calling yet? This would be the time to get Curry and the Doc back
working together on a case.

"Hey Curry, there's brownies at my place." I didn't say they were
microwave brownies with the texture of sewage sludge.

"I'm not very hungry."

"Well, c'mon anyway."

Curry held the orange to his chest, like a portable McGillicuddy he
could pray to, then he put it in his pocket. His thick shoulders heaved
in a sigh. "Okay," he said, as if too tired to put me off. I guessed he
didn't want to go home and face the troubles there. He kick-started his
scooter, I threw a leg over my bike, and we rode up the hill. The
autumn air had reverted to its natural chill now that the sun had set. As
we approached my place, I recognized the shape of a V-dub bug at the
curb, and smiled. We met Keeley coming down from the front door.
She walked right past Curry to within a foot of my face and nearly
jammed a cassette tape up my nose. "This belongs to you, I think."

I pressed my lips together to keep from smiling, and took the tape.
The tape I'd recorded of Curry's reading out past Sturgis's place.
"What'd you think of it?"

Keeley's mouth became a thin-lipped line when she got mad. No
doubt she considered it a shabby trick for me to have put the tape in
her car stereo so her father would hear it. By her glare, I guessed he'd
listened not only to the part about Sturgis's eyes, but the whole thing.
The cosmic stuff. Perfecting yourself over many incarnations. The
three-fold nature of all things. The subconscious roots of diseases.

"Well?"

"Dad wants to see Curry again. Tonight."

As I did a fist-clench, Curry gave me a *why don't you mind your own
business?* glare, but it didn't ruin the moment for me. Mom hadn't
come home from the newspaper office so I left a note. I returned to
find Curry in the back seat and Keeley revving the engine. She dumped

the clutch when I still had one foot on the curb and we were off. It took a while for the clattery engine to push us to top speed, but by the time we hit the rolling hills, I had to fight the urge to grab the panic strap. I hoped Keeley's frustrations would get worked out by driving and it seemed like that's what happened. By the time she got off the paved road, she'd slowed to the speed limit. Then, turning up her driveway, we saw a harvest moon rising, and she slowed, and slowed some more, in fact, slowed until it seemed that only the swollen moon's gravity kept us moving. When she parked, I put a hand on her arm. It felt thin but hard as madrona. "Keeley, you can't stop your dad from wanting to heal people. He's a doctor."

"He can't heal people from a jail cell."

Curry piped up for the first time since we left my place. "Maybe it's like being in jail if a man can't do the job he was born to."

"Bullcorn!" Keeley said. "People aren't born to jobs."

"You'll find out someday." Curry gave me a peculiar look, as if surprised by his conviction.

"If that's so," Keeley said, "then what's *your* job?"

Staring at the moon, he answered, more to himself than to Keeley or me. "Maybe I'm about to find out."

Chapter 35
Under a Spell

*T*he Big McGillicuddy sprawled obesely beside the steps. Curry gave it a tender pat as if it were a loyal dog and not a pumpkin on steroids. Round orange things seemed to be the theme of the evening.

Doc Uncas held the door for us as if we were important, not a pair of pimple-pushing teen-agers. "Darwin," he said, squeezing my hand and looking me in the eye. "You hoist a fair bit of canvas to the wind, don't you."

I scrunched my brows, not quite sure of his drift. Without elaborating, Doc greeted Curry with a warmth that seemed almost suspicious. Inside, Doc poured some juice and spread his arm toward a plate of vegetables. "Fresh from the garden."

Curry and I sat on tall chairs at the breakfast bar, chowed a radish or two to be polite, then listened to Doc Uncas as he stood slightly hunched across the bar from us.

"You have some interesting thoughts about Sturgis and his eyes— the swami has, if you prefer—and I think I know why you arranged for me to listen to the tape. You thought maybe I'd be inclined to drop in on old Sturgis for a talk."

I glanced at Keeley, seated at the dining room table with opened schoolbooks, wiggling a pencil over her homework. She didn't look up. Curry said, "He's not likely to ever ask for help."

"I'll try to arrange it."

"Thanks," Curry said. "But what about..."

"Your sister?" Doc scratched his beard. "I know this has been hard on you, Curry, but I don't know how to make it easy. So I'll get right to the punch line. I can't help her."

I felt the world shifting beneath me, as if my equilibrium had gone haywire, and I gripped the edge of the bar. Curry closed his eyes for several seconds.

"It's not a straightforward case, and I haven't been able to figure it out."

Curry slumped. "There's nothing you can do?"

"Perhaps there's something *we* can do. You've diagnosed Clara Dozier and specified a thoroughly unconventional treatment. Now I've heard you suggest a treatment for Sturgis that intrigues me. One thing I don't understand: why haven't you tried helping your sister?"

The wind-up clock on the mantle ticked slowly. Curry cracked the knuckles of each finger, one by one, as if keeping a different kind of time. When he ran out of knuckles, he said, "What if I come up with a treatment, and Paprika dies? I couldn't live with it."

Doc leaned his forearms on the bar and answered firmly. "Yes you could. I know because I've been doing it for six years."

"The governor's daughter?" Curry asked.

Doc nodded. "I believed Molly was going to die anyway, so I tried something I learned from a Peruvian shaman. It didn't work, and I don't know why. But I couldn't have lived with myself if I hadn't tried. You wouldn't be able to either."

"Do you mean she's going to die?"

"I think so. Death has a certain feel to it."

I felt a metallic chill, as if my skin had turned to aluminum foil.

"Like a black mist?" Curry asked.

Doc's eyes opened wider. "You've seen it?"

Curry nodded.

"Then there's no time to waste, is there."

I went to the car for my drum while Curry accompanied Doc to the study. When I returned, Keeley pulled me into her bedroom and closed the door. Her domain was pathologically neat. No surprise. Shelves filled with books, not stuffed animals. Color coordinated curtains and quilt, heavy on plum and turquoise. What threw me were the colored-pencil drawings of bizarre creatures. Dozens of them like microbes in clown suits. "You do these?"

She didn't answer, just got in my face, hands on hips, her plum sweater making the most of her mosquito-bite figure. "Darwin, this has got to be the end of it."

A little radish burp came up and I blew it aside. "As if I have any control."

"Don't play games with me. I'm not stupid. You're behind this swami business, pushing it, steering it. Why? Because it makes you feel important? A big shot?"

It felt like a kick to the guts. I wanted to get mad, but didn't have the heart for it, and after what seemed like an endless silence, I said, "Is that any reason to let Paprika die?" I turned without waiting for her answer and hurried to Doc's study, where I found Curry getting comfortable in the big chair. I dimmed the lights and positioned myself on the floor, feeling clumsy and distracted from Keeley's accusation, and as I began drumming, I looked up and caught a reflection in the window of her standing behind me. I lost the groove and tried to find it again, tried to get synched with Curry's mantra, tried watching for his breathing to become shallow, tried to think how important this was, how it might change everything for Paprika and the Buckle clan. And how this *did* make me feel important. But Curry's eyes remained half-open. We tried a full five minutes before he finally blinked and sat up.

"It's no good," he said. "It's not happening."

I wondered if it was my fault, and wondered if Doc and Keeley were forming new doubts about Curry. Doc asked, "Would it help if Keeley and I left the room?"

"He's done it before with people watching," I said. "I don't understand...." Then I noticed Curry's feet.

"Your shoes!" I said with a laugh. "You forgot. You always take them off."

"I didn't forget." He eyeballed the Doc.

I laughed, remembering Doc's test. "I won't let him take the pliers to you. Now, let them dogs bark." I pulled his shoestrings and he flipped off his sneakers. I could smell the talc he always dusted his feet with.

To my surprise, Keeley stepped forward, knelt down beside Curry, and began massaging his feet. The more she rubbed, the more Curry melted into his nest of cushions.

"Mmm, can I have some of that later?" I asked her.

"You'll get what you deserve."

I couldn't read her tone, and the big-shot comment still ate at me, but I decided to hope for the best, and resumed drumming before Curry passed out from ten-toed bliss. This time, when his breath-heaves became shallow, his eyes turned up and his lids fluttered and closed. I turned to Doc and nodded. He scooted his chair closer.

"Swami," I said, "Doctor Uncas and his daughter are in the room. We want to ask about the illness of Curry's sister, Paprika Buckle."

A pause, as if the swami needed a moment to locate the patient, then his precise, resonant voice. *"Yes. You may proceed."*

I made a writing motion on my palm to Keeley. She grabbed a notebook and pen.

"We would like to understand what's wrong with her."

"Certain energies essential for assimilation are disrupted because of blockages in the physical and astral nervous systems. The liver is thus rendered ineffective, as certain proteins necessary for breaking down foods are not being synthesized. The condition is exacerbated by accumulated toxins produced by partial breakdown of certain molecules present in medications being administered. The underlying condition stems from a fall suffered while cheerleading. The automobile crash is an aggravating factor, but not the primary cause, as is presumed."

Doc and I exchanged surprised glances. I couldn't wait to tell Curry about the last comment. He'd been feeling so guilty about helping Paprika win the car.

"Please explain the astral nervous system," Doc said.

"All physical things, including the human body, have an astral counterpart, composed of energies too fine for most people to detect. Stubborn diseases can often be dislodged by changing the astral blueprint with the power of mind."

"Swami, how should the physical body of the patient be treated?"

"You will find a nodule between the twelfth and thirteenth vertebrae. This indicates a misalignment that must be cleared. Then twice daily treatments with Oil of Midnight administered by rubbing in the area of the liver, and ceasing all other medications."

"What is Oil of Midnight, for goodness sakes?" Doc asked.

"This is a formulation no longer in use containing a compound for which the present location was once well known—baritonin—derived from the skin of the blue toad."

Doc threw up his hands, his tone rising in frustration. "But there are no more blue toads."

"If the formulation were not available in this instance, it would not have been mentioned. You will find one bottle remaining on the shelves of Drack's Pharmacy."

I looked at Doc Uncas to see if he had any more questions. He told me to wait, then made a phone call.

"Drack? Wesley Uncas here. Sorry to bother you at home, but I need to get my hands on some Oil of Midnight. I understand you have a bottle of it?... Are you sure?... Yes, I know about the damn toads. Can you hold?" Doc covered the receiver. "Drack says he hasn't had any since before his father retired, thirty years ago."

I turned to Curry, confident he hadn't been wrong. "Swami, can you say exactly where the Oil of Midnight is located?"

He didn't hesitate. *"There is a storage room. On the top shelf on the south wall is a blue bottle coated with dust behind various tinctures and decoctions. The label has fallen off, but lays next to the bottle."*

"Drack," Doc said into the phone, "tell me, has Curry Buckle—or any of the Buckles for that matter—ever worked for you? No? Well, I need you to meet me at the pharmacy in fifteen minutes. Yes, it's urgent."

Doc Uncas stood and reached for his coat.

"You two go ahead," I said. "I'd like to bring Curry out of it slowly and explain what's happened."

Doc nodded. "Let's go, Keeley."

But when I heard the car chugging down the lane, I didn't wake Curry. Here was my chance to do something for Ms. Dozier. To raise money for the camp. To restore her will to live. My latest crazy scheme. I chewed on my lip for a while, then asked the question.

The *voice* answered without emotion, as if reciting a recipe, but it felt like a spear had been hurled through me. I managed to ask for an explanation and sat in shock for a long time afterward, trying to digest it. Trying to figure out how I could tell Curry. Or if I should.

Before I woke him, I instructed him to remember nothing of the session, although he never had anyway. He'd trusted me, and I'd explored a new subject without his permission. A subject he had specifically refused before. He blinked, rubbed his eyes, stretched. I couldn't look at him. "Where is everyone?" Then his tone rose with alarm. "It went badly?"

"No," I said, and turned back to him with a smile. "It went fine. Doc is out tracking down some Oil of Midnight."

"Oil of whozits?"

"Midnight. You've never heard of it?"

He shrugged. "Not a clue."

"Blue toads?"

He shook his head. "You're saying Doc can help Rika now?"

"Sounds like it."

"Whew! That's... that's... that's..."

"Awesome?" I suggested.

"Colossal!"

"Yeah, that works."

"It's astronomical!" he declared, his face a lamp of joy. "Tell me! Tell me everything!"

"Calm down and let's get something to eat and I'll tell you."

His tongue involuntarily wetted his lips.

We raided the kitchen. I didn't think Doc and Keeley would mind, under the circumstances. While carrying on about how infinitely wonderful things were, Curry made an avocado, peanut butter and tuna fish sandwich. I'd have to tell Troutigan—he could market them as swami sandwiches after Curry became famous. I settled for an apple.

As Curry crammed sandwich in his gob, I gave him a dump on what Swami Curryban had said about Paprika. When I got to the part about the injury starting with a cheerleading accident, he swallowed a mouthful without chewing and asked, "The car wreck didn't cause it?"

"She would have gotten sick anyway. Know what that means? Means Reverend Fern is hosed when he says there's a demon in you. If you ask me, Reverend Fern is trying his best to... I don't know... keep your soul bottled up."

Curry paused his attack on the swami sandwich. I put stuff back in the fridge while he thought things over. Finally he said, "It's still wrong to use my gift to win things."

"Maybe, but if what comes out of you is truth, how can it be evil?" Curry's exuberance had taken my mind off the other part of the reading, distracted my guilt, but now it flooded over me. I tried to think of anything else—Keeley in her plum sweater—fearful that Curry, in one of his unpredictable insights, might read my mind.

"It's all about how people use the information, I think," he said.

"If Paprika had donated the car to the raffle, like you suggested, then maybe something good would have happened, instead of something bad."

"Maybe. But what about the Swami Curryban routine? I wonder if Camp Bluetoad is a good enough cause? It's just a place for kids to have fun."

"People need fun," I said, raising my voice. "Ms. Dozier thinks Camp Bluetoad is important. In fact, Doc thinks it might kill her if she can't save the place." I had my reasons for bringing this up. Curry didn't disagree, and that would have to do for now.

We waited, each lost in private thought, until we heard an engine roaring up the drive. I watched from the window as Keeley spun the Bug in a ninety-degree drift so it stopped broadside to the house. This would save her the trouble of reversing next time out. I wondered what Doc thought of it, but he wasn't in the car. We collected our jackets and drum and rushed out.

Keeley's dark eyes flashed with excitement. "They found it, behind the other bottles, exactly like you said, Curry. Dad made Mr. Drack look twice, and when he found it, he slapped his forehead so hard, his hairpiece fell off." She giggled. "I left dad at your farm, Curry."

For a minute we stood with arms around each other's shoulders and studied the moon's engraved detail through our frosted breath. I felt a special magic pouring into me from that autumn moon, and when Keeley opened the car door for us, her Bug looked like The Big McGillicuddy transformed into a carriage by a spell.

Chapter 36
Casting Out Demons

"C'mon, dad needs us," Keeley said.

We piled in the car and she spun the wheels getting out of there. Then, to Curry in the back seat, she said, "Did you know that Reverend Fern is at your place?"

"He's been dropping by."

"Well this time he's brought company."

Neither Curry nor I asked for details. Other things to think about. For me, the other thing was the unauthorized part of the reading, and how I should play the new card I'd drawn. Keeley's focus locked into getting the most out of her clatterbox engine.

At the Buckle farm, we parked next to a van I didn't recognize, and joined Doc and Mr. Buckle standing by the porch stairs in the night air. An earnest-sounding hymn drifted from the house: soprano voices quavering around a bold male baritone. *How Sweet is God's Lamb*. It reminded me of my first meal at the Buckle table the night we couldn't wake Curry up.

"I fed your dogs and chickens for you," Mr. Buckle said, sounding miffed.

"Sorry," Curry said, then he saw the bottle in Doc's hand. "Is that the Oil of Midnight? Have you treated Rika yet?"

"Hmmm, it's a bit difficult. Complicated." The bug light on the porch deepened the grim lines on Doc's face. "By law I can't do anything that might be construed as treatment. Not being licensed, what have you."

"They're praying over her now," Mr. Buckle said.

Doc cleared his throat. "Particularly since Mrs. Buckle thought it would be best to get Dr. Slather over here. We're waiting."

The hymn crescendoed with someone trying to hit a harmony note and missing. "I'm going up," Curry said, and we all went into the house. At the same time, Mrs. Buckle, Reverend Fern, and a half-dozen of his faithful descended from the second floor. The reverend—a brisk, angular man wielding a sweat-stained Bible and an oversized gold cross on his chest—stopped to assess Curry with a twitchy frown.

"And here is young Curry Buckle—the other Buckle in need of the Lord's blessing. While the spirit is flowing, my brethren," he said in his pulpit voice, "we may as well cast out the demons troubling this boy. Gather around him and lay on your hands and let's send Satan a message he won't soon forget."

I got elbowed aside as the God Squad took their positions. As he was being surrounded, Curry looked to me. I could only shrug helplessly as his face disappeared in a pyre of hands.

"Oh Mighty Jay-sus, only son of God," the reverend intoned, "deliver this misguided child from the charms of Lucifer. Get thee out, Devil! Get thee behind me Satan! Get thee gone serpent of darkness!"

Then, as the bile had risen to my throat, and I'd looked anxiously from Mr. Buckle to Doc to Keeley thinking someone must put a stop to this, Curry somehow ducked through a gap in the circle and put a safe distance between him and his healers.

Curry turned on them, stood firmly, weight forward, and pointed a finger that froze Reverend Fern in mid-incantation. "You're not qualified to say what's evil. If there are any demons here," Curry said with an authority I'd never heard from him before, "you brought them with you!"

The reverend's jaw quivered and his eyes burned in their sockets. He clutched for the gold cross and held it out as far as its chain permitted. "Such stubborn evil I've not seen in a long, long time. I see we are casting good seed on barren soil here."

He muttered a few more pieties on his way out the door and consoled Mrs. Buckle who kept smoothing her dress in anguish. Curry silently ignored a number of cutting remarks from the faithful, and just kept staring at Reverend Fern until he and his followers were out the door. I wanted to give him a high five and a back slap, but before I could, in charged Dr. Slather on stout, bowed legs.

"Do you mind telling me--love of mud, anyway, all the commotion--what's this about a new treatment?"

"Oil of Midnight," Mr. Buckle offered.

"Oil of Snake," Dr. Slather muttered. She noticed the half-pint blue bottle Doc Uncas clutched to his chest and grabbed it from him. "There's not even a label on it." She unscrewed the lid and sniffed. "Whew!" She recoiled. "Like something crawled in there and died. I do not think... for pity sake. The only thing that's going to be treated with this goop is the septic system." She stomped toward the bathroom.

"Melanie, wait!" Doc Uncas pleaded.

"This is not the way we practice medicine in the twenty-first century."

"Melanie!"

Dr. Slather didn't pause her determined course to the bathroom, the blue bottle held at arm's length before her. The precious Oil of Midnight, possibly the only bottle in existence.

My path to cut her off had a recliner, an end table, two dogs, and Mrs. Buckle in the way. Curry headed there about the same time I did.

"Please Melanie!" Doc raised his hands to his head in panic.

One of the dogs spooked as I tried to hurdle it and I came down on its foot. It yelped and I rolled my ankle and fell. I looked up just as Dr. Slather upended the bottle over the toilet. Then Curry, covering ground with an efficiency I wouldn't have thought possible, grabbed Dr. Slather's elbow and wrested the blue bottle away from her. The potion, being syrupy thick had only partially been lost. He capped the bottle with his palm and backed out of the bathroom. I got back to my feet and looked around to make sure no one else was making a move for the potion.

Curry glared about, furrows converged above the bridge of his nose. To all of us between him and the staircase he ordered, "Get out of my way."

I stepped back as he passed, the force of his will pressing on me like a repelling magnet. Mrs. Buckle covered her gaping mouth and stepped back as well. Mr. Buckle held on to the knob at the end of the balustrade for balance. Curry seemed larger and I felt shaken to see my easy-going friend changed so much. And very proud.

As he climbed the stairs, Dr. Slather called out, "If you let that boy touch my patient... cripes."

Nobody made a move to stop Curry.

"Then I'm off the case. Do you hear? Can't be responsible."

Nobody begged her to stay.

"Uncas, don't think for one minute..." She shook a finger.

"He hasn't done anything," Keeley said, and put an arm around her dad's side.

Dr. Slather gave an angry backward look, then slammed the front door and was gone. Curry looked down at us from the top of the stairs. After we all breathed a few times, Doc reached into the breast pocket of his jacket. "I have some latex gloves."

Curry shook his head. "If this stuff harms her, then let it harm me too."

I looked for Doc's reaction. He gave me an amused smile. We all went upstairs. In the sickroom, Paprika lay as before, eyes half open but without recognition, gaunt, her skin pasty. Curry found a pill organizer on the nightstand, opened the lid and went to the window. I knew what he wanted of me without being asked and I raised the window. Then, before flinging the pills into the night, he stopped and gave a little laugh. "Guess I don't want to poison the chickens." He gave the box to me. "Take care of these, will you?"

I nodded, and spilled them out on a magazine.

Doc smiled with satisfaction, then turned back Paprika's blankets and hiked her pajama top to expose her abdomen. Curry poured Oil of Midnight into his palm, rubbed his hands together—a smell like rotted skunk cabbage—then slowly began massaging the oil into his sister's frail body, speaking to her, scolding her lovingly for getting sick, telling her about blue toads and baritonin, telling her the car accident hadn't caused the problem and asked if she'd remembered being dropped during a cheerleading routine. I held my breath and hoped.

Everyone did.

When he'd finished, Curry kissed her on the forehead. I curled the magazine and poured all the little pills into my jacket pocket so I could flush them down the toilet later. Curry asked Doc, "What about the spinal blockage?"

"We'll take her to Anacortes tomorrow for pictures and alignment."

Mr. Buckle said, "With all the prayers and healing we did tonight, I expect to see her snap out of it pretty quick."

"If she comes around," Doc answered, "It'll be more magic than medicine."

Chapter 37
The Hidey-Hole

I stayed up past eleven that night, hunched over my homework, not making much progress. I kept thinking about what I'd learned from the swami that evening. I finally went to bed, but lay awake for a long time.

The grinding alarm woke me. Though still dark outside, the clock insisted it was morning. As I sat on the edge of the bed, scratching my skull, my mind returned to the problem I'd been worrying about, and to my surprise, little elves had been cobbling away while I slept. Curry wasn't the only one who did good work with his eyes closed.

I got to school too late to find Curry, but we had second period together—geometry—so when the time came, I waited for him outside the classroom. Across the hall, one of Choker's toadies joined a huddle of guys. "Hey, smeggers, looks like the Choker made a clean getaway."

"Awesome!"

"Smegtacular!

"Where to?"

"Who knows? Didn't show at the homestead again last night."

"Maybe he struck it rich, like he said."

"He's off buying Harleys for all of us. Hyuk hyuk!"

I tuned them out when Curry showed. "We need to talk," I said. "How 'bout we cut this stumblebum class. Old Schwartzie moves at the speed of slobber. We can catch up easy."

Curry shrugged. "I didn't do my assignment anyway."

I liked this. Two weeks ago he wouldn't have dreamed of skipping class. Then I saw Schwartzie's thin, nearsighted face peer around the door. I quickly turned my back to him, hoping he hadn't overheard or recognized us, and led Curry away with that prickly feeling of being watched.

"How's Rika?" I asked.

"Doc Uncas stayed all night. He says it's going to take time."

"Did Doc tell your parents where he got the idea for the treatment?"

"I asked him not to."

"Why?"

"He's already got a problem if Dr. Slather reports him. If it gets out he's listening to a strange voice coming from a kid... you get the picture."

I couldn't argue that. "Curry, we need to visit your Aunt Iris. She's probably still at home, right?"

"She doesn't open the shop before the noon ferry. But why?"

"You need to trust me on this one, amigo."

He got worry wrinkles on his forehead. "I trust you, Dar... but I don't *trust* you. Know what I mean?"

"That's all I could ask for. We'll take your scooter."

Curry shouted over the motor as we zoomed through town, "Does this have something to do with Cyrus Twist's treasure?" I pretended not to hear, not knowing how he'd act if I told him.

Sun-cured leaves, six inches deep on Iris's lawn, smelled like butterscotch. We parked at the curb and waded through them under enormous fans of bare limbs. One of the stair treads had broken; we stepped over it, and I tried the doorbell.

"It's busted," Curry said, and he knocked.

I'd nibbled the excess off a fingernail while we waited for Iris to answer; even then, she looked through the porthole before opening up. She looked ready for work—dressed, made-up—but moved with a lethargic stoop as if expecting nothing good to come of the day.

"How's Paprika?"

"We're trying a different treatment," Curry said, not mentioning Doc Uncas.

Iris shrugged a bony shoulder and said, "Poor thing."

She didn't even ask why we'd come, so I started it off. "Iris, we were wondering if that reward offer is still good." She had an uncomprehending expression, so I added, "The ten-thousand dollars for solving Pansy's murder?"

That straightened her posture. Curry's jaw dropped and he stepped back as if to distance himself from the question.

"Well, I suppose it's still good." Her voice bristled with irritation. "But I don't expect to be paying it after all this time, what with Charlie Angostura having an alibi. I suspect whoever did it got clean away. What business is it of yours, young man?"

The *young man* comment seemed intended to put me in my place. I answered, "I notice you don't lock your door. Is that because you're not afraid?"

"Afraid?"

"That the murderer might come back."

"Nobody locks their doors on the island. What are you getting at?"

"I happen to know the murderer has not gotten clean away," I said. "In fact, you'll be needing your checkbook."

"What!" Both Curry and Iris said it simultaneously.

"I don't appreciate you boys joking about this," she said to Curry.

He turned up his palms. "I don't have a clue..."

I tried to look confident, but my insides were wound tight as a golf ball. "I'm not joking. We'll be wanting a check from you this morning." I leaned forward and whispered something to her.

Iris's expression turned to bitter amusement. "Ha! So young Sherlock has it figured out, does he?"

I felt sorry for her, and even sorrier for Curry. As they both stared at me, I wondered if Curry would ever speak to me again. But I'd already decided. Saving Camp Bluetoad might make the difference in whether Ms. Dozier lived or died, and the reward could save the camp. "If you'll sit down, I'll explain. Over here, by the fireplace." Reluctantly, they humored me. I leaned against the stone mantle. The morning fire had died down, but the embers still threw a comforting heat. I felt both cold and sweaty at the same time. "Now, is there anything you'd like to tell us?" I looked directly at Iris.

"Get on with it—you're wasting my time."

"If that's how you want it." I pushed up my sleeve, crouched, and reached up the flue, searching for some kind of nook, the nook Swami Curryban had described. I remembered how Iris had stopped Curry from reaching in there the night we'd blacked our faces. I didn't have to grope long to find a ledge in the brickwork. I ran my hand the length of it until finding something hard and angular. I gripped it carefully and withdrew it from its hidey-hole, heavy and warm. When I turned, Iris had buried her face in her hands, and her shoulders heaved with sobs.

Curry's mouth gaped as he recognized the object in my hand. A family heirloom, of sorts, passed down from his great-uncle Cyrus Twist.

A gun.

Chapter 38
Confessions

I set it on the mantelpiece, taking care to point it away. Curry rose halfway from his chair, sat back again, and began hyperventilating. Iris sat expressionless. I had a falling feeling, like circling down a drain. Curry's look of confusion changed as the pieces fell into place for him. His jaw moved back and forth as if working out a kink. And the kink was me. How could I have known about the gun, if not from his own sleeping voice? I hoped he'd understand I'd done it for the sake of Ms. Dozier. Saving the camp could be her lifeline, though I never dreamed that Aunt Iris would be the price of it. Curry may not have traded the one for the other, had I consulted him; but I had no qualms about deciding the world needed Ms. Dozier's defiance of Mr. Krogstrand, and her fight-to-the-death battle for a cause she believed in, more than the world needed a sister-killer. If it cost me my friendship with Curry... I didn't want to think about it. I just felt heartsick for both of them.

Overnight, I'd played the scene dozens of times in my mind, with different endings. None of the scenarios matched what really happened. Aunt Iris stirred at last, gave a good blow into her hanky, took a deep breath, and held her palms out to me. Their witch-like boniness unnerved me; still I couldn't refuse them, and when I advanced she gathered my hands and kissed them.

"You can't know what it's like to have a burden like this on your soul," she said, her voice breaking. "Every day, a living hell, just getting through it. The dread—oh my Lord the dread!—of someone seeing the truth in my eyes. It's such a relief to have it over."

"What's over, Aunt Iris?" Curry didn't want to believe it. "You didn't... you couldn't have..."

Iris gave Curry a look of pity. Her first glimpse of the family pain to come.

"You might as well get it all off your chest," I said, wanting Curry to have no doubt of the truth.

She nodded, released my hands and dabbed at her eyes. Tears had already tracked through the powder on her cheeks.

"It started with Bumpy Hornseth's funeral."

I recalled the two spinsters, Iris and Pansy, arguing the day I first met them about going to the service.

Iris's face changed as she thought back, becoming rigid and angry. "I thought I'd be big hearted and give the widow Hornseth a pat on the back, though I haven't talked with the woman for forty years. And what does she say? 'Bumpy and I had a wonderful life together. And, in a way, Iris,' she says, 'we owe it all to you.' And I say, 'Oh, whatever do you mean by that?' and she says, 'Well, you turned him down, didn't you,' and I say, 'I did no such thing,' and she says 'Well of course you did. In your letter.'"

Iris clasped a hand to her breast, and tried to go on but the words stuck in her throat. Curry and I waited. When the swami told me the gist of it, he'd sounded so detached; but with Iris unfolding the tragedy fresh from her recollection, it shredded my heart.

"I'm getting emotional all over again. 'What letter?' I ask. 'Why, the letter you sent to Bumpy telling him you weren't interested in his attentions anymore, and that you could never marry a man who always smelled of fish.' Well, this floors me, I can tell you. 'What!' I say. 'I wrote no such letter.' The widow gets this flummoxed look on her kisser and says, 'You may have lived to regret it, Iris Twist, but you sure as heavens wrote it, because he showed me and I kept it. Why? Because it was the greatest stroke of fortune that ever blessed my life. You see, Bumpy proposed to me the very next day after he received it. And I never figured to be anyone's first choice, and the Bible says the last will be first, so I took this letter as a sign from the Almighty and kept it.'"

Iris looked back and forth between Curry and me, pleading with her eyes for us to understand.

"That's when I had the first inkling of what happened, though I could barely make myself think it, much less believe it. 'I want to see that letter,' I say and the widow Hornseth says 'That's no trouble at all because it's been tucked in our Bible all these years, and fell out during the service, and it's here in my purse.' And she's got this purse the size of a half-grown halibut and out comes this letter and I read it and I know the handwriting the minute I clap eyes on it because I've been looking at it for sixty years and more."

Iris sprung to her feet and paced. When she talked, it wasn't to Curry and me. It sounded more like a reliving of what had happened next.

"I took that letter with me. Oh, the widow didn't want to part with it, but I snatched it out of her hands, and I went home and read it over and over and got madder until I thought my spleen would pop."

Even then the purple veins in her temple looked like they could go at any time. She reached into her blouse and pulled out a small envelope. As she scrabbled at the envelope to get out the letter, her eyes glazed with tears, and I suspect she read it aloud more from memory than sight:

> "I fear, Bumpy, we are constitutionally ill-suited for each other, for you want nothing more than to be a fisherman, and I must confess my dislike—no, my abhorrence—for the smell of fish. Although I am flattered by your proposal of marriage, and will be forever fond of you, I prefer to do it from a distance. You would do well to shift your proposal to one of your other admirers at the earliest time, as my decision is final.
>
> Yours truly,
> Iris"

Iris clutched at the page so fiercely I thought her nails would perforate it.

Curry slouched into his chair, hands tucked in his armpits. At that moment, if I could have turned back the clock and restored the gun to the flue, I would have.

"I read the letter over and over and saw Pansy's selfishness in every word, and thought about how she always got her way. The merchandise, the prices, everything. Then to find out she'd stolen my life away. Nobody would marry her, the toad, so she made sure I'd keep her company. What she did was unforgivable, and I couldn't forgive her."

Iris stared blankly and panted as if she'd lost her train of thought, then said, "We didn't always see eye-to-eye, but we loved each other, or so I thought until I read this monstrous forgery, and then I hated her so bitterly that I... I... I couldn't breathe."

"How did you arrange it?" I asked. I could scarcely breathe either.

A false smile jerked across her face. "I didn't, really. But I wouldn't speak to her that afternoon at the shop and she wanted to go home, so I drove her, and then confronted her with the letter. She tried to laugh it off as a harmless prank. 'Water under the bridge,' she says." Iris shook her head sadly. "The next thing I remember was a terrible loud sound and the awful smoke, and I had Uncle Cyrus's gun in my hands, and Pansy was sitting on the floor right there." She pointed at my feet.

I stepped backward and felt a shiver of revulsion travel up my legs to my groin.

Looking at the place on the floor, Iris continued, "Pansy just looks at me and says, 'You hurt me. You hurt me bad.' And then... "

Iris collapsed in her armchair and wept bitterly. Curry started to go to her, but again something held him back. Then, abruptly, Iris sat erect, wiped her eyes, and said, "Well, it's over now, and I'm glad of it. There's no joy left in this life. All used up. Spoiled. I only wish Bumpy could have known how I really felt, and it grieves me he went to his grave thinking I refused him."

We heard rough steps on the porch, a firm knock.

Curry sprung to the window and pulled the curtain aside. "It's Sheriff Biggs."

"So you called him in advance did you?" Iris appraised me with a look, and gave a small nod of approval. "Let him in and I'll sign a confession."

"But we didn't call..." Curry started, then looked at me for confirmation. I shrugged and shook my head.

"Iris," the sheriff called, and he rapped again.

As Curry opened up, I looked for the gun on the mantle, and without really knowing why, moved a framed picture in front of it. Sheriff Biggs swaggered in, towing his deputy—and Dan Klatt.

The Sheriff hitched up his belt, heavy with cop paraphernalia. As he was rounder in the middle than at the hips, a good sneeze might bring the whole works down around his ankles. "Iris, we're looking for Billy Durant—Choker Durant, they call him. Our star running back thinks his cousin went into a tunnel on your property and didn't come out."

"Oh my!" Iris fanned herself with a skeletal hand. "You mean you're not here to arrest me?"

"No joke, Iris."

She looked stunned, but I breathed easier.

Sheriff turned to Dan Klatt. "Now, Danny, where'd you say that tunnel was?"

"Around back, in the shed. Follow me." Klatt thumped a fist on his sternum as if taking a hand-off, and he headed for the door. The deputy followed.

"Reel yourselves in, boys," the sheriff said. "I'm going to ask these people if any of them have been down in that hole. Maybe they can save us some time."

"I can draw you a map," I offered as Iris lowered herself into a rocker.

"Well now," the sheriff said, crossing his arms. "That's what good police work will do for you. You're Conrad Bownes' son, aren't you?"

I nodded.

"You've been in that hole then?"

"Yessir. But I don't see how Choker could know about it. Curry and I didn't tell anyone."

"Well let's see: Danny Klatt here knows about it. And he heard about it from his cousin Choker. What does that tell you?"

Then I remembered the feeling of being watched the night we found the tunnel entrance.

Curry turned to Iris. "Dan and Choker were the ones helping Charlie Angostura dig the holes."

Dan Klatt tilted his head like a parrot trying to work out how we knew. Sheriff Biggs looked interested too.

Curry said, "The picture I took of Charlie had Dan in the background. And we found Choker's footprint. They were digging for Cyrus Twist's treasure."

Dan Klatt's eyes, usually narrow and brooding, opened wide at Curry. "That's nuts! What are you trying to do, cost me my scholarship? My whole life has been screwed up since you started hanging with this clown." Klatt pointed at me with such force that I felt pain in advance.

"What are you talking about?" the sheriff demanded.

"Curry won that car for his sister, who happens to be my girl, who happened to wreck the car and might die. Then Curry looked into my future and said I'd be disfigured by a deep fat fryer, and now Choker's lost in a tunnel and it's the same two little dorkheads involved."

"Calm down Danny. We'll find him."

Curry, standing beside me, raised his hand. "I need to say something."

"We've got a missing boy out there," Sheriff Biggs said.

"It's important." Curry worked at a knuckle until it cracked. "I owe Dan an apology. Dan, when we gave you the reading about your future, well, I... um... I made it all up."

I closed my eyes and shook my head with exasperation at Curry. It took Klatt a few seconds to get it, as if translating the words from a foreign language. Then he began to redden like a hammered thumb. In a microsecond he covered the ground to Curry and collared him.

"You lying little maggot, I'm going to cut you into crab bait."

I would have been glad to help. Whether bothered by his conscience, or inspired by his Aunt Iris's confession, I didn't know—or care. I jumped back when Klatt grabbed for me with his free hand, as I had the distinct impression he intended to bang our dork-heads together. "You too, cretin!" He jabbed a finger at me. "You just wait and see who gets disfigured."

The sheriff hiked his belt and roared, "If it's not too inconvenient, we've got a search and rescue operation underway."

Glad for the diversion, I went to Iris's roll-top desk and sketched out the tunnels, showing the left shaft branching until blocked by water, the main shaft caved in, and the right shaft extending for an unknown distance. I didn't want to admit reaching the hub of tunnels where the mummified body of Buster Henry's wife lay. It might be against the law not to report a corpse. I also omitted the part about the markings chiseled by Cyrus Twist on the wall.

"Let's go," the sheriff said, and Dan led the way.

When they'd gone, I asked Curry, "Are you trying to get us massacred?"

"I had to tell him, Dar. It was tearing him apart. What if a person attracts what they're afraid of?"

"What, like a self-fulfilling prophecy?"

"Yeah. And look how Aunt Pansy's lie turned out—the forged letter."

I looked around for Iris, and found her hunched over the writing desk.

"What are we going to do about her?" Curry whispered.

"You're the one with the hyperactive conscience. You tell me." I had a thought, but wanted to test Curry on this one.

"The law's the law, I suppose," he said, after agonizing for a while.

"Curry," I barked. "A headless chicken has more common sense than you do."

"What do you mean?"

"Can't you understand why Iris did what she did?"

"Of course—kind of."

"Is she likely to shoot anyone else?"

"...Nooo."

"Do you think she's going to feel any worse about it if she's locked up?"

"I doubt it."

"Then what's the point of dragging the family through a trial, and depriving your mom of her last sister?"

Curry stared blankly. It had to be his decision. I wasn't going to be part of a cover-up, then have his conscience start bothering him next month and make a clean breast of it. Before we could finish, Iris rejoined us.

She folded a piece of paper and tucked it into my shirt pocket, turned, looked over the family photos on the buffet, and smoothed the lap wrinkles on her skirt. "What happens next?" she asked, voice trembling.

I looked at Curry.

He stepped over to the mantle, uncovered the pistol, but couldn't bring himself to touch it. "For now, Auntie," he said, "why don't you put this old gun of Cyrus's back up the chimney."

Chapter 39
Fear of the Dark

Curry and I left Iris to her private hell. We nosed around to the tool shed, watched the searchers descend into the tunnel, and sat cross-legged to wait for their return. Curry plucked thatch from the lawn and released it to the wind. Without looking at me, he accused, "You asked about Pansy's murder during one of the readings."

"At Doc's house," I admitted, "when you did Paprika."

"But I told you..."

I felt a jab in my heart. "I know."

"Then why? For the money, I suppose. Why is money such a big deal to people?"

I took the check from my pocket and handed it to Curry.

He looked at it. "Ten thousand dollars."

"Yup."

His brows knitted. "Payable to... Camp Bluetoad Foundation?" He looked at me with surprise. "That's what you whispered to Aunt Iris when you told her to make out a check."

"Doc Uncas thinks that saving Camp Bluetoad might make the difference for Ms. Dozier—whether she lives or dies. But I won't give her the check until you decide about Iris. She might need the money for a lawyer. I swear, Curry, I never guessed it would turn out to be Iris." I plucked a blade of dry grass and bit it. "But, you know, she'd have gone nuts if she hadn't told someone."

Curry polished his glasses with his shirttail—his way of not looking at me.

"I should have asked you first," I said. "I figured the swami thing was a partnership, and we could each have a say in how to use it, and we don't always see eye-to-eye, and... and I'm sorry. It's your gift and you have the right to decide. I just... I'm sorry, that's all."

Curry sat still as a garden Buddha. I thought maybe I should leave, but then he said, "It is, Dar."

I waited for more, but he made me ask. "Is *what?*"

"A partnership."

"Yeah?" I said, the tightness in my chest loosening.

"I hadn't thought of it before. There's so much to think about... everything changing, getting complicated. But one thing feels solid. I've never had someone totally on my side before. Know what I mean? Sometimes I can't trust you, but I always feel like you're on my side."

"Yeah," I said. Curry's eyes looked ready to water the grass, but I felt like laughing.

"Sorry I spilled my guts to Dan without asking you," he said.

Then I did laugh. "When he's done disfiguring us, we'll be the ugliest dorkhead partnership in history."

He laughed too, then said, "I want to help find Choker."

"Help that duck-lipped moron? What for? If he rotted down there, the world would be a better place."

Curry sighed. "Here we go again. I can't explain it, Dar, but I just had this feeling... that even if people don't get along, somehow we're all... tied together, in the big picture."

"That's not the way Choker sees it."

"It's how we see it that matters."

"All right, all right. You're the conscience of this outfit."

Curry began untying his shoes. I didn't have my drum, but found a galvanized tub in the shed that I could get respectable sound out of, and right there on the lawn, with birds chirping and crickets cricketing, I drummed him into his meditative trance.

"Swami," I said, "can you describe the present whereabouts of Billy Durant, otherwise known as Choker?"

Curry lay still for about fifteen seconds, then came the swami's precise voice, which, as always, made my spine tingle. *The subject is presently lying in a limestone cave one-hundred and sixty yards west of southwest from the present position, and some twenty yards beneath the earth's surface.*

From the mapping Curry and I had done, this probably meant the flooded shaft. "What is his condition?"

"He is in abject darkness, of body, mind, and soul."

"But he's alive?"

"There is no alternative to being alive. But yes, his physical form is not badly injured, other than by hunger, cold and fright."

"How can we rescue him?"

"The passage to the chamber in which he lies trapped is flooded with tidewater. By chance, he passed through at an extreme low tide some forty-two hours ago, and became trapped by falling rock, and was thus unable to retreat during subsequent low tides."

"When will the tide be low enough to go after him?"

"It will be yet eight hours before one could pass with safety. However, the subject is nearing the breaking point of hysteria, a crisis which may render him emotionally sterile if he remains for that additional time."

I thought for a moment. "Swami, how far would a person have to swim underwater to reach Choker?"

"Twelve yards, but as the tide floods, the distance becomes greater with each passing minute."

The idea of someone taking risks for Choker still bothered me. "Can you explain why Choker is so mean to people?"

A pause. *"There is a long history of this behavior. He became habituated to such in prior incarnations, but had made progress in the life immediately prior to this one, and showed early promise, in his present life, of further advancement; however, during his sixth year, after viewing a television drama depicting an execution by hanging, he and his brother invented just such a fantasy, which led to tragedy."*

My breath felt punched out of me. I didn't want to believe it. "You mean Choker hung his brother?"

"Yes. Their father had impressed on them that the violence in the film was not real, and that the 'dead' actors walked away when the movie was over."

"Oh man."

"The parents held their son to blame. Billy overheard them telling a relative that he was on a fast track to the penitentiary. Thus he became convinced of this, and fell easily into the ruts of negative behavior he had cultivated in past lives."

I sat for two or three minutes, watching the faintest signs of breath in Curry's chest. I wondered if someone else had tagged Choker with his nickname, or if he'd invented it for himself. Then I asked one more question. "Is there any hope that Choker will change for the better?"

"Everyone must evolve spiritually; it is only a matter of time before a person understands that negative behavior extinguishes joy; however, there is no predicting what trauma is necessary to awaken the desire for change."

In a way, then, is this happening to Choker because of how he's treated other people? Like payback?

"Every person's circumstances are the sum total of their own choices in this and prior lifetimes."

I took that as a yes, thanked the swami, then woke Curry. When I gave him a report, he shook his head. "There's that reincarnation stuff again.."

"So life is weird," I said. "But maybe it's fair after all. What do we do about Choker?"

Curry just looked at me as if it were my move.

I spit out the blade of grass I'd been gnawing, and said, "That's what I was afraid of. Let's find a flashlight."

But before we could act, Sheriff Biggs, his deputy, and Dan Klatt emerged from the shaft. "We need a complete search and rescue operation," the sheriff said. "There're too many tunnels. Danny, you man the hole in case the victim finds his own way out. Deputy and I are going to round up the S & R team."

"Ah, Sheriff," I said. "Curry and I think we know where Choker is."

He shifted his weight onto one leg, his leather gadget belt creaked. "If you knew, why didn't you say so a half-hour ago?"

"We just figured it out. I'll show you on my map." I pointed out where I understood the dry chamber to be, past the flooded tunnel.

"And just how do you figure he got in there?"

"It's salt water. The level goes down when the tide ebbs."

"We know that," Sheriff Biggs said, getting a little tense. "What I want to know is how *you* know where Choker went."

"Um, Curry has ways of knowing things."

Dan Klatt said, "He thinks he's psychic, but he's just a fraudulent little maggot."

The sheriff looked Curry over, then said to Dan, "I swear that little girlfriend of yours is the only worthwhile thing ever to come off the Buckle farm, aside from giant punkins." Turning to Curry and me, he said, "You boys just cost us valuable time when we're trying to save a life."

"Are you going to bring a diver?" I asked.

"I'll get a diver if I think we need a diver, and right now I don't think we need a diver." His glare challenged me to disagree.

I kept my mouth shut. When the sheriff and deputy left, I went up to Klatt. He had one of the sheriff's powerful flashlights, the kind sealed against water. "I need that light."

He smacked the fat end of it into his palm. "I ought to brain you with it, cretin."

His threat lacked testosterone. He seemed truly worried, and maybe felt responsible for getting Choker mixed up in the treasure hunt. It occurred to me that maybe Klatt, after Curry told him he'd be flipping burgers for a living, had schemed with Choker to go after the treasure themselves. Ace out Angostura and Krogstrand.

"Look, we really do know where he is."

Klatt sneered. "Don't expect me to fall for that swami dorkhead crap."

I shrugged at Curry. "I s'pose Choker can stay in that dark cold hole another day or so. Hungry and alone. Out of his mind with fear. Couldn't happen to a more deserving guy. But, Curry, if you want to be the Good Samaritan, we could go down and shine our wimpy little flashlight on the water, and maybe Choker would see it and at least know someone's looking for him. It's not much, but it might keep him from going stark-raving batty."

Curry nodded. We headed for the tool shed.

"Nobody goes in that hole without my say-so," Klatt said.

"Fine!" I said, and sat down.

Curry, hands on hips, said, "I want you to try something, Dan. Go down there, turn off your flashlight for ten minutes, and think about Choker being trapped in the total darkness for almost two days."

Klatt beat his palm with the flashlight a few more times, then said, "You stay put while I call Sheriff Biggs." He headed for the house.

I got up. "Let's go."

Curry descended the ladder first. I grabbed a bundle of clothesline cord from the shed and followed. When I'd reached bottom, Klatt called out.

"Bownes."

I looked up.

"Catch."

He dropped the flashlight down the shaft and I caught it.

Chapter 40

Trapped

*I*n ten minutes we reached the flooded section of the tunnel. The water looked inky and bottomless. It had been rising for nearly a half-hour since the *voice* had measured the underwater distance at twelve yards—thirty-six feet—and during the minute we stood shining our lights on the water, it crept visibly toward our toes. I guessed the distance to now be fifty feet or so.

"I used to swim underwater the whole length of a swimming pool," I said, trying to bolster my nerves.

"But that was warmer." Curry stooped to dip a finger. "Holy pig-snouts! It ain't bath water."

"Nope."

"And you had the side of the pool to push off against."

"Yep."

"And if a person *were* to swim fifty feet underwater, and still couldn't come up, he'd have to turn around and swim back again. All on the same breath."

"Good point."

Curry scuffed at the rock underfoot. "I don't swim very well."

"I kinda expected that."

"I mean, I float fine. But I can't stay underwater."

"Mm," I said, and felt the water for myself. Refrigerator cold.

"I did find him, didn't I?" Curry said. "Does that count for my end of the partnership?"

"Don't sweat it," I said, a little too sharply. My nerves were getting jumpy. "If anyone goes, it'll be me."

"Too bad Sqyrl Marx isn't here."

"Well, she isn't."

"If Choker's already gone off his nut, he could be dangerous."

I imagined Choker in a violent frenzy. If he went off on me, there'd be no one to help.

"We should have made some sandwiches," Curry murmured.

"Jeez, Curry."

"I mean, if you get Choker out, he'll be starving."

"Right. Okay, I'm going." I stripped off my jacket and flannel shirt, shoes and socks. "Take one end of this cord. If I give two strong tugs, then you pull. If it happens in the next minute, it means I'm drowning. Three quick tugs means I made it." I didn't want to think about it anymore, because I was already on the verge of wimping out. But I needed to prove that *I* had something special to contribute to our partnership. I waded in to my knees, unwinding cord from the bundle, wincing at sharp rocks under my feet. The stone walls around me looked like the belly of a whale, and it reminded me of Curry's dream, the one where I'd cut an impossible hole so Curry could escape.

Curry shone the light as I tied the cord around my waist. I waded deeper, my shadow looming grotesque on the tunnel wall. "Wish I had goggles." When the icy water wicked into my crotch, the shock made my breath suck in. So, instead of getting wet a centimeter at a time, I ducked my head to get it over with, and shot up with an echoing hoot. "Dang, that'll curl your nose hairs!" My heart raced and my breath came in gasps. But the longer I stood there, the more body heat would drain away, so I said, "Give me the light." I wanted both hands free to swim, so I tucked the flashlight into my belt, took three deep breaths, and dove, arching my back for depth. I kept my eyes closed for two strokes to get beyond the silt I'd stirred up. Against natural instinct, I forced my eyes open, but couldn't see much. I stroked, thinking if I made it to a count of twenty strokes without reaching the other side, I'd turn around and tug on the line. With each thrust I told myself the *voice* had never been wrong.

Then something conked me on the head and I groaned out some of my air. I'd risen and banged into the ceiling of the tunnel. My scalp stung, and it cost me two strokes to adjust my angle downward. Sometimes the flashlight tucked in my waistband gave me a narrow glimpse of the tunnel; mostly it shone up my nose and lit specks of stuff floating before my eyes. I realized the flashlight's added flotation made it difficult to stay under, and try as I might, I again rose and scraped my shoulder and banged my heel on the rock. Though I'd held my breath much longer in the swimming pool, the cold and the fear burned through my air by the time I'd gone fifteen strokes, and tentacles of panic seized my mind. What if the tunnel doesn't go back up? Is Choker worth it?

I reached for the line to signal Curry to pull me out.

Then something bizarre happened. It may have been my oxygen-starved imagination, but I don't think so.

I heard the *voice*!

Just as if coming from Curry's mouth, except it came from inside my brain. "*Do you trust me?*"

For a moment, I stopped thrashing. In what may have been a single second, thought after thought cascaded through my mind, and I realized this was not only about Choker. It was about me. Was I worthy? Worthy of what?

"*Do you trust me?*"

Was the *voice* calling me to my death? Or testing me. If I turned back, then it's all over. What's over? My partnership with Curry and the swami. What does it mean to trust? Everything. Trusting there were but a few yards to go, that the depleted air in my lungs would be enough. Trusting I wasn't alone.

In that endless second, some part of me, more powerful than fear, more powerful than logic, made a decision. I continued on. Continued with new strength, as if going to my own rescue.

The tunnel seemed never ending, but I seemed to be watching myself from outside my body. Twenty strokes. Twenty-five. Then fear-tentacles started growing back, and each stroke became more desperate, less efficient. Thirty. The harder I kicked, the slower the specks went by. Surely a minute had elapsed and Curry would begin pulling me back and I wouldn't be able to return without passing out and inhaling salty death. I clawed furiously at the water.

I didn't realize I'd cleared the flooded passage until my toes began slapping the surface. With joy, I powered my head up, purged the stale air from my lungs, heard my own panicky gasps reverberating in the void.

I found footing and stood chest-deep, pressed stinging water from my eyes, and pulled the light from my pants. The tunnel sloped up and I waded to dry ground. "Choker," I called, and played my light around the chamber. A natural cave—not a manmade tunnel. It looked like a dead end.

"Help?" said a voice, small and muffled.

"Choker?"

"Help me." I couldn't tell where the plea came from because of the echoes.

"Keep talking Choker. I'll find you." I untied the cord from my waist, gave three sharp tugs, and lashed it on a knob of rock.

"Dan, is that you? I'm up here. Trapped. Get me out."

The beam of my light revealed a rock chamber size of a cellar. The air, which had tasted sweet at first breath, seemed increasingly foul. As Choker kept it up, I followed his voice, puzzled that I couldn't see him.

"Up here."

I found a dark ledge above eye level and scrambled up. Though numb from cold, my bare toes still ached when I stubbed them on the stone.

"Hurry. And don't make any more rocks fall."

I scrambled to the ledge and shined my light into a low, flat hollow propped with a forest of stubby timbers.

"Ah! My eyes!"

Choker draped a forearm across his eyes. They hadn't registered a single photon of light for two days. He shouted in a raw voice, "Danny, what took you so smeggin' long? I could have died and rotted."

"It's not Danny," I said, examining a rockfall that had his leg pinned. Near him lay a flashlight with cracked lens. "It's Darwin."

"Who? Just get me out of here." Then he began sobbing convulsively.

I hesitated, then put a hand under his ear where it rested on the stone. He grasped my arm like a lifeline. It felt like some of the strength that flowed into me when hearing the *voice* now flowed into him, and the shaking subsided.

"What happened, Choker? Cave in?"

"Ha ha. These stupid posts were too close together—couldn't get through—so I had to kick one out—these freaking rocks came down."

"Dang it, Choker, you reek. Have a little accident?" Choker averted his eyes in embarrassment, and I felt bad for rubbing his nose in it.

"Leg busted?"

"It hurts bad. Get me out."

Cyrus Twist. He'd built some kind of a trap to protect his treasure. I remembered the reading Curry had done in Krogstrand's office, about the diamonds being flooded, warning of danger. Cyrus had a love of complex mechanical things. I figured he'd booby-trapped the hiding place for his gems. As Choker had said, the timbers holding up the two-foot ceiling were spaced too closely for a person to wriggle through. Cyrus would know just which supports could be removed safely. The others would trigger another rockfall or some other calamity.

I snaked headfirst around a post to get a look at the rocks heaped on Choker's leg. He'd been able to roll several away, but, because of the awkwardness of his position, couldn't reach the big ones that clamped his ankle down. I couldn't either because of the other timbers.

"One of these posts has to go, or I can't help you," I said.

"No! It'll cave in!"

"Not if I pick the right one."

"You'll kill me. Just pull me out of here."

"You're stuck tight. Let me check things out." I examined each of three possible posts, and found a clue—a scrape mark on the cave floor where one post had been jammed upright. All the posts were tightly lodged, some undoubtedly bearing the weight of loose boulders, like those that had caved in on Choker. But hadn't Cyrus

Twist made periodic trips to Seattle to refresh his bank account? He must have stashed his gems where he alone could get to them and sell them when needed. If the stash lay beyond this booby-trapped passage, then some of the timbers must be removable, jammed in to make them appear to be holding things up. But if a post had been repeatedly removed, it might leave a scrape mark.

"I'm going to knock this baby out," I said, positioning myself.

"No! Just get me out of here, you pinhead. Where's Danny?"

"Here we go!" I drew back my leg, feeling my muscles quivering from the cold, not sure of my choice but anxious to get out of this stone sarcophagus, and drove a piston-like kick at the base of the post, hoping I could scramble fast enough to avoid the booby-trap cave-in if I'd chosen wrong.

The post dislodged—and clumped harmlessly to the ground. My bare heel ached with the bruising blow, but I heard no sounds of releasing stress in the tunnel; only Choker's whimpering.

With room to work, I squirmed in headfirst to examine the overhead cavity that had puked boulders on Choker's leg. Satisfied there were no more rocks poised to fall, I began clearing the rubble from Choker's ankle, taking care not to bump any standing timbers. Using his six-battery flashlight as a lever, I had his leg free in about ten minutes. Then I pulled him out to the ledge by the armpits, where he babied his battered ankle. It didn't seem to be broken

"Gimme a drink." Choker's voice had an edge of animal wildness.

"I don't have any water." I checked for the clothesline cord, fearing Curry had become impatient and yanked it free, and felt a rush of panic when I couldn't see it. Then I realized the rising water had covered it. "We need to get going, Choker. The tide's still coming in."

"It's flooded."

"Yeah, and it's not going to be unflooded for quite a while. If you want to get warm and get fed and get something to drink, we need to go."

"Can't swim!"

I'd noticed that about island kids: surrounded by water, too many of them didn't know how to swim. Sqyrl Marx being the exception. "It's not far, and there's a rope with Curry on the other side to pull you through."

"No! Just get me out of here! Danny, where are you?"

I helped him down from the ledge, thinking some cold water might clear his mind. I waded in to retrieve the cord and returned to Choker. "Why don't you lose those pants—I don't think you'll be wanting them anymore."

I turned my back and tied a slipknot loop, while he did as I suggested, but when I tried to slip the loop around his wrist, he pulled away—as if it were a noose. "What are you doing? Trying to drown me, you dumb smeg?"

"I didn't drown, did I? It's only a few feet. Any candyass can do it." The cheap shot to his manhood seemed to do the trick, and leaning heavily against me, he hobbled down the sloped tunnel, into the water. He stooped for a drink; I chopped him across the wrists as he raised cupped hands to his mouth. "It'll make you sick."

He bared his teeth like a cornered animal, then reached out swiftly and tightened his strong hand at the pinch points of my neck. "What are you up to? Trying to get rid of me."

Fear had reduced him to a near animal. Afraid of what he might do, I twisted free. "I'm not hunting for the treasure, if that's what you think."

"Yeah? Well, maybe that's what I think."

"After seeing what happened to you? Get real."

"How'd you know about the treasure?"

"I know everything about it." Without thinking, I added. "Everything about you, too—Billy Durant."

He lost his balance and grappled me to stay upright. Enough light reflected off the limestone for me to see his rapidly changing expressions—his face tensing, bulging, quivering—leaving me jumpy over what might be going on in his coconut. Like the Wizard of Oz with the curtain drawn aside, some little man inside Choker was pulling all the levers at once. I decided to try a dose of reality on him.

"I know what happened to your brother. How he got killed."

Choker's nostrils flared. "I hung him."

It sounded like he was daring me to disapprove. "Your parents blamed you."

His face twitched. "Why shouldn't they?"

"Just natural-born bad-to-the-bone. End of story."

"This smegging water is cold."

"It's good for your ankle."

"Go back and get some scuba tanks so I can get out of here."

"We're talking hours. Even then, you'd still have to go in the water. You're just one deep breath from being out of here, okay?" I led Choker into deeper water. Because of his gimpy ankle, he needed me to lean on.

"Told you I can't swim!"

"Just paddle as much as you can and keep yourself down from the ceiling. Curry will do the rest." Which gave me an idea. I looked around for some loose rocks I could put in my pockets to offset my buoyancy. I found a deposit of pebbles, flecked with shell fragments, in a natural hollow in the rock, and filled my pockets, wondering, in passing, how the stuff could have washed in. Then Choker began ragging on me again.

"The treasure is mine. I found his hiding place. If you try to steal it, I'll cripple you."

"Yeah, you tried to steal it from Angostura who tried to steal it from Krogstrand, who tried to steal it from whoever owns this property— probably Iris Twist. So you know what? If it's not on your property, it doesn't belong to you."

"Finders keepers, you loser."

I clenched my jaw so hard my teeth stopped chattering. Then I suddenly recalled the day I'd biked to Camp Bluetoad and had imagined Choker dumping his canoe and begging me for help, and how I'd wanted to humiliate him. Had the force of my vengeful daydream somehow caused Choker to be trapped here? But Swami said that every person's situation resulted from their own choices.

Then it hit me. My thoughts might not have put Choker in this situation, but it sure as heck had put me in it!

I had to rescue him, no matter what names he called me. But how? No sooner had I wondered when a new angle came to mind. "See this tunnel Choker? Think of it as being born fresh. You can go through and start all over again in the world. And you don't have to be the old bad-to-the-bone Choker. You can be anybody you want. That's worth more than any treasure. Now, suck it up and let's get going."

I snugged the loop tight around his wrist, pulled the slack out of the line, and gave two stiff jerks. The line tugged back twice, then a steady pull. I tried leading Choker, but he balked when it became crotch-deep. "I hate water!"

He seemed close to wigging out so I broke his arm loose from my shoulder and left him teetering on one leg. "What do you hate most: water... or darkness?" I tucked the flashlight into my belt. "Because I'm outta here. With or without you." I crossed my arms over my chest, as I'd started to shiver.

"You're not going anywhere!" His roar filled the cavern, and as he took a wincing step toward me, I backed away. "You skinny little smeg-head. Come back here or I'll kill you." I stepped into deeper water as he took another lunging stride, this time almost losing his balance. I gave another tug on the line, and Curry understood. He responded forcefully, toppling Choker into the drink. He struggled to his good leg and yanked so hard he fell over backwards as the line went slack. He must have jerked it right out of Curry's hands.

"Come on, you're all wet now, you might as well go for a swim."

"No way." He took the loop off his wrist.

"Then I'm history. See you later—maybe." I waded up to my navel.

"Darwin, wait, I'll share the treasure with you if you stay. Me and you. You'll be my best buddy."

"Why would anyone want to be your buddy?" I turned away, took my deep breaths.

"Don't take the light!" His plea had a girlish squeal to it.

I dove.

Chapter 41
Pockets Full of Nothing

*T*he swim was farther because of the risen tide, but with ballast in my pockets, I didn't have to worry about barking my skull on the overhead. My strokes were efficient and confident, knowing what lay ahead; the birth-canal image stayed with me, and I felt somehow changed by what had happened. Confronting fear, hearing the *voice*, being free of the vengeance I'd been carrying around.

When I broke surface, Curry waded in to help me. "You're getting all wet," I tried to say though chattering teeth.

"I was worried sick about you. Especially when you pulled the cord then didn't come." He toweled me off with my socks and helped me into my dry sweatshirt and jacket. I couldn't do anything about the wet pants except scoop the pebbles out of the pockets.

"Did you find Choker?"

"Yeah, he's there. You'll want to keep hold of that cord—he could be coming any time and he'll need a strong pull." I aimed my flashlight beam at the water. From the pitch black of Cyrus's cave, he'd see some luminescence. Maybe it would be enough to induce him to come. If not, at least he'd know someone would come eventually. "Let's give him five more minutes—then we'd better get help."

"I think I hear voices, Dar."

I heard a distant babble and the scuffle of boots. A minute later, Sheriff Biggs and several others painted us with their lights. "What are you boys doing, causing more trouble? We already got one kid lost in here; don't need more. Now get yourselves on out of here."

"We found Choker," I said.

"You found him? Well, I don't see him."

"Through there," Curry said.

"Through that flooded tunnel? Now just how would he manage

that?"

"It dries out at low tide," I said.

The Sheriff noticed the cord wrapped around Curry's hand and followed it with his light to where it disappeared into the deep water. Then Curry's hand tugged sharply. He signaled back and began pulling. "Think I got a big one." We both hauled on the line, hand over hand.

"What in blazes...?" Sheriff Biggs said, but Dan Klatt got the picture and waded in to grab the line in front of us, bent it around his waist, and pulled like a draft horse. Before long, a shape became visible under the water. Klatt kept pulling until he beached Choker in a foot of water, sputtering and cussing, his arm nearly yanked from its socket.

In the commotion where many hands helped Choker to his feet and wrapped him in dry things, Curry and I dodged out. I needed to get warm.

Curry did his thing in Iris's kitchen with bread, peanut butter, a can of tuna, and a jar of pickle relish. When he got the ketchup out, I retreated to the drawing room. Iris kept her rocker going just enough to creak the floorboards. Her dull eyes tracked me across the room. She'd remade her face, but I'd never seen a living person look so white.

I straddled a chair backwards. "Your Uncle Cyrus set a nasty trap. I think we found his hiding place."

A slight movement of the shoulder. She didn't much care.

"You should lock up that shed, or you're going to have others going after it."

A curl of the lip, averted eyes. In time she said, "I'll have the tunnel blasted shut."

"We think there're diamonds down there."

She pressed her eyes shut. "Diamonds. What use are diamonds, except for rings. Just rocks. Lifeless, cold, rocks." She glanced around the room. "None of these things we spent a lifetime collecting mean anything. It's people—husbands, wives, friends, family—that mean something. Young folks don't understand that." She looked at the backs of her fingers—no rings—then wadded her hands in her lap and took a deep breath. "I tried to tell Sheriff Biggs but he was too busy. Should I just wait here?"

"All dressed up and nowhere to go," I said, drawing a little smile from her. "Don't do anything just now. Curry needs to decide. He likes to get things right, you know."

One corner of her mouth turned up in a smile. "That boy's got enough conscience for the whole family."

The phone rang. Iris recoiled from it, so I answered. "Iris Twist residence... Oh, hello Mr. Buckle."

Iris held up a palm and shook her head.

"She can't come to the phone, but Curry's here. Hey Curry, it's your dad. He sounds excited."

Milk sloshed from the corners of his mouth as he washed down a gulp of sandwich. The whole disgusting mass bulged his throat as it went down. He took the phone, listened, and his eyes widened.

"It's good news! Dad says Paprika is snapping out of it!"

Chapter 42
A Taste of Blood

I knew something had changed at school the next day when classmates who'd ignored me, and closed their circles when I approached, and claimed an empty seat was saved (for someone who never showed up), now gave me long looks, or an occasional 'Yo Darwin.'

I cautiously returned the greetings, but moved on. Recognizing Keeley from behind, chatting with a girlfriend, I tickled her ribs and she nearly spilled her books.

"Darwin!" she scolded, trying as usual to act mature.

The girlfriend said "Hello hero," smiled coyly, said, "Well, three's a crowd. Ciao!" and took off.

"Did you hear about Paprika?" I asked Keeley before she could say anything. "She sat up in bed last night and talked."

"Yeah. Dad thinks she's going to be all right."

"That's great! But what about Dr. Slather? She's not going to like being upstaged."

Keeley grimaced. "Dad's going to say that Dr. Slather's treatment finally started to work."

I rolled my eyes. "People aren't stupid enough to believe that."

"Dr. Slather will. And it should keep her from reporting dad to the medical board. Anyway, I suppose Curry deserves most the credit."

"We're all in it together," I said, then flinched at the thought that Curry's mysticism was starting to infiltrate my personality. It reminded me I hadn't even told Curry about the *voice* I'd heard while swimming underwater.

"Well, he's certainly giving you credit for saving Choker's life."

"Choker's *life?* He wouldn't have died." Keeley looked just a little let down, so I added, "Probably not. Gone insane, most likely. Anyway, I need to stuff a sock in Curry's cake hole."

But I didn't look for him. Now that other people were warming up, they shouldn't think Curry and I were joined at the hip. I needed room for others in my life too, didn't I?

Choker didn't come to school that day, or the next, though I thought I saw him peeking over the fence during touch football. On Wednesday, I sat next to Curry in social studies as usual, though I shot the bull mostly with other guys. Then, during English comp, I noticed how pasty Ms. Dozier looked, and how loose her muumuu hung on her, and how she half-sat on her desk while lecturing instead of stalking about and wheeling her arms. Curry's treatment for Paprika may have been working, but Ms. Dozier seemed to be losing traction. I wondered how much the stalled campaign to save Camp Bluetoad weighed on her mind. I'd given Curry the check for ten-thousand bucks, but he'd done nothing with it.

After class, Ms. Dozier stopped me on the way out. "I understand you're quite the hero."

"It keeps getting exaggerated."

She nodded. "By the end of the week, you'll have saved western civilization."

I laughed. She had a way of connecting that made you feel... connected. "Yeah, that's the way it's headed. Hey, you still doing the treatments with Doc Uncas?"

She looked away. "When I can."

"You need to be regular about it. I know you've been busy with Camp Bluetoad."

Picking at the chipped polish on a thumbnail, she said, "There doesn't seem to be much point to it anymore."

I wanted to tell her not to give up—on Camp Bluetoad, on life—but I didn't know how to say things like that to an adult, even though she always tried to make her students feel like adults. I saw Curry lingering near the door, so I said goodbye to Ms. Dozier and joined him. In the hall, I whispered, "You haven't given her the check yet, have you—the one from Aunt Iris."

"No. I'm not sure..."

"Curry, she's wasting away. I know you can't decide whether to turn Iris in, but the check is good either way. She offered the reward to find out who killed her sister. We found out. We collected the reward. We give it to a good cause. What's there to think about?"

We walked, pausing at the graph with the jumping blue toad. The toad had mostly jumped sideways lately, and was about to smack into the deadline wall. Curry shook his head. "Everything's simple to you. Black or white."

"It *is* simple—it's a no-brainer. You turn Iris in, your whole family suffers. The trial, the publicity. Your mom's already lost one sister—you want the other one to spend the rest of her life in a cage? How's it going to affect Paprika? And the reward—I bet she can afford the ten grand, and it's for a good cause. Everyone comes out ahead."

Curry turned on me, looking flushed. "You're not even considering the bad stuff that can happen."

"Okay, worrywart, lay it on me, the worst case scenario."

"Let's say the sheriff finds out the truth—"

"How's he going to find out?"

"Maybe he figures it out himself. Maybe two months from now Aunt Iris turns herself in. Maybe two months from now she's still depressed and leaves a note and..."

With a shiver, I said, "I get the picture. Go on."

"Okay, Sheriff Biggs finds out we hid the truth. That makes us guilty. Especially since we took money—like a bribe to keep quiet. I might take that chance for me, because it's my family, but I can't put you in that situation. And if I turn her in, wouldn't she need all her money for legal expenses? We can't let Ms. Dozier cash that check."

I stuck a pinkie in my ear as far as it would go, and gave it a few cranks. The image of a suicide note splattered with brains slowed me a bit. "Okay, there are complications. But remember, we're just teenagers, obviously too stupid to know the law. Heck, they'd never believe we solved the crime in the first place. Arrest us? Get real. So please, don't try to protect me. And I'll bet your Auntie has wads of money squirreled away in pickle jars." I gave Curry a stern looking over, then pointed to the deadline on the chart—a week from Monday. "You'd better make your mind up soon."

I saw even less of Curry the rest of the week. Some guys on my touch football team invited me to their lunch table, and sat with my back to Curry so I wouldn't have to see him sitting alone. Just sensing his presence made it tough to keep up my share of the BS, but I felt entitled to more than one friend. Curry could mix if he wanted to; he didn't have to act like someone in a parallel universe who didn't care about ordinary stuff.

Ms. Dozier held one last bazaar on Friday afternoon. The weather turned cold and windy, so she moved it inside to the hallways. It had no chance of making enough money to save Camp Bluetoad, but everyone enjoyed running their little shops and coming up with new things to improve their businesses. The girl who'd started a hat booth with one design, now had six people working for her, a dozen different hats, and a custom operation. They'd booked orders into December.

Swami Curryban Bucklananda had folded his tent, never to reopen, but we'd spawned an imitator who read palms and tarot cards. I bought a cup of Moe's Famous Mulled Cider and walked aimlessly past the booths. At the door I poked the cinnamon stick in my mouth to chew on, tossed the cup in the trash, and stepped out into the biting wind. Students weren't supposed to leave the grounds until three-thirty, but I didn't feel much like staying, so I headed for the bike rack. Then I saw someone walking in from the ball field, and I paused to make sure it wasn't someone who'd rat on me. I didn't recognize Curry at first because he always walked in an erect, absent-minded shamble, and this kid hunched and held something to his face. But the meaty chest and large head were Curry's and I ran toward him. His glasses were missing and his breath blew out in rapid puffs of vapor. When I saw gouts of something dark leaking down the front of his jacket, the base of my spine tingled with alarm.

"Dang it, Curry! What happened?"

He tilted the handkerchief away from his nose, then quickly plugged the fresh gush of blood. He shook his head, leaned over to spit a strand of crimson saliva, and said, "Nothing." He had his mouth open to breathe and I could see his tongue pushing on a loose tooth.

My jaw so tense I could hardly talk, I demanded, "Who did this?"

Curry shook his head. "He thought I made him look like a coward. I shouldn't have said anything about you rescuing him."

Then I knew who'd pulped his face, and why. Also I knew Curry had only been trying to help me become accepted in this new place. Trying to make me look good, instead of keeping quiet to protect his monopoly on my friendship. Queasy with anger and guilt, I scrutinized the area he'd come from. Through a mist rising off the ball field, a dark figure walked away with a swagger I had no trouble recognizing. I balled my fists and began striding on an angle that would cut him off. I'd bit the cinnamon stick and spat slivers as I walked. He saw me, I think, and changed course, heading for the fence and the alder thicket beyond.

"Choker!" I called, and broke into a stiff trot.

He stopped, crossed his arms, and faced me, cap on backward, denim jacket snapped only at the waist. I slowed to a walk.

"Hey, smegman," he said, pushing up a phony smile. Then he must have read the look on my face because the smile went away. "Your little buddy was flapping his lip and somebody needed to button it for—"

He didn't get a chance to finish before I drove a fist toward his midsection. He twisted aside, so the punch mostly glanced off. He pushed me and, unbalanced from my lunge, I had to put a hand down to keep from falling. I squared off, feeling a fury that had to be unleashed no matter how much punishment it cost me. I cast off my jacket, turning sleeves inside out.

"Now Darwin..." Choker held his palms up and stepped back.

I charged, swung under his hands toward his belly, missed, then rained fists at whatever part of him his forearms weren't covering. He retreated a step and I pressed all the harder. Then he lifted a knee to my groin, connecting, driving the air from my lungs. Quick to seize the advantage, he hooked a foot behind mine and shoved. I tripped over backward, rolled on the wet grass, and fended off a kick with my feet. He dodged my legs and aimed another kick that got through to my ribs. Groaning, I curled into a ball, rotating to get my feet between us.

Choker circled, huffing clouds of steam. "He shouldn't of made me look bad. He had to pay."

The knee to the cookies took some vinegar out of me, but it hadn't landed direct and the effects were wearing off. I played it up a bit, rocking and holding my lower parts, though my ribs hurt far more.

A crooked smile appeared on his face. "Shouldn't play leapfrog with a unicorn, Bownes."

I rolled up to one knee. "You're the worst kind of coward!" The ache in my ribs turned my shout to a croak. "You don't have the guts to grow up. In my book, that makes you a spineless wuss."

I hoped he'd retaliate with a kick, and he did. I was ready. I dove inside the arc of his shin before he could generate much power, seized his shoe with both hands, and twisted the ankle in a direction it didn't want to go. He shouted and I felt the thickness of elastic wrap above the shoe, remembering this had been the ankle pinned under the rocks. He swiveled to protect it and went down. I rolled up the back of his legs, crossed his bad ankle behind the other knee, then levered the leg back until I had the bad ankle clamped. I'd seen the move on pro wrestling. I got in better position and leaned hard on the leg. Now flat on his stomach, Choker bellowed in pain, encouraging me to lean all the harder.

I felt hands on my shoulders. "Let him go, Dar." Curry sounded like he had a mouthful of marbles.

"This one's for Curry's nose," I said, reefing on the leg.

"Owwwww!"

"Don't let anger control you," Curry implored.

"Too late," I said. "And this one's for Curry's lip." I leaned again, getting a feel for how much strain the knee joint could take without coming apart.

"Yeeeooooowww!!"

"Dar, please!"

"And this one's for Curry's tooth." This time Curry jumped me before I could sit on the leg with all my weight.

"What's going on here boys?" The deep voice boomed from behind me. A strong hand grabbed me under the armpit and dragged me off Choker. I hadn't had my full pound of flesh yet and reflexively swung my elbow to break free. I connected bone to bone and the hand dropped me. When I looked up to see who'd butted in, my stomach turned into a bowling ball. Mr. Krogstrand loomed tall in his black overcoat and tweed hat, rubbing his chin where I'd speared him with my elbow. Curry helped Choker to his feet. Curry had stuffed a piece of tissue up his nose to stop the bleeding; his upper lip looked fat and yellow as a full-grown banana slug. Choker gingerly put weight on his bad ankle.

"What's this all about?" Krogstrand demanded.

"They jumped me," Choker said. "Two against one."

"I see," Krogstrand said.

"Wait a minute," I said. "That's a crock."

Krogstrand raised a finger at me, and made a smile that looked like it must have hurt. "Mr. Bownes, in my eyes, you are already a convicted liar. Do you want to dig yourself a deeper hole?"

"Yeah, and you're a born egg-sucker." I snatched my jacket off the ground. As I did so, dozens of colored pills rained from the pocket, falling at Krogstrand's feet. Paprika's medicine.

"What do we have here?" Krogstrand said. "My oh my."

Chapter 43
Disgrace

Curry explained the pills, but Krogstrand just kept picking them from the wet grass, muttering, "My oh my."

I drove Curry home on his motor scooter. The faster I went, the deeper the chill penetrated, so I backed off the throttle. I had the shakes in my arms anyway as my body tried to deal with all that spent adrenaline, making my steering a bit wobbly. At the Buckle's farm, thousands of pumpkins glowed in the field among frost-blackened vines. Near the barn, three blue-jeaned backsides were hanging out from under the hood of Mr. Buckle's pickup.

Curry and I slipped inside the house without drawing attention, and found Paprika snuggled under an afghan in Mr. Buckle's recliner, attended by her mom and Aunt Iris, who had an early start on the traditional Friday evening amontillado. Rika had a tiny glass of the stuff, too; her elders seemed to be grooming her to fill the vacancy left by Aunt Pansy. Rika looked pale, but the light was back in her green eyes. As Curry rushed into the bathroom to clean up, I noticed that Iris's hand began trembling and she put her drink down. She smoothed her dress with knobby fingers, looking at me, eyes asking *have you two decided anything?* I returned a subtle shrug and nodded toward the bathroom. *It's his call.*

"Heavens to Murgatroyd!" Paprika said, adopting one of Aunt Pansy's favorite expressions, when Curry returned. "Did you chop down a tree with your face?"

As Curry gave her a hug, I helped out. "He ran into a doorknob."

Paprika smiled knowingly. "And what's the doorknob's name?"

"Choker."

She wrinkled her face in anger. "I'll have a word with Danny about that. His cousin needs to learn some manners."

"Don't bother," Curry said, fat lip blurring his words. "Dan is sorta peeved at us for something."

Paprika giggled behind her freckled hand. "Oh, that thing about getting disfigured by a deep-fat fryer? Well, rescuing Choker ought to count for something."

Curry had saved Paprika's life too, but she didn't know. While Mrs. Buckle and Aunt Iris fixed dinner, and Curry showered, and Paprika yakked on the phone, I stared at the TV news without hearing a word of it. In time, I tuned in more to Paprika's conversation; it sounded like news of the fight had spread. She continued yammering even as Mr. Buckle and Dan carried the recliner, with Paprika in it, to the dining room so the recovering invalid could eat with the family. By the time the roast beef and winter vegetables came from the oven, my stomach had settled enough to tolerate food, and—as usual—they'd set a place for me.

I phoned mom when Paprika finally hung up.

"Staying for supper? Okay DAR-ling. I was just going to nuke a meatloaf, but I can re-group. By the way, Mr. Krogstrand left a message asking us to call. What could that be about?"

My stomach soured all over again. "Maybe he wants to renew his subscription." Then I thought it would be better if she heard the worst of it from me. "Of course, there was a little thing on the school yard this afternoon. No big deal. I settled a disagreement with some guy."

"Oh, Darwin! No one was hurt?" Mom always assumed the best, as if by doing so, nothing bad would ever happen. It made my life easier.

"Everything's cool."

"Not that same gang that hit you at the football game?"

"Just one guy. I think it's all over now." A little wishful thinking. I knew somehow there'd be a price to pay for my mindless rage.

At dinner, I mostly pushed meat and squash and Brussels sprouts around my plate. Maybe Krogstrand had tried calling the Buckles, too, but with the phone GooeyGlued to Paprika's ear...

When the phone rang during dessert, Rika answered. This time, though, she handed it to her father.

"Yes? Oh, hello principal." He sat up straight and brushed dinner crumbs off his shirt. Then his carefree expression sagged as if he'd had a stroke.

"You don't say..."

"You don't say..."

"Well, I know but... " He shot a stern look at Curry.

"Oh... you don't say."

Mr. Buckle hung up.

"What was that all about?" Mrs. Buckle demanded.

"We've been officially notified, that's what."

"Officially notified of what?"

"That he's expelled from school." He bent an accusing glance toward Curry.

My body went rigid and my eyes lost focus.

"Expelled?" Mrs. Buckle said. "Expelled for what? Don't make me drag out every last detail. You exasperate me."

"All kinds of things, it seems. Fighting, and lying, and disrespect to a teacher, and cutting class, and something about drugs, and... dang, I can't remember the whole of it."

"What! Buckles have sometimes been flunked, but they've never had drugs and they've never been expelled!" She dipped a napkin in her drinking glass and pressed it against her forehead. She snatched the apple crisp away from Curry. "No dessert for disgracers."

She hadn't noticed that Curry's swollen lip, the cuts inside his mouth, and loosened tooth had kept him from eating anyway. Curry just sat there looking detached, as if all this was happening to someone else.

"Come on, stop holding back," Mrs. Buckle said. "How long is he out for?"

"Why," Mr. Buckle said with stunned eyes, "for the whole year."

Mrs. Buckle turned to me, her small eyes sharply focused. "You! The first time I saw you, I knew you was trouble."

Chapter 44
The Rendezvous

I dialed home before Paprika could get on the phone again, but the line beeped busy. I considered alternatives like signing on an Alaska-bound crab boat, but decided to borrow the scooter and get home and throw myself on the mercy of my parents. Maybe Mr. Buckle got it wrong somehow.

At home I came in through the kitchen door and found mom wadding up balls of cookie dough. When stressed, she made cookies. And these were full of nuts and chocolate chips and God-knows-what. Big ones, quarter pounders. It didn't look good.

Dad sat me down in the living room. They'd received the same notification: expulsion. Before I could explain, he said, "Son, I want to apologize for what's happened. It's all politics, you know." I hadn't noticed before how old he'd begun to look, bags under his hawkish eyes, the beginning of jowls. Always a deadline and never enough sleep. "The old timers here don't appreciate outsiders moving in, especially taking over the newspaper, because it's so important to a community. Emil Krogstrand throws a lot of weight around here and he sees me as a threat, because we don't see eye-to-eye on some things. So he's taking it out on you. But don't worry, we're going to fight it."

Dad could be a major embarrassment at times, but right then I really needed his support. But I couldn't have him discovering later that I'd held out on him. "Dad... there's more to it. There's stuff going on."

"I know. You cut a class or two. Nothing worse than what your old dad used to do. In fact... well, I'd better not give you ideas." He laughed through his nose.

"We had Paprika's pills because we didn't want the chickens eating them, so Krogstrand probably thinks... it's sorta complicated."

"Things always seem complicated to teenagers. But it's really simple: whatever you did, it doesn't deserve expulsion. Certainly not for the whole year."

I wanted to explain everything, but realized my thoughts were too jumbled, so I gave up and asked, "What can we do?"

"I've already done it," he said, looking smug. "I called Thelma Duff, head of the school board. I told her what happened and said I'd be raising holy hell in the newspaper if the board didn't—"

The phone rang.

"Maybe that's her now. Hello? Ms. Duff. We were just... good... yes." Dad frowned a little. "Well, I'd hoped to get the whole thing overturned... A hearing?" He listened intently for a minute, then put his hand over the receiver. "Darwin, this is critical: she says if we appeal, Krogstrand is likely to seek prosecution for drug dealing and assault. Level with me. Do we have a problem here?"

Though my brain locked up at these grotesque accusations, another part of me felt proud of my dad's willingness to take my word for it. "He's full of beans," I said.

Dad looked me in the eye for a moment, then nodded approvingly. "Let's schedule it," he said into the phone. "I understand, no promises... Yes, I have every confidence in the board's judgment."

Mom came in with a plate and a forced smile. "Hot cookies."

I tried to call Curry that night, but his mom said he'd gone to bed, and that he'd be busy with chores all day tomorrow. I got the message.

But the following afternoon he phoned. "My folks told me not to see you. They think you're a bad influence."

"I am. And proud of it. When can you sneak away?"

*   *   *

A gully snaked along the east border of the Buckle farm. The next morning—Sunday—I leaned my bike against a fence post, stomped through thick brush down the bank and made my way a hundred yards up the gully's mostly dry streambed. I waited five minutes at the rendezvous spot before Curry thrashed out of the underbrush, legs of his corduroys studded with cockleburs.

"Holy pig-snouts!" he said, plucking off the burrs. He had a livid bruise under one eye, and swollen cheek and lip from the beating Choker had given him.

"What are you all dressed up for?" I asked.

"I told mom and dad I was going to church."

"Oh boy. Guess I am a bad influence." We sat on a fallen tree. "What did they think about the hearing?"

"I don't know, Dar. They really don't want the family's disgrace out in public."

"So they're going to let you sit out a whole year? C'mon! Krogstrand is just getting even because we wouldn't help him find Cyrus Twist's diamonds."

Curry looked away. "Maybe I should have helped."

"Have you been smoking pumpkin seeds? You need to be at that hearing."

"It's... it's not just my parents. Krogstrand is going to make a big deal out of me telling fortunes, and I don't want to go there."

"Why not? It's nothing to hide."

Curry cleared one pant leg of burrs and started on the other. "I don't want to be a freak show, that's all."

"So you'll give up a whole year of school without a fight? Dad thinks we have a great chance to get the thing cut down to a suspension."

Curry flicked burrs into a frog pond.

"What if I win and you don't try?" I said, my apprehension growing. I didn't seem to be getting through to him. "We'd be in different classes from now on."

He chewed on that a few seconds, brushed his pants, and slid off the trunk. Without looking me in the eye, he said, "Sorry, Dar," and began running away. Just before reaching the sticker patch, he stopped and turned and called out, "Thanks for what you did—kicking Choker's butt. I'll never forget it."

*T*he school board scheduled my hearing for the following Thursday evening at the Community Hall. The board originally wanted it in Krogstrand's office, but my dad insisted on neutral ground, and he wanted it open to the public so there wouldn't be any shenanigans. I didn't know what kind of shenanigans he expected, but when he got his way, I felt like we'd won something, and felt more confident than ever that he'd get the best of Krogstrand.

It never occurred to me that Krogstrand might want a big audience, too.

The air seemed unnaturally calm that day, warm, almost balmy, although purplish clouds massed to the southwest. By mid-afternoon, the wind struck, tumbling leaves through the streets. The rain came a few minutes later, and by that evening, became a horizontal barrage that made umbrellas useless.

In the parking lot of the community hall, dad dropped a bombshell.

"Son, you understand your mother had her reasons for not coming tonight."

"She's not good with conflict."

Dad shifted in his seat to face me. "That's part of it. But there's something else, and she's kind of upset. We've been talking it over the last few days, and we've made a decision. We can't have you fall back a whole school year. You've always been near the head of your class, and you need to move forward. You need the challenge. If things don't work out tonight, we're going to sell the paper and move."

"Move!" I shook my head with disbelief. "Move where?"

"There's a town in Oregon with a paper for sale."

"No!" I tensed until I shook. Rain splattering on the windshield fractured the lights from the hall into a million slivers. A month ago, I probably would have gone along with it. Now, leaving seemed inconceivable.

"It's hard on all of us, but we have to keep your long-term interests in mind. And, I think you know, we're struggling financially. But forget that—let's go in and give 'em heck."

Dad, in his greatcoat, walked upwind of me to block the rain, but my jeans still soaked up a lot of it. Inside, people didn't begin recognizing us until we hung our dripping coats on the rack. Then they backed away, leaving a circle, and the babble of voices fell to a buzz.

The number of people astonished me—maybe eighty or ninety. Adults, mostly, though I saw Keeley, arm-in-arm with her dad. Ms. Dozier, muumuu now looking too large, rubbed her hands together over the wood stove at the rear of the hall, talking to Mrs. Muldoon, Krogstrand's gray-topped secretary. And I recognized Troutigan, Leon the albino who ran the Take It Or Leave It, Gretchen (whose father Curry had found), Dr. Slather, the rich guy who'd invented GooeyGlue, and others. Rows of folding chairs went up. I couldn't believe all these people had come out on a blustery night just to see me drummed out of school. Maybe islanders used any excuse to get together. Curry would have freaked, being at the center of all this.

Dad wanted to meet my friends, so I led him to Keeley and Doc, then to Ms. Dozier. They all wished me luck and it helped me to relax. Some men arranged a long table in front. I wondered where I'd be sitting and kept looking at the door, hoping Curry would come after all, but he didn't.

Shortly before the hour, a door at the head of the room opened and Mr. Krogstrand held it as five men and women filed out. I felt confused, almost dizzy, that I had somehow set all this in motion.

The school board sat behind the long table. "That's Thelma Duff," dad said, pointing to the woman in the middle with the no-nonsense expression, glasses stowed in her hair, and a purple scar below one eye, shaped like West Virginia, where a cancer had been burned off. Two other women and two men, in a range of ages, completed the line-up. One of them looked familiar—a squinty-faced woman—who smiled at me. I don't know what I'd expected, but they all looked like regular people.

Krogstrand, though, appeared regal in a three-piece suit, gold pin under the knot of his tie. The smile he made at the board members looked out of practice. Then he scanned the room, found me, and pointed me out to Ms. Duff with his pinkie, as if I deserved only his least significant finger. I would have returned the gesture with a different finger if Ms. Duff hadn't been looking.

Ms. Duff motioned dad and me to a side table. Krogstrand stood behind his own table, opposite us, hands clasped behind his back. At the stroke of seven, Ms. Duff chimed the water pitcher with her glasses. As the crowd quieted, the pelting rain sounded louder.

Ms. Duff cleared her throat. "We're here to consider multiple allegations of student misconduct, for which our superintendent and principal, Emil Krogstrand, has expelled Darwin Bownes for the remainder of his sophomore year. The board has granted the student's request for review, as expulsion would delay his education for a full year, thereby rippling through his life for many years to come." She uncapped her pen, looked briefly at me, then asked my dad, "Mr. Bownes, will you be speaking on behalf of your son?"

Dad stood and bowed slightly. "Yes ma'am."

I rubbed my sweaty palms over the damp thighs of my jeans.

"You and your son have been advised of the charges, specifically," she lowered her glasses into place and read, "possession and distribution of drugs on school grounds; fighting; cutting—"

The wind blew the front door open and I felt a draft on my chilled legs, then heard murmuring.

Ms. Duff peered over her glasses. "Ahem, Curry Buckle, is it?"

My heart kicked and I rose to look. Just inside the front doors, Curry stood, mopping rain from his broad face, Aunt Iris standing behind him, a full head taller. He located me and gave a goofy wave.

Chapter 46

"*T*ake a seat up front, Curry," Ms. Duff said. "That is, if you want these proceedings to apply to your case."

Curry and Iris came forward and I shook his hand, and felt that special kind of energy that seemed to swirl around us. As a team we could take on the whole town. His mom had given him a scissors-cut for the occasion, doing a shaky job on the sidewalls, and he smelled of fresh talc. Though the swelling had gone down on his cheek and lip, some bruising remained under his eye. Nevertheless, his eyes sparkled and he cracked an elfish grin.

"What changed your mind?" I asked.

He gestured toward his aunt. "She had a long talk with me. About not living like a victim."

"I'm glad—"

"Iris," Ms. Duff said, "I take it you'll be speaking on behalf of your nephew?"

"Curry can speak well enough for himself." She took a vacant seat in the front row. Curry sat next to me.

"As you prefer. I'll continue reading the charges, which mostly apply to both boys." She enunciated precisely: "Possession and distribution of drugs on school grounds; fighting; cutting class; disrespectful conduct toward faculty; endangering another student; cheating; and, specific to Darwin Bownes, striking Mr. Krogstrand and vandalizing school property." She lowered the paper and looked at our table. I had only the vaguest idea what some of these charges referred to. "Mr. Bownes," she said, "would you care to make a statement before I turn the floor over to Mr. Krogstrand?"

"Yes, ma'am." Dad stood. "These charges are mostly false, invented to attack me through my son. Certain people want to force our family off Kluge Island, and that's exactly what's going to happen unless you overturn this expulsion. I know our family would be a great asset to this island if you'll give us a chance, but I will not have Darwin's education interrupted."

Curry looked at me with alarm. I nodded back. He'd heard right.

Ms. Duff scowled. "Mr. Bownes, whether or not Mr. Krogstrand holds any animus toward you is irrelevant if your son is guilty as charged."

"My son is not a drug pusher. Whatever else he might have done, the penalty is too harsh."

"If the board sustains the charges, we're disinclined to substitute our judgment for his."

Dad sat down slowly, looking discouraged.

Ms. Duff offered Curry a chance to speak—he shook his head—then she spread her palm toward Krogstrand. He stood, opening a leather-bound notebook.

"Last month, our biology teacher, Mr. Flatski, brought Curry Buckle to my office for cheating on a quiz. Buckle claimed he had a vision of the answer—verbatim from the textbook—by divine intervention."

I jumped up. "He never said that!" I remained standing, frowning at Krogstrand.

"Not his exact words, but close enough," Krogstrand explained to the board.

"What were his exact words?" Ms. Duff asked.

"Something about seeing it in his head."

She looked at me but I couldn't dispute it. "Continue."

Dad pulled me down to my chair.

"Then Darwin Bownes barged into my office—you just saw his belligerent personality—and he backed Buckle's story. Naturally, I warned them both that if they were lying, they'd be punished equally. They refused an opportunity to prove their story, and Mr. Flatski docked them one grade for the quarter. I also warned them that a second offense would result in suspension. It's all in my notes."

"And was there a second offense?"

Krogstrand's words twisted out of his mouth like soft ice cream. "In a manner of speaking. They portrayed themselves as psychics and accepted money in return for telling fortunes. If necessary, I can produce a witness, Dan Klatt, our starting senior running back, to testify that Curry Buckle and Darwin Bownes conspired to give him a false prophecy with the intent of creating fear for his future health."

"What do you say to that, boys?" Ms. Duff asked.

Dad leaned over to me with a look of concern. "What about it?"

Before I could explain how Dan had been greedy and wanted lottery numbers, Curry piped up. "What he says is true about Danny. We made it all up."

I said, "But there were reasons, and all the others were legit."

Krogstrand put his palms together like an undertaker. "So you admit lying to Dan Klatt and cheating him of his money."

Neither Curry nor I answered.

"Yet you claim everyone else got a genuine revelation for their money."

"Go ask them," I challenged. "See if any of them want their five dollars back." Curry patted my arm, indicating I should calm down.

Ms. Duff gave me a crusty look and said, "You may continue, Mr. Krogstrand."

He turned a page in his notebook—"Cutting class"—and came out from behind his table to strut before me. "Darwin Bownes, do you deny cutting geometry class no less than eight times?"

Probably closer to eighteen, I thought, counting the days I'd slipped out after Schwartzie took roll.

Dad crimped his eyebrows and looked me over.

"But the class is so slow, it's a waste of time," I explained to him and Ms. Duff. "I haven't missed a single test question—"

She cut me off. "We're not interested in your opinion of the class, just whether you attended it."

"I attended once in a while, but it was a waste of time."

A sneer curled Krogstrand's lip. "And you, Buckle, how many times did you cut class?"

"Just the once."

Curry would tell the truth at the cost of his life, and Krogstrand knew it, and would use it against Curry if he could.

Krogstrand turned his attention back to me. "And if cutting geometry wasn't enough, you openly disparaged your teacher, Mr. Schwartz. Does this sound familiar?" He read from his notebook, "That old stumblebum Schwartzie moves at the speed of slobber."

That got a round of chuckles from the room, but the eyes staring at me from the front table weren't smiling. Dang that Schwartz. His hearing must be way better than his eyesight.

"True?" Krogstrand boomed. He grabbed the lapel of his suit coat and struck a pompous pose. The same pose he'd struck in his office when he'd demanded that Curry and I discover where the diamonds were hidden.

"Don't know if I said *slobber.* Might have said *drool.*"

More chuckles.

"We take that as an admission," Ms. Duff said. She did not seem amused.

Krogstrand said, "Although we have an admission here, I'd like to call Mr. Schwartz forward to testify on a separate charge."

"What charge is that?" Ms. Duff asked.

"Vandalism."

"We never vandalized anything," Curry whispered to dad and me.

I could only shrug. We'd never so much as stuck Blubbergum on a desk. Meanwhile Schwartzie tottered to the witness chair and raised his hand to be sworn in. Ms. Duff explained, "This is an informal hearing, Mr. Schwartz, so we aren't administering an oath."

"I swear to tell the whole truth, and nothing but the truth," Schwartzie said anyway

"Yes. Now what did you see or hear?"

"Well, before class, I heard them call me a stumblebum, and—"

"No, Mr. Schwartz. Regarding the vandalism of school property."

"Oh that, well, it was at the football game—I don't remember who we were playing but the score was thirteen to seven, with two minutes left in the first half—I'm good at numbers. It's my job, you know, heh heh."

"What happened at the football game?"

"I wanted to use the restroom before it got crowded at half-time, but when I got there a young man said it was busy inside, so I waited. Then I saw Bownes come out. He looked guilty, like he was trying to hide his face."

Swartzie's small, spiteful eyes stared at me through rimless glasses. I felt a sick feeling coming on.

"The young man waiting outside didn't go in, so I said, 'Someone came out therefore there must be room for one more. Basic mathematics.' He didn't go in, so I did."

"What did you find when you entered the restroom," Krogstrand asked, glaring at me with triumph.

"Two boys were flushing one of those continuous cloth towels down the toilet."

Ms. Duff scrutinized me, then asked Schwartzie, "Did you recognize these boys?"

"Either Bownes or the short boy outside called out to warn them, and the two flushers ran out and bumped me, and in all the confusion, I didn't get a good look at them."

"But you did get a good look at Darwin Bownes, correct?"

"Yes, indeed."

"What about Curry Buckle?" Ms. Duff asked.

Schwartzie squinted at Curry. "Might have been the short boy standing outside."

"Your witness, Mr. Bownes," Krogstrand said.

I whispered to dad, "I can explain."

He nodded.

I stood. "Mr. Schwartz is correct. Except I wasn't part of the gang doing the vandalism, and it wasn't me that called out the warning, and Curry wasn't there."

"Who were the other boys," Ms. Duff asked.

"Choker Durant and his friend Goof—I don't know his real name."

Krogstrand rose. "You saw the vandalism taking place?"

"Well, yes. They tried to make me—"

"And what did you do to stop them?"

"Stop them? Well, nothing, but—"

"You watched school property being destroyed, did nothing about it, and when you encountered a faculty member, you failed to report it? Instead, you slunk away in a big hurry. Now why would an innocent person act like that?"

"You're making it sound—"

Krogstrand threw his hands up. "No, that's the way *you* made it sound. Mr. Schwartz, would it be fair to say that Bownes slunk away in a big hurry?"

"Fair enough," Schwartzie agreed.

I shook my head in disgust and sank to my chair.

"Thank you Mr. Schwartz. You're dismissed," Ms. Duff said. "Next charge."

Krogstrand sucked his teeth and consulted his notebook. "Endangering another student. Specifically, Billy Durant, commonly known as Choker Durant. Bownes and Buckle knowingly enticed him to enter a condemned tunnel, luring him with a cock-in-bull story about hidden treasure. But they failed to tell him the tunnel flooded with the tide. You all know the consequences. Young Durant nearly paid for this deception with his life."

Curry and I looked at each other with gaping mouths. He must have seen my hackles rising because he reached with both hands to keep me from coming out of my chair. But nothing could have held me down, just as nothing could have kept me from rushing Choker when he'd beat up on Curry.

"That's a crock! Choker found the tunnel by spying on us."

My vehemence forced Krogstrand a step backward. Nonetheless, he seemed pleased. "Oh, I see. But you knew he was observing, didn't you?"

"I thought someone was, but—"

"And you could have locked the entrance to the tunnel, but you didn't."

"I suppose, but—"

"And you knew the tunnel was dangerous."

"Duh, it's an old tunnel. Anyone could figure—"

"But you did nothing to deter him from entering. In fact, you told him Cyrus Twist had hidden something valuable down there, and tempted him to find it."

"That's a lie!"

Krogstrand nodded at me with a pathetic frown, then took a sheet of paper, folded lengthwise, from his breast pocket, and handed it to Ms. Duff. "I have here an affidavit signed by Billy Durant, which supports the charges."

Everything went quiet and seemed to waver in slow motion as if I'd been plunged underwater. I felt hands on my shoulders—dad standing behind me.

"We object to this affidavit," he said. "If this Durant boy has any testimony to give, then let him come forward and give it. I can't cross-examine a piece of paper."

Ms. Duff looked only briefly at the document then folded it back up. "He has a point, Mr. Krogstrand. Is Billy Durant in the room?"

"He had homework tonight," Krogstrand said.

"Homework! Choker?" I said, but dad pressed me into my seat before I could say something truly rude.

Curry put up his arm to speak.

Ms. Duff said, "I'm going to rule this affidavit inadmissible because there is no compelling reason the witness couldn't provide live testimony."

I relaxed a bit. Curry's hand remained flagpole straight. Krogstrand reached for a cell phone. "Perhaps we can get him here." While he poked at numbers, Ms. Duff recognized Curry.

He rose, looking like a gnome, feet splayed, ears large against buzzed sidewalls. But he had an air of calm about him that hushed the crowd.

"We never talked with Choker about the tunnel or any treasure. He got into trouble on his own, and Darwin risked his life to save him. And that's the truth."

I thought it sounded convincing, and I think Krogstrand did too, because he immediately jumped all over Curry. "One word against another. And remember," he pointed, "this one is already a proven liar, voices in his head giving him test answers and all that. And it's all well and good to claim that Bownes rescued Billy Durant, but there's a witness who can testify otherwise. I call Danny Klatt to the stand."

I hadn't seen Dan come in, but now I heard his firm stride on the planks. He swaggered forward, arms stiff as if he'd just come from the weight room. He took the witness chair, glancing only briefly at Curry and me.

"You all know Danny," Krogstrand said. "After all, he's averaging three touchdowns a game. Now Danny, I want you to answer me yes or no. Understand?"

"Yes, Mr. Krogstrand."

"Good. Now, Billy Durant is your cousin, is he not?"

"Yes."

"You were present, were you not, when he escaped from the flooded tunnel?"

"Yes."

"Did you see Darwin Bownes assist your cousin in any way?"

"Well, I didn't see—"

"You didn't see him help."

Klatt paused. "No."

"Who pulled Billy Durant out of that flooded tunnel?"

"Well, I guess, I sorta did."

"Thank you, Danny. You're dismissed."

Dad raised his finger. "Wait a minute, we might have some questions."

"Go ahead Mr. Bownes," Ms. Duff said.

Dad whispered to me, "Does he know what really happened?"

"He knows."

Dad nodded, and asked Klatt, "You know that my son played an important role in finding and rescuing your cousin, isn't that true?"

"I object!" Krogstrand said. "He's putting words in the witness's mouth."

"He's your witness," Ms. Duff said. "So Mr. Bownes may put whatever words he likes in his mouth; the witness may take the words out of his mouth if they're not true."

Klatt said, "Well, Curry and Darwin said they knew where to find Choker but I had to stay behind and guard the shaft, like Sheriff Biggs told me. And when I finally got down there with the sheriff, Choker was just coming, so I grabbed the line and pulled him out. I found out later—"

"We're only interested," Ms. Duff said, "in what you personally saw or heard, not what somebody told you later."

"I guess I didn't really see or hear anything."

"Fine. Any more questions?" she asked dad.

"I have one," I said, rising slowly for effect. "Dan, we know that you and Choker and Charlie Angostura dug all those holes over by the Twist property. Who hired you to do it?"

"Irrelevant!" Krogstrand blurted. Just the sight of his knotted forehead should have made it clear to everyone he had something to hide.

"Just what is the relevance of this question?" Ms. Duff asked me.

"Ah... " I wanted to explain how it was the key to everything, but I didn't know where to start. "Don't you see? It's a conspiracy. They're all in cahoots and Curry wouldn't help and I interfered and Mr. Angostura tried to cheat Mr. Krogstrand and Choker tried to cheat Mr. Angostura—"

"Darwin," Ms. Duff said, holding a hand up.

I felt the heat of disbelieving eyes on me and my brain seized up but I kept talking anyway. "And it all has to do with diamonds that Cyrus Twist found in British Columbia and hid before he went mad from mercury poisoning—"

"That will be quite enough," Ms. Duff said. "Objection sustained."

I raised my voice. "So don't you see, he's retaliating against us because he's greedy and he's on this huge power trip and can't stand anyone, especially students, who won't—"

"Witness dismissed." Ms. Duff said sharply.

My energy suddenly felt used up. I knew I'd sounded like an idiot and that no one believed me.

Dan Klatt opened his mouth like he wanted to say more, but heaved his chest, rose from the witness chair, and ape-walked toward the back of the room. I heard the door open, then slam shut.

Chapter 47
Mrs. Muldoon's Knitting

Krogstrand smiled, licked a thumb, and turned the page in his notebook. "The next charge is fighting. Specifically, Curry Buckle and Darwin Bownes ganged up to beat Billy Durant on school grounds last Friday afternoon." He sniffed. "I saw it from my office window, and went out personally to break it up. And I might add," he gripped his jaw as if testing whether it still moved right, "I took an elbow to the chin for my trouble."

"Did you see who started the fight?" Ms. Duff asked.

"Bownes charged the Durant lad and pummeled him with his fists. Before Durant could recover, Buckle jumped in and completely overwhelmed him."

"Oh sheesh!" I said, cuffing myself on the forehead.

"Save the dramatics," Ms. Duff said to me. "You'll have your chance to talk."

"But he's lying!" I looked to Curry for support, and found him staring sadly at Krogstrand.

"Enough!" Ms. Duff shook her pen at me. "I think we can quite rely on Mr. Krogstrand's word, as he has no reason to fabricate."

"See what a hothead he is?" Krogstrand rubbed his poor jaw for emphasis.

"Your point is taken," Ms. Duff said.

I scowled and said to Curry, "Does the term 'kangaroo court' come to mind?" I might have said it a bit too loudly, judging by the appalled expressions on the board members' faces.

Dad stood immediately. "I apologize for that comment, your honor, I mean Ms. Duff." Then he chastised me privately. "Lose your cool, and you lose your credibility too."

I sighed and nodded. But Curry and I were wasting our time.

Then dad asked Krogstrand, "Where exactly did the fight take place?"

"Out by the ball field."

Dad cleared his throat. "Your office is up in that third floor bell tower, isn't it? It must have taken two or three minutes to come all the way to the ball field. So how could you have seen everything you've testified to?"

Krogstrand narrowed his eyes at dad. "I rushed down the stairs, Mr. Bownes, and practically ran to the fight. They couldn't have been out of my sight for as much as a minute."

"So you admit you didn't see it all."

"I saw the important parts."

"But you didn't see why my son charged Choker."

"I didn't have to see. I know why."

"Oh?"

"When Choker—ah, Billy Durant—refused to buy drugs from these two hoodlums, and threatened to report them, they ganged up to silence him. Why, they beat him so severely, Durant could barely walk. I had to help him back to my office."

I gripped the edge of my chair to keep from flying out of it.

"It's all in Billy's affidavit."

Dad spread his arms in appeal. "Ms. Duff, I object!"

"Sustained, Mr. Bownes. This amounts to hearsay. Perhaps if Billy Durant was here..."

Krogstrand, looking unconcerned, said, "There *is* another witness to the fight, including the few seconds I took to descend the stairs. My secretary, Mrs. Muldoon."

Ms. Duff scanned the crowd and crooked a finger. "Would you please come forth, Mrs. Muldoon?"

"Gladly," she said in a thin but firm voice. And when she did, she brought her knitting bag. She looked a little unsteady, so one of the board members helped her to the witness chair.

"Now, tell us what you saw, Mildred," Ms. Duff said.

"Last Friday at about half-past two, Mr. Krogstrand called down from his office. 'Mildred,' he says, 'tell me who those boys are, fighting out there.' Well, I don't have a window, so I went upstairs to his office, and I recognized Curry Buckle because of his, um, distinctive shape, and I figured the tall one must be Darwin because they stuck together. And Choker—you can almost assume that if there's a fight—"

"Nobody is interested in what you assume," Krogstrand interrupted. "So you looked out the window and saw these two ruffians beating up the Durant boy. Now, did I miss anything important during the time I was going down the stairs?"

"Well... " Mrs. Muldoon scratched her temple and her entire poofy hairdo vibrated. "For a while, I would say that Choker was getting the best of the altercation."

"He defended himself valiantly, but Bownes and Buckle overwhelmed him. Thank you Mrs. Muldoon, you're dismissed."

"Wait," Ms. Duff said, "Mr. Bownes, Curry, do you wish to question the witness?"

"Yes," dad said. "Mrs. Muldoon, does Choker Durant have a history of fighting?"

"I should say he does."

"Objection," Krogstrand blurted. "Durant has no official record, not that it matters one bit. The issue is two boys beating up on one. And Mrs. Muldoon testified that Bownes was bigger than Durant."

"Taller," Mrs. Muldoon corrected.

"The point is the same—two against one."

"Is that all, Mildred?" Ms. Duff asked.

The shrunken-looking secretary squirmed in her chair, gaze shifting between the board members and her boss and back again.

"Well, no, actually. I wasn't planning to do it this way, but now seems like the appropriate time."

"Appropriate time for what?"

"To give you this." Mrs. Muldoon withdrew a bulging three-ring binder from her knitting bag and rose from her chair to present it to Ms. Duff. "You're aware I reached retirement age almost five years ago. Shortly after Emil Krogstrand became principal. But I saw something in his character that made me want to stay on."

Krogstrand straightened and hooked a thumb in his vest pocket as if posing for a portrait.

"I saw he was a *prima donna* who felt the rest of us were dirt under his feet."

Krogstrand did a double take, and as I leaned forward to hear every word, his smug look drained down his turkey neck, past his loose collar.

Mrs. Muldoon continued. "He ran off some of our finest teachers because of his dictatorial style. I decided to stay on just because the staff needed a friend in the front office. And the things I saw and heard in that office," she shook her head, "would burn your ears off."

Krogstrand made a cutting motion at his neck. "This is hardly the place—"

Ms. Duff dinged the water pitcher. "Mildred your, um, surprising, opinions of the principal don't seem to have any bearing on this case."

Mrs. Muldoon shook a finger back at Ms. Duff. "But don't you see? It has everything to do with it. It's part of Mr. Krogstrand's pattern of retaliating against anybody who doesn't grovel to him. These boys stood up to Mr. Krogstrand and his ego couldn't tolerate it."

"Missus Duff!" Krogstrand stood with arms spread.

Pumping with excitement, I looked to Curry. He simply stared at Mrs. Muldoon without visible emotion.

"I'll handle this," Ms. Duff said to Krogstrand, then turned to the witness. "Now, Mildred, are you saying these two young men failed to do the principal's bidding? In what way?"

"Something to do with hidden treasure."

The board members exchanged amused glances."

"Treasure," Ms. Duff said, voice flat with disbelief.

"Yes! It's all in that file, tabbed and indexed. Along with the rest of his monkey business, like doing personal things on the job, and hiring Charlie Angostura to dig those holes, and scheming with buyers for Camp Bluetoad."

"Hold on," Krogstrand said, taking two long strides to the front table.

He picked up the binder and shook it at Mrs. Muldoon. "You've been spying on me and writing things down?"

Mrs. Muldoon thrust out her fuzzy little jaw. "Darn right I have. For five years. And I've got the dirt on you. It's all in here."

I inched forward until I had only a token amount of rear-end on my chair. Dad leaned too, the beginning of a smile on his face.

"And you've been doing this during working hours, when you should have been doing your job? No wonder your performance has been so atrocious, correspondence always messed up, nothing ever done on time. Mildred, I've kept you on because I thought you needed the money, so I put up with your odd obsessions and your refusal to learn your computer. I'm afraid what you need, more than a job, is professional care."

Mrs. Muldoon's little face became so screwed up with anger she couldn't answer.

Krogstrand stepped forward, snatched the binder, opened it, and showed a page to the board members. "See? Just a bunch of gibberish." Before they could look further he took back the binder. "Of course anything produced on school time belongs to the school. And I'm afraid I must relieve you of your duties for incompetence and for misuse of official time and materials. You'll find your personal items on the front steps of the school tomorrow morning, and you're banned for life from entering the building because you obviously can't be trusted not to steal things from the files."

My chest inflated with rage against Krogstrand. Mrs. Muldoon had always treated me kindly. Face pale, lower lip quivering, she looked to the board members, who were whispering among themselves, shrugging, shaking their heads. Curry placed his hands over his face. I knew him well enough to understand he was blaming himself for Mrs. Muldoon's predicament. With the board huddled in debate, Krogstrand strode briskly to the rear of the room, binder under his arm. As dad and I stood to watch, he walked directly to the wood stove and jerked open the firebox.

"No!" Mrs. Muldoon shrieked. "That's five years of my life! Stop him, someone!"

Ms. Duff looked up. "Mr. Krogstrand!" she called, but he ignored the summons and thrust the binder into the blaze.

While I stood rooted to the floor, Ms. Dozier sprung from her chair to intervene but stumbled and went down with a thump that I felt in my own tailbone. People jumped up to help her, and others went to the fire, seemingly with the idea of saving the binder, but they could find no tool to use. Dad stepped out from behind our table, jaw set.

"Save that file!" Ms. Dozier urged from the floor.

Chapter 48
Dad Smells a Hot Story

*D*ad charged the stove, skirting the front row of seats, picking up speed down the narrow isle, and then to my amazement, he leaped up on a chair seat and hurdled from one empty chair to another on a diagonal line toward the wood stove. He stepped squarely on the first two chair seats, but landed too far back on the third, and it folded up, swallowing his leg and sending him crashing into the back row. I cringed and rushed to help untangle my dad and see if he'd broken a leg. But before I could get there, he scrambled out of the pile of arms and legs and chairs and surged toward the back of the room.

Krogstrand closed the stove door and made a show of steadying Ms. Dozier, though others had already helped her up. When he saw dad coming, he took a big step to block the stove. Dad brushed him aside and threw open the stove door; the fire roared with fresh oxygen. He, too, searched for a fireplace tool and, finding none, hesitated. But then he darted his bare hand into the fire and pulled the flaming binder onto the floor. He slipped off his best cardigan to smother the fire, then stood over the smoking mess as if daring Krogstrand to make a move.

Then he curled his right hand to his belly and covered it with the other.

"Dad!" I yelled, pushing through a confusion of people. I reached him and pulled the left hand away, revealing a blackened cuff and his flesh already an angry red. "Doc!" I cried.

"Here." Doc Uncas had arrived at my elbow. He hustled my dad toward the drinking fountain to cool the burned hand. "Keeley, get my bag from the car."

Keeley nodded and broke into a gawky run, all knees and elbows.

I remembered the binder just in time to see Krogstrand stooping for it. He'd pulled on thin leather gloves. But I couldn't let my dad's heroics go for nothing. As Krogstrand pulled away the ruined sweater, I hooked the binder with my foot, soccer-kicking it toward the coat rack, then scrambled to retrieve it ahead of him. Not knowing who would be loyal to him, I rushed out the door into the rain, clasping the smoldering thing between my elbow and side to avoid being burned. A pair of headlights swung into the parking lot, illuminating Keeley leaning into her car. I glanced over my shoulder and saw Krogstrand's silhouette rushing through the doorway. I darted in front of the moving vehicle and sprinted toward the Bug.

"Keeley," I yelled. She'd just straightened up with her father's medical kit. "I'll take the bag. You get this file out of here. Someplace safe. Hurry!" I looked back toward the hall.

She followed my glance to the dark shape splashing through puddles toward us, then climbed behind the wheel. I hugged Doc's satchel and wove through the cars, trying to create a diversion. It worked. Krogstrand followed me. By the time he brought me up short by the collar, Keeley was peeling furrows of gravel through the lot.

Krogstrand had two handfuls of leather bag before he realized he'd been snookered. "Damnation! I suppose that smarty-pants girl has the file."

"That's right," I said, elated. "And you don't stand a prayer of catching her."

"We'll see." He shoved me away, took a slim phone from his pocket, and punched some numbers. In seconds he had someone on the line. "Biggs, Emil Krogstrand here. I'm reporting a theft. A binder-file stolen by a girl named Keeley Uncas... right, Doc's kid. She's underage and she drove off in an orange Volkswagen. It's urgent you go after her. She shouldn't be driving anyway. All right... yes... I know you'll get the job done. Thanks sheriff." He walked off, muttering, "Hah, we'll see what becomes of her precious four-point average."

I ran the medical bag into the building, taking advantage of a puddle to splash Krogstrand's pant legs. As Doc applied a burn gel I told dad the binder was safe, but I regretted what it might cost Keeley. The hall had become a zoo, nobody in their seats, people crowding to watch

Doc at work, others replaying the action with wild gestures, opinions flying about. Smoke lingered in the open rafters. Someone restored the crashed chairs; others began folding and stacking them, assuming the hearing was over. Then Krogstrand skulked in, face looking nearly as red as dad's hand. Steam rose from him as he dried his spoiled suit before the stove. As Ms. Duff joined Krogstrand for a word, the front door opened again, and they both looked with interest as Choker Durant made a stumbling entrance, nudged along by his cousin, Dan Klatt.

Ms. Duff conferred with her board members. This time, no one quieted when she called for order, so she removed her shoe and struck the table with the stubby heel until the riot subsided.

"Please people. The hearing will re-convene in five minutes."

Only then did I realize I hadn't seen Curry since the excitement. I looked everywhere. No Curry. I tried the bathroom and—sure enough—saw his clodhoppers showing under the stall door. "Mrs. Muldoon's file is safe," I said.

"Oh, it's you." I couldn't detect any enthusiasm in his voice.

"You were expecting Elvis?" No answer. "Keeley drove off with it, but Krogstrand called Sheriff Biggs." I took my soggy shoes off, and wrung my socks in the sink. Still no response. "Speak to me O Swami."

"Don't call me that."

" Well, put a taper on that thing, will ya? We gotta be out there in one minute."

"I'm not..." He paused. "Dar... this isn't where I belong."

It sounded too much like giving up, and I didn't like it. We had no choice but to fight; couldn't he see that? "Are you cracked? Of course you belong. You've lived here all your life. If anybody doesn't belong, it's me."

"I mean... not Kluge Island... it's this *life*, people suffering, hurting each other, telling lies. What's wrong with this world?"

I wanted to kick in the stall door and drag him off the pot by his gnome ears. "Tough beans, Curry. What are you going to do, live in a cave?" I waited for an answer and it gave me a chance to calm down a little. "My dad always says this Latin thing: *Accipitridae non carburendum*. It means don't let the vultures grind you down." I put my clammy socks and shoes on. The clodhoppers didn't move the whole time. Then I heard Ms. Duff call the hearing to order. "C'mon Curry, they're starting. Oh, and Choker's here, and dad's hand is burnt to a crisp, and Mrs. Muldoon's been fired because she tried to help us, and Ms. Dozier got knocked on her keester, and you'd better get your keester in gear because we're a team, and if we don't go out there swinging everything we got, we might as well lay down at Krogstrand's feet and get used to being doormats because we'll always be somebody's doormat forever." He didn't answer. "Curry?"

I tried his stall door. Latched. "Curry?" Suddenly worried, I opened the next stall and stood on the commode to peer over the partition. There Curry sat, fully clothed, on the toilet seat, completely motionless. "Curry?"

The bathroom door opened and dad called out, "Dar. Son, are you in here? Curry? We're starting."

I showed myself. "Yeah, we're here, but Curry's in a trance I think."

"What do you mean?"

"I'll show you." I crawled under his stall door far enough to release the latch, then got to my feet and swung the door open. Dad and I both looked in to find Curry sitting perfectly still, frozen in place, his eyes half-open but turned up so we could see only the whites."

"He's having a seizure," dad said. "I'll get the doctor."

"No," I said. "He's okay. I can bring him back." Maneuvered into the cramped cubicle, I began to chant OM in his right ear.

"Whatever are you doing?" dad asked. "We have to make sure he doesn't swallow his tongue."

I ignored dad and kept chanting, and in half a minute I heard Curry make a small but sharp inhalation. Then his eyes closed completely for a few seconds, and when they opened, I could see that Curry had returned from wherever he'd gone. "What was that all about," I asked, after he'd blinked and resumed breathing normally.

"Are you okay, Curry?" dad said.

Curry looked at him a moment, as if weighing how much to tell, then said, "It just came over me. A vision. The same as the dream I had before." He looked at me with such otherworldliness that it raised goose flesh on my arms. "The dream where I'd been swallowed by a something huge and you were cutting off pieces and eating them to make a hole for me to escape. I..."

Before he could finish, someone poked his head in the restroom and said everyone was waiting.

"But what does it mean?" I asked Curry.

"The hole was there for me to go through, and I put my head through, but it looked so vast and weird outside. Yet I knew I had to go out because... because there's a job I have to do. *We* have a job."

"*We* need to go," dad said.

"Can you tell them it'll be a minute?" I asked, uncertain about Curry's willingness.

Dad nodded. "Hurry."

"Okay."

When dad left, Curry emerged from the stall. He had a new air of certainty to him, a luster in his eyes, chest expanded with determination.

"Our job is to save ourselves," I said, "otherwise my family is going to move away, and we'll never see each other again, and... and I'll never get to see Paprika in her underwear."

Curry cracked a Big McGillicuddy smile. "Sicko. Your dad's hand... is it bad?"

"Pretty toasted."

"Why'd he do it?"

"Dad? Easy. He smelled a story. And when he smells a story, he clamps on like a wolf eel. You'd have to cut off his head and pry his jaws loose to get rid of him."

"Well, I think he made some friends."

I stood taller. "Yeah, I suppose he did. C'mon, they're waiting."

He caught me by the arm. "And what's Choker up to?"

"You're the psychic. I just saw Klatt's truck drive up. He must have twisted Choker's nipple and dragged him here."

Curry nodded knowingly. "It's all happening the way it needs to happen." Then he slapped me on the back and said, "*Acceleratus mine carburetor*, or whatever it was you said."

Chapter 49
All Choked Up

A roomful of eyes tracked Curry and me to our seats. Though dad looked pale from shock, he sat balanced forward as if ready to hurdle the chairs again if necessary. Aunt Iris, from the front row, clenched a bony fist and threw a little uppercut. *Go get 'em.* I winked back.

Curry and I sat. He pulled his Tibetan amulet from under his shirt and clasped it in his hand. His eyes closed, his lips moved with the powerful Sanskrit words written on it—*Tat Savitur Varenyam Om*—and when he opened his eyes, they were lit with a calm glow. He patted his shirt pocket as if checking for something and seemed reassured.

Ms. Duff said, "Now that we're all here, Mr. Krogstrand, I think you have one more charge."

"Indeed I do. And this charge alone warrants expulsion, if not prosecution. Possession and distribution of drugs... *on school grounds.*" Krogstrand paused to let the horror of it sink in. "Immediately after the fight, Bownes grabbed his jacket off the ground and," with a dramatic flourish Krogstrand spilled the contents of a plastic bag on the front table, "these pills fell out of his pocket. Eight different kinds of prescription drugs. The board is well familiar with the school's zero tolerance policy. I suggest you summarily reject the appeal, and we can all go home."

"Everything in due course, Mr. Krogstrand." Ms. Duff turned toward our table. "Mr. Bownes, boys, this is an extremely serious charge. How do you explain these drugs?"

A familiar voice called from the audience. "May I examine those pills?"

I turned to see Doc Uncas standing.

"Of course," Ms. Duff said. "If you think you can identify them."

"I suspect so," Doc said, working his way to the aisle. Keeley hadn't returned and I hoped Sheriff Biggs didn't have her in custody. She wouldn't have approved of her father getting involved, but it felt great to have a well-known member of the community stand up for us. After a moment's examination, he picked up a handful of the pills and said, "Yes, these meds were prescribed by Dr. Slather for Paprika Buckle. We have muscular analgesics, anticataplectics, antispasmodics, anti-inflamatories, none of which, I assure you, have any recreational value."

Krogstrand seemed to have anticipated the argument. "Whether kids could get stoned on these drugs is beside the point. These boys have a history of lying to their classmates and cheating them of their money. No telling what claims they were making for these drugs. Why else would they bring them onto school grounds? And, by definition, prescription drugs are dangerous. Poisonous in the wrong hands."

Curry rose to answer, but Doc Uncas beat him to it. "The answer is simple. I intervened in Paprika Buckle's treatment, and suggested these drugs be removed from the household. Darwin was following my orders. I'm sure he simply forgot to throw them away."

I nodded to the board, hoping they'd believe it.

Krogstrand again pulled Choker's affidavit from his pocket. "It's all in here. Billy Durant says they approached him to sell him drugs, and beat him up when he refused."

Dad and Curry both grabbed my belt to keep me in my chair.

"Objection!" Dad called out.

"Sustained," Ms. Duff ruled. "The board will disregard the purported content of the affidavit, as we have previously ruled it inadmissible."

"Fine," Krogstrand snapped. "Anyone in this room can add two and two to get four. Drugs plus school equals expulsion. I rest my case."

"Thank you Mr. Krogstrand. Now, Mr. Bownes, do you have anything to say in defense? Perhaps some mitigating circumstances?"

Dad rose slowly, as if not quite ready. Then hailed a stout voice from the back.

"Ms. Duff, Choker has something to say."

Dan Klatt's voice.

Ms. Duff squinted into the crowd and scratched her melanoma scar. "Is that right, Billy?"

I stood to see over the crowd and saw Choker nod. Klatt stood directly behind him.

"As Mr. Krogstrand has rested his case, Mr. Bownes, you may call Billy Durant to testify if you please, but you don't have to."

Dad looked at Curry and me. I could only think of having another go at punching his lights out, but Curry, with a knowing smile, said, "Of course."

So Choker took the witness chair, trying to look cocky. "Billy, are you here to tell the truth?" Ms Duff asked.

"Either that or Danny's gonna make me a soprano. Guy's gotta do what he's gotta do." Choker gave his braying laugh.

"Skip the levity. Now, are you are aware of the charges against your two classmates?"

He nodded, sneaking a quick peek at Curry and me. I wondered why Dan Klatt had gone out of his way to make Choker testify. Was he for us or against us?

"Speak up, Billy. Is that a yes?"

"Yeah."

"What is it you wish to say about these charges?"

He squirmed and his Adam's apple bobbed. "Well, first of all, they rescued me from the tunnel and second of all I started the fight."

Choker looked truly ashamed. If I'd been chewing Blubbergum, I would have swallowed it.

Krogstrand gave exaggerated shakes of his head as if to call Choker a liar.

Ms. Duff asked, "Mr. Krogstrand testified he saw these two boys ganging up on you. Are you saying that's not true?"

Choker popped a knuckle. "I pounded Curry because he said things that made me look bad. Then Darwin came and I defended myself, and we each landed some good chops. I didn't really want to fight him, because he tried to help me."

"In the tunnel, you mean?"

"Yeah."

Dad jumped in with a question. "Did Mr. Krogstrand question you after the fight?"

"I had to go to his office and write out what happened."

"Did you write it in your own words, or did Mr. Krogstrand suggest things to you?"

Choker stole a glance toward the principal; Krogstrand had purple veins standing out at his temples. I wondered if veins ever popped.

"We want the truth, Billy," Ms. Duff said. "You needn't worry about anything if you just tell the truth."

"I... I tried to tell him, but he said that someone had to get expelled because of the fight and the drugs, and it would be me or them. So he told me how he saw it and asked if that's how it was, and I said yeah, and he told me to write it down and sign it."

"So they weren't trying to sell you drugs?"

Choker glanced at Krogstrand and cracked another knuckle. I was bursting, wanting to get inside of Choker and make the truth come out. Finally he said it.

"No ma'am."

Krogstrand leaped to his feet, took a gold pen from his pocket and wagged it at Choker. "Ms. Duff, this boy will say anything he thinks you want to hear. I insist his entire testimony be disregarded as unreliable. My own eyewitness testimony stands as the most credible account of what happened. And even if the witness initiated hostilities against Buckle, as claimed, this does not justify the vicious and unfair attack by these two hoodlums."

"Does not justify?" Dad pounded his bandaged hand on the table. Despite his obvious pain, he continued. "Is our principal suggesting it's wrong to stick up for a battered friend? Is this the lesson we want our kids to learn? Ms. Duff, this man should be tagged and monitored so he can't come within a quarter-mile of a school."

The crowd erupted with gasps and comments. One woman cried out, "Amen!"

"Mr. Bownes!" Ms. Duff reached down for her shoe and gave the table a whack. "This is becoming personal, and I want it to stop." She admonished both sides with a look, then faced Choker, whose heel tapped nervously. "I think I know the truth when I hear it. It wasn't easy for you to come clean, was it?"

Choker blinked.

"Sometimes a young man can grow years in a single minute. You're dismissed."

Choker rose from his chair, paused, then angled over to Curry. Instead of his usual scornful look, he seemed to be assessing his handiwork.

"Sorry I smegged up your face, man."

Curry shrugged. "Spoiled my good looks."

They both managed a trace of a smile. When Choker looked briefly at me, I said, "Thanks." He nodded, then beat feet, sidling past Ms. Dozier who came forward, hair in disorder, feet shuffling under the hem of her muumuu. My heart ached with regret; how could I have failed to check on her after Krogstrand had knocked her to the floor?

"I wish to speak on behalf of these boys."

"Of course," Ms. Duff said. "But briefly, if you don't mind; it's getting late."

Ms. Dozier stood behind us, resting one hand on Curry's shoulder, the other on mine, leaning rather heavily. I sat up straight to offer as much support as she needed.

"I've taught both these young men, and I've come to know them personally, and I can vouch for them as students and I can vouch for them as decent human beings."

A shiver passed through me. I don't know if it came from me or from Ms. Dozier.

Ms. Duff waited. "Is that it? Nothing specific?"

Ms. Dozier sighed, and seemed to wobble a bit. I gave her my seat; she eased into it and continued. "I had wanted this to be my little secret, but perhaps if I made a clean breast of it... You see, I'm dying of cancer." The strength drained from my muscles and it was my turn to wobble. When the murmurs subsided, she continued, her words filled with all the fire her tired body could muster. "These boys, they've helped me to find a treatment which is giving me some relief, and, I suspect, will prolong my life through the end of the school term. I tell you this because there are no finer boys in our school, and it would be a mistake of the highest order to expel them. To portray them as liars and thugs is ludicrous to anyone who truly knows them."

I turned away and bit hard at my lip, and saw Curry wiping the corners of his eyes.

Krogstrand stood. "We're all saddened over Ms. Dozier's illness, and I find her testimonial touching. I must remind the board, however, of the strained relations between Ms. Dozier and myself over the difficult decision to sell Camp Bluetoad. She's led a commendable campaign to save the camp, which has had my full support. However, the campaign has fallen short, and I'm afraid she lays the blame at my door. I suggest, therefore, that her testimonial is tainted by these sentiments."

Ms. Duff replied, "You can rely on the board to consider that possibility. And thank you, Ms. Dozier."

Curry raised his hand.

"Yes, Curry?"

He stood—which didn't net him much additional height—pressed his lips together, and looked at Aunt Iris. I looked, too, and saw her nervously shredding a tissue in her lap. Curry dipped his thumb and forefinger into his shirt pocket, and brought out a folded slip of paper.

"I, um...." He sighed, then went to his aunt and reached for her hand. He tried to get Iris to stand, but she wouldn't. "I think everyone knows my Aunt Iris. She's a good person who's taught me something important. She told me I had to come here this evening because how a person deals with problems determines his character. Anyway, this really doesn't have anything to do with being expelled, but the deadline for raising money to save Camp Bluetoad is tomorrow, and Aunt Iris wanted me to give this check to Ms. Dozier, and since I'm expelled from school, I won't have another chance, so..." He walked back to Ms. Dozier, smoothing the reward check. Aunt Iris watched with wide eyes.

"Here, Ms. Dozier."

She accepted the check graciously, but without enthusiasm. Until she read it.

And burst into tears.

Chapter 50
The Verdict

Curry handed his hanky to Ms. Dozier. He always had a clean hanky. Clean and pressed. When I remembered to stuff one in my pocket, it wasn't in any condition to be handed to a lady. How do people get all that disgusting stuff out of hankies? Anyway, I had to make do with a shirtsleeve.

Blotting her eyes, Ms. Dozier read the check again and laughed. "My God. I had to make sure I read it correctly." She looked at Iris. "But this is for ten-thousand dollars. Are you certain?"

Iris looked at Curry as if not quite sure what this meant. I knew what it meant: Iris wouldn't be spending the rest of her life in prison, at least not to satisfy Curry's scruples. Of course, Sheriff Biggs might solve the crime—yes, and he might invent an anti-gravity belt to keep his pants up. Curry just gave her a little smile, the first time I'd seen him smile at her since she'd admitted killing her sister. A first try at forgiveness. Iris shrugged and said, "It's got my signature, doesn't it?"

"Oh, you dear, precious woman. This puts us just up to what we need." Ms. Dozier rose and walked shakily to Iris, arms spread for a hug.

Iris tried to wriggle out of it. "For goodness' sake, it's just money. You're the one who did all the work, so just cash the check and leave me out of it."

With everyone's attention on the two women, I gave Curry a little punch on the shoulder, and a wink.

"The universe can settle Aunt Iris's account without my help," he said.

A cracking sound drew my attention to Krogstrand. I found him looking down at his reading glasses, now broken in two, one half in each hand. I smiled, and he saw me smile, and I showed him every last tooth in my head.

"Well," Ms. Duff said after the excitement had passed, "I suppose that was worth getting off-track for. But allow me to summarize. The possession of prescription drugs charge is uncontested, but appears to be more a serious lapse of judgment than any attempt to sell or distribute. Regarding the fight: as Billy Durant has clarified the nature of the altercation, that charge is dismissed." She added, "'Choker looks more than capable of handling himself anyway—was he held back a grade?"

I laughed into my hand.

"Also, the charges of endangerment and vandalism are based on unsubstantiated conjecture. And Mr. Krogstrand did not indicate that being elbowed in the chin by Bownes was deliberate, so we'll consider that an unfortunate accident. That leaves us with what? Disrespectful conduct, cutting class, and cheating. The remark about Mr. Schwartz, to my understanding, was made privately, and while he may have been distressed to overhear it, it caused him no public humiliation until he, himself, reported it. He might better have accepted it as constructive criticism."

The spectators chuckled. I gave Curry a thumbs up. Ms. Duff caught it—she didn't miss much.

"Ahem, Darwin Bownes. Cutting class: the charge is uncontested and presumed true. I think we can deal with Curry Buckle's single violation with an oral rebuke." She aimed her gaze at Curry. "Consider yourself rebuked."

Curry nodded.

"Yours is a more serious matter, Darwin. This geometry course appears to lack any challenge for you. A school that fails to challenge is a bad school. Therefore I suggest to the board and to Mr. Krogstrand that you be immediately enrolled in eleventh-grade algebra, where you will be responsible, by independent study, to catch up with the class. Can you handle that?"

"Yes, ma'am," I said, determined to handle it or die trying.

Krogstrand's hands seemed to be groping for something else to break.

"And," she said, pointing a cautionary finger in the air, you will also be responsible for completing your geometry course work. You may choose to attend Mr. Schwartz's class when you feel it beneficial. You do understand: any failures will become a part of your permanent scholastic record?"

"Understood." Joy bubbled from within like carbonation.

"Lastly, the most troubling charge—at least to me—*cheating*. Are we to understand, principal, you've already punished these boys for cheating? Mr. Krogstrand?"

He jerked his head. "What?"

"Did you not dock these boys' grades for cheating?"

"As a warning."

"That seems a more than sufficient penalty. Refresh my memory, why are we now considering additional jeopardy for the same offense?"

Krogstrand's lip curled. "They portrayed themselves as Swami Buckle-knuckle or something and cheated their schoolmates of hard cash."

"Oh, yes." She nodded. "And would you feel cheated in a Chinese restaurant because the price of a meal includes a fortune cookie? Most people consider these things entertainment and believe them at their own peril."

Krogstrand snaked his body around to confront her. "I object to your tone, Ms. Duff. In fact, I object to the way you've conducted this entire hearing."

"Your objection is noted, and will be given," she lowered her voice a notch, "its due consideration."

Krogstrand opened his mouth but said nothing. After drying his tonsils awhile, he stood and stalked to the side door but didn't exit. Ms. Duff polled her board in confidential tones. One by one they shook their heads no. Then, facing Curry and me, she said. "The matter of expulsion is dismissed."

I cranked my fist in delight as the crowd erupted in applause and mayhem. Dad wanted to join in, but remembered his bandage just in time. Curry pressed his eyes shut for a moment before cutting loose a smile.

"However," Ms. Duff continued, holding up her hands for silence. "As it stands, the board is in no position to overturn the original finding of cheating by you, Curry, and falsely backing him up, Darwin, leading to the docking of your grades. This, Curry and Darwin, would remain as blots on your otherwise unblemished records. And quite serious blots to anyone who values their integrity."

No mention of the bogus quiz I'd written for Choker on natural selection.

I see only one way around it," Ms. Duff continued. "I don't believe, Curry, that you've had a fair chance to prove yourself. That is, did the quiz answer truly come to you through—how should I say it— paranormal means? So in the interest of fairness, we now offer you that opportunity. Though I am skeptical, one of my colleagues informs me you were instrumental in locating her daughter's cat."

So that's where I'd seen the pinch-faced school board member. Mrs. Juniper. Squeaky the cat.

"Would you care to give a demonstration, Curry?"

The words had barely left her mouth when I began hatching a compromise. I knew Curry would never go for a demonstration before the busybody population of Kluge Island, but maybe we could work something out; however, one look at Curry and I began to doubt. His eyes downcast, he sat motionless except for his thumb tracing the bird shape on his amulet.

"Curry?" I said.

He made a soft whistling sound, glanced briefly at me, then answered Ms. Duff. "We appreciate the hearing. Dar and I are very grateful. But a demonstration... well... it's not a parlor trick—you know what I mean?—it's a sacred thing... or should be."

When several people began chuckling, my guts knotted.

Someone called out, "C'mon Curry, show them!"

His face remained stony.

"This is your final answer?" Ms. Duff asked.

Someone in the audience flapped his elbows like a chicken. "Bok bok bok ba-ok."

I looked to dad, but he just watched to see what we'd decide.

More voices encouraged Curry to do it. His chest rose and fell heavily and he turned to me. I didn't like being docked a grade, but what I hated most was Krogstrand winning the last skirmish. "Can't we can do it privately with the board?" I suggested.

"That's not the point."

I tried to think of a way around the point. To wipe the last trace of smirk off Krogstrand's face. "The truth needs to come out."

Curry shook his head. "They might be entertained, but it wouldn't help anyone. Nothing would change, and that's the truth. Can you forgive me, Dar?"

I knocked my teeth together a few times before giving up. "Forgive you for what? Listening to your conscience?"

So, to put the best face on it, I said to the board, "I've just known Curry since school started, but it only took me about five seconds to understand him. He'd lose everything before he'd tell a lie." And he's stubborn as a mule, I almost said.

Ms. Duff took off her glasses and squinted at me, shook her head, then leaned back in her chair. "Then we have no basis for overturning that charge. But, as the expulsions are reversed, you boys are to return to class tomorrow, Friday morning."

Krogstrand's murderous glare seemed directed at me in particular.

Chapter 51
A Warning... and a Proposition

The floorboards creaked their usual greeting, and I sniffed the familiar pig-in-a-blanket smell wafting from the cafeteria. The day might have been gray, but not Ms. Dozier. Climbing on a stepladder, steadied by a throng of kids, her flowered muumuu rose like a hot-air balloon above us. When she pinned the blue toad in a heroic leap off the chart, someone started the unofficial school cheer:

Gazilla gazilla gazzam
Look at that monster clam
Loser sucks hockey pucks
Nobody beats the Gooeyducks
Rah rah weasel guts!

Someone else gave way so I could grab a piece of the ladder, and we pressed around Ms. Dozier, a victorious phalanx of Spartans, guys hooting in their deepest voices, the girls' hair smelling washed and perfumed. I wanted it to last forever, except I wanted Curry to be there, but I knew he'd feel smothered in this crush of people, his face being at armpit level. And I wanted to be smelling someone else's hair—short, black, with a swirl at the nape—but she wasn't there either.

Ms. Dozier descended the ladder, reaching a hand for support, finding mine among many. I felt an unexpected strength in her grip that gave me hope she would not, after all, die.

I went looking for Curry and spied his gouged sidewalls in the cafeteria, bent over a sheaf of stationary written with purple ink. He tried to hide it, so I went for it like a blood-crazed shark. Holding him off with a stiff-arm, I read aloud what turned out to be the last page:

> Like I said, I'll be home the weekend after next, so maybe I'll run into you at Troutigan's. I'm dying for a murderburger.
>
> Your Devoted Friend,
> Sqyrl

I waved the pages over my head with delight while Curry jumped for them. "Your Devoted Friend! Whoa! You got quite a mackerel on the hook there, bubba." I smelled the pages. "Mmm. Lilac!"

Curry launched a fist toward my stomach and snatched the pages. "Sensitive," I croaked. The punch slowed my laughter, but didn't stop it. "Jeez, Curry, guess I better make other plans for that weekend, because you'll be up to your non-existent neck in murderburgers and God-knows-what."

The bell rang and we hurried to get our books.

I had a note on my locker from the algebra teacher, and when I stopped in later between classes, she gave me a book and the name of a student willing to tutor me. She acted pleased to have a willing pupil, and I knew I could handle it. Later, after bolting our lunches, Curry and I went to the auditorium where Keeley always nibbled her lunch and read. But she didn't mind us interrupting.

"How's your dad?" she asked me.

"He's thinking of taking up firewalking." Keeley had a V-shaped grin that made it worth the effort of amusing her. "Your dad did a good job patching him up."

"Mostly second-degree burns."

"Yeah."

"I dropped Mrs. Muldoon's file off at the newspaper office this morning."

"Great!" I said. "That reminds me: Krogstrand called the sheriff on you for driving."

Keeley couldn't have looked more pleased. "A certain sheriff's wife is receiving certain medical treatment by a certain doctor."

I nodded. Keeley wasn't just book-smart.

"So you guys really got docked a grade?"

To Keeley, this would have been like having an organ removed. "Yeah."

She set her jaw in determination. "The school board better change it. If they don't, I've made up my mind. When they give me the Golden Gooeyduck award for finishing at the head of our class, I'm going to accept it under protest."

Curry laughed. "But you haven't won it yet."

"The only one with an outside chance is Darwin." She said it as if I wasn't there. "And only if he really applied himself, which doesn't seem likely."

"I wonder," I said, "If I ace eleventh-grade algebra, do I get extra credit? That could bump me back up to a four-point average."

That clammed her up. I didn't mention how Krogstrand, in the parking lot, had threatened to spoil her perfect grade-point average. Keeley said finally, "You really think Mr. Krogstrand is going to let you succeed? Like my dad says, you two made a powerful enemy last night."

"So he got slam-dunked," I said. "He asked for it, right?"

"He won't see it that way. Remember, you've got three years at this school and he's in charge of your life. Don't think he can't mess it up. You saw what happened to Mrs. Muldoon. He fired her on the spot. Nobody stands up to Krogstrand Almighty without paying the price."

"But the school board... "

Keeley rolled her eyes as if talking to a moron. "Believe me, the guy is connected. You can't hide behind Thelma Duff for three years."

I hadn't given it much thought, but Keeley's warning chilled me. "What are we supposed to do? Lick his boots? That's not our style, is it Curry?"

"I didn't know we had a style."

"Well, if we did have a style, it wouldn't be boot-licking. So, Keeley, what else does your dad say?"

"Oh, that's right, dad needs to talk to you, Curry. Can you come for dinner?"

"Food?!" Curry said, and laughed at himself.

I must have looked like a kicked puppy because Keeley looked at me and added, "Can't see any harm in you coming too."

"Beats nuking a veggie-burger at home," I said, getting over the slight.

After school we piled in her car. Keeley missed her record time by two seconds. "Bullsnot! Too much weight."

The Big McGillicuddy greeted us, a face now carved into him, lit from within by candles. A broad, sly, pleased face, alive in the dimming light.

"Did you carve it?" I asked Keeley, while Curry examined it up close.

"Do you like him?" Her eyes sparkled with delight.

"It looks like he wants to speak."

"What's he trying to say?"

I cupped a hand to my ear. "Food?!"

She laughed. "I did capture that big toothy grin of Curry's, didn't I."

Curry turned and obliged with his best imitation.

"And you've got the shape of the head just right."

"I can't take credit—it grew that way, remember."

"Keeley, have you noticed that Curry's head seems a little swelled lately?"

"Now that you mention it... " Keeley raised her index finger. "A mild case of hydrocephalus perhaps."

304   *Awakening Curry Buckle*

Curry's expression turned to vexation.

"Close. He's had a letter from Sqyrl Marx."

Curry's hairline must have begun to itch, because he started raking at it.

"Sqyrl Marx? She's an animal! Ah... b-but a *nice* animal."

"Curry has a way with animals," I said. "Dogs drool all over him. Bunnies come hopping up. Worms poke their little segmented heads out of the ground when he walks by."

Curry endured the abuse until Keeley and I had milked it dry, then we went in, and found Doc wrapped in an apron, hacking vegetables in rhythm to some dead composer, smell of sizzling onions rising from a wok, steam billowing when he added new stuff. His goblet of Burgundy went from full to empty to full again, with a glug for the wok.

Doc rattled on about the benefits of olive oil and omega fats and tofu. Curry and I looked at each other like *it'll never replace pizza*. Mom wouldn't dream of owning a wok unless they invented a microwave model, and dad was a total klutz, so it intrigued me to see Doc humming with pleasure, chop-chopping so dangerously close to those educated doctor-fingers. Keeley got the table ready without being asked. They made a good team. When Doc left the room for a minute, I poured a slug of wine into a measuring cup, swirled and sniffed like a pro for Keeley's amusement, and swallowed just as Doc returned. It tasted like sour owl spit and I couldn't believe people made such a big deal about wine. At least I had a bit of a glow on by the time we sat for dinner. Maybe that's why I launched a question at Doc about Krogstrand. "Do you really think he'll try to get revenge on us?"

He took the question more seriously than I'd expected, smoothing his chin whiskers in thought. "Emil Krogstrand was humiliated last night. Men of his type can't tolerate losing. Probably the reason he became a school principal is to be in a position to dominate others."

"But what can he do to us?" Curry asked.

"He'll isolate you, set you up, turn your teachers against you. Plant things in your lockers." He shook his head, his deep-set eyes looking—chillingly—as if they'd seen terrible things done to people. "Let your imaginations run wild. And it's not just what he can do to you: he'll find ways to strike out at your families. I'm hoping your dad can do something with Mrs. Muldoon's notebook to run that vindictive jackal out of here."

"They're busy at it right now," I said. "If anyone can do it, Wolf-eel Bownes is your man."

"Let's hope so."

Doc didn't say anything at dinner about why he wanted to see Curry. After dishes were cleared, Doc lit the fireplace and settled us into the furniture and got around to business.

"I like to ponder things before making a decision," he said. "I'm a private man. I enjoy the small pleasures of life, and don't particularly like change. Except, of course, in the field of medicine, where things don't change fast enough. Physicians still treat the body like a piece of machinery, instead of... let's not get into that."

He lit a straight-stemmed pipe and sipped at the smoke. "I've been thinking about something, Curry, ever since you diagnosed your sister's condition. I went to your hearing last night, prepared to vouch for your psychic abilities if I thought it would make a difference. But you two managed nicely without me. In fact, one thing impressed me very much." He pointed his pipe stem at Curry. "You didn't fall into the trap of demonstrating your powers to that bunch of Philistines. I thought, ah, here's a soul who doesn't thrive on glory. It made me wonder if there were things we could do as a team. Things that none of us could do alone. Are you following me?"

"Maybe," Curry said.

I glanced at Keeley and she returned a tiny shrug.

"You're aware," Doc said, "that I'm no longer licensed to practice medicine."

"Oh, sure," Curry said. "Everyone knows that."

Doc made a face as if something bitter had leaked out his pipe. "You don't say. Well I certainly hope everybody doesn't know how I dabble, you might say, for those who haven't found relief elsewhere. This places me at some legal risk, you understand. However, I've yet to find any other useful purpose for my life, and so I do it. As long as I keep a low profile, I suspect I'll be tolerated."

A look of grave concern crossed Keeley's face.

"Okay, here's the punch line. Sometimes I see cases that other doctors consider hopeless. Sometimes my experience or intuition suggests a treatment that helps. All too often, I confess, it's educated guesswork... and I can't afford to be wrong."

A strata of fragrant pipe smoke had formed over our heads and we were all still for a moment. Then Curry said, "But Ms. Dozier said she's dying, so my treatment must not be working."

"A person must have a reason to live," Doc said. "They need to battle. A person with no purpose can die of a head cold."

Curry brightened. "You mean there's hope for her?"

Doc nodded. "After what happened last night, I'd say so. Let me ask you something Curry: have your psychic readings ever been wrong?"

"Not once," I answered for him. "He's found the Juniper's cat and won the Blubbermobile and cured my plantar wart and found Choker underground and"—I thought about Aunt Iris's murder—"and lots of stuff."

Curry sighed. "Something came out about past lives. That must be wrong because I don't believe in such things. My church doesn't believe in it."

"Mm," Doc said. "What does it feel like when you go into your trance?"

Curry turned his eyes upward. "At first I'm aware how my body wants to keep moving and I tell it to be still. And my brain is like a caged parrot that wants to keep talking, but I say *Tat Savitur Varenyam Om* until the parrot shuts up, then Dar's drumbeat becomes like a ladder that I climb until there's no more gravity and I spread out and feel connected to everything, and then..." He cracked a sheepish grin. "And then I wake up and want a sandwich."

Keeley giggled, and I did too.

Doc leaned forward. "Those words, the mantra, what do they mean?"

"Sanskrit," I began, then realized I'd run out of bright answers.

Curry said, "It has to do with summoning the light of creation."

"Fascinating." Doc rose from his chair and began pacing behind it. After three or four passes, he leaned on the chair, and said, "What I'm proposing, Curry, is—"

"The answer is yes," Curry said.

Doc's eyes widened. "Yes? You mean you'll give diagnostic readings—on the hard cases?"

"Yes." Curry's voice sounded unrushed and definite. "On three conditions. First, Darwin is always there. That's because of condition number two, which is that I won't be asked questions about the stock market, or lottery numbers, or hidden treasure or anything like that. I trust Darwin to make sure."

I'd been biting the inside of my cheek at the idea of Doc and Curry collaborating without me, thinking it probably didn't take any special skill to do my part. As Doc looked me over, I sat up straight and worked the tension kinks out of my shoulders.

"Fine. What's the third condition?"

"That we don't do it for money."

Doc chuckled. "Curry, I can't accept money anyway because of my status. If I'm paid at all, it's in barter, understand? Apples and live chickens and repair work on the car. A load of gravel. People pay for their own medication and equipment, like that ultraviolet contraption for Ms. Dozier."

Keeley added, "People want to show their appreciation. It's important to them."

Curry laughed. "Like The Big McGillicuddy. Okay, money for expenses, then, and reasonable gifts."

"No Lamborghinis for Keeley," I said, trying too hard. No one even smiled.

"Agreed," Doc said. "Now, I'm afraid I have to ask a big condition, too. And I'll be blunt. It would finish me as a doctor if it became known I was consulting a sleeping schoolboy. Right? You'd have to stay out of sight, and keep your abilities secret. You do this because you care about people and want to see them get well, but you never get any of the credit. Crazy Doc Uncas gets the credit, and the more hopeless cases we cure, the more they think I'm a miracle worker. Meanwhile, you're just a common student. How's that going to feel?"

Curry and the doctor studied each other. "I can handle it," Curry said at last. "I just want to help people—especially kids. But one thing I don't understand: why do *you* want a big reputation?"

Doc shook his head. "Ah, but I don't. But, if we're any good, you see, it can't be helped." He spread his palms in a gesture of inevitability, then thought of something. "You knew what I was going to ask before I asked it."

Curry nodded. "I had a strong feeling when we were at the hearing last night. I suddenly knew Dar and I were being prepared for something. That we had a job to do."

Chapter 52
Hatching a Plot

Curry remained silent the whole drive home. Keeley had something on her mind, too, because she kept to the speed limit. I let my imagination run wild about Krogstrand getting even, but kept thinking that dad would use Mrs. Muldoon's file to get rid of Krogstrand forever. Investigative journalism fired up Wolf-eel Bownes like nothing else. As we neared the Buckle farm, I asked Keeley if she'd read through the file.

"Some."

"And?"

"Couldn't make much sense of it. Notes about phone conversations and dates. Mrs. Muldoon uses a lot of shorthand. Photocopies of phone bills, expense accounts, appointment book pages. Performance evals for teachers. It didn't seem to tie together." As we approached the Buckle farm, she put on her turn signal though we hadn't seen another car the whole drive.

"Keeley," I said, "take us into town, will you? I'll bet my dad's still at the paper. You coming, Curry?"

"Why not."

Keeley put it back in fourth gear and had us in town in under five minutes. The lights were on at the *Whalebone*, so she stopped. I let Curry out the back seat, then told him to go ahead into the shop, I'd be a minute.

Then, feeling clumsy, almost disconnected from my arms and legs, I got back in the car.

"What?" Keeley said.

She had the clutch in and her hand on the stick. I put my hand over hers and pulled the stick down to neutral, then jerked on the parking brake. She let up on the clutch. The motor sputtered tamely and she didn't look at me, though I still had my hand over hers, and she didn't ask *what* again. The dash lights glinted in her eye and softly revealed the curves of her nose and mouth, and they seemed perfectly formed. I took her hand into both of mine, and she let me do it, but didn't give me any kind of squeeze. Her hand felt warm and damp, and she blinked, but still wouldn't look at me. I felt dizzy and dry-mouthed and at a loss for what to do next, so I just fondled her hand, looking for some kind of response one way or another.

Finally, still looking forward, she said. "Well, Darwin?"

"You have a little callous on your hand from shifting."

"I'm glad you find that fascinating."

"The other parts are so soft."

"I thought Curry was the palm reader."

I shifted awkwardly in my seat until I wound up where I started.

She sighed. "Are you going to kiss me, or what?"

I had to twist and bend to get there, and she didn't meet me halfway, but when I arrived, she made it worth the effort. And I might have got more if I hadn't propped an elbow on the steering wheel and blew the danged horn. That made her laugh, and she laughed in a way that made me laugh too. The horn brought Curry back outside. I got out and stood next to Curry on the curb as the Bug revved off, and he didn't say a thing, as if knowing I wanted to hold on to the moment and listen to the clattering engine fade into silence.

Inside the stuffy shop I found dad, hand taped like a boxer's, and Mrs. Muldoon, documents from her binder spread everywhere. They looked blurry-eyed and slumped.

"Hi Dad. You going to nail that slime-dog Krogstrand?"

Dad looked up, grimacing at my lack of finesse. "I don't know, Dar.

We've got some rocks to turn over, but no smoking gun." He looked at the clock; the hands nudged toward ten.

Mrs. Muldoon stubbed her index finger on a note-sized paper on the desk. "This isn't a smoking gun? It proves he was going to collect a big payoff if that Camp Bluetoad property sold."

The sheet had been rubbed with a pencil to bring out writing pressed into it from another sheet above it. Along with some doodles, it read:

C. B.

750K

10%

"What does it mean," I asked.

Mrs. Muldoon said, "The first week of school, a man phoned asking for Mr. Krogstrand. I got his name, a Mr. McShari. He wouldn't tell me what the subject matter was, so I got suspicious and brought coffee up to Mr. Krogstrand so I could hear, and he said, 'Very interesting, perhaps we can work something out.' He'd been making notes, but tore the page off before I could see it. However," she jutted her jaw at me with pride, "when he left the office, I took this page. When I found out two weeks later that Camp Bluetoad had failed a building inspection and that the founder of DataRip had offered to buy it, I did some sleuthing, and right there in the annual report it listed under Assistant General Counsel none other than Frank McShari."

I tried to follow. "So the C.B. on the note stands for Camp Bluetoad?"

"That's what I've been trying to tell your father!"

"What's the 750K?" Curry asked.

"DataRip offered seven-hundred and fifty thousand dollars for the property. The *ten percent* is Mr. Krogstrand's illegal commission."

"We can't prove that," dad said. "Besides, it looks like the sale is off."

"But it's obvious!" Mrs. Muldoon insisted, face flushed. "He's a crook. No doubt he paid off Grant Roundy—the building inspector—to exaggerate the problems... with some of the seventy-five thousand bucks he stood to make on the deal."

"Mrs. Muldoon, if I print that, his lawyer's going to be back, this time with a libel suit that'll suck every nickel out of me."

"*Back*?" I asked, alarmed.

Dad nodded. "Krogstrand sent him this morning to collect the file. I told him to get a court order. He beat his chest for awhile, but, as you can see, we still have it." Dad drank some coffee and made a sour face at it. "He phoned an hour later, threatening an injunction."

"That means he's scared silly," Mrs. Muldoon said gleefully.

Dad sighed. "No doubt he's pulled some shady business. But without a clean shot at him... A lot of people on this island wish the Bownes family would just go away. If I start swinging blindly at pillars of the community, I'm liable to hit a hornet's nest." He took off his glasses and rubbed his temples. "Dar, you need to keep your nose clean. Krogstrand's likely to make life rough on you, to get back for what happened at the hearing."

Where had I heard that before? Curry and I exchanged glances.

Mrs. Muldoon meanwhile had cycled up to a fit. "Are you telling me you're not going to print this? I've devoted my retirement years to putting this file together."

Dad shook his head. "Can't go to press with it. I'll keep digging, but we need an airtight case that he's done something seriously wrong."

"What about all these documents?" She banged her tiny fist on the table.

"A lot of them amount to covering his fanny for the record."

"Bownes," she said in a voice wavering with emotion, "I thought you had guts. And since you pulled these papers out of the fire, plenty of other people are under the mistaken impression that you have guts.

Let me tell you something about Emil Krogstrand. I've watched him for five years, and I know him inside out. He'll lay awake at night thinking of ways to destroy you and destroy these boys. He's an evil man, and if you don't get him, he'll get you!"

Mrs. Muldoon panted a few times to catch her breath. "But he's also a coward. And he's close to cracking because of what I know about his shenanigans. You've got people in this town that will back you, but if you don't print it, Mr. Bownes, then you're history around here, because when Krogstrand comes after you, you're going to be all alone."

She began gathering the papers and stuffing them into her knitting bag.

I sat stunned by her outburst. Dad didn't move either. It began to hit home that perhaps we'd won the skirmish, but might lose the war. If the *Whalebone* lost more subscribers or advertisers, I knew we'd have to fold up and move. Dad and mom couldn't afford a lawsuit, and it would be foolish to risk one without that smoking gun.

Smoking gun...

Mrs. Muldoon headed for the door. I wanted dad to stop her and tell her not to lose hope, but he didn't. She vanished into the night, muttering to herself.

Several minutes passed. The wind rattled a roof vent.

Smoking gun... smoking gun. It made me think of what I found up Iris Twist's chimney. "Curry, you found a lost cat. Do you suppose you could find some dirt on Krogstrand? Some solid evidence?"

Curry gave me a withering look that said it all.

"Is that a no? Okay, well, no harm asking."

Curry and his rules. Shouldn't have used the word *dirt*, but *smoking gun* would have been even worse. Smoking gun... Iris Twist... Pansy Twist. I felt the itch of a crazy idea coming on. Despite the hour, dad made a fresh pot of coffee. Curry covered a yawn, but I suddenly felt wide-awake, man-the-battle-stations. By the time the coffee maker had slowed to a drip, the itch had become a full-blown rash.

But when I explained it to dad, omitting an important part that I couldn't tell him, he shook his head. "Won't work. If I try to negotiate with Krogstrand, he'll know I'm doing it out of weakness."

"That's why Curry and I have to carry the ball."

Curry stopped yawning.

"No Darwin. No no no. I can't have you boys involved in something like that."

"What? We're not already involved? You heard Mrs. Muldoon. Krogstrand is coming after us. He'll run us off the island. Maybe bankrupt us too."

"Mr. Bownes," Curry said. "You might say Dar and I have a partnership, and we need to do something to keep Krogstrand from busting it up."

Hearing that from Curry convinced me all the more.

Dad plopped sugar cubes in his coffee and stirred. "I appreciate how you boys have a lot at stake—we all do—but a man like Krogstrand is too dangerous to get careless with."

I could see where this was going, so I cut it off. "Maybe we'll figure something out tomorrow."

Curry crashed at our house that night.

Between thinking of Keeley and refining my plot, I didn't sleep much.

Chapter 53

Scamming the Man

Curry is not the kind of guy who thrives on confrontation. On the other hand, he thinks there's a special hell just for animal abusers and greasy slimeball hypocrite high school principals. So when I revealed the perfected plan in the morning, he simply asked, "What about your dad?"

"He wouldn't understand the best part of the plan, because he doesn't know what we know about Aunt Pansy's death, and we can't tell him, right?"

"I suppose not."

"So he doesn't think it'll work, but it will. Better to ask for pardon than permission."

"But he said no."

"He didn't exactly forbid it."

"Now I'm sure you're going to be a lawyer when you grow up."

"Desperate times call for desperate measures."

Curry shook his head at me, but he had an amused bend to his lips. He went to my bedroom window. Now that the leaves had fallen from our big maple, I had a far view of the boarded-up turret on the old Twist house. "What Doc asked us to do... it feels right somehow. It almost feels like Krogstrand is a dark force trying to prevent it."

A cold shudder passed through me. I didn't much like the thought of a dark force, but cold shudders must mean something. "I know we can do some good, but not if Krogstrand drives our family off the island."

Curry breathed on the window and, in the patch of fog, traced an

OM symbol. "Okay Dar. What do you need me to do?"

"You write the letter. You can phone Mrs. Muldoon to get the details right. I'll work on the headline story. Maybe we can get Ms. Dozier to critique it because it's got to sound like dad's writing."

Curry wanted to put off the scam until sometime during the school week, but I insisted on doing it Sunday. In his bell tower above the school, Krogstrand had godlike power. Taking him by surprise in his own home might help. Also, I just wanted the stomach-churning to be over with. If we put it off, Curry might change his mind; or, I might lose my nerve.

Curry's folks dragged him to church on Sunday morning so we met afterwards at Troutigan's. We ordered the special—mock turtle soup—which I tasted and put aside, and tried the crackers. Nothing seemed to agree with my stomach. I huddled in my jacket, as the sun cast no warmth, and watched Curry finish my soup. We ran through the scheme again, then headed to Orca Lane. There Krogstrand lived with a wife no one ever saw, in a modern two-story squeezed between two fine older houses. A Rottweiler patrolled a spotty patch of lawn behind a wire fence.

It got excited as we approached, trampling the near-dead roses planted along the fence. "What's got four legs and an arm?" I asked Curry.

"What?"

"A Rottweiler on a playground."

"Don't worry about him."

I didn't know how he could be so calm. As we approached the gate, the dog's barking vibrated my chest cavity. Curry simply lowered his hand over the fence for the beast to sniff. Soon it stopped barking, and listened to Curry's sweet talk, and finally, licked his hand. Curry lifted the gate latch, and I followed him in, though Ripper seemed to have his doubts about me.

The brass knocker on the door probably didn't have a single fingerprint on it. While Curry made friends with Ripper, I knocked. After the third time, the deadbolt turned and a once-pretty but now anorexic-looking woman in ratted hair and stretch pants answered in a Brooklyn accent. "Yeah?" She looked dazed, as if trying to comprehend how there could possibly be unshredded people at the door.

"We're here to see Mr. Krogstrand. We're students."

"Never would of guessed." Bobbing her head slightly, she glanced at the folder under my arm, and shrugged. "C'mon in." She pointed down a hallway and said, "In the war room."

I rapped on the 'war room' door and opened it. My eyes swelled like Blubbergum when I peered inside and saw what Mrs. Krogstrand had meant. A battlefield diorama, the size of two Ping-Pong tables, dominated the room, with hundreds of painted soldiers, artillery pieces, horses, and model buildings, all arranged in heated battle on a landscape complete with wooded hills, a bush-lined stream snaking through a meadow, a camp scene detailed down to a stew pot over a fire, smoking cannonball craters and gruesome casualties. Krogstrand remained hunched over a table lit with a gooseneck lamp, airbrushing paint on yet another lead soldier.

We entered. "Guhh—," I started, then swallowed the gob in my throat. "Good morning—I mean, afternoon."

Krogstrand jerked around as if under attack.

"Wha? How'd you get in here?" Only then did I see that Krogstrand wore a goofy-looking red uniform with gold braid and rows of medals.

"Front door, wasn't it?" I asked Curry, but he'd planted his hands on the edge of the battle scene and leaned in to study it.

Krogstrand rose, arms stiff at his side. "This space is off-limits."

"Um, sorry." I had the feeling of talking to someone other than Mr. Krogstrand.

"Sorry, *sir*," he corrected me.

"Whatever." Then, telling myself to sound confident, I said, "Curry and I have business to discuss. We can go to another room if you want."

"Bownes?" Krogstrand asked as if just returned to the twenty-first century. "Buckle? What do you mean by disturbing me at home?"

It had been a good strategy to catch him off-guard, I thought, and flexed the folders to draw attention to them. "We have a proposal—to settle our differences."

"A proposal? Huh huh huh." His laugh sounded like a chain saw that wouldn't start. "Get your mitts off that general!"

I turned to see Curry holding a horse-mounted officer in a fancy blue uniform. Krogstrand bore down on him to snatch it from his hand. "Don't touch!" Krogstrand replaced the figure on the hilltop, adjusting it with precision.

"That's General Robitussen," Curry said softly, as if to himself.

Krogstrand froze, still bent over the table.

Curry surveyed the scene intently. "And this is the massacre of the Hedgehog Battalion in Northern Crimea."

Krogstrand straightened. "What did you say?"

Curry looked at me with the oddest expression, and I felt strangely disoriented.

"Who told you that?" Krogstrand said, then frowned. "My wife?"

Curry shook his head. "I just know."

"You just know."

Curry blinked, pointed at the scene and shook his head. "This isn't right. General Haryluk wasn't mounting an offensive. His men were cooking a few beans with nettles collected from the woods when Robitussen attacked." Curry pointed to a mounted officer and spoke with a force that blew me away. "The Hedgehogs were betrayed by Major Kipper-Langosta. Is that supposed to be him on the white stallion? Fighting valiantly? I don't think so. Kipper-Langosta was a perfect coward, as well as a traitor. But with the whole battalion wiped out, except him, who would find out?" Curry shook his head with disgust.

"Are you mocking me?" Krogstrand asked. "What do you know about it? I did my thesis on this battle, and I happen to be the world's leading expert."

Curry faced him, tall as he could stand, eyes squinted with what appeared to be bitterness. "But it's wrong."

Krogstrand flushed red and his jaw muscles bulged.

This was not the same Curry I'd dumped from his chair in September. He had the same shape, all right, but he was no longer made out of mashed potatoes. Worried that we'd get thrown out before getting down to business, I said, "We didn't come to debate history."

Curry worked his fingers as if they'd stiffened. "No." Then he took the thinner of two manila folders from me, not according to our script. I'd expected little more than moral support from Curry. But I'd gladly hand him the ball if he wanted to run with it. "Mr. Krogstrand," he said, "we've prepared a letter for your signature. Mrs. Muldoon helped, so it should be proper." From the folder, Curry took out a single sheet of stiff bond with its neatly typed paragraph.

"I'm not interested in any letter from Mrs. Muldoon."

Curry held out the letter. "Like I said, it's from you, addressed to the Kluge Island School board."

Krogstrand grew a smile. "Do you think the school board can protect you? That you can come into my house and wave letters under my nose? Oh, I think I'm going to enjoy this."

"Probably not, sir," Curry said, matter-of-factly. "Shall I read it?" He cleared his throat. "Dated today:

Dear Madams and Sirs:
For personal reasons I hereby resign my positions as
principal and superintendent of the Kluge Island
School District, effective as of the date of this letter.

"It just needs your signature."

Krogstrand snatched the letter, wadded it to a ball, and began his
slow huffing laugh. "Huh huh. This is rich." He tossed the ball in the
trash. "For personal reasons. What personal reasons would those be?
Funny, I can't think of any personal reasons." But then he looked, first
to Curry, then to me, with a suspicious tilt to his head.

Though I'd expected a reaction, the violence of it and the fire in his
eyes shook me to the core. But remembering the plan, I tapped a
finger on the other folder. "Maybe we should find a place to sit."

Krogstrand controlled his anger well, but allowed a sneer to curl his
lip. "Does your father know you're here?"

"No."

"I'm going to phone him and see if he approves."

I tensed, but tried not to show it. "You might want to hear our idea
first."

He sawed his jaw back and forth as he thought. "Does this, by
chance, have anything to do with diamonds?"

I'd written off the diamonds since Sheriff Biggs had secured the
shack over the tunnel entrance to keep fortune hunters out. He and
Aunt Iris planned to have the tunnel blasted shut. If Charlie Angostura
had really discovered an entrance, it would have been on the other
side of the cave-in we'd found, so it wouldn't do Krogstrand any good.
"As a matter of fact..." I said, as bait for him to listen.

Krogstrand replied in a voice he might have used on a dumb
animal, but with a menacing undertone. "Then let's go have our little
chat." He took his uniform coat off, hung it up, tugged his sleeves

straight, and led us to another room: his home office decorated with model ships. Curry and I pulled straight-backed chairs up to his desk. Krogstrand unfolded a pocketknife and leaned back in his swivel chair to clean his nails. "Okay, boys, your nickel."

I'd spent two restless nights imagining this moment, but now felt sickeningly out of my depth. Somehow Curry mustered enough composure for us both. "Let's talk about Charlie Angostura," he said.

Krogstrand's expression didn't change. "What about him?"

"You hired him to dig holes on the property next to my aunt's house."

"Hm."

I added, "And Angostura hired Dan Klatt and his cousin Choker to help. That's why you expected loyalty at the hearing. You probably owe them money."

Krogstrand shook his head. "Now why would I pay anyone to dig holes?"

Curry said, "For the same reason you had us up to your office, Mr. Krogstrand: to find Cyrus Twist's treasure."

Krogstrand gave Curry a pathetic smile. "I happen to own that property. If somebody's digging holes on it, I really don't give a ripe rip."

"We wouldn't care either," I said, "except that when Angostura couldn't find the tunnel, you authorized him to cross over the property line."

"Nonsense."

"C'mon," I said and took exhibit B from the folder. "This is a map of the holes. It's obvious how the pattern repeats. Angostura dug exactly where you told him to dig. And you based it on something you found in Cyrus's trunk, which you bought at auction this summer."

Krogstrand snapped, "Get to the point. Where's the diamonds?"

"Right where Cyrus left them, I suppose," Curry said. "Problem is, right after my Aunt Pansy reported the holes to the sheriff, and started watching for intruders, then someone shot her dead."

Curry glared accusingly at Krogstrand. I couldn't have glared better myself.

Krogstrand rasped the meat of his thumb sideways across the knife blade. "Am I supposed to know something about that?"

Now came the part Curry had a problem with. A moral problem. He had reluctantly agreed it wasn't a lie—merely a deception. But, to save his conscience, I took over. I'd remembered Aunt Pansy claiming that a man had been in the house because she'd found the toilet seat up. "Like Curry said, you bought Cyrus Twist's things at auction, looking for a clue to his hiding place. Maybe you found something, but maybe an important detail was missing. So, you sent Angostura to break into the Twist house to look for more clues."

"Balderdash!" Krogstrand blurted.

"C'mon," I said. "You can't hide anything from Curry. Between him and Mrs. Muldoon, we know everything. We know that when Pansy came home early and caught Angostura, he pulled a gun and it went off."

Krogstrand froze. Only for a second, but long enough to show we'd hooked him. I'd been betting he didn't know that Angostura had an alibi. He jerked at a kink in his neck and said, "Preposterous! If that's what you think, then why aren't you talking to Sheriff Biggs instead of me?"

Krogstrand scraped under a nail he'd already cleaned twice. I turned to shield a wink at Curry. We were gaining momentum. "We wanted to collect more evidence against Angostura first," I said, "to make sure we'd get the reward. But now we've got some hard proof. Show him the picture, Curry."

Curry placed on the desk the photo he'd taken that night in the field.

"Charlie Angostura," Curry said. "He's worked at the school since before you came."

Krogstrand took his feet from the desk and grimly studied the photo.

"This shot was taken on Twist property," I said. "With this picture, the sheriff won't have any problem getting a search warrant to look for a gun, and for the things Charlie stole from the house. Dad says Sheriff Biggs is under a lot of pressure to crack that shooting."

Krogstrand leaned toward us, the skin on his face tight enough to split. "You're not here to talk about diamonds. You're trying to paint me as an accessory to murder!"

We let him worry about that for a moment before throwing the next sucker punch.

"Should we show him your dad's article?" Curry asked.

"Yeah. Just the first page should do it."

Curry opened the folder and handed over the double-spaced article. Krogstrand snatched it from his hand. Watching his eyes, I could see him scanning the lead paragraph. I knew it by heart, because I'd written it:

Krogstrand to Profit from Camp Bluetoad Development

Documents turned over to the Kluge Island School Board indicate that district superintendent and principal William Emil Krogstrand stood to benefit financially from the sale of Camp Bluetoad to private developers. Island County building inspector, Grant Roundy, has admitted that his structural inspection of the Bluetoad lodge building may have been "overly severe." His condemnation of the lodge led to the Kluge Island School Board's decision to sell the camp property. A shorthand transcript of a prior phone conversation between Krogstrand and DataRip attorney, Frank McShari, suggests a ten-

> percent commission was offered Krogstrand if he
> could arrange for the property to be sold. Based on
> the $750,000 sales price of the camp, Krogstrand
> stood to pocket $75,000.

Krogstrand lowered the page, all color drained from his face. A thrill rose in my chest and I made a fist, as I thought we had him. But then Krogstrand blinked rapidly about five times, and was back to his old self. "I'll have my lawyer on your father like stink on crab bait. He can't prove that."

"Mrs. Muldoon did a very thorough job," I said.

"That senile conniving old biddy! Who's going to believe her? Besides, the sale is off."

"Maybe," I said. "But dad thinks the school board will have to fire you anyway."

"Then why didn't your yellow-bellied father come here himself?"

Fighting back anger, I said, "I told you, he doesn't know we're here."

"Just a minute, what are you trying to pull? Why should I resign if the newspaper is going to run this story anyway?"

This was the part I'd worried about most. I had to be as good a liar as Krogstrand. So I'd scripted it close to the truth. "I can get him to kill the story. If I've made a promise, he'll stand by it. I know my dad."

"Now that's interesting. Why would you do that?"

"Curry and I just want to finish school, but we don't trust you to leave us alone. Mrs. Muldoon said you always get revenge. But the other thing is that I know your lawyer came by the print shop threatening to sue. The last time dad got sued, he had to get a second mortgage to pay the legal fees. We won the case, but it cost a pile of money." I leaned on Krogstrand's desk and met his suspicious eyes. "He'll beat you, too, but there goes my college fund down the toilet. So

I figure it's better to just get it over with."

"What's your dad's number. I'm going to call him."

A hot flush of panic came over me. We'd come so close, but if Krogstrand phoned and found out the news article was a hoax, the house of cards would collapse. "You can call him, but dad is really cranked up about doing this story. There's only one way he's going to back off, and that's to protect me. Only if we've already made a deal and he has to honor my promise."

"Bunch of nonsense. He's not going to—" Krogstrand picked up the phone.

"I'm an only child."

Krogstrand seemed to take my meaning, then turned a skeptical eye on Curry. "You want me to believe you'll withhold evidence against someone who might have murdered your aunt? I don't buy it."

Curry scarcely hesitated. "You forget, I have the power to see into the murderer's heart. I don't think we have anything to fear from Charlie Angostura, and everyone pays for their sins eventually. If the choice is to stop you from ruining people's lives—especially Darwin's... " Curry took another letter from his folder and centered it on the desk. "We made a spare resignation—in case the first one got damaged."

I gave Curry a trace of a smile to tell him he'd played his part perfectly. Then I clicked a pen and placed it on the letter.

I heard the cracking of bone as Krogstrand adjusted his neck.

"So, in a nutshell," he said, "I walk away from my livelihood, or you'll destroy my reputation and get me fired."

"In a nutshell," Curry said. "Major."

Chapter 54
The Bell Tower

I took back the photo and bogus newspaper article from Krogstrand's desk. His glassy eyes didn't even track us out the door. I said goodbye to his skeletal wife, Curry patted the Rottweiler on his bony head, and we literally ran to the print shop, ridiculously amped. I jumped a bike rack and a planter box; Curry ran around the bike rack and mowed a swath of flowers when he jumped the planter. And we laughed and whooped it up. By the time we barged into dad's office, we'd burned off some serious pimple-pushing hormones. But now I had something new to worry about: what to tell dad in case Krogstrand called.

"You did what?!" he said, coming out of his chair when I told him we'd been to see Krogstrand. "I thought I told you—"

"Yeah Dad, you did, but—"

"But what?"

"But, um..."

Curry said calmly, "It's just something we needed to do, Mr. Bownes."

Dad ran a hand through his mussed hair, sat down, and shook his head slowly. "Are you saying Krogstrand fell for it?"

"He didn't sign the resignation, but he didn't crumple it up either." Then I handed over the draft article. "This is what really put blood in his stool."

Dad frowned at the expression, and became seriously grim at reading the article. "You wrote this?"

"Think there's any hope for me in the newspaper business?" I asked, trying to lighten things up. "I told him you'd drop the story if he resigns."

Dad stared blankly at me, looking dazed with exhaustion. "You might have just ruined me in this town, you realize that? Krogstrand is probably on the horn to his lawyer as we speak. You have no business impersonating me. It was wrong, and I won't stand for that kind of behavior from you."

It usually took dad a few minutes to adjust to something new. After a tense minute, Curry asked, "Mr. Bownes, have you found anything else to use against Mr. Krogstrand?"

"Unfortunately no. The Angostura thing might pan out, but it's doubtful. He's got a record—petty crime mostly. Drunkenness, fighting, breaking and entering. An automatic garage door closed on his head as a child; let's just say there's no bait on his hook. But he's clean since getting that handyman job at the school."

"Oh," Curry said, looking uneasy. "I have to tell you Mr. Angostura had nothing to do with my aunt's death."

"Well, I don't see how you can say that, Curry." Then a light of suspicion came on in dad's eyes. "Are you telling me—"

Time to change the subject. "So whatcha got for the front page this week?"

"Well, there's Camp Bluetoad, of course. But, Curry, you were saying—"

"Have room for another feature?" I butted in, then traced a bold headline with my hand. *"Mummy of Lost Woman Found in Limeworks Tunnel."*

Dad rolled his eyes. "Let's make it: 'Mummy of Space Alien...'"

"Dad, I'm serious. Have you heard about Buster Henry's wife? She got lost after her cow fell into a sinkhole back in the 30's and she went looking for it. We found her down in the tunnels, and Curry has a locket for identification."

"You're serious?"

"Yeah! We can go get a picture, right Curry?"

Curry swallowed. I knew he'd be game—with a little persuasion. "But Aunt Iris is going to have the entrance blown up," he said, "so no one else gets trapped."

"When?" I asked.

"Tomorrow, I think."

"Then we go see Sheriff Biggs today and see if he'll let us in. Dad, can we borrow a camera?"

Sheriff Biggs scrutinized the locket, and when he heard about the human remains, he hitched up his belt and said, "Let's go." To my surprise, dad went with us. Down below, Curry took the photos, then Sheriff Biggs arranged for recovery of the corpse. It took our minds off Krogstrand and it felt great to do something for dad after he'd supported Curry and me at the hearing. Of course, we stood to get our names in the paper, too.

But the next morning, the bike ride to school seemed even gloomier than the tunnels had been. Darkness lingered longer every morning, and the day started half-heartedly with fog and drizzle. Cold as a clam's you-know-what. The tower looming over the school grounds glowed with sickly fluorescent light. I found Curry waiting for me at my locker, drooping as if from lack of sleep. If my nightmares showed on my face, I must have looked even worse.

"Dar, I've been thinking a lot."

"So what else is new?"

"I'm worried about Charlie Angostura. What if Krogstrand fires him because of what we said yesterday?"

"Why would he do that?"

"Krogstrand probably thinks that Angostura blabbed about who hired him to dig the holes."

"But he didn't blab. We figured it out ourselves."

"Krogstrand doesn't know that. And Charlie has had it pretty rough. He needs this job."

"Curry, don't you ever think of what *you* need?"

He looked flummoxed by the question.

"What can we possibly do for Angostura?" I asked.

"Tell Krogstrand the truth."

"Sheesh." I rubbed the back of my neck. "How much of the truth?"

"That Charlie didn't blab... and that he didn't hurt Aunt Pansy."

I threw my arms out. "C'mon Curry. What does that do to our scam? You just can't appreciate a good honest deception, can you? Jeez Louise." The first bell clanged.

Curry stood rooted like an oak. "I've made up my mind, Darwin."

I shook my head in exasperation. "Well, don't do anything until we talk some more. I need to get to class."

"After first period, then. We've got geometry after that, which you can skip, remember?"

In an hour we met again. In history, I'd zoned out most of the Teapot Dome scandal except for a general understanding that corrupt people tended to get away with all kinds of crap. Mostly I kept imagining ways Krogstrand might hurt me and ruin dad's business. After yesterday, I never wanted to see him again if I could help it. We'd taken a good poke at him, but now I felt like a shooting gallery duck.

"You still want to blow our chances for Charlie Angostura's sake?" I asked Curry.

"I couldn't live with myself if he got canned."

"Dang it Curry! Your conscience must look like the Big doggone McGillicuddy." I sighed. "Well, you put up with a lot from me, crazy ideas and everything, so I suppose... " Then I had an idea. "Okay, if we tell Krogstrand that Angostura is innocent, he'll never sign the resignation. The only reason for Krogstrand to sign is because he thinks he's responsible for Pansy's death because he sent Angostura to burgle her house. But what if we take one last shot? Tell him he has a deadline of four o'clock today, or the deal's off."

"That might be too late for Charlie."

"Noon then."

Curry pursed his lips and placed his hand over the place where his amulet hung under his shirt, and after a pause said, "We can give him fifteen minutes."

Better than a flat no. "Deal." I shook my partner's hand and we wove through the throng of students. "Hey Curry, I forgot to ask. Yesterday, those toy soldiers on the battlefield, when you contradicted Krogstrand and called him *Major*. What the heck was that all about?"

He paused at the foot of the bell tower stairs. His eyelids fluttered. "I'm not sure. It's just that I somehow knew. It looked real, but not exactly right."

"So you've read about the massacre? Saw a movie?"

Curry shook his head. "I don't think so."

"That uniform he wore—how did you know it was a major's?"

"That was a general's uniform."

"But you called him—"

"Major. Did I really say that? I thought maybe I'd imagined it."

"Curry, you're giving me goose bumps. You told Krogstrand that Major Crapper-Linguini-or-something betrayed his side and was a coward."

"Major Kipper-Langosta," Curry said, a dreamy look in his eyes.

The hall had grown quieter, just the hurried footsteps of the last student scurrying to class. I grabbed Curry by the shoulders. "You were there! It's the only explanation."

"But..."

"I know, you don't believe in reincarnation. Well maybe you'd better start believing."

"But Darwin, there's five billion people on the planet. What're the odds I'd run into someone I knew before?"

"Maybe because you hated him so much." I didn't know where the idea came from, but I liked the sound of it.

"But I don't..." Curry's words dissolved into an expression of wonder.

And I had the eerie feeling of knowing his thoughts before he said them. "Maybe not hate," I said. "Disgust?"

Curry whistled silently. "This is getting too weird."

"You and I need to have a long talk with the swami," I said. Then the tardy bell rang in the empty corridor. I looked up the steep stairs, and climbed them, the creaky treads starting to sound familiar. But this time the smell of furniture oil on the wood paneling didn't make me sick to the stomach. Whatever happened up there, we had nothing to lose.

A woman sat at Mrs. Muldoon's desk. Young, big eyes, big hair. She talked to her computer screen as if it wasn't behaving, and didn't see us until Curry toed up to her desk. "We need to see Mr. Krogstrand."

She inspected us up and down. This part of her new job description she could handle. "Well, you can't. He left a note saying he's not to be disturbed until four o'clock. See?" She held up the note to prove it.

Curry looked at me, and, again, a telepathic thing happened. I nodded, and as he broke for the spiral stair leading to Krogstrand's office, I blocked the secretary's path in case she tried to stop him. I heard Curry's steady chuffing up the iron stairs while she fumbled with the intercom switch but couldn't seem to figure it out, and finally called up in a shrill voice, "I tried to stop him Mr. Krogstrand. It's not my fault."

I listened for Krogstrand's response but heard nothing. I'd thought I'd gotten over my fear of him, my heart beat like a dribbled basketball.

I started after Curry.

Then Curry rushed to the railing. "Dar!"

The urgency in his voice sent me bounding up the circular steps two at a time making the iron staircase ring like a gong. When I reached Curry, his eyes were big but devoid of answers.

"What?" I demanded.

"See for yourself."

I did. Stepping past him, I entered Krogstrand's office. Though it was mostly as I remembered it, something felt wrong. The garbage can looked like the janitor had been on strike for a month. File drawers stood open. Things were missing: the Oriental rug, the ship models. Clean rectangles on the paint where diplomas and stuff had hung.

I glanced around the room to make sure Krogstrand was really not there and stepped behind the big walnut desk. Cautiously I opened the top desk drawer. That's when bubbles of joy began rising through my body because the drawer was cleaned out except for some paper clips, blunt pencils, a few dirty pennies.

I accidentally nudged the computer mouse bringing the monitor to life. The screen saver sent an eight ball bouncing off the edges in endless bank shots.

An envelope lay on the desk.

Curry picked it up and read the address.

"Kluge Island School Board, attention: Ms. Thelma Duff."

Feeling almost dizzy, I clapped Curry on the shoulder, and he turned it into a hug. Over his shoulder, I saw the secretary peeping into the room from one or two stairs down. We broke off the embrace in our own good time. Then I suggested to the secretary that she might want to look for another job. I didn't trust her with the envelope; Curry and I would hand-carry it to Ms. Duff.

While the secretary practiced her pout, we went downstairs and walked the noisy wood floors of the main hall and breathed the air, rich with the smell of pig-in-a-blanket and hot radiators. We about-faced at the far window and walked the hall again, feeling incredibly light, as if a curse had been lifted from the place.

Epilogue

Curry and I found Ms. Duff in her yard in a flannel shirt and denim overalls, chopping her spent flowerbeds to the ground with a riding lawnmower. We stood by as she tore open Mr. Krogstrand's letter. She squinted at it, then read it again with her glasses, then said, "You never know where your first surprise of the day is coming from." She looked us both over so hard I began to think the letter had accused us of something new, but then she handed the letter to Curry, saying, "I'm guessing you already know what this says." We read the signed letter of resignation—not the one we'd prepared, but one similar enough that he might have spared himself the extra trouble. And the next morning Ms. Duff called a school assembly where she announced the resignation and the saving of Camp Bluetoad, and the whole school raised a cheer that lasted all day. It seemed we'd skipped winter and gone straight to spring.

Principal William Emil Krogstrand didn't return to Kluge Island High. He didn't return to his wife or his Rottweiler either, or to his miniature soldiers. The surprise resignation, and everyone's befuddlement over what had become of Krogstrand, took the headline in that week's paper, pushing the mummy story into the following week's edition. A good thing, as enough ads had sold to expand the paper to twelve pages from the bare bones eight.

A few days after Krogstrand's disappearance, Curry and I got a call from Doc Uncas, and that evening Swami Curryban Bucklananda and I went to work and diagnosed a boy's constant fatigue and mental dullness as an allergic reaction to foods contaminated with plastics. Afterwards, when I asked Curry what he'd be doing Saturday, he hummed evasively—something about tuning and waxing his motor scooter—and no, he didn't need help with it. Then I remembered Sqyrl's letter, reeking of lilac, and had the manners to say I'd be busy all weekend, too.

In fact, the only thing I did that weekend of much use was to visit Troutigan when he opened his stand Saturday. He hadn't decided on the day's specialty and my suggestion appealed to his basic weirdness and lack of business sense. So he wrote on his chalkboard: *SWAMIBURGER*, and went to the store for avocado, peanut butter, and tuna fish (and his own special touch: kimchee) while I minded the stand. And he seemed pleased to report, later that afternoon when I checked, that he'd actually sold two of the disgusting things—to my friend and that wildcat of a girl that had her nails dug into his belly as they rode up on his scooter.

I did a long bike ride Sunday morning, and felt bored enough that afternoon to help mom with the laundry. I did it in self-defense really: I needed clean jeans and skivvies for school the next day, and mom never did laundry until the closets and drawers were empty.

"Be sure to turn the pockets out," she said. "I'm tired of picking tissue off my clothes."

"Yes, mom."

And as I pulled out a pocket from my old black jeans something flew out and rattled on the floor at mom's feet. She stooped, picked it up, held it to the light. "Where'd this come from?"

"What is it?"

She handed me a pebble the size of a marble, translucent and slightly yellow, with an angular grain running through it, smooth except for a sheared edge. "Don't know... probably wore these pants the day we got Choker out of the tunnel. Yeah, I stuffed gravel in my pockets for ballast." I turned the other pocket out and got only a teaspoon of sand.

"Well, it's a pretty rock," she said and resumed humming as she sorted clothes. I put the pebble in my pocket.

It wasn't until later that afternoon, after feeling the lump in my pocket and fingering the smooth, almost oily, pebble, with one sharp edge, that it added up. I went upstairs to my room and used the rock to scratch a small X in the corner of my window. It scored the glass easily.

I held the stone to the light for a long time, and with a helpless laugh thought about the tunnel entrance being blasted shut only days before. If another entrance existed, it had been long forgotten. Then I realized that the booby-trapped passageway had been a sly trick by mercury-crazed Cyrus Twist. He'd cleverly mixed his treasure of uncut diamonds with ordinary beach gravel and left it within easy reach. I wondered what Cyrus understood about greed that made such a deception a safe bet.

Then I rolled the diamond between my fingers remembering poor Aunt Iris, her tortured face when she'd said *what use are diamonds... except in a ring*. Which gave me yet another crazy idea. Back to the window, I scratched something else into the corner. Small, my secret.

A name.

About the Author

Having served as head of labor relations at the Naval Submarine Base, Bangor, Michael Donnelly now writes novels, is involved in community mediation, grows rare plants, meditates, plays the guitar (rather badly), and kayaks to islands no one has heard of. He may be contacted through his website, www.donnellybooks.com

Bonus Features

It's not your favorite premium DVD. It's a Blue Works novel for young adults. We pack every Blue Works novel with "extras" because our books are created at premium quality — no wasteful mass-production, no newspaper print pages, no formula stories. With every purchase of a Blue Works novel you'll receive some or all of these incredible features:

Downloadable from our webcenter:
- A full-color poster.
- An extensive study guide written by the author.
- A "Making Of" interview with the author and others.
- Deleted or extra scenes not found in the novel.
- Fan-fiction links where readers take the story further.
- A limited edition, official trading card for the book.
- A full-color bookmark, door-hanger, club card and more.

By sending us your purchase receipt:
- An autographed Blue Card™. This archival-quality, deep blue, luminescent, mica-speckled card is hand-signed by the author.

www.windstormcreative.com/blueworks

Blue Works
Attn: Bonus Features
c/o Windstorm Creative
Post Office Box 28
Port Orchard WA 98366

For a partial listing of other great Blue Works novels, turn the page.

Blue Works Novels

Take 20% off every book at our webcenter. And while you're there, use eTalk™ to ask your favorite author a question, download or request the first chapter of any book, and much more.

Fiction

And Featuring Bailey Wellcom as the Biscuit (Peggy Durbin)
The Brute (Mike Klaassen)
Makoona (John Morano)
Mrs. Estronsky and the UFO (Pat Schmatz)
Out There, Somewhere (John Morano)
The Pirate Queen (Christina Bauer)
Present from the Past (Janet & Mike Golio)
Puzzle from the Past (Janet & Mike Golio)
Way Past Cool (Jess Mowry)
A Wing and a Prayer (John Morano)

Science Fiction & Fantasy

2176: Birth of the Belt Republic (Ted Butler)
Menace Beyond the Moon (Ted Butler)
The Rune of Zachary Zimbalist,
The Connedim: Book One (Pamela Keyes)
The Legend of Zamiel Zimbalist,
The Connedim: Book Two (Pamela Keyes)
The Mythfits (Gary Goldstein)
On a Distant World (Joseph Yenkavitch)
Merlin's Door: Book One, Outside of Time series
(Wim Coleman & Pat Perrin)